High Praise for *Exceeding Expectations* and Author Lisa April Smith

"fantastic characters" "well told, well plotted out and executed perfectly." "I was absolutely trapped by this book. " . . . held me right to the very last page." "a surprise at the end that will have you sitting with your mouth hanging open."
Natalie Hillier
http://booksfromthepurplejellybeanchair.blogspot.com

"Smith . . . has woven an intriguingly rich tapestry of delightful well-developed characters into a perfectly balanced plot bursting with riveting mystery, crimes of the petty and the horrible sort, suspenseful twists, and romantic tension complete with love scenes that sizzle and pop."
Cari Pestelak http://audacityshewrote.com

"5 Soaring Stars" ". . . it's the authentic details of the time-periods that make it fun to read . . ." "historical and fictitious characters work in sync as they are perfectly set in these time frames, and midst the transitory madness of WWs I and II Paris." "It's witty, fun and sassy."
Deborah Previte: http://abookishlibrarian.blogspot.com

"This book has it all! . . . romance, mystery, sex and crime. . . . a story that you will not be able to put down."
Charla Wilson http://booktalkswithcharl.blogspot.com

"If you like a thrilling read pick up this book."
http://Alaskanbookcafe.com

"Smith's books have the pace and heat of Jacqueline Susann and the style and sophistication of Dominick Dunne." **Amazon reviewer**

". . . twists, turns and adventures, it keeps readers on the edge of their seat." ". . . suspense, family drama, romantic tension and more, then you want to check out this e-book!"

And for *Dangerous Lies*

"This is the closest novel I've read to Mario Puzo's "Godfather" in decades . . . one of the best finds of this year! . . a story that won't allow you to look away, and it's one that will cause you to laugh and cry right to the last sentence."
The Bookish Dame

"Seduction. Crime. Revenge. One woman's life on-the-edge . . ."
The Morning Call

"This riveting novel is fast-paced and full of intriguing characters. I found myself picking this book up every chance I got just to see how it would end."
Four Stars, Excellent *Romantic Times - Mainstream Fiction.*

"The book is laced with suspense, humor, emotion and lots of twists and turns . . . racy new thriller has two unforgettable protagonists."
Palm Beach Post

" . . . a thriller with just enough steam to captivate . . ."
Parkland Press

". . . a tale of suspense, heartbreak, humor, and love. Smith has style, class and a gift for story telling."
Amazon.com readers award *Dangerous Lies* **Five Stars**

"If Mary Higgins Clark looks over her shoulder she may see Lisa Smith following closely behind. Their books have the same ingredients . . . page turning suspense and a plot that grabs the reader from the first page." ". . . Smith's sly sense of humor puts the frosting on the cake."
Spotlight Magazine

Exceeding Expectations

Lisa April Smith

Windgate Press

Other books by Lisa April Smith

Dangerous Lies

Paradise Misplaced

For more about the author
and her books
visit her website http://www.LisaAprilSmith.com

Acknowledgments

Common knowledge. Writers spend a lot of time alone. Nevertheless, I believe that no project that takes longer than two hours is done entirely without help. I am indebted to so many people who helped and encouraged me over the years.

My husband, He-Who-Wishes-To-Remain-Anonymous, who knows that when I'm staring into space and don't respond to his questions, I'm not intentionally ignoring him, I'm simply somewhere else. Also, after a marriage that began when I was eighteen and he was twenty, unprompted, the man tells me that I'm beautiful. You can't put a price tag on that.

My kind patient friend Lois Lineal, a former magazine editor who came out of retirement to do so much more than edit my books multiple times. You can't put a price tag on that either.

Many thanks go to my dear friend of twenty years, photographer and graphic designer Sandra Friedkin, who designed the cover of *Exceeding Expectations* as well as its sequel, *Paradise Misplaced*.

How would I have managed without Dr. Len Pace who graciously advises me on all medical issues in my books?

And then there are my kids, who lovingly believe that their mother is incredibly gifted. That's what they tell me and I'm not about to argue.

Exceeding Expectations

By Lisa April Smith

Chapter One

January 2, 1962

Glancing down at the Porsche's speedometer Jack eased up on the gas. The nearest car was a mile back, but a cop could be hiding around the next bend. Being stopped by the police did not fit into Jack's plan. He blamed the excitement and guilt. Composing the single page to his daughters had been agony. There was no nice way to say he intended to kill himself. There were no comforting euphemisms for suicide. No words to excuse a mortal sin. And worst of all, no way to ease the pain his beloved girls would experience. But they, and everyone else, had to believe his intention was absolute and irreversible or the plan would fail. After several miserable gut-wrenching attempts, Jack wrote of how much he loved them and said that this was something he had to do to protect them.

Knowing he could rely on Petal's steely strength, Jack's letter to his wife was more direct. He had explained that he was doing this to save her and his girls from scandal and disgrace. As he was making this noble sacrifice, he knew she could be relied on to be good to his daughters. Petal might not be the maternal sort, but no one could accuse her of being tight-fisted. After reading the letter, his dying declaration, and waiting for two Chivas Regal's straight to take effect, she would call a few select members of her powerful family, and her attorney. The results of those calls would be a discreet obituary in *The New York Times*, another in the local paper, hinting at a long-term debilitating disease, and no further investigation. A quiet memorial service would be held in Manhattan, Petal's preferred place of residence, and she would be stunning in black for the next six to ten weeks, depending on her social calendar.

The best thing about his plan was its simplicity. He would wait until two or three in the morning when the roads would be deserted, park the car on the middle of a bridge and disappear into the night. The bridge and town had been carefully selected – less than a five-mile walk to the railroad to prevent someone later recalling giving a lift to a stranger. The town had to be small – an insignificant speck on the map. The smaller the town, Jack had reasoned, the less sophisticated the police force. Fielding, Florida, a town that lacked a drug store, supermarket, bank, and beauty parlor was ideal. Serious crime in Fielding probably consisted of intimidating the kids who tipped over outhouses on Halloween and jailing the same town drunk every Friday night. A costly abandoned car, coupled with the later discovered suicide notes, guaranteed Jack would be the topic of intense gossip for years, and the object of a bumbling investigation for no more than a week. The Porsche would get more attention than the lack of a corpse in an area where alligators outnumbered house pets, and a Ford with all four fenders intact was considered a damned fine automobile.

Once he boarded a train he'd be safe. Men who rode the rails kept secrets. They were members of a tribe of vagabonds who preferred the town around the next curve – adventurous men ready to share a pot of tramp stew with another kindred spirit. He was eager to join them. For the last two and half decades, his life had revolved around his girls. Jack had chosen that life and never once regretted it. A man couldn't have finer daughters than Amelia and Charlotte. But they were grown now and maybe he had earned himself a change. He thought he might head for Texas, a leviathan-sized state where a man's past was not apt to be questioned. Texas was known for its horses. He loved horses — riding them, watching them trot, canter, toss their heads, nurse their foals. Gorgeous, glorious creatures they were.

After several hours of driving through towns too small to boast a stop sign, Jack reached his destination. A weather-beaten building with a concave roof housed the grocery that doubled as Fielding's post office. He gave his letters to a leathery man behind the counter and gazed at a jar of pickles with interest. He had been so focused on reaching his destination he had forgotten to eat lunch. "Is there a place around here to get something to eat?"

"Just Wiley's. Kind of a bar/restaurant down the street. Lost its sign in the last hurricane, but you'll find it."

An orange neon light in the window erratically flickered *Budweiser*. Jack glanced inside. It was more bar than restaurant, and grimy. Lacking an alternative, he entered. A wall of vacant knotty-pine booths faced a long bar backed by a mirror so streaked with fly droppings and smoke that reflected images appeared cloudy. Five or six patrons turned to note his presence and then quickly resumed what they had been doing. Jack proceeded to the bar's last booth and took a seat where he could oversee the comings and goings. The gym bag containing twenty-seven thousand dollars he stowed under the table.

A blowsy overweight waitress with an elaborate hairdo and a too-tight skirt approached. "Need a menu?" she asked as she wiped the table with a dingy towel.

"What time do you stop serving food?"

"The kitchen closes at eight."

Jack removed his buck suede jacket and placed it on the seat beside him. Assuming this place closed at midnight, he had five long hours to kill. "Bring me a draft beer and a hamburger. And if you could spare a newspaper, I'd appreciate it."

She soon returned with his beer and a ten-page weekly tabloid filled with notices of church events, and feed and grain ads. It was a typical weekday night in a small town bar: plenty of griping and boasting, lengthy recitations of what could have been and should have been, a few stale jokes, more men than women, a lot of talk, little action.

"Would you turn up the radio?" a customer called from the far end of the bar. "That's me and Wanda's favorite song."

The bartender adjusted the dial. A twangy melancholy western tune drowned out the dull background noise.

"Turn it down! Turn that blasted thing down!" several customers shouted in unison.

The bartender found an agreeable level of volume and conversation resumed. It started to rain about nine — a light drizzle at first and then a steady hard-driving downpour. On her return trip from the ladies room, a woman in her late thirties, attractive in a tired way, paused to inquire if Jack would be in town for a while. He politely explained that he was just passing through and she rejoined her companions at the bar.

"That would be eighty cents, including the beer. Would you mind settling up now?" the waitress asked at nine-thirty. "I'm leaving in a few minutes. Buddy, that's the bartender, he'll take care of you. I'm going home to my kids."

Jack handed her a dollar and told her to keep the change. At ten o'clock Jack went to the men's room and ducked into a stall. Removing the bills from the gym bag Jack distributed them around the money belt. Twenty-seven thousand dollars. Money painstakingly gleaned from his checking account in amounts that wouldn't later arouse suspicion. It wouldn't finance the way of life he had been enjoying very long, but it could buy ten new Chevrolets. More than enough for a fresh start.

Customers, who had been checking their watches and shaking their heads for the last hour or more, decided the rain was not going to let up. One by one, they finished their beers, turned up their collars, cursed the weather and dashed into the street.

"Last call," the owner announced to Jack and two stragglers. "Closing at eleven cause of this miserable weather."

"No more for me. I gotta go to work tomorrow," the older of the two remaining men announced. He wiped his mouth with the back of his hand and paid his tab. Jack closed his eyes and listened to rain pounding the wood roof. The last customer drank his beer and stared out the front window at the unrelenting downpour. He was about Jack's size and weight, somewhere in his twenties – a kid. His light brown hair was home-cut and in need of a trim. His pants were deeply creased and stained with what Jack guessed to be grease. A handyman, or maybe a mechanic who worked nearby.

Jack grabbed the empty gym bag, handed a dollar bill to the bartender, and headed for the door. The kid blocked the exit.

"My truck's about a mile or so down the road. It weren't raining when I started out. I'd be grateful, mister, if you could give me a ride," the kid said.

Jack appraised the kid grinning back at him. Crooked teeth vied with one another for space, and his tired green eyes spoke of a resilience born of hardship. The faded denim shirt he wore over a grimy T-shirt, would provide no protection from the cold and rain. Jack looked at the bartender owner hoping for some indication that this kid was a local, but the bartender was busy counting the day's receipts.

"You having any trouble with that truck?" Jack tapped his chest. "This old ticker of mine doesn't work as good as it used to," he lied. "If you need a hand with that truck, I'm afraid I'm not going to be able to help."

"I got no trouble with the truck. Runs dandy," he assured Jack. "I left it at a farmhouse to be unloaded. Sold them folks a cord of firewood. But they had to unload and stack it theirselves. That was the deal. They unload it and stack it theirselves whilst I go into town."

Jack weighed the risk. He had twenty-seven thousand dollars in the money belt, but this kid didn't know that. All he knew was that it was pouring, it was cold and he needed a ride. Eleven o'clock was far too early for Jack to carry out his plan. All that awaited him was two or three hours sitting in a parked car. "What's your name, kid?"

"Folks mostly call me Iowa."

"My name's Jack and the Porsche across the street is mine. Wait here. No sense both of us getting soaked." By the time Jack reached the car and jumped in, his hair and clothes were drenched. Mostly Iowa had fared little better. "Which direction?" Jack asked his passenger.

"You're headin' the right way. Just follow the road a piece. I'll tell you where to turn."

"Is it on the left or the right?"

"Left."

"I expect you live around here."

"Just passin' through."

They soon left the residential part of town. The driving rain and incessant flip-flop flip-flop of the windshield wipers blurred his vision. Jack tried the high beams and quickly switched back. Pointing to a dim light on what appeared to be a house he asked, "It that it?"

"Nope. That ain't it. It's up yonder a bit."

"When I first saw you, Iowa, I said to myself, now there's a fellow who knows his way around cars. You a mechanic?"

"I fiddled with cars some. Nothing as swanky as this."

For the next two or three miles there wasn't a break in the road — not a path, planted field, farmhouse or shed, only endless sawgrass and pine trees. "That had to be some hike into town. Are you sure we didn't pass it? You did say it was on the left?"

"Yep. On the left."

While Jack had been struggling to locate the elusive house and truck, Mostly Iowa had been facing right. Damn! What an idiot he had been! A solitary man wearing expensive clothes and a flashy gold watch. A new Porsche – obviously his. A mysterious gym bag that had never left his side. A transient loner who needed a ride. "We must have passed it. I'm going to turn around."

"Just pull over here!" Mostly Iowa's eyes were cold. His right hand expertly cradled a knife.

Targeted like a deer by a hungry kid. Stalked! Jack's foot remained on the accelerator. "You don't want to do this, Iowa. How about I slow down to ten, fifteen miles an hour and you jump out? We part friends and forget this ever happened."

"You stop this here car or I'll stick you like a pig. It wouldn't bother me none to kill you."

Now Jack was a man who liked a good laugh as much as the next guy, but irony had its place. Dying the very night he scheduled his fake suicide was not his idea of a joke.

Iowa grabbed Jack's right arm. "Stop this car or I'll cut out your gizzard and leave it for the birds."

"I'm not stopping the car as long as you got that knife," Jack said in a calm friendly voice. He could feel the frightening tip of the steel blade through his suede jacket. "Toss it out the window and I'll stop the car."

Iowa grabbed the steering wheel. The Porsche hydroplaned and fish-tailed, barely avoiding trees on both sides of the road.

By intuitively releasing his grip, the finely engineered racing car realigned itself. Jack glanced at his passenger looking for some hint of humanity, still hoping to change the kid's mind, yet very much aware of the danger. "You're going to get us both killed. We're doing twenty miles an hour. The ground is soft from the rain. Open the door and roll out."

"Not a chance in hell, you miserable fuck. You're going to die."

The knife slashed the jacket and dug into the money belt. If it weren't for the thick wad of bills, the blade would be boring into his rib cage. Jack deliberately swerved the car right and then left. Iowa grabbed the wheel. Using the butt of his right fist Jack smashed his attacker's hand. Iowa howled with pain and dropped the knife. He alternated curses with punches aimed at Jack's head.

Jack fought to simultaneously keep the car on the road with his left hand and ward off his attacker with his right. A pothole caught Iowa off balance. He slid away. Jack used the opportunity to use the bent right arm, that had been guarding his chest, to lash out, landing an explosive blow with his clenched fist. He could feel the bridge of Iowa's nose collapse, hear the bones crack.

"Goddamn you! You jackass. You busted my nose!" Iowa fumbled beneath the seat.

Seeing the dreaded knife reappear, Jack made the only decision left. "Don't say I didn't warn you." He braced himself and floored the Porsche, aiming the passenger side at a massive oak tree. Iowa reached for the wheel again, too late. The car hit the tree with a violent jolt, throwing both men forward. A branch smashed the windshield a microsecond before Jack's head reached it. The glass shattered harmlessly, but his chest had struck the steering wheel with an impact that left him gasping for air. The motor groaned and sputtered as Jack waited with his eyes closed. His chest ached with every breath. Tentatively touching his forehead he discovered a swelling throbbing bump. Jack opened his eyes. Mostly Iowa had not fared as well. He lay slumped against the door. Blood from the broken nose bathed his face, neck, and shirt. Jack didn't know if he was dead or unconscious, but he wouldn't be a threat for a while.

"Why didn't you jump when you had the chance?" Jack asked the limp figure. "Soon as I find out what kind of shape I'm in, I'll figure out what I'm going to do with you. If I can walk back to town, I'll send someone out to help. And that's better than you deserve, you dumb bastard, considering you were trying to kill me."

Limb by limb, joint by joint, Jack tested his extremities. His arms, hands, and fingers moved, painfully, but they didn't appear to be broken. He flexed one leg and then the other. "My legs seem okay," he informed his silent companion. His chest and shoulders ached. "Probably cracked a few ribs and there's a buzzing in my ears. Going to be sore for a while, as well as black and blue, but I'm alive. What about it, Iowa? You going to make it?"

Jack leaned across the inert body expecting to hear a heartbeat. Nothing. Silence. The kid was dead! Jesus Christ! He hadn't intended to kill the kid. His goal had been to prevent his own imminent demise.

"Now look what you did, Iowa. You tried to kill me and you ended up killing yourself. God damn dumb kid!" he said to keep his teeth from chattering. "God damn dumb kid!" His entire right side throbbed and he was trembling. "Got to get out of here."

He tried the door handle. It turned, but the bowed door would not budge. He threw all his weight against it and grimaced. It groaned in sympathy and swung open causing him to crash onto the muddy ground. The rain had subsided to a trickle. Jack wiped his hands on soggy moss and sat down to think beside the demolished car.

There was nothing more that could be done for Iowa. His problems were over. Jack's problems had tripled. In a day or two, Petal and the girls would read the letters he had mailed. A first-class plan wiped out because he wanted to help out a dumb kid.

Okay, he told himself, if faking his suicide by leaving the Porsche on a bridge was no longer possible, he simply needed a new plan. A new plan. Jesus, Mary, and Joseph. The Porsche would be traced to him. They would find a dead kid in his car. If he disappeared now he would be accused of murder. Unless . . . Unless . . . Iowa was about his size. The police would assume the body belonged to Jack Morgan if – if it was unrecognizable. But how? The car and its contents would have to be burnt beyond recognition. He could do that. Provided he kept calm, and no one came along in the interim, it was a good alternative plan.

Jack removed the ruined suede jacket. It could go on the corpse. A scrap of burnt suede would add to the illusion, as would his wedding band. He had intended to sell it before he reached Texas, but it would be better used now. As he removed the ring he noticed his prized gold watch. They might look for it. It was too bad about the watch, but it too had to go.

The tight quarters inside the crumpled Porsche, coupled with Jack's reluctance to touch the bloody corpse made the exchange time consuming, exhausting, and grisly. As a final touch, Jack traded shoes with the dead man before shoving him into position behind the wheel.

An hour had passed since the crash and no one had driven by. His luck was holding. Now he needed matches. Matches or a cigarette lighter. His pockets yielded neither. His plan would fail because he lacked a pack of matches that every bar and restaurant supplied free. Think, he told himself. There had to be a solution. The Porsche's cigarette lighter. Would it still work? Leaning over Iowa's body, Jack located it and pressed it. Thirty seconds later it popped out glowing red. God bless the Germans! Every twenty or thirty years, it took a war to remind them who was boss, but they sure knew how to build a car. Jack looked for something to start the fire. Downed branches were too wet. A dry rag. He kept a towel in the trunk.

Jack walked to the rear of the car to unlock the trunk but it wouldn't release. He kicked it with his heel. Another sharp kick. The trunk creaked open. A white, still-folded hand towel lay tucked in a corner. A few more minutes and it would be over.

He stuffed as much of the towel as would fit into the gas tank, then replaced the ignition key. As he was about to press the cigarette lighter he remembered the knife. What if it were found with the remains? Palm Beach socialite Jack Morgan didn't carry a switchblade. He would have to find it. Ten minutes passed as he searched the car and the corpse. He was about to give up when he felt it lodged under the passenger seat. He folded it, tucked it into his belt, and inserted the dependable lighter.

Half a football field away Jack leaned against a tree and waited.

Several times the flame appeared to die, only to flare up again. And then the rag ignited with an enormous *pop* – followed by *ear-splitting thunder.* Roaring flames, the height of a church steeple leapt from the car's rear. Jack could no longer make out Iowa's silhouette in the flames. Just a few more minutes, he told himself. The smoke and heat from the blaze reddened his face and seared his lungs.

When it was time to leave Jack strode away in Iowa's ill-fitting shoes, away from the wrecked Porsche, the town of Fielding, and his past. Then he heard it. A train whistle. The magical hollow sound of a train whistle. And it wasn't far off. Damn, if he wasn't a lucky so-and-so. One of God's favorite children. Jesus tolerated the pious, sober, and abstinent. Yes, He tolerated the tiresome righteous and their smug unforgiving Christian smiles. And He had little pity for the tyrant, the merciless, and the cruel. But Jesus loved the ordinary sinner. Isn't that what the bible taught? The Almighty loved sinners. Without sinners there would have been no reason for Jesus to come to earth and experience the joy and pain of mortals.

Intoxicating freedom mingled with the chilling air. Jack could forget the chafing money belt, cheap ill-fitting shoes, sore feet, and aching muscles. He had a new name and a thousand new possibilities. The next time he found himself with a drink in his hand he would remember Iowa and raise his glass to the tragic dumb kid.

"This one's for you, Iowa, you miserable misguided creature," he would say. "May the good Lord take mercy on your soul and your time in Purgatory be brief."

Chapter Two

The last time I saw Andrew Regis, my stepmother's attorney, was six weeks ago at my father's funeral. I assumed the reason he had invited me to his office was to discuss my father's will. Normally, Regis smiled, a broad smile meant to assure the listener of his sincerity and pure intentions. Today his expression was suitably grave. I, on the other hand, appeared composed. I could do that, hide my emotions – look calm when I was agitated, or angry, or grief-stricken, as I was now. It was a keystone of my social set, a trick we'd been trained to perform from infancy, in the same way children of circus performers are taught to juggle or ride a unicycle.

"Mrs. Morgan contacted us from New York," Regis said. "I understand she plans to spend the rest of the season there."

My stepmother had left town the day after the funeral — scarcely after Palm Beach's winter social events began.

"No doubt she had some urgent business to attend to," I said, hoping to move our conversation to the real reason for my presence. I had been seated in his office for thirty minutes and Regis had yet to say anything meaningful. I estimated the time to be thirty minutes, but it could have been five. Since my father's death time advances at an agonizingly slow pace.

"Ah, yes, business. Very sad." Regis waited for me to nod my acknowledgment of his considerate distress. I complied and he continued. "This is particularly awkward to do at this time, so I'll try to make it as brief as possible. Naturally we were shocked to learn about your father — the accident. Tragic. How old a man was your father? Fifty-five, I'm told. Every member of this firm thought highly of him. Splendid sportsman. Dreadful loss. I'm sure you're anxious to get on with things — know where you stand – financially and otherwise, so you can make plans for your future."

"Yes. Thank you."

"As you know, Mrs. Morgan is very fond of you and your sister. She assures me that you will always be welcome in her home. This must be so difficult for you — and of course Amelia. How is she progressing? Well, I hope. No doubt, she'll mend quickly. Young people do."

My sister Amelia currently receives callers at Silver Glades, a private clinic euphemistically termed a rest home. If only Regis would get to the point. His babbling was chipping away my veneer of control. My throat was dry and my eyes were threatening to betray me. The idea of blubbering in front of this stranger was appalling. I did my blubbering in private.

"It would help if I could make plans for our future," I prompted.

"Yes, yes, of course." Regis swallowed and deadened his face. "I regret to say that your father left no will. Nor was one necessary. He had no holdings other than a small sum in his checking account, and his personal effects."

I willed my stomach to settle while I corrected what had to be a mistake. "My father had to have a will. Perhaps it was misplaced."

"No will was filed. Records have been checked. Your father held no assets beyond those I've described."

"What about stocks and bonds?"

"There were none."

"A small trust fund? He was an only child. His parents died before I was born. He had to have inherited everything."

Regis shook his head. "I'm sorry. There is no record of a trust fund from any source."

"That's impossible. My father wasn't employed. How did he support us without an income? What about the allowance he gave us?"

"He wrote checks to you and your sister from his checking account. Mrs. Morgan's accountant made monthly deposits to that account."

"That can't be. My father was a wealthy man. I know our homes belong to my stepmother, but we never had to concern ourselves with money." Feeling queasy and lightheaded, my brain attempted to focus. "What about the horses and riding equipment?"

"All belong to your stepmother, and either have been, or will be, sold as per her request. Mrs. Morgan doesn't ride and doesn't wish the unnecessary expense. She intends to sell the estate in Virginia, as well."

"But how are we to live?" I stupidly blurted before I could stop myself.

"For the next three months, your allowance and the expense involved in maintaining Amelia at the" – Regis glanced at his notes – "Silver Glades, will be provided by Mrs. Morgan, which I'm sure you'll agree is very generous of her. She is under no obligation to do so. Your charge accounts, naturally, have been terminated. Oh yes. And you may stay on at the house here in Palm Beach until next season. Mrs. Morgan intends to stay in New York. So that's it. All of it. I'm sorry if this all comes as a shock."

A shock? My legs had turned to Silly Putty and my upper body had fossilized. Forcing air into my lungs required all my concentration. I could taste rancid baby food, which had somehow managed to remain lodged in a crevice of my stomach for the last twenty-two years.

"I can imagine what you must be thinking. Would you like me to repeat any part of what I've said?"

"No. Thank you," I replied in a voice barely audible to myself. "I'm quite certain that won't be necessary."

Exiting Regis' office I walked faster than my normal pace, temporarily unconcerned if I was seen limping in my quest for the Ladies Room. Mercifully, it was empty. I had the luxury of regurgitating into the porcelain bowl in privacy. I flushed several times during the process to muffle the sound. When I turned to the sink, the mirror corroborated my expectations. Like the Italian flag, I was red, white, and green. I bathed my face with cold water, rinsed out my mouth, and applied face powder before exiting.

On my way past thickly carpeted offices and conference rooms, I decided to forgo all earlier resolutions regarding self-pity. Learning I was a pauper entitled me to a three-month orgy of self-pity, or until the last dollar of my allowance was spent. After that, Amelia and I would convert to Catholicism, join a convent, preferably one with good wine, minimal requirements for self-flagellation, and an abbey with a dazzling view. I had visited several lovely facilities in France. Escape was within my reach until I felt a hand touching my shoulder.

"Wait! Please. We should talk."

I turned and stared directly into a man's eyes. He was a few years older than I am and an inch or two shorter. I could hear him speaking. The language was English, but the rhythm and deep cello undertones were foreign. With the exception of Richard Burton and a few other Brits trained for the theater, English-speaking voices lacked that resonance. He had to repeat himself before I understood.

"I'm sure I could be of help if you could give me a few minutes."

I stared at the man – dark wavy hair, skin the color of a pecan, and dark chocolate eyes. And he wore a suit. A Latin man. A Latin man wearing a suit, doubtless a common sight in Barcelona or Madrid, an imaginable occurrence in Manhattan, but not in Palm Beach. In Palm Beach, residents employed Latins as gardeners and household staff. But this man with the long sweeping lashes and glacier-white teeth seemed completely at ease in his suit.

"Raul Francesco." He extended his right hand. "I'm an attorney with the firm. Neville Byrd is my uncle. He's asked me to speak with you. My uncle considered your father more of a friend than a client. As dreadful as things may appear at the moment, there may be some way we can help."

Neville Byrd was the firm's founder. My father hadn't abandoned us, hadn't left us destitute. Andrew Regis had been mistaken. I shook the proffered hand. "Nice to meet you, Mr. Francesco."

"My uncle thought you might appreciate some assistance, letters of recommendation, advice on employment. We'd like to help in some small way. And please call me Raul."

So there wasn't any money. Advice! I didn't need advice. I needed my father and hard cash. In lieu of that, I needed to be alone. At the very least, I was entitled to a good cry and the half bottle of sherry I had stashed in my bedroom. "Perhaps some other time. I'm in a bit of a hurry."

"What about tomorrow? How about lunch? We could meet at Taboo."

"Tomorrow? Lunch? Ah, that would be impossible." I responded, hoping to dissuade my persistent pursuer with a thin pasty smile.

"Then coffee or a drink in the evening?"

"I've made other plans."

"What about later this week? I absolutely promise to be helpful."

Realizing this insistent man would simply continue suggesting times and days, I decided to name a day. "I'm free on Friday." That gave me three full days to invent an excuse.

"Where and when?"

"The Sandbar, three o'clock."

"Three o'clock, Friday, the Sandbar," he replied, once again flashing those outrageous teeth.

*   *   *

When I returned home the house was empty. Carlos and Maria, the couple my stepmother employs, had gone out for the evening. I was alone in my lilac and cream flowered bedroom that now seemed sickeningly precious. I opened the white wicker dresser that held what remained of the sherry. It was the last alcoholic beverage not under lock and key. Over the past six weeks, I'd drained three decanters of after-dinner liqueurs I'd found in the living room, five bottles of table wine from the butler's pantry cooler, a silver flask my sister kept filled with cognac for emergencies, and a bottle of scotch my father stored in his library.

I remembered the day we learned of my father's death. Petal had been in a tiff because Daddy had left without advising her of his plans. Amelia was spending a chaste weekend with her fiancé Hal, at his parents' home. It didn't occur to me to be overly concerned. I assumed that he had left a note explaining his absence and it would soon be found. Daddy often made trips to and from New York.

We were having breakfast on the lanai that faced the pool and rear garden. The doorbell rang but we ignored it until Maria informed us a man from the Sheriff's office wanted to speak with Mrs. Morgan. Curious, I took my glass of orange juice and followed Petal to the front door.

"I'm sorry to have to tell you this, Mrs. Morgan, but your husband's car was found a couple of miles outside of Hamilton Grove. He had an accident," the grim uniformed man said.

"Go on," Petal ordered, squaring her shoulders. "Has he been hospitalized?"

"No, ma'am. It was too late for that."

I remembered hearing the loudest, shrillest scream and the sound of glass shattering. It wasn't until later that I realized that both the scream and glass were mine.

Daddy's letters arrived the following day as we were preparing to leave for New York for the funeral. I didn't see Petal's reaction to her letter; she took it to the small study adjoining the master bedroom to read privately. Amelia and I sat in the breakfast room and held hands as we read ours. Amelia was calm, chalk white, but calm. I sobbed uncontrollably until I threw up. The family's physician was summoned. He gave me a shot to sedate me and left pills. The next ten days were a blur. I either slept, wept, or woodenly obeyed Petal's orders.

As I disintegrated, Amelia grew more and more serene. People compared her to young Princess Elizabeth after her father died, until my sister was found huddled in her closet, catatonic, and had to be carried away. No one dreamed that she would collapse, least of all me.

Amelia was the girl with the Shirley Temple dimples and irresistible smile. She wasn't the sister who called the police when she was thirteen, because she saw escaped convicts lurking in the trees. She wasn't the one who heard lions prowling in the tall grass when other people heard house cats. It's not that I'm phobic. Bats, cockroaches, centipedes, spiders, worms, mice, rats, ghosts, vultures, vampires, snakes, lightning, and thunder don't frighten me. It's simply that I have an overactive imagination. It was only reasonable to assume that I would be the sister in a cloistered room and Amelia would be dealing with this nightmare.

Seated in my favorite chair, I glanced down at one of our family photo albums that had not left my room in weeks. Most nights I could find some comfort in the pictures of the three of us. Mother died when Amelia was four and I was two. No image appeared when I tried to imagine her, nor could my sister provide one. We knew nothing of my mother or her family. Any reference to her caused my father to leave the room.

Nevertheless, Amelia and I had never felt neglected. Daddy was always there to lavish us with attention and affection. But being a motherless child did set one apart. For example, Amelia and I still referred to the area we sat on as *down there*, as in "Wash down there, Charlotte." I'm certain my mother could have provided a better term than *down there*. I turned to a photograph I particularly liked, taken at a horse show when I was twelve. In it, I was holding two of the three ribbons I'd won that day. The date beneath read May, 1950. Learning to ride was my father's idea. He encouraged me to participate in sports where my limp wouldn't be a disadvantage. My right leg was partially immobile, the result of a birth defect. Daddy had offered no sympathy. "Throw your head back, Charlotte, and stand tall. You're Jack Morgan's daughter and you can do anything you set your mind to."

Stand tall. When one stood a mere inch shy of six feet in stocking feet, what other choice remained? Memories of being the last girl chosen at Mrs. Medford's Dance Academy still plagued me. I'd always been the tallest girl in my class. The only thing I truly envied of my sister's was her height. I often felt like Alice-in-Wonderland after she ate the cake, her head jutting out of the roof, her feet the length of a coffee table. Lucky Alice. Her tears caused her to shrink to her original size. My tears have thus far proved futile.

The photo on the facing page showed the three of us that day.

Daddy and I were in riding clothes; Amelia wore a navy dress with a full skirt and a white lace collar. She had lost all interest in horses a year earlier. Amelia the Beautiful. Immediately after losing their hearts to my father, two stepmothers and countless others fell in love with my sister's pale blond curls and bluebonnet eyes. In the photo, a hat hides my waist-length braid, which had darkened to muddy blond. Like Amelia, my skin was fair and scorched easily. No bluebonnet eyes for me, My eyes never could decide whether to be blue or green. At fourteen, Amelia was petite, feminine, and shapely. At twelve, my chest was mirror smooth. Except for the addition of breasts, which still require "a hint of lining" to fill up a B cup, I looked pretty much the same. Amelia's lips are bow shaped and neatly defined. Mine are full and oddly shaped – particularly my upper lip.

I stared into the photograph. You, the most loving father ever, had no right to run your car off the road and kill yourself – your body so hideously burned that you had to be buried in a sealed casket. No right to abandon us! No right at all. Without saying good-bye. How could you do this to us? How could you do this to me?

Do you remember, Daddy, I asked his photograph, when Amelia and I both came down with the chicken pox? I was seven and Amelia was nine. Lucky Amelia had two pox on her back, one on her stomach, one on her forehead, another on her chin, and no more than two on each arm and leg. I, conversely, had no area larger than a half-dollar devoid of itchy red blotches. They invaded my underarms, my inner ears, and eyelids. We were forbidden to scratch. Scratching left scars, you warned us, and since you never left our side that endless week, the relief scratching might have provided proved impossible. Other parents doused their children with calamine and left them to amuse themselves by listening to Arthur Godfrey or Art Linkletter on the radio. When we complained we were bored, you tinted the calamine with food coloring and painted pink, red, and magenta anemones on our spots. With her measly dozen or so pox, Amelia was merely attractively embellished. I, on the other hand, was an ambulatory floral display.

I reached for the sherry. The bottle was empty. Closing the album, I climbed into bed. The image of the three of us surviving chicken pox faded. I fell asleep once more trying to figure out why my father killed himself and how I could have prevented it. Why hadn't I seen the signals or symptoms? If I'd done this or said that. If I'd known what demons haunted him, surely I could have done something.

*   *   *

I glanced again at my watch. It read 3:15. I was not fond of people who kept me waiting, and Raul Francesco was late.

The Sandbar was a local spot to have lunch or, later in the day, to stop for drinks. I had deliberately selected three o'clock, a time too late for lunch and too early for cocktails. In the restaurant's dim interior, an elderly couple appraised me when they believed they wouldn't be observed. The pair was attired in the expected Palm Beach mode for their generation. For the lady, a long-sleeved frock buttoned to the neck, stockings, wide-brimmed summer hat, and sensible shoes. For the gentleman, navy blazer, tan slacks, panama hat, and loafers — no socks. I wore my generation's local feminine attire: cotton skirt, blouse, sandals, and Episcopalian features. Raul arrived at 3:25. The couple noted his presence by openly staring their disapproval.

At Raul's suggestion we ordered the Sandbar's legendary martinis.

"How are you related to Neville Byrd?" I asked, making certain I could be heard at the next table.

"My mother is his wife's sister," he replied in that hypnotic voice. "When my mother was young, she went to Cuba with two girl friends. It was Carnival. People in Cuba go a little crazy during Carnival. My parents saw each other across a crowded plaza and fell in love. Romantic, no?"

"When did they leave Cuba?" I said, trying to keep the topic away from myself.

"When I was in my final year of law school, just after Castro took control. Since my mother never gave up her American citizenship, it was easier for us to get out."

His eyes insisted I was intriguing and attractive. Doubtless a well-rehearsed act, but as I was in desperate need of reassurance, I nodded in the appropriate places while he talked. He had attended college and then law school in the States. As for his reasons for returning to Florida he explained, "I have two older sisters, but I'm the only son. In a Cuban family an only son has obligations."

The martini was growing on me — both the taste and the effect. "Do you like being a lawyer? Working with clients?"

He dropped his gaze and smiled. "I don't see many clients. My work is mostly research, done where I can't be seen. I took the job because it'll look good on my resume. I can never hope to a partner at Byrd, Regis and O'Dell. At some point I'll have to leave the firm, and either go out on my own, or join one with a more diverse list of clients."

"Oh." Did he have to be so blunt? I decided to ignore the pointed remark as he continued staring at me with those provocative eyes.

"Someday, I'm planning to do something more interesting than help rich people hang onto their money."

He moved when he spoke — with his hands, with his head, with his shoulders. I was accustomed to men who stayed fixed, but his gestures were graceful and masculine.

"Charlotte! Charlotte is more than a beautiful name. It should be sung, accompanied by a guitar."

"Frankly, I've always hated it. Maybe you should just call me Charlie." When Raul crooned *Charlotte* with his cello-like voice and slight Spanish inflection, the effect was . . . Distracting. Unnerving. While I was unhappy about volunteering something so personal as my nickname, I wasn't about to risk becoming a slack-jawed, wide-eyed schoolgirl every time he said my name. "Unfortunately, you forgot to bring your guitar. But that's not why we're here, is it?"

"No it isn't. I promised to help you. So, what are your plans, Charlie? Maybe I can give you some ideas."

Plans? I had no plans other than the deal I had offered God every night since Daddy died. I would devote my life to charity and good works, and He would put everything back as it was — my father would be alive and the events of the last six weeks would be a bad dream. "My plans are sort of vague right now."

"Okay. Let's start with college. What was your major?"

"Ski weekends. I minored in sorority teas."

"It's great that you haven't lost your sense of humor."

Having made a joke I got to see those outrageous teeth again. "I have a bachelor's degree in art history. Any ideas?"

"Umm. How would you rate your skill at drawing or painting? Honestly! Don't be modest."

"Honestly? Good enough to get through classes." I'd liked this man better before our conversation took this unsettling turn — when I could simply study the fine bone structure of his face, listen to his musical voice, and pretend that he was taller and richer. I didn't need anyone to remind me how totally unprepared I was. When I wasn't battling guilt and fear, that little tune repeated endlessly in my brain. "It was always understood, when I was ready, I would meet the right man and get married."

He glanced down at the simple pearl ring on my right hand and grinned. "You're not wearing an engagement ring, so I assume that you're not engaged."

"True, but I'm sort of seeing someone," I lied. There was no point in encouraging this man who shared my father's easy charm. At the moment, I had no interest in dating anyone. Raul Francesco could be as innocent and pure as a saint, or as evil as the Marquis de Sade. I no longer trusted my judgment.

"Sort of seeing someone. Just a promise not to date other people?"

"Right."

"Then we'd better come up with a marketable skill until he makes up his mind or you decide that he's not the right guy for you. What about modeling? Have you ever considered modeling?"

I glared at him. I'd heard too many jokes at my expense to find the remark amusing. In the past five weeks I'd lost eight pounds that I could scarcely afford to lose. "You mean I'm tall enough to be a model. In my opinion, the only thing good about my height is being able to reach objects on high shelves."

"You're not just tall. And I not going to say you're beautiful, because it's obvious that you're not going to believe me. You're interesting looking – different – exotic. Most blonds are wishy-washy."

I raised my brows, pursed my lips, and shook my head — the accepted way a lady signals that a subject was closed. But this man would not take the hint.

"Come on. You can't deny that you've got terrific skin. I bet you have a few freckles on your shoulders. Some men find them sexy."

Freckles sexy? I adjusted my collar. How dare this stranger toy with me. "I'm sure you mean well," I said, feeling increasingly uncomfortable.

"Okay, forget modeling. What about hobbies?"

"I ski. I play golf and ride." I omitted mentioning my eight years of ballet lessons – another one of Daddy's ideas to correct my limp. The mental image of me in tutu was too absurd to share. I instinctively tucked my size eleven sandaled feet under the table. "And I sculpt. Anything marketable there?"

"Maybe. Are you good enough to teach any of the above?"

I mentally compared myself with former instructors and shook my head. "I doubt it."

"I suppose it's useless for me to ask if you can type or take dictation."

"Useless."

"What about a musical instrument? You don't play the piano, do you?"

"The flute."

"Well enough to be in an orchestra or a band?"

"I sincerely doubt that an orchestra exists that's desperate enough to hire me." I'd never thought I'd have to rely on a job to support myself. Right before Daddy died, feeling useless with so much time on my hands, I'd seriously considered returning to college, so that I could teach art – in high school. But that was out of the question now. Rapid heartbeat and nausea, my personal panic symptoms, were rapidly returning.

"I've upset you. That wasn't what I intended."

"I'm sure you mean well, but I haven't been able to think clearly . . ." I swallowed in an attempt to regain my composure. "Not since my father's . . . Not since . . ." Appalled that I was about to lose control in front of this stranger, I stopped and forced myself to smile.

Raul leaned toward me and gazed at me with empathetic soulful eyes. "Suicide is a horrible thing to do to the people left behind. I can't even imagine how you feel."

"I'm not myself today. Please excuse me," I said, reaching for my handbag and rising. Apparently, this recent import from sunny Cuba was aware, not only of my financial devastation, but of my father's decision to end his life. "You're trying to be helpful, but I'm just not ready right now."

If he said anything as I raced off, I was moving too fast to hear.

Chapter Three

I maintained a steady monologue in my car as I drove home. If Raul Francesco was aware of Daddy's suicide, how many others knew? How many pitying faces and morbid questions would I be forced to endure? I might never leave the house again. That convent in France grew increasingly attractive. I possessed few worldly goods to surrender. Nor would it be tragic to take an oath of chastity. Based on my experience sex was highly overrated. On the other hand, I'd never had an orgasm. I'd read about them, of course. In novels, they sounded dream-like. But that was in novels.

I'd lost my virginity, or if one insisted on being technical, given it away to Dickie Allbright the night of the spring formal in my junior year at William Smith. Dickie was my roommate Dina's older brother and had graduated from Hobart the year before. Dina was worried that I might not get a date and we always looked out for each other. On the way home Dickie drove into a parking lot and stopped the car. We both had had too much to drink. At first, I thought he might have to throw up, but he had other ideas. He wanted to pet – which we did. He was particularly adept at breathing into my ears and sucking them, something I hadn't found arousing before, but did that night. As the Shirelles sang *Will You Still Love Me Tomorrow?* on the car radio, I allowed Dickie to remove my bolero jacket, unhook my bra and fondle my breasts. When it became apparent he planned to go further, I stopped him.

"Aw come on, Charlie, what are you waiting for? You're the only virgin in your class."

"How would you know?" I challenged. But Dickie was a brother in Sigma Phi, a fraternity notoriously popular with girls.

"Name one girl that's a junior who's still a virgin."

"Mary Ellen Ritchie and Brenda Hellenbeck," I said with reasonable certainty. It was a small class. Mary Ellen had told every girl who would listen that she would absolutely and positively not French kiss unless she was pinned, engaged, or married. As for Brenda Hellenbeck – poor Brenda was, without argument, the homeliest girl in school.

"Okay," Dickie said. "I'll give you Brenda Hellenbeck, but you can forget Mary Ellen Ritchie. Mary Ellen was giving hand jobs at thirteen. She was screwing anyone who asked before she turned seventeen."

It didn't require much imagination to decipher hand jobs, and screw was already part of my unarticulated vocabulary. That did it. Being linked with Brenda Hellenbeck, for all eternity, wasn't the kind of distinction I craved. I'd wanted the first time to be more like my daydreams, with someone I was madly in love with, someone who made my lips tremble, my breasts heave, and set my loins afire. He would have yard-wide shoulders and granite muscles and be breathtakingly handsome, like Rock Hudson, who appeared regularly in my fantasies. Alas, Rock hadn't made his real-life entrance, and I'd always been curious about male equipment and mechanics. So I did it. Unfortunately, Dickie didn't remove his shorts, so I never did get the opportunity to expand my knowledge of the equipment, and just as I seemed to be recovering from the shock of sitting on Dickie's plunger with my skirt going everywhere, it was over.

It wasn't much better with Bruce, I decided as I parked my car at the back of the driveway, unwilling to enter the silent house just yet. Bruce and I had been dating since we met at a horse show the summer before my senior year. Having been foolishly impetuous once, I permitted petting with breast fondling privileges until we had discussed marriage and Bruce had given me his fraternity pin – about eight months after our first date.

The problem was that I attracted few men. They preferred curvaceous women like Sophia Loren and Marilyn Monroe to 5' 11" girls, who needed a hint of lining to fill out a "B" cup bra. Give a man a few drinks, mention Sophia Loren and watch his eyes glaze over, his jaw go slack, and his lips curl into the most ridiculous smirk. He was imagining Sophia Loren, with her improbable tiny waist and enormous boobs, ready to fulfill his wildest sexual fantasy. Women admired lithe Audrey Hepburn, with her enormous brown eyes and elfin face, but you'll never see a man's jaw go slack at the mention of her name, no matter how much he's had to drink. Unfortunately, I bore absolutely no resemblance to the voluptuous Miss Loren and Miss Hepburn possessed a waif-like quality that eluded me.

So when tall, extremely eligible Bruce Hoffstat said and did everything he could to get me into bed, including discuss marriage,

I was willing to overlook his boring horse-centered conversations and limited interests. I kept waiting for an orgasm, but it wasn't to be. I ended our relationship. The initial excitement of finding a tall extremely eligible man who met my father's standards, and found me desirable, no longer seemed enough.

*　　*　　*

The following day I drove to Silver Glades to see my sister. Visiting days were torture. I had to paste on my unwavering smile and steel myself for what I would find. I had to assure myself that other patients had been admitted with serious problems and had left cured.

As soon as I located Amelia I led her to a bench and talked while she sat mutely beside me. A deserted and neglected, weed-invaded tennis court separated us from the single story, pale pink stucco main building. Notwithstanding the sad looking tennis court, the facility and grounds at Silver Glades were tranquil and parklike. I didn't know if Amelia was aware of the placid beauty surrounding us, nor did I know if she heard any part of my forced cheery monologue, but I steadfastly continued in the desperate hope that it would bring her back to me. I didn't know what else to do.

A hundred yards away, under twisted gaunt pines draped in gray-green Spanish moss, a man and women occupied another bench. Although they were too far away for me to see their facial expressions, it was apparent the woman was the visitor and the stooped man was the patient. A number of residents at Silver Glades came looking for help with alcohol abuse. This one hadn't. After weeks of visiting Amelia, I could distinguish the seemingly normal alcoholics from the more troubled patients, like my sister. The man was indifferent to his surroundings and his visitor's presence. The woman's bearing spoke of weariness and frustration — a language I understood too well.

I opened the bag I'd brought with me, removed a chocolate chip cookie, and handed it to Amelia. "Maria baked these for you." Receiving no response, I placed the cookie in Amelia's hand, lifted it to her mouth, and was rewarded with a small bite. No emotion, just a small bite. Amelia's silky hair was clean and combed. Someone had taken the trouble to dab pale pink lipstick on her lips, I reminded myself, trying to find comfort in signs of care.

"What can I get you? Would you like me to bring you some

things from home?" I asked. Instead of answering Amelia turned away.

When the ninety minutes I had allotted to spend had passed I was relieved and guilt ridden that my twice-weekly visit was over. I kissed Amelia's cheek, led her to an attendant and headed for the director's office.

"I assume you'd like to discuss Amelia," Dr. Mendelson said, as I sat facing him. A cigarette burned in an ashtray on his desk and a ceiling fan circled slowly. His head was shaved and his dark eyebrows were high and arched. Books were strewn about his desk and shelves. Blinds kept out the sun and hid the view.

"Amelia still doesn't speak or respond," I said. "How long is this going to last?"

"As I explained to your stepmother, we still have much to learn about acute depression. Amelia had a nervous collapse triggered by your father's death. You, no doubt, were able to grieve – as you should. Your sister is one of those people who hold things in and pretend everything is fine. When reality clashed with her dream world, she turned her back on reality. However, I do see progress."

It was hard to imagine the progress he saw. I saw none.

"She doesn't participate in conversations," he continued. "But she does say an occasional word or phrase. She allows the staff to bathe her and to comb her hair. She'll feed herself with a little urging. When she arrived she wouldn't do any of those things."

I nodded.

"Have you been in contact with her fiancé? When Amelia first arrived" – the doctor lifted a sheet of paper to study the one beneath – "her fiancé, Mr. Harold Holmes, came to see her twice. Is there any way you can persuade Mr. Holmes to visit? It might be helpful."

I'd called Harold "Hasty" Holmes, heir apparent to the Romanoff Furs fortune, several times and left messages for him with servants. From the first day we met, I found Hasty's charms elusive. He wasn't a bad looking fellow – no jug-handle ears, beaver teeth, or disfiguring scars, and my sister was so infatuated with him that I feigned enthusiasm. Now I detested him. Two days after Amelia's collapse, when he took back his ring for safekeeping, I added spineless and shallow to my list of adjectives to describe him. "I fear Mr. Holmes has given up."

"Regrettable." Dr. Mendelson slowly lifted the cigarette to his lips.

"Dr. Mendelson, what drives a person to kill himself?"

"Hmm, if you're referring to your father, I'm afraid I can't help. I never examined him or even met him. But, if you are looking for a general answer, people kill themselves when life is too filled with pain to continue."

"Wouldn't a close family member notice this?"

"Sometimes." He formed a triangle with his hands. "Sometimes they misinterpret subtle changes like loss of appetite, increase in alcohol consumption, or detachment from family and friends. Did you notice any of these symptoms?"

"It's hard to say. Mostly I was away at college, wrapped up in my own life," I admitted, feeling guiltier than ever. "I always considered my father and Amelia stronger than I am."

"Perhaps they were better actors." Dr. Mendelson walked to my side of the desk. "Amelia's file indicates you have no other living relatives. Perhaps your father had close friends you could speak with."

I rose to leave. "Thank you for your time."

"What you uncover may be painful, but it could help you better understand your father. Amelia's illness is her way of avoiding reality. I'd be interested in hearing anything you learn."

I smiled and nodded. At this particular moment, reality stunk.

* * *

Since I was the sole family member left in the cavernous house, I'd taken to eating with the staff, which now only consisted of Maria and Carlos. We ate in the kitchen, situated in the rear and side of the house.

Maria and Carlos had worked in this house for as long as I could remember. They had cooked, swept, mopped, dusted, and taken care of us, but I knew little about them until recently. Born in Puerto Rico, with three grown children who all held "good jobs", they were short sturdy people with patient faces.

When I returned to my room I found my laundry washed, ironed, and neatly stacked on my bed ready to be put away. I suddenly realized that soon I would have to do all those things that I took for granted. It wasn't only washers, driers, and irons that I would have to learn to negotiate, I brooded, as I sat on the side of my bed. I would have to pay bills, cook, clean, find a job. And what about a place to live — a home for Amelia and me after she recovered – if she recovered? Provided I had money, how much could I expect to pay for rent? I had no one to help or advise me. No one! My girlfriends were as ignorant as I was. Washers. Driers. Irons. Apartments. Electricity. I never even bothered to balance my checkbook. The list expanded with every second that passed. Taxes. Telephones. Food. Food! I can't live on potato chips and candy bars. I don't know how to cook. What about insurance? My heart was racing. I could feel my pulse pounding in my head. I was so dizzy straight edges, like walls and furniture, appeared to be wavy. Rather than fall I decided to sit down, missed the bed, and landed bum first, elbows second, on the carpet. I'd forgotten to breathe. If I didn't force myself to inhale and exhale, I'd die. Inhale. Exhale. Inhale, I told myself. Slowly. Deeply. I crawled to my dresser and the newly purchased bottle of sherry, opened it, and took a long swallow directly from the bottle. Inhale. Slowly. Exhale. The panic slowly subsided. Inhale. Exhale. My god! If I survived, I would never allow myself to be this helpless again.

*   *   *

With the brilliant sunlight pouring in my window and flooding my room, I found it impossible to be gloomy despite the terrifying panic that I'd experienced the night before. Determined to prevent a relapse I decided to have Maria teach me how to operate the washer, drier, iron, and vacuum, as a start. In a few hours, having mastered the basic skills, I was feeling rather pleased with myself when the telephone rang.

"It's Raul Francesco calling to apologize," a deep resonant voice said.

"You have nothing to apologize for."

"Then how about giving me another chance?"

I imagined him grinning at me mischievously. "How did you learn my father's death was a suicide?"

There was a long pause before he answered. "It's a small town. People talk."

"In that case, have you heard any theories as to why he did it?"

"Only baseless rumors and idle speculation. Are you sure you want to talk about this?"

"Look, I realized this morning that before I can worry about finding a job, I have to find out why my father killed himself. I keep wondering if there was something I could've done to prevent it."

"Have you spoken to his doctors? There's always the chance your father chose a quick death over a long drawn out illness."

"That's the one thing I did do. His doctor assured me that my father was in great shape for fifty-five."

"Was he acting odd or drinking more than usual? In private, when others weren't around, was he moody in the last six months?"

"I was at school. I don't know," I admitted, impressed that in less scientific terms, Raul's questions echoed the learned Dr. Mendelson's.

"Are you feeling guilty or just curious? It could get unpleasant."

"Horribly guilty. The doctor that's treating Amelia is curious. He thinks it might be helpful."

"Then it's going to take some detective work."

"What sort of detective work?"

"Digging into his life and looking into his past. Rifling through his papers. Calling people he knew and asking questions. Remember, I did offer to help."

"Shall I assume you can be trusted?" I joked, rather than admit I was as frightened as I was determined.

He laughed his deep musical laugh. "I knew behind that genteel debutante exterior you had a trace of spit and vinegar in you."

I replaced the phone feeling nervous, but unquestionably better.

*   *   *

We met as agreed, near the Middle Bridge on Royal Palm Avenue — or almost as planned. Raul was twenty minutes late again. He parked his beat-up Plymouth station wagon in the only space available, between an Austin Healey and a Jaguar.

"A shiny red MG," he said, opening my car door. "A graduation gift or did you have to promise not to smoke?"

It had been a graduation gift from my parents — a gift, I now realized , my stepmother had paid for. "I realize that in your eyes getting a car as a gift makes me an overindulged, spoiled brat, but at least I'm a punctual, overindulged, spoiled brat."

"Do you know you pout? You stick out your upper lip and pout. It's very attractive in an overindulged, punctual, spoiled brat sort of way."

The smile I tried hard to suppress escaped. We crossed the street to be nearer the ocean for the view. We leisurely strolled past homes on Ocean Avenue, with their Spanish Colonial/Moorish architecture, barrel-tile roofs, bell towers, and courtyards hidden behind dense impenetrable ficus hedges. It was an overcast windy day. A dark cloud threatened a drenching south Florida deluge. Along the beach, intrepid sun-worshipers worked on their tans. The wise ones had set their chairs and blankets farther from the water, by the saucer-leafed seagrapes, turtle grass, and creeping railroad vines that shielded them from the blowing sand.

I was about to speak when I recognized a familiar silhouette approaching. It had to be Harriet Bannister, a girl I remembered from elementary school. Harriet was the first girl in the sixth grade to have a bosom, one that had grown until it was remarkable by any standard. I introduced her to Raul and watched her give him an admiring once over. I knew exactly what the most promiscuous girl in the class of '56 was thinking as she aimed those amazing matched cannons in his direction. Unless he was unimaginably rich, his Latin origin precluded anything serious, but that wouldn't stand in the way of a quick and dirty fling. I was tempted to reach for Raul's hand for spite.

With yet another meaningful glance at Raul, Harriet asked if we had heard that Mattress Jack Kennedy was fooling around with Marilyn Monroe? Predominately Republican Palm Beachers loved repeating rumors about the President, even though they admired Jackie's style and considered Rose Kennedy one of their own.

"The acorn didn't fall far from the tree," Harriet assured us. "Joe Kennedy is a womanizer. Everyone knows he humped Gloria Swanson on his yacht, right under poor Rose's nose."

I pretended to listen. Raul turned to watch a freighter off shore.

Harriet surveyed his compact backside, while she continued regaling us with regional dirty secrets.

I offered no encouragement until Harriet finally gave up and moved on.

When she was too far to hear us, Raul said, "I didn't think you were the kind who enjoyed gossip."

"Haven't you heard? Gossip is Palm Beach's favorite form of entertainment," I joked defensively. Instead of being amused, he continued walking without comment.

"You want to know why your father killed himself," he said at last. "The most common reasons for suicide are bad health, money problems, and being jilted. Occasionally, a criminal will kill himself when he's cornered rather than go to jail. We can try to keep things quiet, but there are no guarantees. What we uncover might make you Palm Beach's next hot topic."

I blushed. With my fair skin, when I blushed I could light an area of ten square miles, and toast marshmallows for a hundred with the heat. What if my father had done something awful and people found out? I would be humiliated — mortified. If Amelia was well enough to understand, she would be too.

"What do you say, Charlie? We can forget about looking into reasons for your father's death and go back to concentrating on getting you a job. I've made some inquiries. A decorator I talked to is ready to take you on as an apprentice. It doesn't pay much to start, but there's room to advance."

His gaze slid from my face, down my blouse and back to my face. He smiled mischievously when he realized he'd been caught. He was flirting again. But he had found me a job, and he'd ignored Harriet and her twin missiles. Despite every resolution, Lord-have-mercy-Miss-Scarlett, if I didn't drop my lashes and smile up at him. "A decorator's apprentice?"

"You have a degree in art history. It was a logical jump."

"Don't think I'm not grateful. It's very tempting, but I'm trying to take hold of my life, and guilt is giving me more trouble than the practical." I wasn't going to delve into the satisfaction of mastering the washer, drier, iron, vacuum, mop, defrosting a refrigerator, and balancing my checkbook as compared to frustration, remorse, and regret.

His eyebrows rose in mock alarm. "So you decided to trust me."

The clouds had shifted and the setting sun warmed my skin. "I have no choice. You're the only one that offered help."

"What about the man you're sort of seeing?"

I froze. Fortunately, my panic produced a set of plausible lies. "He's in Iran – on an engineering assignment – a contract for a year." I did have a friend with a degree in engineering that had accepted a job in either Iraq or Iran – one of those oil-rich desert countries.

"Nevertheless, I'm honored. I get the impression you don't trust many people."

"More so lately," I admitted. I was once again surprised by his insight and half-ashamed of my fabrications. "There's something else you should know. A day after we were notified by the police, Petal, Amelia and I received letters he mailed before he died."

"What did they say? In a general way, you don't have to be specific unless you want to."

"Petal didn't tell me about hers. The one addressed to Amelia and me only said that he loved us, and he was doing this to protect us."

Raul frowned. "Protect you from what?"

"I have no idea."

"Have you checked his appointment book?"

"For what?"

"It could tell you a great deal — who he was seeing and when. Appointments scheduled after he died would mean his decision was sudden rather than planned. In fact, you should go over all his papers: checkbooks, bank statements, mail, his address book. They might all contain clues."

"What kind of clues?"

"Names, checks written for unidentified reasons. Frankly, I see blackmail as a strong possibility. A man with no assets of his own, who's married to a woman like your stepmother, is an easy target."

"I don't understand."

"Forgive me for saying this, but your father had a reputation as a ladies' man."

To hide my face I bent over, removed my sandal and brushed nonexistent pebbles off my foot. "You can rule out blackmail. As long as they didn't interfere with her plans my stepmother was indifferent to Daddy's outside activities." Raul didn't reply but his disapproval was apparent. "Maybe we should be heading back to the car. It's getting late."

When we reversed direction, I spotted a magnificent sailboat, white sails filled with wind, darting through the waves.

"Do you like to sail?" he asked, when he turned to see what had caught my attention.

"I adore sailing." We silently watched the boat skip and yaw until it was out of sight. "The house in Virginia is for sale. Daddy kept things there — we all do – did. I think I should drive up before it's sold. After it's gone it'll be too late. Checkbooks, letters, address books, calendars, what did I forget?"

"Bring back anything you can pack in the car that's looks interesting. We can decide if it's important later."

I leaned against the MG, reluctant to leave the tranquility of the beach. "I feel very stupid. Other than calling his doctors, I never considered doing a single thing that seems so obvious now."

"Your world was upended. You can't expect to think clearly for a while."

"You're just saying that to make me feel better."

"Don't get too comfortable. I plan to tease you every chance I get." Raul pressed the end of my braid against his upper lip to form an absurd mustache. "You don't intend driving to Virginia in this thing, do you?"

"Of course."

"After you pack your toothbrush and a change of clothes, you won't be able to squeeze a paper clip into this windup toy."

I hadn't considered the limited size of my car. "It would be tight, I suppose."

"Take my station wagon," he offered, absently brushing the loose ends of my braid against his cheek.

I gently retrieved it and received a sheepish grin. "Will that crate of yours get me up and back without leaving me stranded on some deserted road?"

"Don't be fooled by Esmeralda's looks. This noble chariot possesses a brave heart and sufficient stamina for a long lovely ride."

"You can use my car while I'm gone," I replied, ignoring his suggestive tone.

"And have people think I'm a rich playboy? No, thank you. I can walk to work. If I need a car, I'll borrow one." He opened my door. "I suggest you call me daily while you're gone."

"Please don't think I'm unappreciative, but I'm over twenty-one and mentally competent. I hardly think I need to check in with anyone."

"What if Amelia's doctor needs to reach you? Someone should know where you are and how to reach you."

I just hated when he was right.

Chapter Four

At Raul's suggestion, I left both his day and evening numbers with the switchboard at Silver Glades. While I'd hardly describe my mood as euphoric, I felt more hopeful than I had for weeks.

The first few hours of driving I sang along with the radio, watched the billboards that lined the highway and congratulated myself for being a gal with spunk. The sky was clear, the traffic was light, and the breeze from the open windows ruffled my hair. The next hour or so I listened to the radio and looked for a service station that might have a clean rest room. Around one o'clock, a legion of squashed bugs on Esmeralda's windshield radically impaired my vision, and her gas gauge indicated near empty, as did my stomach. I chose a service station with a small restaurant next to it that boasted in cheerful red writing *Country Style Food Served Here.*

After refueling and debugging, I headed for the restaurant. While seated in the booth waiting for meatloaf, mashed potatoes, and fried greens, I checked my position on the map. When my order arrived I wasn't certain what on my plate constituted greens, but I knew that Country Style Food meant greasy. Less enthusiastic, I climbed back into the station wagon. Esmeralda sputtered a few times before starting. Raul had warned me that she occasionally coughed and I was to ignore it, unless she became flooded and refused to start entirely. I found myself saying "good girl" and "you can do it" at what I considered critical times.

At seven o'clock, an hour after I passed the last decent motel, I realized I was too tired to continue. I stopped at the first vacancy sign and requested a cabin close to the highway. Through the uninsulated walls I could hear heavy trucks thundering past – a small price for peace of mind. Traffic noise was infinitely better than imagining myself being strangled by the escaped convict who lurked in the rear dense forest waiting for unsuspecting travelers to fall asleep. The one room cabin was clean, sparsely furnished, and dreary. As there was no television set, I tried the radio. It produced either fierce static or two stations with nasal western music. I sat on the bed until I summoned the energy to take a shower. Luckily, the cabin did feature a working telephone. Thanks to Raul's insistence, I had an acceptable reason to call someone.

I inquired about Amelia. Raul assured me he hadn't been summoned. He asked how Esmeralda and I were getting along, I explained that we had formed a working relationship based on mutual dependence. Five minutes of teasing and another five during which he flirted and I pretended not to notice, provided the calm I needed to sleep.

In the morning Esmeralda forgot the lovely bond we had established the day before and stubbornly refused to start. Or maybe I gave her too much gas and flooded her engine. Whatever the reason, I had to wait twenty-five minutes while she cooled off, or dried off, or whatever it was mechanical devices did when they were flooded. Not one to hold a grudge when I get what I want, after she started, I resumed praising.

The second day's journey was a virtual repeat of the first. It had been dark for an hour when I reached Treetops' imposing fieldstone parapets. Immobilizing memories assaulted me. I might have sat there brooding, had it not been for Esmeralda's wheezing reminding me that if I permitted her to idle too long she would stall. I drove up the driveway, bordered on both sides by towering pines planted decades earlier, past rolling green lawns, and approached the massive brick Tudor dwelling. It had been built by a shipping magnate. Petal had added the neat white fences behind and to the sides of the house, to allow for grazing and riding.

"Mrs. Morgan left me to look after the house and the grounds," Clarence "Woody" Wilson roared when he greeted me at the arched front door. Woody was hard of hearing and tended to shout. "The horses are gone, so's all the stable boys. Mrs. Morgan got rid of them right after we lost Mr. Jack. The grand lady herself, told me that no one's allowed on the premises except people the real estate folks bring by."

"I'm sure she didn't mean that to include family. I've come to sort through my father's things. I have my stepmother's permission to take anything of his I want." Which was more or less the truth. Besides, I had been driving for two days. Ten sumo wrestlers couldn't make me leave.

Woody shook his head, picked up my bag, and thumped into the house. "I expect you're right about that."

I followed the man with the nose that looked like it had been broken more than once down the hall to my room.

"Shipped Mrs. Morgan's clothing and such to her right after the funeral, like she asked," Woody bellowed. "The rest of the family's things are right where you left them. Hope you ate before you came. I had my supper and there's nothing waitin' for you. Just some cold cuts and fresh bread if you have a mind. There's also most of a peach pie that the widow-lady housekeeper next door gave me, cause she's looking to catch herself a husband. It isn't half bad if you like peaches."

"Go on and watch your game shows or your westerns. I'll help myself."

"Guess you know I like westerns. Like game shows too. But tonight, it's wrestling. There's this Nameless Avenger that's a hoot. G'night, now."

I went into the kitchen and fixed myself a sandwich and a cup of tea. The homemade peach pie looked wonderful, but I decided to leave it for Woody and not spoil the chances of the widow-lady-next-door. After I rinsed my dish I headed for my father's library. My curiosity overpowered my fatigue.

As I sat in my father's desk chair, my hands on the armrests, I felt his presence. I was sorely tempted to halt my investigation. I could think of a hundred excuses to do so and only two reasons to continue. To stop now meant accepting defeat – I would never know why my father killed himself. I'd been spending my days feeling like a beached whale, or the sole survivor on a desert island, or an alien abductee. So little was under my control. I needed to know why. The second reason – less dramatic, but no less distasteful – was that unless I was prepared to lie, I would have to admit to Raul that I had failed. It wasn't a hard decision. Two days of eating greasy food and listening to Esmeralda's tubercular cough would not be for naught.

I slid open the top drawer. It contained my father's 1959 appointment book and a silver letter opener with his initials. Success! I would not have to admit defeat or lie. I set it aside and resumed my search. The second drawer furnished a thick manila envelope containing canceled checks.

In the cabinets beneath the bookshelves and behind grilled doors, I discovered an assortment of unrelated items: a humidor, ashtrays, an atlas, several old copies of *Life* magazine, Scrabble, two packs of cards and a pad used to score bridge. A square men's hatbox caught my attention. I opened it to find it was filled with an assortment of ancient, yellowed paper — letterheads from unknown companies and personal stationery — some blank, some not, some written in French, some in English. Interesting, but useless.

I reached for the canceled checks, intending to analyze them as Raul and I had discussed, but within minutes one's looked like seven's and the script blurred. I'd leave the checks for tomorrow.

*　*　*

The following morning, pleased that I had remembered to pack a few warm outfits, I found the dented pot Woody had left on the stove and poured myself a cup of hot coffee. That and some reheated oatmeal took care of breakfast. From the rumble of the motor, I knew Woody was fertilizing the lawn, or reducing downed branches to woodchips, or one of his other many chores that would occupy him until lunch. I steeled myself and returned to the library and the canceled checks. They were dated from August, 1959 to November, 1961, two months prior to my father's death. Many of the recipients' names were familiar to me, but lacking the associated checkbook, I could only guess at their purpose.

The library shelves beckoned. I fanned the pages of the leather-bound books, no doubt selected by Sister Parish, my stepmother's decorator, for their size, color, and gilt embossed covers. No telltale notes or cryptic treasure maps fell out. There were a dozen or so art-related books that I knew had belonged to my father. They were now mine. I was about to give up on the shelves when I spotted a small antique chest inlaid with ivory. It was just out of reach. Using a stool to supplement my height, I removed the chest and set it on the desk. Inside, I found scissors, household glue, tweezers, matches, and various writing equipment: feather quills, pen points, three bottles of discolored ink, black, brown, and blue. I wondered how many years it had sat there, its odd contents untouched. The box would be a nice keepsake, either for me or Amelia. I added it to the take-home pile.

I made my way to the stables for one last look while I possessed the courage to do so. The familiar pungent odor of horses greeted me well before I reached my destination. My father and I had spent many happy days here, riding or preparing for events. Bruce was a part of its past. I walked the long concrete corridor. No horses whinnied or stomped. No voices, only my footsteps echoed off the bare walls. Bridles, saddles, crops, framed newspaper clippings, saved programs — all gone, sold, scrapped, given away. I passed the empty stall of my father's horse, Errant Prince, without stopping, then paused to gaze into the bay that had housed Bluebell. Bits of hay were the sole traces of the former inhabitant. Bluebell had been my first jumper and trusted girlhood companion. She was nearing twenty – too old to jump competitively, but still fit to ride. What had become of her? It was only now that she was gone that I regretted neglecting her these last few years.

I returned to the house and went directly to the bedroom my stepmother and father had shared. The French provincial chests and dressers were merely decorative, as were the pair of easy chairs covered in an earthy plaid. Bedrooms were to be used for reading or sleeping. Petal preferred storing clothes in the his-and-hers dressing rooms that flanked the large room. Hidden in the alcove that faced my father's dressing room was a wall covered with photographs of Daddy, Amelia, and me taken at riding shows. Rather than let myself be distracted I opened the closet door to hide them.

Jackets and suits were on upper racks, slacks below, all organized by color and season. Built-in drawers held smaller items. The sight and smell of my father's clothing swept over me. Ignoring the stinging tears, I grabbed the nearest jacket and plunged my hand into the pocket. It yielded a lollipop stick – an odd item for some adults, but not for Daddy.

Further burrowing produced movie stubs, a bank deposit slip, cigar wrappings, two dimes and a nickel. His jewelry box held collar stays, two pairs of gold cuff links, and a silver dollar. I gently closed the lid, located one of my father's hankies, wiped my eyes, and blew my nose. I was about to leave when I remembered my father wasn't returning. I went back to the jewelry box and slipped the cufflinks into my pocket without looking at them. As I closed the closet door behind me, my father's handsome face was grinning at me. I yanked the frame from the wall and hurled it at the large plate glass window. It hit the drapes and slid harmlessly to the rug.

*   *   *

"If you find any photographs or letters, to or from my father, I'd appreciate it if you sent them to me," I told Woody that evening as he stoked the fire. I had suggested we bring our coffee cups to my father's library after dinner.

"What?"

I pointed to the chair near mine, motioned for Woody to sit, and repeated what I had said. "Take whatever you want of Daddy's clothes. Anything you don't want, give to any charity that will take it."

"That's what Mrs. Morgan told me, except the part about my keeping what I can use."

"All Daddy's personal belongings are mine to do with what I want. His sweaters and jackets will fit you, and maybe his shirts."

"Yup. That's what I thought."

"What's going to happen to you after my stepmother sells this place? Is she going to find a position for you in Manhattan, or will you look for a job around here?"

"Don't much care for big cities, and I'm too old to start working for someone else."

"So you're going to retire. Has my stepmother provided for you?"

"Got a little pension. Put some aside. Don't need much. Going to live with my sister. Upstate New York. Nice there."

"I didn't know you had a sister."

"Got three sisters. This one's a widow. She's lonely now that her boy Amos is gone. One of them Mongoloids, he was. Good boy, but slow. Essie misses him something terrible. With me there, it'll be company for her."

After the longest single declaration I had ever heard from Woody, we sat watching the fire in silence. His nephew had Down's Syndrome and was missed. And Woody had a place to go and means to support himself.

"Funny thing about Mr. Jack," Woody confided, as the fire crackled and spit. "Said he grew up in Vermont. But he sure did know Philadelphia. Knew every street, store, and park."

"Philadelphia? I thought you come from Maine."

"Born and raised in Maine. Worked for a Philadelphia family for almost twenty years. Got to know the place real well."

"And you discussed Philadelphia with my father?"

"Yup. Mr. Jack liked to talk about Philadelphia. Maybe he went to school there. A lot of society folk send their boys to U of P."

My father did not attend the University of Pennsylvania, nor, I suspected, any college. He was unfamiliar with academic jargon: grade point averages, doctoral dissertations, majors, minors. The only academic subject that he'd been knowledgeable about was art. Growing up, Amelia and I were dragged to and lectured at every art museum within traveling distance. At twelve, Amelia's pleas to be excused were heard. Thrilled to have Daddy all to myself for a few hours, I continued to accompany him. Eventually my enthusiasm matched his.

"Good man, your father. Knew how to treat regular folks."

*   *   *

When I returned to my room I called Raul and was irrationally pleased to find him home.

"How did you make out?" he asked, once again reminding me how sensuous a voice could be.

"Nothing too exciting. I found some canceled checks for the last year and a half and some personal mementos." I leaned against the headboard. "Our caretaker believes Daddy may have lived in Philadelphia at some point in his life."

"Any significance in that?"

"Just that he never mentioned it to me." I switched the phone to my other ear. "Will you be able to manage without Esmeralda a while longer?"

"She does have a certain indescribable charm, like her owner."

"She rattles like a locomotive and she guzzles gas like an eighteen-wheeler, but I'm hoping you can manage without her for another few days. I'd like to go to my stepmother's home in Manhattan. The checkbook has to be there and so does my father's address book. They weren't here and they weren't in Palm Beach."

"It's cold in New York. I wouldn't want you to freeze your tootsies off. I hope you packed your long underwear."

Long underwear. I caught sight of myself in the mirror wearing a bra and panties. For a split-second, I foolishly thought he could see me and blushed.

"Are you planning to stay with your stepmother?" Raul asked.

"I thought I would call and tell her there's an art exhibit I want to see and only plan to stay a few days. Just long enough to snoop."

"It would be better to show up unexpected."

"Why?"

"I just learned that after your father's death your stepmother made it clear to the firm that she wanted any investigation squelched. That's why there was no autopsy and the police backed off so quickly. But you have to promise to keep this to yourself. No one is supposed to know, not even me."

"Typical lawyer. Impossibly devious. If your firm learns that you're helping me, they'll fire you. You'll have no job and a lousy recommendation."

"Let me worry about that."

"Neville Byrd never asked you to help me, did he?"

Another rumbling laugh. "Would you believe I'm doing this because I see you as a potentially valuable client?"

"No."

"Then let's just say I have a weakness for stuck-up leggy blondes who are sort of seeing someone."

"That doesn't bother you?"

"I'll let you know when it bothers me."

An hour after replacing the phone I was still trying to decide if I found Raul's bravado a sign of confidence and attractive, or hopelessly egotistical.

Chapter Five

My stepmother's pied-a-terre, part of the divorce settlement from her first husband, was conveniently located just off Fifth Avenue. It was a four-story building — five, if you count the sub-basement that contained the boiler, air conditioning units, and such. An elevator in the rear of the building was used for luggage, heavy articles, the infirm, and the weekly-delivered flower arrangements. The rest of us, including Petal, used the stately staircase. Seven steps above pavement was the main floor, which contained the entrance foyer, two small adjoining rooms, twin powder rooms, and an elegant formal area primarily used for parties.

The kitchen and breakfast room, which led to a rear garden

patio, were a level down. The formal dining room, butler's pantry, library, and family sitting room were on the second floor. The third floor consisted of bedrooms — six, I think, and my father's sitting room. Quarters for live-in staff and additional storage were on the fourth floor. My stepmother favored the word "cozy" to describe the house. It was also Petal's favorite residence, no matter the season or weather. I think she liked the city's pace, power, and immediacy.

I arrived after eight and was greeted by Joseph, Petal's houseman.

"Mrs. Morgan is out for the evening," the gaunt swarthy man informed me. "I'll take your bags to your room. I wasn't told to expect you. Have you had dinner?"

After I assured him that I had eaten and was certain he was gone, I proceeded directly to the master bedroom. The "three C's" that exemplified Sister Parish's work – chintz, colors, and cushions, were everywhere. I was disappointed when I entered my father's closet. Shirts, pants, suits, shoes, hats, underwear, all gone. Petal had wasted no time disposing of everything that said my father had lived there. I had no right or supportable reason to be annoyed by her practical decision, but I was. The only item that had been overlooked in the cleaning blitz was a neatly clipped section of newspaper stuck to an upper shelf, no doubt unnoticed by someone shorter than I am. I read it.

Michael Hagen, a plumber, had been found scalded to death by a burst steam pipe. No one had witnessed the horrific event and the police had labeled it an accident. Mr. Hagen's wife, Fiona Hagen, and their three grown children insisted foul play was involved, and were asking for an investigation. They cited Mr. Hagen's participation in the local plumber's union, in which Mr. Hagen was a founding and influential member, as a possible motive for an attack. The *Philadelphia Inquirer* clipping was dated June 12th, 1953. I folded the disturbing article and put it in my pocket.

My next stop was my father's sitting room. His desk was empty but his bookshelves were just as I remembered them. The leather-bound, gold embossed books were mostly decorative props. Those about horses or art had been purchased for or by Daddy. Still determined to find the hidden treasure map or telltale letter, I opened every one, decorative or personal, and looked for anything: a highlighted line, a dog-eared page, a note, a keepsake and found nothing. I set aside a dozen or so books on art for myself and glanced at my watch. Damn! Eleven o'clock. Too late to call Raul.

*   *   *

"Joseph told me that you were here. What a pleasant surprise," Petal declared when I entered the breakfast nook the following morning. Fully dressed and made up, she smelled of Shalimar, her favorite scent. "How long are we to have the pleasure of your company? I've accepted several dinner invitations for the next few days with close friends. Should I ask to have you included?"

"Thanks, awfully, but I'm here to catch an exhibit at the Guggenheim I couldn't bear to miss, and see a few friends before I have to dash back. I hope that won't be inconvenient."

To visualize my stepmother, picture the Duchess of Windsor. There was a resemblance. Both were slender, stylish, plain women, seldom seen without pearls. Petal was somewhere in her sixties, eight to ten years older than my father, but still, as they say, handsome. Frown lines and laugh lines eluded her as Petal rarely frowned or laughed; she preferred an elusive, thin-lipped smile. She had only one incomprehensible quirk, at least, one I found incomprehensible. She encased herself in a waist-length, steel boned brassiere and an equally formidable boned girdle — a crotchless girdle that she wore minus panties.

When I'd mentioned her strange choice of undergarments to my father, he warned, "Charlotte, there's one thing that I've discovered, women defy logic."

"She doesn't wear panties, and the girdle doesn't have a bottom. Doesn't she get cold? And what about —"

"Frankly, I don't know – and I'm too much of a gentleman to ask. I expect you and your sister to wear appropriate underwear at all times, and to keep your curiosity to yourself."

Petal kissed the air above my cheek and left me to go to fittings, or cards, or the theater, or whatever she had planned.

*   *   *

Petal stopped by my room before she left to go out that night. "I'm on the board of several charitable foundations which distribute clothing to the poor. I donated your father's things. I thought you would approve."

"Thank you. That's exactly what I would've done."

"I saw that you set aside some of his books. Take as many as you wish."

"Thank you. That's very kind. But I didn't see any of his personal papers."

Petal paused as if to assess my motive before answering. "I had them packed and stored in the attic. My accountants might need his financial records."

"I was trying to find his address book," I improvised. "There's a few numbers I need."

"I expect that it's at Casa Buena."

"Not that one, his old one."

Petal turned to leave, then stopped. "Your father gave me the small landscapes over the settee in my sitting room." He did them when he was a young man living in Paris. I was hoping you won't object to my keeping them."

"If Daddy gave them to you as gifts, I wouldn't dream of taking them."

After I heard Joseph close the front door behind her, I went into Petal's bedroom to look at the paintings. Other than little cartoons and sketches Daddy drew to amuse us, I'd never seen a single example of his work. Over the blue damask settee hung two small but impressive landscapes. French with Italian influence. Pre-Impressionist. I moved closer for a better look. Students often copied masterpieces to learn technique. Had my father copied the work of a gifted artist of the mid-nineteenth century? They were excellent. Had Daddy been this talented? And if so, why and when had he stopped painting? Or was the story he'd given Petal another example of his gift for fabrication? In either case, I almost regretted surrendering the pair so quickly.

While Joseph and the rest of the staff were downstairs having their dinner, I went to the attic to search for the packed papers. I soon located two small cartons containing Daddy's things and triumphantly carried them back to my room. The first carton contained a checkbook and canceled checks. I scanned several rubber-banded clusters and found nothing of interest. The second box held his appointment books from 1957 and '60, two small leather address books with well-worn bent pages, both done in Daddy's elegant hand. My father was a fastidious man. When an address book became messy from too many corrections and additions, he copied it into a new book and saved the old one.

I was about to bypass the discarded address books and concentrate on the calendars when an extraordinary idea came to me. Find people from Philadelphia. Woody had insisted that my father was unusually familiar with Philadelphia – a city we'd never visited. The newspaper clipping I'd found was about a man who had died in a freak accident there. I picked up the newer of the two address books and skimmed the pages, bypassing names, concentrating solely on cities and states. Not one entry had a Philadelphia address. Scanning the older address book, I nearly dropped it when I reached *Fiona Hagen*. Just to make certain I wasn't hallucinating I found the clipping and compared the name. Fiona Hagen was the dead plumber's widow. I dialed Raul's home number, eager to brag about my findings, and anxious to hear his theory on the meaning.

"Call her," Raul suggested after we chatted a bit. "Tell her your father's name and see what she has to say.

"I was thinking of doing that, but her name was left out in the later book, so how important could it be? Anyhow, how's the weather down there? It's freezing here. Icy cold, high winds, and a chance of snow."

"Too bad. We're having great weather – high seventies to low eighties. If you're back by the weekend, I'll take you sailing. You did say that you love sailing."

"Where are you going to get a sailboat?"

"I'll borrow one."

It was pleasant to visualize myself on a sailboat, the wind tossing my hair, the sun warming my shoulders. "Can I bring a friend?"

He laughed his rich musical laugh. "No."

I didn't need a psychic to tell me where this conversation was headed. "You really think I should call Mrs. Hagen?"

"Her name was in your father's address book and he saved a newspaper clipping with her name in it. A five minute conversation and you'll know whether you're wasting your time."

It was too early to go to sleep so I turned on the television. I couldn't stop wondering why my father had kept the article. Was his suicide in some way to linked to the nightmarish accident? Poor Michael Hagen. Scalded to death. Boiled like a lobster. The horrific pain. Screaming for help. Something pleasant. I needed something pleasant to replace the grisly image. A waterfall. A stream. A sailboat. Sailing. Water misting my face. A light breeze. A far more agreeable tableau, even if it did include a man with dark chocolate eyes and a smile capable of melting an iceberg.

*   *   *

In the morning, after Petal left for her usual flurry of activities, I prepared a little white lie for Fiona Hagen and dialed her number.

"This is Charlotte Morgan," I said. "You don't know me, Mrs. Hagen. My father disappeared suddenly and I'm very worried about him. I have reason to believe that you might know him. His name wa — is," I corrected myself, "John Morgan, but everyone calls him Jack. Is the name 'Jack Morgan' at all familiar to you?"

"Jack Morgan. I don't recall anyone with that name. Can't help you."

She was going to hang up. To stop her I blurted out the most compelling mixture of fact and fiction I could invent. "I found an article about your husband's death in my father's things. Your name and phone number was in his address book. My father is the only family my sister and I have. I'm afraid something dreadful may have happened to him."

I could almost hear her thinking as I waited for a response.

"To tell you the God's truth, I'm not very good with names," she finally said. "I'm better with faces."

"What if I showed you some pictures? Maybe you'd recognize him. If you'd be willing to meet me, I would be happy to pay for your time."

"You don't have to pay for my time. You get yourself here and I'll look at your pictures."

Chapter Six

I considered turning back a half dozen times as I made the drive to Fiona Hagen's house. It was only the combined force of the clipping and her name in my father's address book that kept me following the directions she had given me, instead of heading back to Palm Beach.

I reached her two-story framed house and pulled into the rutted driveway shortly after three o'clock and rang the front doorbell. A large-boned, ruddy faced woman with steel-gray hair opened the porch door. Fiona Hagen was surprisingly tall.

As we picked our way through the toys, galoshes, and school bags that littered the worn parlor and a dining room badly in need of dusting, finally arriving in the kitchen, I tried to imagine Mrs. Hagen at eighteen or twenty. She might have been pretty. It was hard to say.

Two school-age children, a girl and a boy, made room for me at a scratched brown metal table. A younger boy played on the floor near a sink filled with pots and dishes.

"Just give me a chance to give these bandits their cookies and juice or they'll give us no peace. They come home from school hungry enough to eat the legs off a piano."

The red-haired boy seated next to me grinned shyly.

"These three belong to Peggy, my youngest. I look after them until she comes home from work."

The children finished their snack while Fiona prepared our tea. Within minutes she was buttoning coats. "Now go play outside until I call you. And stay away from the Flynn's dog or she'll bite you again." Fiona closed the door and addressed me. "If I've told them once, I've told them a thousand times to leave that blasted animal alone."

I waited for her to sit down, add milk to her tea, and carefully adjust her glasses, before handing her one of the photographs I had taken from the house in McLean.

"Jesus!" What she actually said was "Jaysus" but I had no trouble understanding her. "Jesus in heaven! It's Alan himself. It can't be. Alan Fitzpatrick himself, after all these years."

"You must be mistaken, Mrs. Hagen," I said, trying to calm the confused agitated woman. "Many people resemble one another. That's my father, Jack Morgan."

Fiona took the photograph and inspected it again. She shook her head. "There's no mistaking it, Deary. I should know my own brother. That's Alan Fitzpatrick. So he took off on you, did he? Took off on the lot of us. It must be — something like twenty years ago."

"Your brother looked like my father." I felt the blood soaring to my ears. This silly woman had gone mad.

"You must be Michelle, from the size of you. My father wasn't much. He drank and he was quick to give us the back of his hand, but he didn't take off on us either. Died in his own bed like a man's supposed to."

Michelle? Who was Michelle? "Here's another photo. This one was taken about eight or nine years ago." She had to be wrong. My father's name was Morgan. My name was Morgan. I heard a buzzing noise inside my head. No oxygen was reaching my brain. "Stand up and tell the class your name," the teacher would say. I would respond, "My name is Charlotte Morgan."

"I don't need to see any more of your pictures," Fiona Hagen said. "This is you, Michelle, standing next to your father. And this has to be Maggie, all grown up. I have a picture of the four of you upstairs. I should have seen it straight away, but you've grown so. What could have made Alan go off and leave his two little princesses? Jesus knows, he worshiped the pair of you."

"My name is Charlotte Morgan," I said, rising, rushing to escape, blind to the school bag I tripped on as I raced through her parlor.

"Maybe you're a darned sight better off without the rascal," I heard her call after me as I flung open the front door.

I drove until I could no longer see. My eyes were blurred with tears. My hands, my legs, my jaw were trembling. I sat by the side of the road, staggered and hurt. The tall woman with the blue/green eyes and the messy house was my aunt. My father had been born Alan Fitzpatrick.

"Son-of-a . . . " I screamed as I fumbled with my purse, the tears pouring down my cheeks and nose. "You must have done something horrific, you dumb — dumb — dumb son-of-a-bitch! Took us from the only family we had and then killed yourself! Left us to wonder how we had failed you. Left me with nowhere to live, no income, a sick, helpless sister and destitute. Stupid son-of-a-bitch! Why? Why in Jesus' name did you do it?" I sniffled loudly as I upended my purse. "Why didn't I bring more tissues?" The one I'd had in my purse was soggy and rapidly disintegrating. No tissues! Why did the entire universe have to crash around me at once? "Is it too much to ask to have a simple tissue?" I shouted, as I grappled with the glove compartment that held nothing useful. I might have a handkerchief hidden somewhere in my luggage, but that was piled in the back of the station wagon beneath cartons of books.

"This is all your fault, Daddy!"

I sniffled again and blotted my cheeks with my sleeve. The area behind my eyes ached. My throat felt as though I had gargled with double-edged razor blades. And I had no tissues. It had been senseless to dig up the past. What had I gained? A crabby aunt who lived in a dusty dilapidated house. Instead of answers, I had more questions than ever.

I sniffled twice more, but it was obvious that no amount of sniffling was going to prevent the inevitable runny mess. Which garment was expendable? My half-slip. I reached beneath my skirt and tugged and wriggled until I managed to step out of it. I sank my face into its satin depths and soundly blew my nose.

"I want you to know, I'm not going to forget this," I cried, waving my soiled slip. "Look at me! This is your doing." I adjusted the rear view mirror to view eyes that looked like oysters on the half shell, and a face that resembled chopped meat — perhaps a tad too aggressively. The wretched thing landed in my lap. Esmeralda had joined the conspiracy. This was the last straw. Even a single-celled amoeba had its limits.

"I am not taking this lying down!" I shouted, using her rearview mirror to repeatedly bludgeon Esmeralda's dusty upholstery. "I, Charlotte, or Michelle, or whatever my name is, I am not taking this lying down. Do you hear that, Daddy? I'm not taking this lying down. Don't imagine for a moment that I'm going to say nice things about you to your grandchildren. I'm going to tell them you were a liar, a scoundrel, and a coward. How many times did you pass your sister's name in your address book without calling her? When did you decide to leave it out forever?"

Thankfully, Esmeralda was able to withstand my rage with a serenity honed by years of use. Thirty minutes later, I fell back exhausted and watched the haloed lights from oncoming cars streak past. Drops of rain trickled down her windshield, joined others, and raced to the cleft below. Fiona had said, I have a picture of the four of you. Four. Amelia, Daddy, and me was three. Four could only mean that Fiona had a picture that included my mother. If I returned to that house, would I be in for another disappointment, another horrible shock? My watch read 6:15. I located my compact, dabbed some powder under my eyes, then glared at the mirror lying next to me. Expecting nothing, since I lacked both tools and know-how, I held the mirror's base against its socket with my left hand, made a fist with my right, took a deep breath and landed a single mighty blow. I heard an agreeable pop. I cautiously adjusted the mirror. It held. My hand ached, but it was a good pain. I had repaired an automobile. I was not a feeble helpless girl. I was a woman capable of repairing automobiles. I could turn one around too.

Chapter Seven

Paris, 1934

It was more than the sunny warm May day that had convinced Parisian pedestrians to stroll the boulevards, to take their time savoring sights and sounds. Perhaps, it was an awareness that they stood on the precipice of a bold new era. Memories of the last horrific war were fading. Cars, buses, trains, and yes, airplanes, could speed a man anywhere he wished to go. Horns and engines had almost entirely eliminated the slow clip-clop of horse's hoofs. The light bulb was replacing gaslight at an electrifying pace. Indoor bathrooms, central heating, motion pictures would soon be a universal birthright. As for the diseases that plagued mankind, they would soon be a thing of the past. Miracle drugs, aspirin and penicillin, would cure any ailment that vaccines hadn't prevented. Women in the United States had been granted the right to vote fourteen years earlier. French women were certain their day would come soon. Jazz, that remarkable, pulsating, musical import from the brash United States, could be heard on the radio and at nightclubs.

Among the throng of people viewing Notre Dame was Alan Fitzpatrick and his good friend Henri Puissard, both in their twenties. The men had set up their easels that morning hoping for a sale. Behind Alan two comely young shop-girls studied, or pretended to study, his efforts — yet another uninspired rendering of the famous Gothic cathedral. Alan immediately dismissed them as too poor to buy a decent meal, let alone a painting. The bolder of the pair attempted a flattering remark. He simply nodded and went on dabbing at the canvas before him. Five years had passed since the stock market crash. The United States was deep into the Great Depression. Like so many young men Alan had left his homeland to seek his fortune. Some expatriates would fulfill their dreams. But two years after his departure, though he might convince the occasional unsophisticated tourist to purchase one of his efforts, Alan knew his works would never grace museums, mansions, or even tasteful villas. His paintings were destined to collect dust or be covered with another effort. Still, he had learned to speak French with a credible accent within a year.

Ten feet away Henri paused to correct an errant brush-stroke. Alan noticed his plump, balding friend glancing enviously at his two admirers. A middle-aged couple approached. From their well-cut, conservative attire Alan knew they were either American or English tourists — even the poorest Frenchman possessed more flair. Hoping to attract their attention, he made a great show of stepping back and clearing his throat while appraising his work. The ploy succeeded. The couple stopped, first to inspect Alan's effort and then Henri's. The two shop-girls drifted away.

"This chap has caught something. Rather nice painting, wouldn't you say, Eloise?" the man wearing the gray fedora asked his wife, in a decidedly upper-class Boston accent.

The dour looking matron with a large black hat and ponderous bosom agreed. "Nice. Very nice. Notre Dame and all that."

"You have an excellent eye, sir," Alan declared, joining them as per his agreement with his friend. "Henri Puissard's work is the most sought after on the Left Bank. Look at the way he depicts the sun's rays without losing the fine details. Outstanding, wouldn't you agree, madam?" He gave Eloise his warmest smile.

Eloise smiled back from under her hat. .

Her husband nodded. "Just so! Precisely what I was saying to my wife."

"Investors are snatching up Henri's work as fast as he can he produce it," Alan confided.

"Investors, you say?" Eloise repeated.

After fifteen minutes exchange on the merits of Henri's effort — and a bit of polite haggling — the sale was finalized. The gentleman handed Alan a deposit. Later that afternoon the completed oil would be delivered to the couple's hotel.

"Well done, Alain," Henri said in colloquial French when they were once again alone. "We will eat well tonight, and be able to pay the rent as well. America lost its best salesman when you left."

"You dare suggest that I engage in honest labor? Blasphemy! Quick, cross yourself and spit three times, or you will be damned in hell for all eternity."

Henri shook his head and laughed. "Did you have to be so brusque to those two angelic creatures? I would have insisted you have your pick, even though I had already given my heart to the little one with the saucy brown eyes."

"Why didn't you speak up, my friend?"

"Me? I'm much too shy. But you could've persuaded them to model for us. I would much rather paint nudes than churches."

"You can paint nudes in the winter when it's too cold to be outside. In May we stand on the sidewalks where we can paint churches and be seen. They sell better than nudes. American tourists are self-righteous, pious prudes."

Henri dipped his brush in solvent and wiped it with a rag. "Are there no young women for whom you would make an exception?"

"Young women are either saving for their dowries or they're looking for rich patrons. Young women have scowling papas who are waiting for them to get married. They want to be courted, flattered, and indulged. Young women do not interest me."

"No. You prefer married ladies in their thirties, forties, or even fifties who are bored and looking for amusement. What has it gotten you besides a meal, a good bottle of wine, or an afternoon in some fancy hotel?"

Alan used his finger to blend and soften a cloud. "Is that so bad?"

"What about me?" Henri insisted. "I'm a man in need of a woman's company. Is it my fault I possess talent and lack manly beauty? Are you so selfish that you think only of yourself?"

"Look! There. The charming lady who admired my work only yesterday." Alan waved at a stylish woman in her late forties, wearing a lavender dress with a ruffled hem that flattered her shapely legs, a matching cloche hat, and a small fox fur draped about her shoulders.

"The one who claimed that you resembled Errol Flynn. You're a lucky dog. Elegant, chic, the nose a trifle too long, but all in all, most attractive."

"We meet again," the lady announced when she reached them. "This appears to be your favorite spot, monsieur."

"Yours too it would seem. And as this is our second meeting, may I ask your name? I should be so pleased if you called me Alain."

"Alain, you may call me Celeste. First names are sufficient, don't you agree?"

"Most definitely. Henri, let me present the delightful and lovely Madame Celeste, a lady who has the good sense to dispense with out-dated formality."

"Enchanted, Madame," Henri declared.

"I was just telling Henri," Alan said "that a glass of wine would be so pleasant this spectacular spring day, but Henri had to decline. He must finish his latest commission for an impatient client. Would you consider accompanying me?"

She wrinkled her brow, enough to suggest deliberation but not enough to spoil her appearance. "A glass of wine would be refreshing."

"Perhaps my good friend Henri would take care of my things while we are occupied?"

Henri's shrug assured them that he would be happy to be of assistance.

A scrawny waiter in shiny black trousers was there to observe, as they sat at the sidewalk cafe, sipped their wine, and exchanged flattering glances. An hour later Alan confessed that he would love to take Celeste to his humble flat, where they could continue their conversation in private. Alas, there was a problem.

"I have not one, but two flat-mates. Not men, pigs really. It's no place for a cultured lady like yourself. And I have a busybody for a landlady. How I would adore escorting you to a fine hotel, but an artist's life is hard." He presented a grave face.

Celeste smiled her understanding, opened her purse, and looked around. The waiter hiding near the awning turned away. Beneath the table, she slipped two bills into Alan's waiting hand.

The afternoon's activities were so enjoyable for both parties that another meeting was arranged. It was on their second liaison that Alan conceived his plan. Apparently, Celeste had a recurrent need which required regular fulfillment and the lady was a generous partner in so many ways. Alan waited until their fourth rendezvous, or about a month, before proceeding to the next step. That afternoon as they made love he did everything in his power to please her, testing both his imagination and his stamina. As they lay next to each other on the narrow bed he confided, "We cannot go on meeting in hotels. It's too dangerous. Someone is certain to remember a beautiful lady like yourself. A jealous maid or doorman might confront your husband."

"But we never stay at the same hotel."

"We're running out of hotels." Alan gave her a minute to absorb this. "But I have a simple solution. I've found a most suitable apartment — convenient, clean, with a very discreet concierge."

"An apartment, Alain? Do you intend to live there?"

"My dear, it would just be for the two of us. For painting, I will keep the studio I share with Henri."

"What does this apartment cost?"

"It's a tiny thing — just big enough for our purposes. Our love nest will cost less than engaging a hotel room once a week. Hotels are horribly expensive, are they not?"

"Horribly," she agreed, stroking his abdomen.

Alan hoped she would not demand more of him. A late night followed by the afternoon's activities had left him drained. He removed her hand and kissed each successive finger. "We can pretend we are Bohemian lovers, the tortured artist and his exquisite tempestuous model."

She giggled. "Star-crossed Bohemian lovers. Tell the concierge we'll take it."

"May I make one more suggestion, my love? Would you allow me to handle the transfer of funds? The concierge knows me. That way you won't have to provide your name."

"Always you are so thoughtful, Alain. So thoughtful and so loving." Celeste slid her manicured hand down his abdomen once more before rising. "Too bad there isn't time for more, but I really must go."

Alan sank back against the pillows and silently thanked several saints for the lack of time.

* * *

Two weeks after moving his belongings to his new residence, one of the many women who paused to contemplate Alan's mundane efforts met his stringent requirements for an invitation for wine. Georgette Pelletier wore a wedding band, was attractive, older than he, and rich.

"A glass of wine?" she repeated. "I was planning to do some shopping, but I suppose that can be done later."

At the very same cafe where he had taken Celeste, Alan learned that Georgette was married to an elderly government official who had a mistress and little in common with his vivacious wife. As the waiter poured the last of the bottle into Georgette's glass, it would have been logical to suggest retiring to his apartment. A less enterprising man might have done so. As Georgette rearranged the neckline of her deeply-cut dress, it occurred to Alan that what had succeeded once might succeed again. Besides, Celeste's desire for him might fade. So Alan again suggested a hotel, one that regrettably he was too poor to pay for. And the romantic farce, with its second leading lady, proceeded much as it had before. Soon both women provided the rent.

One evening, as Henri and Alan were dining on a sumptuous meal, Alan was feeling particularly magnanimous. "Thanks to my two lady friends we can pay off LeBlanc. That way we can buy supplies without having to listen to his complaints or his wife's endless whining."

Using an end of bread, Henri wiped the last bit of gravy from his plate. "Never mind LeBlanc. His wife is a shrew who overcharges unmercifully. Let the old swindler wait. It's more important for you to buy yourself new clothes."

"For you too, Henri."

"No, my dear Alain. I'm an artist. I'm expected to look shabby. My shabbiness does not detract from my appeal. You are a lover. Women are fickle creatures. You cannot risk offending the sensibilities of your gracious benefactresses."

Alan congratulated himself for having such a wise and generous friend. At Henri's insistence Alan purchased a few new items — underwear, shirts, two pair of trousers. A month later he added a fine new hat and shoes. The investment paid off. Not only did Celeste's interest continue unabated, the new wardrobe enabled Alan to attract Brigitte, the wife of a newly rich financier. Brigitte soon unknowingly joined Georgette and Celeste in supplying the rent.

Alan saw nothing disgraceful about his unorthodox ménage a

quatre. He didn't regard his lovers with contempt, nor did he feel used or exploited. The women were no less attractive to him than their younger counterparts. He had been raised in a motherless home by a volatile abusive father. Following eleven pregnancies in thirteen years of marriage, Margaret Noreen Fitzpatrick used her last measure of strength to give life to Alan before joining her heavenly Father. She left behind five sons and one daughter — one lone female responsible for making their meals, washing their clothes, and cleaning up after them. Alan had seen all that he wanted of poverty and neglect. He preferred the company of women who wore expensive perfumes and elegant clothes – cultured women, women who would indulge him rather than expect to be indulged. So Tuesdays at 2:30 and Fridays at 3:15, Alan considered himself fortunate to behold Celeste's lovely carved-ivory arms, tiny waist, and curvaceous legs. Every Monday at 4:00, except in August when she vacationed with her husband, Alan found Georgette's graceful long neck and luscious white bosom irresistible. Brigitte's adorable mouth, so eager to find a hundred delightful ways to please (Thursdays at 3:00 and alternate Saturdays at 1:00) more than compensated for the tiny lines around her eyes.

Ah, Paris. Ah, the wonderful, sensuous nature of Parisian women. How fortunate, Alan thought, that Paris was filled with philandering husbands who left their poor wives with no one to appreciate their charms. It was so easy to condemn the former and toast the latter.

Around the time Brigitte unknowingly joined the ménage, Henri found Mimi, a crafter of silk flowers, with handfuls of strawberry-red hair and a plump young body to inspire him. That Christmas Mimi brought her belongings to the shared studio. Henri's studies of Mimi easily outsold his commonplace renditions of churches. Although neither man had to rely on the other to survive, they continued their informal work arrangement.

*   *   *

One cold cloudy evening in January, Alan chose to stroll the banks of the Seine prior to returning home. Street traffic was light. In the murky haze ahead, he saw a lone shadow on the bridge. From the silhouette he decided it was either a small woman or a child. Before turning into the street that would take him home, he paused. Horror struck, he watched the figure climb over the railing, hesitate a second, then dive feet first into the river. Pulling off his heavy overcoat as he ran, he could hear splashing. She had attracted the attention of others as well. Voices were calling for someone to help. By the time Alan reached the bridge several people had gathered and were pointing at the water. He quickly removed his shoes and jumped in.

The icy impact simultaneously numbed his limbs and cleared his head. He scanned the water's surface and saw that she was the length of a streetcar away. He swam toward her only to watch her sink beneath the murky water before he reaching her. He dove repeatedly where he had last seen her. The foul water stung his eyes and its vile taste sickened him. The frigid temperature deadened his limbs and stole his breath. Alan plunged for what he knew would be his last attempt. Just as his lungs were about to explode he headed for the surface; her elbow struck his head. Before he could lose her again he managed to grab the back of her heavy coat. She thrashed angrily, either in an attempt to free herself, or from fear. Alan held fast. Using his pumping legs to stay afloat he waited until she had expended the last of her energy. When she was too weak to resist he dragged her to those waiting to assist on the river's bank. Many cheered as he and the girl were lifted out of the water. Others reproached.

"Foolish girl. Foolish girl with so much to live for!" a woman with a gray shawl shouted.

"Bravo! Bravo, the gallant hero!" another called, waving her arm.

"Did you see how fearlessly he dove in?" an old man demanded of the others. "You are a brave man, monsieur. One can only hope she is worthy of such daring.

Alan feared, if the young woman lying next to him didn't rid herself of the water she had swallowed, she would die. He turned her onto her stomach and gently applying pressure to her back. While those watching offered encouragement she sputtered, coughed, and threw up repeatedly.

"She'll be all right now. I'll look after her," Alan told the onlookers. One by one they dispersed. As she lay on the pavement regaining her strength Alan noticed the quality of her waterlogged clothing, her ruby earrings, and a delicately worked gold bracelet. Nor was he blind to her physical charms. His artist's eye noted the symmetry of her face, the pouted upper lip, the thick long lashes and dark blond hair, and when at last she was able to sit up, the curve of her young breasts.

"You did me no favor saving me, monsieur," she said, her sad eyes focused on the ground. "I have nothing to give you. I am a poor girl with no family to reward you. You would be better off throwing this skinny fish back."

This soggy creature was no orphaned peasant girl. She was lying. "I'll decide when it's time to throw you back. Just sit there and don't move while I find the rest of my clothing."

"Behind you."

He turned and looked down. Someone had gathered his things while he had attended to the girl. Only his new hat was missing. He assumed it had blown away. "Did you have the good sense to remove your shoes before you jumped?" he asked the girl. "You'll need them to walk."

Still unwilling to meet his gaze, she shook her head. "Leave me here. I don't need shoes."

"Leave you to jump again as soon as I'm out of sight, after all the trouble you've given me? I think not." With minimal effort Alan threw her over his shoulder. Literally soaking wet, she weighed scarcely a hundred pounds.

"Where are you taking me?" she demanded.

"You say your life has no value. What does it matter?"

*　*　*

"Take off your wet clothes and get into the tub." Alan pointed at his bathroom. "One more minute in those wet things and you'll surely catch pneumonia and cause me all sorts of grief."

"You're an American. You speak French well, but I can hear it in your accent."

"Yes, I'm American. Americans are impatient. Now get out of those clothes."

"You must give me a robe to put on and promise to leave me alone, or I shall scream loud enough to be heard from one end of Montmartre to the other. I will tell the police that you tried to have your way with me."

Alan laughed at the stubborn girl. "You ungrateful brat. I have no intention of touching you. Who would want a half-grown water rat like you? You can't be more than sixteen."

"I shall be eighteen in . . ." She silently counted. "In seven months and there's no need to be rude. A gentleman doesn't take advantage of a lady in distress."

He handed her one of his shirts. "Here, put this on. This isn't a hotel. I don't supply robes."

"My name is Nicole."

"Don't use up all the hot water or dilly-dally too long. I plan to get in there next. You're not the only one who needs a bath."

While he waited and considered how to proceed, Alan stripped, placed his wet clothes in the washbasin he used for dishes, and wrapped a towel about himself. It was obvious that Nicole came from a wealthy family. Her clothes and jewelry, even her bearing told him that. Poor girls didn't have her arrogance. But why had she tried to kill herself? Young women were romantics. Unrequited love? Perhaps. Or parents who wouldn't permit her to see a boyfriend they considered unsuitable? No. That sort of hysterics would be done at home and calculated to be unsuccessful. So, what reason would a beautiful girl from a wealthy family have to kill herself? In time he would find out. He intended to use what he had fished out of the Seine to his advantage.

She emerged from the bathroom encased in two towels plus his shirt. "What do you want me to do with my wet clothes?"

"Put them in the sink next to mine. You can hang them in the bathroom after I'm done. I left bread and cheese on the table. Having emptied your belly so effectively, no doubt you're hungry."

The guarded look in her eyes told him she would be there when he finished.

*   *   *

As was his habit, Alan left early and returned with food he had purchased. Nicole had been sleeping on a makeshift banquette when he'd left. The flat was neat and she was waiting for him with anxious eyes. The healthy glow of youth had returned and her brushed hair formed a gauzy golden halo around her head. She was even lovelier than he remembered. Fortunately it was Sunday and Alan expected no visitors. He had yet to devise a strategy for what to do with his unplanned guest when he entertained his expected ones.

"I'll give you this gold bracelet if you let me stay two weeks. You can sell it or give it to your fiancée."

Alan went to his demi-kitchen and took out a knife to slice the sausage they would have with lunch. "Ah, you're bargaining with me. I assume you've decided to live."

"Thanks to you I have no choice. Are you going to let me stay or not?"

It occurred to him that she might be pregnant. What other reason would a girl of her class have to kill herself?

"Is there no one who will take you in until the baby comes? Can't the father be persuaded to marry you?"

In an instant her newfound strength abandoned her. Her eyes lost their resolve, her mouth slackened, and her shoulders fell. She raced toward his front door. Alan caught her as her hand reached the knob. Tears cascaded freely down her cheeks and chin. To his astonishment the slight figure collapsed into his arms. She clung to him as she sobbed — massive body-racking sobs. A new emotion overtook him, flooded his being like a powerful narcotic. Growing up with four older brothers, an alcoholic father to knock him about, and only an overburdened sister to look after them all, Alan had never been the object of compassion or warmth. If pressed, he could not explain what he felt as he held Nicole in his arms. He had known passion and desire. He knew the companionship of friends. He knew pain and laughter. But simple tenderness had eluded him.

"Let me die," she whimpered. "I want to die. I can't disgrace my family."

She tried to pull away but he wouldn't release her. "Stupid girl. Stupid ignorant girl. I've never seen a problem that money couldn't solve. If this man won't marry you, there are other ways. If it isn't too late, a doctor can help you. Or your parents can send you to the country, to some poor relative where they'll find a home for the baby. You can marry someone else."

The tears ceased and her upper lip protruded into what the French called a moue. "Who? Who could I marry?"

"You could marry me."

"You would be willing to marry me?"

"I am not offering to love, honor, and cherish you. I would marry you so your child would have a name. It would be a business arrangement. After the baby was born your father would give me some money and I would disappear. You could tell your friends that I was dead — a brave soldier who died a heroic death."

"You're not a Jew. My father would rather I kill myself than marry a gentile. Besides, we have no money. We are poor people."

"If you're so certain, why don't you ask your father whether he'd prefer a Christian son-in-law or a dead daughter? Be sure to mention that I'm a lapsed Irish-Catholic on my father's side and an irreverent Presbyterian on my mother's. Perhaps that will convince him."

"It's easy for you to make jokes."

"When are you due? The baby, when is the baby coming?"

As she approached the window the sunlight shone through the shirt he had lent her. She was half siren, half water sprite. He turned away.

"I don't know. Maybe July."

"You don't know? Are you so ignorant you don't know it takes nine months to have a baby?"

"July. The middle of July. Why are you so mean to me? And who are the women in the drawings?"

She had found the sketches he had hidden. For their amusement, and as keepsakes for himself, he had taken to sketching his paramours. "So you are a snoop as well as a fallen woman."

"I'm not a snoop. I found them when I put away the blankets. Are all three of them your lovers?"

"My sketches and my lovers are my business. The women are patrons of my work and they visit me from time to time. Naturally I expect you to be out when I entertain — and not to leave your belongings about either."

"You make your living as an artist?"

"And you? You're an art critic?"

"I'm sorry. I didn't mean to imply that you're not talented. I think the sketches are quite lovely. I'm jealous of your ability to support yourself, to live the life you want. I have no gift for art. Our house is filled with many beautiful . . . "

She had stopped herself, Alan thought. She came from a house filled with beautiful objects — just as he suspected. She would come around. Her belly would become distended and ugly. She would miss her family and familiar surroundings.

"Can you cook?" he asked. She shook her head. "Then you'll learn. What's more, you'll keep this place clean and do my laundry and shopping. Do you understand?"

"Am I expected to be your lover as well?"

Despite himself he smiled. She looked so comical with that outthrust upper lip and glaring at him with those oversized tiger's eyes. "I don't take half-grown girls for lovers."

Chapter Eight

Euphoria with my success in repairing Esmeralda's rear view mirror, coupled with my hysterical outburst, had left me ravenous. I stopped for something to eat before returning to Fiona Hagen's home. It was well after seven when I reached her front porch.

"Would you look what the tide brought in?" Fiona declared when she opened her door and saw me. "I didn't think we'd be seeing you back tonight."

"I'd like to apologize for running off. I hope I'm still welcome."

"Now that you're here you might as well come in."

I followed her to a brown couch with shredded arms. She turned off the television and sank into the chair facing me. The book bags and toys were gone. "Where are the children?"

"Home. Their mother comes to get them when she finishes work. Don't you look like a drowned rat," she said, crossing her arms. "You must have spent the entire time weeping and wailing."

Looking at Fiona, her tired eyes were the exact blue-green as mine. "Weeping, wailing, and cursing."

"Cursing, eh? I guess this house has heard its share of cursing. I found a few things to call that blackguard brother of mine after he took off without so much as a 'by your leave.' So what made you come back? Still think I can help you find him?"

"I lied to you. My father isn't missing. He died just after Christmas."

"Mary, Mother of God." She quickly crossed herself. "What could have took him? I'm sixty-seven. That means Alan was fifty-five. Was it a heart attack?"

"I'm sorry, but there's no easy way to say this. He killed himself."

Fiona shook her head in disbelief. "Alan Fitzpatrick kill himself? Don't you believe it, dearie. Alan loved himself far too well."

"He drove his car into a tree."

"Then it was an accident."

"It wasn't an accident. Two days later we received letters he wrote saying that he intended to do it."

"Jesus," she said, shaking her head, "if that don't beat the band. My baby brother killed himself. Well, I'll be damned. He must have been sick or crazy."

"You mentioned that you had a picture of the four of us. I was hoping you knew my mother. My father never spoke of her."

"So Alan was that angry at Nicole for dying that he wouldn't tell his daughters about their own mother. What a wicked thing to do, not to tell you about your mother. He'll pay for that in Purgatory, he will." She patted my shoulder with her red-knuckled hand. "I can tell you the little I know, but I never met the woman. She died in France during the war while searching for her brother. I know that for certain, I do. Your father went on a two-day binge when he got the news. It wasn't long after that the three of you disappeared."

"My mother was in France looking for her brother?"

"Your mother was French. You and your sister were born there. If I live a thousand years I'll never understand that man. As a boy, Alan didn't give me half the trouble his brothers did, but he was the strange one — a spinner of tall tales and a wanderer. Told everyone he was going to France to be a great artist. Me father always said there was a bit of the gypsy in Alan – from our mother's side. The Fitzpatricks were solid stock. They had no patience with drifters and dreamers."

I observed the faintest guilty smile pass over her face. "But you did."

"How could I not have a special place in my heart for that rascal? Maybe the world needs a few drifters and dreamers."

"Is there anything you can tell me about my mother? Anything at all. You mentioned a picture."

"All I know is that Alan was waiting for her to come to the States, but she never made it. I've got two pictures upstairs. Wait here. I'll bring them down." Fiona disappeared up the stairs and returned a few minutes later. "Lord have mercy, you're the spitting image of her. I should have seen it straight away."

I took the black and white photograph from Fiona. In it was a girl who could not have been older than eighteen. She was standing on a sidewalk in front of a large arched door. Nothing could have prepared me for the first sight of my mother. I was tall; she was petite. I was plain and she was radiant. My hair was drab and hers shimmered. Amelia didn't resemble her at all. I had her eyes, mouth, chin, nose. "I look like my mother," I whispered.

"Now isn't that what I just told you?" Fiona chided, sitting beside me on the tattered couch that now seemed weary and worn from use, not neglect. "Here, take a gander at this one."

It was a picture of the four of us. My beaming young father, with a pencil-thin mustache, held Amelia, who appeared to be about three. Seated on a park bench next to him was my mother holding the infant I knew was me. I searched for signs of tenderness in my mother's smile, the tilt of her head, the soft curve of her arm as she cradled me. I didn't realize I was puddling again until Fiona thrust a large man's hanky into my hand.

"I thought you might be needing this. Now don't be going on too long, mind you, or I'll be wanting one myself."

I pressed Fiona for whatever information she could recall. After the Nazis invaded France my father somehow had managed to get us here. My mother had stayed behind to look for her brother who had been wounded fighting the Nazis, and died not long after we returned to the States. Fiona could tell me nothing about other family members, not even their last name. It seemed even before my mother's death my father was reluctant to talk about her.

"After we moved away, did the police ever come by to ask you about him?"

"The police? No, indeed! But I can't say I blame you for what you're thinking. Have to admit the thought crossed my mind when you said he killed himself. But make no mistake, your father wasn't a thief. I'd swear to that." She sighed. "You better bring in your things. It's nearly one o'clock. I'll fix up a bed for you in the guest room."

Too tired to argue, I obediently did as I was told. My sleep was filled with a recurring nightmare. My mother was standing under the Arc de Triomphe and waving at me across the deserted boulevard. Between us was my smiling father, his arms extended ready to embrace me. I begged and pleaded with him to let me pass, but he wouldn't permit it. I didn't need Sigmund Freud to interpret that dream.

*   *   *

As we drank our first cups of coffee, Fiona offered to show me photos of my father and his family taken when he was a boy. I flipped though the small album looking for a familiar face among the strangers. I knew I would later regret not spending more time, but I was too distraught to concentrate. My father had to have done something truly heinous to take off with two young daughters and sever all relations with his family.

I thanked Fiona for everything and kissed her good-bye. She made me promise I would call her soon. It was a promise I wasn't certain I could keep.

Heading south, stopping only at gas stations for whatever provisions their pumps and vending machines provided, Esmeralda dined sumptuously on high test while I made do with a Baby Ruth and a couple of bags of stale pretzels. When we reached Washington, I pulled into the first motel with a vacancy sign.

The room was lifeless and cold. I found the thermostat, turned the dial, and waited only long enough for my fingers to thaw sufficiently to dial the phone. It was Saturday night — America's official date night. There was no point worrying what I would say. Raul would be out.

"I'm glad you called," he said in a voice that warmed the room far more effectively than the sputtering radiator. "If I didn't hear from you tonight I was going to report Esmeralda kidnapped. The last I heard you were going to call the plumber's wife."

"I drove to Philadelphia to see her. We got to talking and then it was too late to call."

"You uncovered something— something that upset you. Are you all right?"

"I'm fine. Everything is fine."

"Are you going to tell me what she said or do I have to pry it out of you?"

Either I was transparent or he was clairvoyant. An idea came to me as we spoke. A rather good idea. "Can you manage without Esmeralda another day or so?" I took inexcusable selfish pleasure that Raul was home and apparently dateless on a Saturday night. "I'm not in New York. I'm near Maryland, less than thirty minutes from my father's second wife – the stepmother who preceded Petal. I'd like to stop off and talk with her before I drive home."

"Do you think she'll be willing to meet with you? I mean, was it an angry divorce?"

"I don't know the real reason they split, but they parted friends. Norma Dawson is a lovely woman."

"Good. Then turn on the charm and ask questions. There's a lot about your father we still don't know."

Like the fact that his name wasn't Jack Morgan and he disappeared with his daughters twenty years ago. "I might stay an extra day. I'm very tired."

He paused before speaking again. "The guy that you're sort of seeing, he wouldn't happen to live in or around Maryland, would he?"

"No," I responded, hoping the questioning had ended and I wouldn't be forced to tell another lie.

"Good, because I borrowed a boat for the weekend. The weatherman is predicting perfect conditions for sailing — gentle breezes, full sun, warm enough for a swimsuit. You do own a swimsuit, don't you?

I could swear I heard the sensuous, seductive rhythm of a tango when he spoke. Perfect conditions for sailing — gentle breezes, full sun, warm enough for a swimsuit. You do own a swimsuit, don't you?

"Meteorologists don't do seven day forecasts," I reminded him.

"You listen to the wrong stations."

*　*　*

Daddy and Norma met in Palm Beach, but she had been born and raised in Maryland. I'd heard, when Clay Dawson had died some years ago, Norma had sold the sizable estate they owned and purchased the more manageable brick home she now occupied. Like its owner, the Chevy Chase home was warm, tasteful, and unpretentious.

I'd timed my arrival for eleven a.m., when I knew I would find her sitting in a ruffled silk robe at her breakfast table, smoking a cigarette and reading the newspaper. Everything about Norma was soft and round: her dark eyes, full bosom, gently curled hair. There was nothing angular or forbidding about her. Though surprised by my unscheduled visit, Norma's welcome had been genuine. I was not to fuss about anything and to stay as long as I wished.

While my motive for the visit was to pump Norma for information, I found myself unable to mention my father, let alone ask questions. My charming ex-stepmother was the perfect hostess – there for companionship when I wanted someone to talk with, and occupied when I didn't. Mornings, the hours from dawn until two, I was expected to entertain myself. We would meet at four o'clock for drinks and to make plans for the evening. I should have enjoyed this floating pressure-free existence. Instead, I felt as though I was being dragged under to drown in a sea of lies. Waves of anger alternated with depression. My nightly calls to Raul, explaining that I needed one more day only added to my confusion.

"Are you seeing anyone special, Sugar?" Norma asked on the third afternoon, as we sat on her sun porch.

"I have a silly crush on a totally unsuitable man. Frankly, I don't know what to do about it," I found myself confessing.

"Unsuitable? Gorgeous, sexy, and broke, or wanted in three states for murder?"

Norma could be relied on to be direct. "The former. That beat up old station wagon I'm driving is his. He has nothing: no trust fund, no inheritance, no family business waiting for him to step into."

Norma watched the ice cubes circle as she rotated the glass she held in her hand. "Your father had a shiny new car, two adorable little girls, and the clothes on his back when I married him. He had to borrow money from a friend to buy me an engagement ring." She looked up at me with impish glee. "You can imagine who repaid the loan."

I rose to refill my glass with white wine. "You knew Daddy had nothing before you married him?"

"Jack Morgan wouldn't be the first man with the good sense not to hold a woman's wealth against her," Norma confided in a husky voice. "When we met, your father told me he was a stockbroker who had loaned money to a client and was waiting to be repaid. I was just getting over the loss of my son. As the weeks passed I began to have doubts about your father, but by that time I was head over heels mad about him and not ashamed to say so."

I'd never met her son Jason who tragically died in a boating accident. "Would you be upset if I asked why you and Daddy got divorced?"

Norma rose to refresh her glass with bourbon. "In the beginning, I thought that I had enough money for all of us. That's where I was wrong. Economics forced me to divorce your father, Charlie. Economics. Like a fool, I made some bad investments. The four of us were going through cash like a shipload of drunken sailors. No man spent more gracefully than your father. Not for himself. He bought little in the way of clothing, nor did he need to. Jack Morgan looked better in a pair of trousers and a turtleneck than other men did in a tuxedo. One car sufficed him. True, he preferred a Bentley to a Mercedes, but only one was necessary. However, if your father heard the maid's brother had died and left six children, or that the gardener's baby was sick, he was an easy touch. For you and Amelia there were no limits: private schools, ski trips, camps, the finest horses, trainers, your sister's singing lessons, and of course nannies and tutors."

"Clothing, gifts, parties," I added. "All the things Amelia and I took for granted. I feel like a selfish idiot. I've gone through life spending money, never thinking about where it came from."

"As long as there's plenty of it, who does?" she said, giggling. "It was my fault as much as your father's. I loved buying things for you. Lord knows, I'm not known to be prudent. But some nine years after we were married, things were completely out of control. My accountant told me in no uncertain terms that if I didn't stop, I'd be flat broke in no time. The only advice he had for me was to find a man with holdings that exceeded mine. I pleaded with him to find another solution, but he told me that it was too late for that. I had no choice, sugar. I was fifty and no longer a blushing young thing. My face, my backside, my tits, everything I'd relied on, were all heading south, if you know what I mean. I had to be practical. If I waited until I was flat broke, how would that have helped you and your father? As it was, I had to look for an older man. Clay, bless his dear heart, was a good man, but he was also fourteen years my senior and unattractively stout. When I was your age, I wouldn't have given a man with his looks a second glance." Norma drained the last few drops in her glass. "Shortly before the divorce became final your father told me he would be coming into a great deal of money. He pleaded with me to reconsider. He begged me to tear up the papers."

"And you refused?"

"Your father possessed infinite charm; no man was more attentive. Maybe I shouldn't say this to his daughter — but Jack was a wonderful lover. Lord how I miss that man."

Naturally I turned scarlet. I wasn't, however, going to stop now. "But?"

"The plain truth is that your father didn't put much value on the truth. I refused. I simply didn't believe him. I was wrong. I regret it to this day. I heard from friends that Jack rented a grand chateau in Cannes that summer for the three of you, and the Dom Perignon was flowing like bath water."

I recalled both Cannes and the freely spent francs.

"He told me that he had sold a painting that he'd owned." She leaned closer. "A masterpiece."

"A masterpiece?"

"That's exactly what I thought. But Jack claimed it was part of a collection he owned. I'm afraid I didn't believe him, sweet pea. You have to understand. I had caught him in so many lies before. Where would your father get a masterpiece? And if he had one, why hadn't he sold it earlier?"

"Did you ask him who the artist was?" I prodded.

"He told me, but I can't remember. Someone famous. Even I recognized the name."

"French? Italian? Flemish?"

"French," she said, clinking the ice cubes in her glass again. "Yes, definitely French. But that's all I can remember. Is it terribly important?"

"No, I guess not." As we sat watching squirrels playing tag on her sheltered back lawn, I wondered if the mysterious masterpiece could have anything to do with my father's decision to end his life. "There's talk that Daddy deliberately drove his car into a tree."

Norma turned to me in utter shock. "That's crazy! You pay that sort of talk no mind. Your father didn't kill himself."

I smiled at her. There was no point in further distressing this kindest of women.

*   *   *

"You can move in with me. I'm serious, Charlie," Norma told me for the third time as I lifted my suitcase into the back of the station wagon the following morning. "When Amelia is back to her old self, you can bring her here too. You can both stay until a handsome prince on a white horse carries you off, or we all turn into eccentric recluses with a hundred nameless cats."

"Don't think it isn't tempting, Norma, but there's something I have to do."

"You looking forward to seeing that heart-stopping hot-blooded young fellow who owns this wreck? Remember, sweet pea, you don't have to buy. Ask for samples."

Blushing again, I kissed Norma's soft rouged cheek and climbed into the car.

"Darlin', I almost forgot to tell you. Last night I remembered the name — the name of the artist your father mentioned. You wanted to know if he was French and that got me to thinking. I can only name three French artists – Manet, Monet, and Renoir. Well I know for certain it wasn't Manet or Monet. So it had to be Renoir."

"Are you sure?"

"My memory may be slow on the uptake, but give me twenty-four hours notice and I can tell you which sheiks carried flasks and which didn't. Sheiks, that's what we called dashing young bucks thirty-something years ago. Those flasks contained hard liquor. Oh, this girl had some fun in the wild and wicked Twenties."

Renoir, I thought, climbing into the car. Ridiculous! Where would my father get a Renoir?

Chapter Nine

What was I doing? I thought as Raul led me down the hall to his office and closed the door behind him. I should have driven directly home and called later — told him that I had returned safely, thanked him for the loan of Esmeralda, and offered to exchange vehicles when it was convenient. Instead, I was trying to invent a reasonable explanation for my unscheduled and unnecessary appearance because I was rattled, confused, and wanted a man to take me in his arms and tell me everything was going to be all right. Which I knew was utterly irrational and potentially dangerous.

"I thought I would see if there were any messages for me," was the best I could do.

"I'm glad you stopped," he said, grinning at me with all thirty-two teeth in that self-satisfied way. "Amelia's doctor wants you to call him. It's not an emergency. Just something he wants to discuss with you. I can't stay long. I've sort of been promoted."

"That's great."

"Remember I said, *'sort of been promoted.'* That means that I see low-level clients when a partner isn't available. I'm expecting one any minute. And your step-mother called. You won't like what she has to say. I'll tell you about it later at dinner.

"Dinner?"

"This isn't a date, not while you're *sort of seeing* the mystery man. This is just a chance for us to discuss what you learned and to decide what to do next."

What I'd learned? I learned that there wasn't going to be any more investigation. No one was going to learn about father and our alter egos. I had two precious photographs of my mother. I knew her name and the tiniest bit about her. Someday, when Amelia was well, I would share it with her. "We have to exchange cars."

"I'll pick you up at seven-thirty. Put on your sexiest dress and wear your hair down."

The look I shot across the room left no doubt of my opinion of that suggestion.

He grinned at me and shrugged. "I like looking at beautiful women. Shoot me."

"I'll leave you to your low-level client and congratulations on your semi-promotion." I turned the doorknob. "And for the record, I wear what I please and seven o'clock is better. Try being on time."

*   *   *

I called Amelia's doctor as soon I reached home.

"We've been observing a gradual improvement. Amelia's been more outgoing, talking with the other patients and staff. But progress is slow. I'd like to try shock therapy. There's been very interesting work done in the area. To proceed, I'll need a family member's signed permission."

"Shock therapy. I've heard the term, but I'm not sure I understand what it means. It involves electricity, doesn't it?"

"Correct."

"Mild electric shocks? Like the kind you get when you touch something after walking across a rug?"

"Not that mild — stronger. Strong enough to eradicate painful memories."

"Would Amelia have to be tied down?"

"She would have to be restrained. But as I explained, it could prove very —"

Electric shocks. Restraints. I felt sick. Not for my sister. Not Amelia. "I'm sorry, but I have to refuse for the time being."

"I think the therapy would be helpful or I wouldn't be suggesting it."

"I appreciate your professional concern, but I don't think I'm ready to try anything quite so drastic yet."

I hung up, my hands shaking. It would take half a bottle of sherry or a hundred laps in the pool to regain my composure. I considered the remedial effects of both, and after due deliberation, chose the latter.

*   *   *

Having being instructed to wear something sexy, I wouldn't, even if I owned a blatantly provocative outfit. On the other hand, I didn't want to look schoolgirl prissy. I thought I'd achieved a nice balance with a skirt that was loose enough not to pull, soft enough to cling. The filmy peasant blouse I chose had a tendency to fall off my shoulder in a way I hoped was alluring. My hair proved a problem. For years, I'd ignored it, relying on an easy single braid or ponytail. Coiling it around my head made me look like a nineteenth century Swiss matron. Undone, it fell well below my waist, making me look like a gangly Rapunzel. Finally, I brushed it into long waves and loosely tied it at the base of my neck with a flowing silk scarf. I checked my mirror and compared myself to the models I had seen in magazines – a crushing exercise. Cream blouse, cream skirt, pale pink lipstick, I resembled a huge peeled banana. I located a soft brown eye pencil and darkened my brows — a slight improvement. The effect encouraged me to draw a line along my lashes and smudge it. Now my eyes looked interesting, but my lips had disappeared. I tried playing with my limited stash of makeup until I was reasonably certain Banana Girl had been replaced by Attractive Confident Woman.

As instructed, Maria let Raul in and invited him to sit down and wait when he arrived at seven-twenty – a predictable twenty minutes late. When I entered the room, his broad grin convinced me that my efforts had succeeded. I instantly forgave the transgression. As for my escort, charcoal gray slacks worn low on his hips, white sport shirt opened at the collar, which contrasted dramatically with his tanned skin and dark hair — he was indisputably gorgeous.

My shiny MG was parked next to Raul's mud splattered station wagon, which I realized now I should've had washed. The situation called for diplomacy. "Poor Esmeralda looks exhausted. And we've spent so much time together. What if we took my car tonight and gave her a well earned rest?"

"I'm sure she appreciates your thoughtfulness."

Minutes later we were driving down Worth Avenue. I'd assumed that Raul would take me off the island, to a less expensive spot, one where our presence would provoke less attention. But before I could think of an apt polite protest, we were walking down the alcove into Petite Marmite, one of Palm Beach's more pricey restaurants. As we followed the maitre'd to our table, I spotted two girls seated at the bar that I'd known since high school. Naturally I smiled. Both immediately engaged their escorts in conversation.

My feet refused to move. I'd been snubbed. I hadn't been snubbed when Amelia required hospitalization. Silver Glades has been the temporary abode of a number of Palm Beach's finest citizens when they needed a place to dry out. Nor were residents ostracized for late payment of bills. It was well known that some of Palm Beach's most famous residents maintained long overdue balances. I'd been snubbed either because of Raul's Latin heritage or because everyone who counted in Palm Beach was aware of my new financial status. Or both. And unless I quickly latched onto an acceptable rich husband, or some other means of reversing my economic predicament, this was only the beginning. Amelia and I would be persona non grata — permanently inscribed on the list of invisible people, uninvited and unwelcome. I considered bolting before hearing Daddy's voice. "Throw your head back, Charlotte, and stand tall." I leaned into Raul and tossed my head in the time-honored manner of femme fatales everywhere.

Raul responded as if on cue. He pulled me close and led me to our table with the bravado of a conquistador. "Did I mention that you look particularly beautiful tonight?" he said as he helped me with my chair. "I'm the envy of every man in this room."

What if he was a flirt and a shameless flatterer? I thought. A compliment delivered at the exact moment when it was most needed, demanded a warm smile. I smiled. Warmly.

"I don't want to put a damper on a lovely evening," he said once we were seated, "but I'll feel better after I get this out of the way. Your stepmother called the office. She suspects that you're looking into your father's death and she's not happy about it. She's threatening to cut off the last two payments for both you and Amelia if you continue."

Intent on keeping my displeasure private, I leaned forward to whisper. "This, after I agreed to let her keep the only two existing examples of Daddy's hidden talent. What made her suspicious?"

"You took some of your father's papers. I think she's bluffing, but you never know. It's up to you to decide if you want to go on with this."

"Let her try and stop me. I'll sell my jewelry." I said just loud enough for Raul to hear. Diners throughout the room were surreptitiously observing us.

"We can talk more freely Sunday. I promised to take you sailing."

Our waiter arrived. I ordered the bay scallops and Raul ordered the Beef Wellington – both house specialties. The food was excellent. Conversation was better. Raul asked about my childhood and laughed when I supplied the often told family anecdotes. I wanted to know what it was like growing up in Cuba.

His intense eyes softened as he described acres and acres of green fertile farmland, mountains, rain forests, and picturesque fishing villages. His homeland was a country of tiny churches, grand cathedrals, forts, and corridas, many built when Spain ruled.

"And the people," he continued. "North Americans are great, but they're always in a hurry. Cubans take time to be hospitable, warm – warm like the Cuban sun."

"So there are no criminals in Cuba?" I teased. "I suppose a jail is totally unnecessary."

"Before I left there was one jail with ten, maybe twelve prisoners. None that I'm related to."

I watched him waiting for my smile, caressing my bare shoulders with his eyes. And in those minutes, I wasn't impossibly tall and gawky. I was glamorous, stunning, fascinating, alluring. I was Grace Kelly captivating Cary Grant in *To Catch a Thief*, brilliant cascading fireworks filling the sky behind them.

We were among the last people to leave.

"You don't have to wear flats when you're with me," Raul said when we reached my front door. "You can wear four inch heels for all I care. I'm perfectly at ease with your height. I'm five foot ten and tall enough where it matters."

I blushed scarlet.

"Perhaps I should clarify that. I meant that I'm tall in character."

"I know what you meant," I snapped. As I reached into my handbag looking for my keys, Raul gently removed my scarf, lifted my hair and kissed the back of my neck. Oh my God! A bolt of electricity ricocheted down my spine, spiraled my legs and melted my sandals. I checked the sky for lightning.

"I wanted to do that all evening," he said, lacing his fingers through my hair and fanning it over my shoulders.

What had he wanted to do all evening — kiss me or undo my hair? Was he going to kiss me again? Certain the single kiss was responsible for my reaction the top of my spine tingled with anticipation. My lips were prepared.

Instead, he handed me my scarf. "I'll pick you up at nine Sunday morning. Bring a jacket."

"A jacket," I managed to croak.

"It could be cool."

"I could make sandwiches," I added, unwilling to see him leave.

"Great. You can make sandwiches; I'll take care of the rest."

*　*　*

Since I'd be responsible for the cost of Amelia's care, I thought I should consider all possible options. I set off early on Thursday to assess the county's mental facility. The prison-like wing I was shown was filled with shouting unattended patients. Moving Amelia to that horrendous place was unimaginable. Two private and distant treatment centers were only slightly better. I returned to Casa Buena exhausted and depressed.

The next day, as I passed the library, cheerful sitting area, arts and crafts room, and friendly staff, I decided that Silver Glades was the best facility available. I would have to find a way to keep Amelia here as long as necessary.

Although the room held a comfortable chair, I found my sister sitting on her bed and staring absently. The radio was silent. I looked for magazines, newspapers, a book. There were none. How did she pass the time?

"It's a lovely day," I said. "How about a ride in the car? We could go to an ice cream parlor," I suggested with forced animation, knowing my sister's weakness for sweets. "What do you say, Amelia? Doesn't an ice cream sundae with chocolate syrup and nuts sound delicious?"

She shook her head. "Well then, we'll just go for a nice walk."

I led her outside, along a tree-shaded path, chatting as we proceeded. Her movements were slow and clumsy. She answered my questions, when she chose to speak, in monosyllables. I could see no improvement since my last visit. After fifteen minutes, Amelia woodenly refused to go on. She allowed me to take her to a bench under a misshapen pine. I began to question my refusal of shock therapy. What if Dr. Mendelson was right?

When we returned to the main building a nurse in a starched white uniform was waiting for us. "There you are. It's time for your medication."

She handed Amelia two capsules and a glass of water. My sister obediently took both and downed the pills.

"What are those for?" I asked.

"Doctor's orders," the nurse said before she briskly strode away.

I left Amelia with a group of patients playing a listless game of bingo and headed for Dr. Mendelson's office. A receptionist requested I take a chair. I stared at the door for the next twenty minutes. No one entered or left. He finally opened the door.

"What sort of medication is Amelia being given?" I asked, as I entered his office.

"Nothing to be concerned about. Amelia gets a mild sedative to calm her," he said, as though he were speaking to a child. "Patients admitted with her symptoms always receive mild sedatives."

"There were two pills."

"Let me check my records," Dr. Mendelson said, frowning. He opened a file cabinet, removed a folder and spent an inordinate amount of time lifting and replacing pages before he answered. "She also receives a multiple vitamin."

He was lying. I took a deep breath and delivered my best impersonation of an indignant Bette Davis. "I don't want my sister given any medication."

"I prescribe a mild sedative for every patient I feel might endanger themselves or others," he cautioned in a cold voice.

"Do you really think Amelia is a threat to anyone?"

"Are you so certain that she isn't? You've refused my recommendation for electric therapy and now you want your sister's medication stopped. Mrs. Morgan has entrusted me with your sister's care. I think we should contact her before considering any changes."

"I am Amelia's closest relative and legally responsible for her." I once again called on an irate Bette Davis for help. "You are to consult with me about Amelia's treatment."

"Mrs. Morgan placed Amelia here and is billed accordingly," he said more conciliatory. "I'm sure you can understand our position."

I understood full well. He who pays the piper names the tune. "Next month you can bill me. Mrs. Morgan has informed me that she intends to stop treatment May first. I, on the other hand, will continue as long as I consider it necessary."

He leaned back in his chair and knit his hands over his stomach. "I suppose we could try dispensing with Amelia's medication for a while and see what happens. As you point out, Amelia is unlikely to harm herself, and we'll be extra vigilant."

I smiled. "Thank you, Dr. Mendelson."

Exiting Silver Glades' hedged entranceway the enormity of my impulsive decision hit me – followed by accompanying fear and nausea. I had assumed responsibility for expenses I couldn't pay. The jewelry I had cited to Raul consisted of my pearl necklace and ring, a gold charm bracelet, and the Tiffany tank watch Daddy and Petal had bought me when I turned eighteen. I had no inkling of their initial cost, or what their sale would provide, but I doubted it would be much. What I did know was that I desperately needed a job – a job that paid well – multiples of what a decorator's assistant was likely to earn. As I drove home, one side of my brain supplied endless reasons for failure, while the other side supplied overwhelming reasons for trying. Even I knew that modeling paid well. If I succeeded, I'd be able to take care of Amelia and myself, and rid myself of this incessant panic. If I failed, I would be no worse off than my present miserable condition.

Fighting back the urge to heave, when I arrived home I raced up the stairs into Petal's sitting alcove, selected several fashion magazines, and brought them to my room. After riffling through pages of glamorous models and celebrities, I dove into my small stock of makeup trying to recreate that one magical moment at Petite Marmite when I'd imagined myself beautiful. Thirty minutes later I bore little resemblance to the models in the glossy photos. Nevertheless, I searched the Yellow Pages until I located the sole listing I considered useful: *Peter Brent, Portraits, Special Occasions, and Events — Model's Portfolios*. Desperation drove me to dial his number. This wasn't for a special occasion, I explained to Mr. Brent. It was for a portfolio.

"I don't get many calls for portfolios anymore. You ever done one?" he asked.

"No."

"Never needed one or never modeled?"

"Neither."

"Well then, you'd better come by and let me take a look at you. It wouldn't be right to waste your money. It'll take five minutes — ten minutes tops."

"Could I stop by this afternoon?" I asked, before I could change my mind.

"I guess so. Anytime after three and before five."

The tired little studio was in West Palm Beach, across the bridge and a world apart. I feared that Mr. Brent might laugh when he saw me. I'd prepared an imaginative story about losing a bet in the event that he did. Brent, the name he preferred, didn't laugh, nor did he offer encouragement. Instead, the lean, almost emaciated man in his forties, with wispy brown hair and owlish eyes, ducked his head behind the camera. While wispy smoke from his cigarette floated toward the ceiling, I was appraised from every angle. When I thought I couldn't bear another second of scrutiny, he left his camera and delivered the following instructions: next Tuesday I was to bring four changes of clothing – a gown, suit, sports outfit, and a bathing suit, plus related accessories. I was to have makeup, combs, brushes, and a hundred dollar deposit. The deposit alone was more than double the fee that Brent charged for a portrait.

"And get your hair cut, styled, and lightened by the best hairdresser in Palm Beach you can find — someone who knows high fashion."

'I'll have it cut, but I'm not sure I like the idea of changing the color." My father had always discouraged lightening my hair. He'd claimed it would make me look common.

"Your hair isn't dark enough for contrast. It's drab. It's doesn't reflect light. It doesn't shoot well. I suggest that you go really blond. But suit yourself. It's your money."

"Do I have a chance?" I asked, hoping for some reassurance.

"You have the body and you've got good bone structure. But we won't know anything until we see the proofs."

I had the body and good bone structure. The words were exciting until I reached the door with the peeling paint, and realized that Brent might be indulging me because he needed money.

*   *   *

"Mr. Vincent is ready for you," the shampoo girl said.   I proceeded to the designated chair to await my fate.

The highly renowned Mr. Vincent lifted my braid with undisguised disgust. "What do you do with this? Hair this long went out with spats and high button shoes."

"What do you suggest?"

"Cutting it. Giving it some shape. Bringing you into the sixties."

Apparently, highly sought-after hairdressers didn't consider common courtesy necessary. Even so, I persisted. "I was considering lightening it as well."

"Yes!" He snapped his fingers, both hands, over my head and delivered his first smile. "You're going to love, love, love it!"

"What are you going to do?"

"Relax!" He undid my braid and brushed my hair until it draped over my back and shoulders. "Your hair has divine texture and body. When it isn't being dragged down by all this useless weight, it'll be stunning." A single snip of his scissors and a decade of growth fell to the floor.

For the next two hours, my hair was dyed, washed, shaped, redampened with setting lotion, stretched over giant rollers, and blown on by a noisy hot hair-drier.

"It's very light," I said, when I was again in Mr. Vincent's chair and staring in shock at my reflection.

"Don't you just love it? It's absolutely dynamite. You're absolutely dynamite." His knowing fingers prodded and urged my hair into soft waves that ended two inches below my shoulders. It bounced and glistened when I moved. My face had changed as well.

My cheekbones were more pronounced, my jaw was softer, and my eyes were moist. I realized now why Daddy had discouraged me from lightening my hair. The resemblance to my mother's dated black and white photograph was eerie.

*   *   *

Raul met me at my door. "Wow! What did you do to your hair? You look great. You look better than great. You look sensational."

"It looks brassy, doesn't it? The hairdresser made it too light. Wait here, I'll be right back." I handed him a basket filled with sandwiches and Maria's oatmeal cookies, and returned inside for the widest straw hat I owned, delighted at the response the change had elicited.

"Why are you going to cover it with a hat?"

"I have to. Without a hat and sunblock I turn into a giant blister," I admitted, all the while lapping up the delicious flattery.

It was a fifteen minute drive to the Mirabella, the thirty-foot sailboat Raul had borrowed. A half-hour later and five miles out, the sunlight reflecting off the water warmed the air and reminded me of what I loved about sailing: the crisp breeze, the mist hitting my face, the tranquility, the hypnotic repetition of the waves. I removed my jacket but left on the white pants and shirt that covered the swimsuit I intended to keep hidden. Raul pulled off his shirt and stripped down to his trunks.

As he was busy negotiating the large wake from a nearby yacht, I permitted myself the aesthetic pleasure of studying him. For once reality surpassed my imagination. The base of his neck was sturdy but not thick, extending gracefully to broad shoulders and defined arms. His broad chest tapered to a narrow waist. When he turned to steady the mast, my eyes dropped to his solid upper thigh and slid down his curved calf. I remembered the sole scorching kiss on the back of my neck, the longing to return that kiss – and then Amelia who had no one to rely on but me, my desperate financial condition, my father's death and his secret past life.

"Everything okay?" he asked.

"Yeah. Fine."

"Would you like me to put some of that sunscreen on your back before you burn?"

"Maria took care of that before I left home," a truth I immediately regretted sharing.

"Now, tell me what you learned from your first stepmother."

I confided what I'd learned from Norma.

"She divorced your father in 1951, when you were thirteen. How long after that did he marry Petal?"

"Let's see. After we left Cannes, Daddy rented a small apartment in Manhattan. That's where he met Petal. They didn't marry until I was fifteen."

"Have you given any thought to how much money he'd need to support the three of you between wives? I don't know anything about the value of art. Is it possible the money from the sale of a painting could support the three of you lavishly for that amount of time?"

"Beats me. Despite my interest in art, I have no idea what fine paintings sell for. But I have to assume a Renoir would command a colossal sum or every fine home in Palm Beach would have one."

"How do you suppose your father acquired it? Norma said that your father claimed to be a stockbroker before he met her, and that a client owed him a large amount of money. Maybe he took the painting in lieu of cash."

"My father wasn't a stockbroker. Finance bored him and I stopped asking him for help with my math homework when I got to algebra."

"He had to have some source of income. You learn anything from the plumber's wife?"

"The plumber's wife?"

"The woman you drove to Philadelphia to see."

"The drive was a waste. She didn't recognize my father's picture." The lie had dried my mouth. I took out two bottles of soda and gave one to Raul. We listened to the sound of the waves until the wind abruptly changed direction. When the mainsail swung free and Raul rolled into me, his thigh hard against mine, I fought back an insane desire to run my hand all over his rippled torso. I felt my face and neck get hot and red. Luckily, he was busy righting the boat and didn't notice.

"You gave Petal two paintings your father did when he was young," he said, when both the wind and I became calm. "Did you remember seeing them when your father was married to Norma?"

"No. I thought they'd always belonged to Petal."

"You told me they were good, copies done in some old style.

You have to know what I'm thinking."

"How can I know what you're thinking?" I knew exactly what he was thinking.

"Avoiding the truth won't get us anywhere. We're looking for a crime. Say it! Say the worst thing you can think of, and maybe we can prove it isn't so."

"You're wondering if my father was capable of producing a counterfeit Renoir."

"Was he?"

"Truthfully, I don't know."

"It would be nice to find out if a Renoir sold around that time. Is there any way to check?"

"Sales of really important paintings usually appear in the newspapers."

"Would they say who sold or bought it?"

"Auction houses and public institutions are always identified. Sometimes private parties demand anonymity."

"The library has access to old newspapers. You know the approximate date the Renoir was sold. A little research might be helpful."

"But if Daddy was that talented, why did he stop painting?"

"How can you be so certain that he stopped? Perhaps he deliberately hid his talent to protect you."

"Where? He would've had to maintain a studio."

"He could've rented space. Look at his checks and receipts. See if you can find anything that might be a monthly payment, gas and electric bills, telephone bills, for any address other than your homes."

Why did this man have to be so logical? And why did I have to be so pathetically feeble? My father's papers, which I so conscientiously retrieved, were neatly stacked in his library. I'd been unable to go over them. "I'll get to it tomorrow," I said, genuinely determined to carry out the promise. "And I'll check with the library."

Almost within reach, a dolphin poked his nose out of the water to gawk at us. I'd seen dolphins in the intercoastal waterway many times, but never this close. The playful fellow dove, performed two arching leaps, pivoted and flipped his tail in midair. When I turned to see if Raul had witnessed the unexpected aquatic show, I caught him exploring the swimsuit I wore beneath my damp, now translucent clothes. I flushed. He didn't. Nor did he avoid my eyes. I looked away. He was honest. I was a fraud. He let his interest be known: with his concern, his flattery, and unconcealed staring that said what I felt. How long would he wait before giving up?

Chapter Ten

I headed to my father's library immediately following the morning news. Seeing the daunting pile of cartons I decided organization was my first priority. Books on art I added to Daddy's Buena Casa collection. Personal calendars were stacked, most recent on top. Innumerable checks, floating freely or held together by rubber bands, bank statements, and checkbooks were placed in their own carton. His two small address books went on his desk, for easy reference. I carried personal mementos and photographs to my room and checked my watch. It had taken less than an hour and no emotional outbursts, to accomplish the first stage of the project.

Since I considered the checks and checkbooks the dullest job, I tackled them first. It took until noon to sort the mess, and then match checks to the meager information provided by checkbook entries. Many checks lacked entries and vice versa. Around noon, I brought a sandwich and glass of milk back to the library. Just before two o'clock, I stopped. I'd found no evidence that Daddy had written checks to rent or lease any space, no expenditures to the telephone, gas, or electric companies. My father was not a counterfeiter.

I rewarded myself by bicycling to town to purchase the extra makeup I needed for the following day with Peter Brent.

* * *

Brent had set out an impressive array of spotlights, cameras, props, and reflective silver umbrellas in his dreary studio. While he puffed on his cigarette and adjusted equipment, I ducked behind a sagging drape and put on the evening gown I had brought with me. Five minutes later I emerged.

Brent glared at me critically. "You need more makeup."

"More makeup? I'm wearing three times what I normally wear."

"Yeah, I noticed. Listen to me, kid. Strong light bleaches out color. If I shoot you the way you are now, your eyes will look like two raisins on vanilla ice cream. As for your mouth . . . You know what I see when I look at your mouth under the lights? A pink noodle. You need lip liner. Oh for god's sake," he swore, seeing my confusion. "Take one of those small brushes, dip it in a darker lipstick and outline your lips. Don't forget mascara, thick with no clumps. You've got to exaggerate everything."

Exaggerate everything! I returned to my newly purchased makeup. Mascara required three applications and exasperating clump removal. When I was certain that I looked like a cartoon character, I returned for inspection. "Is this what you had in mind?"

"Better. Now stand over there."

I positioned myself at the designated location, in front of a mottled gray screen.

Brent dropped behind the camera and returned frowning. "Okay, now relax. Drop your shoulders. You're too tense. Try swinging your arms and letting them fall."

I swung my arms as directed and felt the tension leave.

"Good. Now make believe you're playing a role."

"Who?"

He stopped to squint at me suspiciously. "Any woman you'd like to be."

I tried emulating Princess Grace of Monaco.

"That's not going to work. Think seductive – even trashy."

Trashy. Elizabeth Taylor in *Cat on a Hot Tin Roof*, vamping Paul Newman in the tightest, best fitting white silk slip ever made.

"Now you look like Joan of Arc being led to the stake. Don't think of anything. Let your mind go blank."

How does one not think of anything? I was told to lift my chin, drop my shoulders, arch my back, twist, turn, pose, point, pout, tousle my hair, and moisten my lips. I had to smile: shyly, seductively, coyly, girl-next-doorly — and stare: wistfully, dreamily, sleepily, defiantly. I was told to look two feet to the right, to the left, and above the camera. Between shots, Brent changed cameras, replaced film, adjusted backdrops and umbrellas, and I changed clothes, repaired my clownlike makeup, and fixed my hair. An exhausting three hours after we began, we stopped. I thought the last hour went better than the previous two. "It that it?" I asked, thinking my humiliation was finally over.

"That's it for the indoor shots. Did you bring a bathing suit like I told you?"

"Yes." I'd hoped he had changed his mind or forgotten. "My neck is too long. I look like a giraffe in a bathing suit."

"There is no such thing as a model's neck being too long. In this business no one would mind if you could graze off the ceiling. Go! Put on the bathing suit."

I slunk back to the closet-turned-dressing room and donned my bathing suit.

Brent draped a third camera around his neck and pointed to the door. "Grab what you need for your hair and your face. Don't forget a mirror. We're off to the ocean. The light should be perfect by the time we get there."

We drove until we reached a deserted section of beach hidden from the road by dense seagrapes and brush. Dark clouds pleased Brent, for the shadows and interest they provided, and worried him, because they indicated rain. Takes came closer together, his moves more efficient, and his directions terse. I was ordered to stand with my legs apart, place my hands on my hips, kneel, touch the brim of my hat, play with my hair, smile, pout, and growl. Yes, growl. Dissatisfied with all my attempts to look sexy, Brent ordered me to growl. I repaired my makeup while he cursed the blowing sand and threatening rain. We worked another two hours. I was too weak to protest when he informed me that I still owed three hundred dollars.

Four hundred dollars! The haircut, coloring, and assorted makeup had cost an additional ninety. I was a tall gawky girl with big feet and I had wasted nearly five hundred dollars — seven weeks allowance – on an impossible dream.

*　　*　　*

Raul and I hadn't spoken since Sunday's sailing. Having found nothing of interest to report, I lacked an excuse to call him. Single women don't call bachelors without good reason. Longing to hear his voice and missing his presence wasn't something I could possibly admit. On Wednesday, I reasoned the only way to find a legitimate excuse was to continue poring over my father's things. And the most likely items to yield information were his yearly social calendars.

I had the books spanning nineteen fifty-six to sixty-one – minus nineteen fifty-eight. I wouldn't have had nineteen fifty-six, except that Maria had retrieved it from a garbage pail, because my father had done some rough sketches of her visiting children on its opening blank pages. I found it impossible to believe the same man had done the two landscapes he'd given Petal.

In his calendar entries, my father used a code that incorporated initials, symbols, and assigned nicknames. Evening appointments usually revolved around Petal's activities and were relatively easy to decipher. Charitable events indicated the recipient followed by a dash, the time, and the attire. So "TB – 7:30 B/T" and "MS – 8 B/T" were the Tuberculosis and Multiple Sclerosis black tie balls at seven-thirty and eight, respectively. A heart indicated the Heart Association, an "R" preceding a "X" was the Red Cross. "J/ NO T" meant jacket, no tie. Suits were either "S" or "DS" for dark suit. "Dumbos" were Republican fundraisers; "Jackasses", those involving Democrats. I knew this because Daddy enjoyed sharing his low opinion of politics and politicians with Amelia and me.

Morning and afternoon appointments were particularly cryptic. Obviously, Daddy wanted to keep his daytime activities secret. Servants could snoop and so could daughters. Some had to be romantic trysts. Using what I knew about his habits, friends, and routine, I worked backwards. Daddy got his hair cut on Tuesdays at ten, so I felt certain "Scarecrow – 10" was his weekly barber appointment. Scarecrow was Floyd, his barber, sometimes called that because he bore an uncanny resemblance to the movie character in *The Wizard of Oz*. Entries on Tuesdays and Thursdays, "Gabby – 5", was a five o'clock appointment with Daddy's taciturn Palm Beach masseur Victor. It took time and patience to finally decipher, "BB M4S – 11" was Brooks Brothers, measured for a suit at eleven. Twice in nineteen fifty-six, while we were in Manhattan, I found the word "Crab." In nineteen fifty-seven, there were four meetings with Crab, irregularly spread over the year, when we were in Manhattan. Meetings with Crab increased over the years. By nineteen sixty, there were thirteen entries, and not just when we were staying in Manhattan. Which meant Crab was either: male or female, disagreeable or congenial, and increasingly popular as time passed. Knowing Daddy's playful sense of humor, my guess was

Crab was an attractive, charming lady-friend, who kept a New York residence, but was willing to travel to see Daddy as things heated up. I wondered if she was someone I knew. In nineteen sixty-two, I found several social invitations that had been received and recorded, that would have taken place after Daddy's death.

All that remained unexplored was the inlaid parquet box. After rifling through its contents once again, my only explanation was that Daddy might have used it for our photograph albums. That would explain the glue, ink, assortment of scissors, and perhaps even the tweezers. It didn't explain the various quills, pen points, matches, and the dried-up bottle of nail polish. Or maybe it did. Perhaps I was overlooking the obvious.

I had no theory concerning Daddy's decision to leave Philadelphia and change our names and identities. None. Did I ever really know the man who called himself Jack Morgan?

*   *   *

Following a grueling day at the library, I literally did a dance step when I lifted the phone and heard Raul's voice. And then I remembered my decision not to get involved.

"How are you making out? You learn anything interesting?"

"Not bad. It's hard to say what might be important."

"Would you like to have dinner with me tomorrow night?"

"Only if you let me pay my share."

"Are you trying to insult me?"

"I'm trying to be fair. Dinner at Petite Marmite had to cost a fortune. Helping a friend shouldn't involve going broke."

"Meet me at the Sea Shanty in West Palm Beach at 7:00. Even a young underpaid attorney can afford to take you there."

Which left me with no argument.

*   *   *

I pulled into the parking lot at 7:15. The Sea Shanty was at the end of a pier. It had been a popular after-school hangout for hamburgers and root beer floats. A wholesome pug-nosed girl with a copper ponytail led me to a waterside table.

The restaurant looked entirely different in the evening. Lit by table candles and dim dock-lights, the weather-stripped, gray wood structure, more roof than sides, took on a primitive beauty. I studied the yellowed one-page menu as I waited for my dinner companion.

"Am I late?" Raul asked, when he set a bottle of wine on the table and dropped to the chair beside me.

"Ten minutes. That's early for you."

"This place only serves soda and beer, but if you're a good friend of Big Momma's, you're allowed to bring wine."

"And you're a good friend of Big Momma's?"

"Of course. And put down the menu. You don't need it. Big Momma's from Louisiana. Order the Cajun fish and dirty rice and you won't be disappointed."

"What kind of fish?"

"Any fish Momma's serves is fresh and seasoned to perfection."

I ordered the Cajun fish and related the mysteries of my father's calendar and my semi success at deciphering his codes.

"What about his checkbook? Anything to indicate a rented studio?"

"No. And the same goes for paint, brushes, and canvas."

"Excellent inference!"

The waitress brought our dinners, which turned out to be scrumptious. As we ate, I noticed an interesting phenomenon. As my height was largely due to the length of my legs, a man with a long torso, when seated, was taller than me. Raul's head was higher than mine. Which meant, were we to kiss when seated, I would be looking up and not down.

"A man who uses a code in his personal calendar has to be hiding something," Raul said, interrupting my reverie. "Maybe he was an international spy."

Although he was joking, Daddy's alternate identity fit the accusation better than Raul realized.

"Should I assume that you've been too busy with your father's papers to get to the library?"

"Busy, but not that busy. According to the *New York Times*, a Renoir was sold the same year Norma divorced my father. The seller was 'a prominent American businessman' and the buyer was 'a German industrialist'. The cost? One hundred and fifty thousand dollars."

"One hundred and fifty thousand dollars!" he said, raising his brows and looking impressed. "That would explain how your father supported the three of you between wives. First-class detective work – first-class."

"Provided the 'prominent American businessman' was my

father," I reminded him, unwilling to let him see how pleased I was with the lavish praise.

"Pecan or key-lime pie?" Raul asked, when our waitress came to remove our dinner dishes. "Both are great. Choose one."

"Which one do you like best?"

"Pecan."

"Then I'll take the pecan and we can split it."

"Two cups of Big Momma's special coffee, one slice of pecan pie, and two forks."

"Big Momma's special coffee?" I asked.

"You'll see."

The waitress soon returned with two mugs of coffee and a slab of nutty oozing pie that filled the entire plate.

I cautiously sipped my coffee and identified the addition. "Rum. Delicious."

"It's a shame we know nothing about your father prior to his arrival in Palm Beach."

I hid my blood-read face behind my hands.

"What is it? Something your father did? Didn't do? He didn't kill anyone. How bad could it be? Talk to me!"

"I've been keeping something from you that I learned in Philadelphia."

Raul listened quietly as I relived my meeting with Fiona Hagen, from my initial disbelief to the supporting photographs.

"Amazing! Your father had another life. Something out of a movie. Absolutely amazing!"

"I'm sorry I lied to you. I kept hoping it wasn't true."

"Do you think your father's death was in some way connected to leaving his family and changing his name? That someone or something from his past came back to haunt him? It reeks of blackmail."

"I don't know. I try not to think about it."

"Look at the bright side. You have family: cousins, aunts, and uncles."

"It's hard to think of Mrs. Hagen as my aunt. That's a terrible thing to say, isn't it?"

"Then let it rest until you're ready."

* * *

I nervously paced my bedroom until ten o'clock when I knew

Brent opened his shop, and then found a dozen reasons to delay calling. He had promised to finish my proofs today. By ten thirty, I couldn't wait any longer and dialed Brent's number.

"They're ready any time you are," he said.

"How do they look?" I held my breath.

"You're gonna like the ones we shot in the blue evening gown. Strong colors are good on you. I figure you got as much of a chance as any."

As much chance as any. As much chance as any! "I'll be right there."

It fifteen minutes I was at his studio.

Brent spread eight glossy photographs before me on a table: four of my face and shoulders, four full-length shots, including one in my bathing suit. It was difficult to believe I'd posed for them.

"Well, what do you think?" he asked, apparently pleased with himself.

"I think you're a miracle man."

"There's plenty more." Brent handed me the first of four thick stacks of what appeared to be hundreds of photos.

I frantically went through the pile. When I could view the photographs as though looking at a stranger, the makeup I'd thought ridiculously excessive was flattering and not overdone. The poses I'd considered bizarre and contrived looked intriguing, natural, artistic. I could see the vast improvement in shots taken when I was too tired to be tense or self-conscious, from ones taken earlier in the day. The woman in the photographs looked professional.

"Before you pick the ones you want for a portfolio, did you have a particular agency in mind? Different agencies like different kinds of shots."

"I don't know anything about modeling or agencies," I admitted, my voice fading. My newfound confidence collapsed like a punctured tire. "I really need a job. A friend suggested that I try modeling."

"Well, if I have to say so myself, your proofs are damn good, kid. It's like I always say, it's all in the bones. A photographer can only do so much. You gotta be born with the right bones."

"You know a hundred times more about this than I do. What do you recommend? Is there anything you can do to help me?"

"I suppose I know a few people I could send these to. But what does a classy girl like you want with a job? Find yourself a nice guy, settle down, and raise kids. Modeling is one tough business. A lot of good looking girls like you get kicked around."

I despise baring my troubles to those I know well. Exposing my problems to a stranger was unthinkable. But I was desperate. "I wish I could. My sister needs expensive medical treatment and she only has me. Both our parents are dead. I have to find a job that pays well."

"Drop off what you owe me and I'll do what I can."

I repressed the temptation to flick the cigarette out of Brent's mouth and kiss him.

Chapter Eleven

"**A** black-and-white ice cream soda," Amelia whispered to the counterman with the thin mustache.

I was so glad that I remembered this homey, old-fashioned luncheonette/ice-cream parlor with its gray marble counter, rotating stools, and tile floor. This was the second time Amelia had agreed to leave Silver Glades' grounds with me, and the thousandth time I mentally thanked the angel who'd told me to demand her medication be stopped. She was still timid, but I could see small but encouraging improvement each time I visited.

"And an all chocolate one for me," I said, as pleased as if I personally had invented the concoction. Amelia and I smiled knowingly at each other as we watched the counterman plunge his arm into the stainless steel cavity and pry scoop after scoop from the freezer. We took our sodas to a booth near the back, past two women in their fifties exchanging confidences. As we leisurely sipped our sodas and spooned our ice cream, children on their way home from school selected penny-candies from the glass display cases.

The bell attached to the luncheonette door rang and I looked up. Harold "Hasty" Holmes and Fred Parker entered. My sister's former fiancé was a prize-winning jerk, but Fred Parker was an idiotic clown. Amelia, facing me, hadn't seen them. I immediately looked away hoping they wouldn't spot us. For a few blessed moments I got my wish — until I saw Fred's sorry face leering at me. I pretended not to notice. Fred said something to Hasty, who turned and waved. I scowled.

"Who's there, Charlie?" Amelia asked, pivoting to see.

"Nobody. Nobody important."

Too late. Hasty approached. Fred trailed close behind.

"Hi Amelia. Charlotte."

"Hi," Amelia breathed, with a smile that broke my heart.

"There's four seats in that booth." Hasty said, ignoring me and looking at Amelia. "What do you say we join you?"

My sister immediately made room for our uninvited guests. I stayed put. "Amelia and I were just leaving."

"What's the rush? You got a hot date? Anyone I know?" Fred flipped a key chain around his index finger, clockwise, counter clockwise, clockwise — a habit I found infuriatingly infantile.

"We can stay a little while, can't we, Charlie?" Amelia said. "I haven't finished my soda."

I pretended to scrutinize my watch in preparation for the next lie. "I'm sorry, sweetie. I have a very important meeting at four."

Amelia's eyes pleaded with me.

"All right. Take two more sips and then we have to go."

"So how are things going, Amelia?" Hasty asked, sliding in next to her. "I mean, are you still at that hospital?"

"Clinic," I corrected. "Silver Glades is a clinic and Amelia is doing just fine."

"That's what I meant to say and I'm glad to see you're doing better," Hasty responded. "That's a very pretty dress you have on."

"Thank you."

"Did you hear that I came in second at our club in Men's Singles?" Hasty continued. "I would've taken first, but I twisted my ankle in the fourth set. I had Dell Lowery down four one."

"Hal should've walked away with first," Fred assured us. "Dell was puffing and panting like a steam engine. It would never have gone to five sets if Hal hadn't tripped."

"That's a shame, Hasty," I cooed. "I'm so sorry you tripped and came in second, but we really have to go now."

Hasty rose and helped Amelia to her feet.

Fred had positioned himself between us and the door, still playing with that ridiculous key chain. "Don't do anything I wouldn't do," he stupidly warned, grinning as though he'd said something funny.

I took my sister's hand and dragged her around Fred, toward the exit.

"Second place is still nice, Harold," Amelia said, reluctantly trailing behind me. "Congratulations." "See you, Amelia," Hasty called after us.

Over my dead body.

*   *   *

It took three conversations with the Holmes' house staff before I finally reached Hasty. "Amelia is slowly recovering, with no thanks to you," I said, wasting no time. "Stay away from her. You couldn't wait to retrieve your ring when she collapsed. You took off when she needed you most."

"What can I say, Charlie?"

"Don't say anything! You walked away. Do us all a favor and keep walking." I waited for Hasty to answer. I'd shocked him. Good, I told myself. He deserved it.

"You're right to be angry," he said. "I was a shit and I'm sorry."

"I couldn't have said it better myself."

"What can I do to make it right?"

"You want to make it right? Leave Amelia alone! Take your tennis racket and — and — and find yourself another partner." I replaced the phone and congratulated myself. I couldn't believe that I'd been so assertive. That was something the ever-so-proper Charlotte Morgan wasn't capable of doing three months ago. I couldn't wait to tell Raul.

*   *   *

I called Brent every Friday to see if he had anything to report and receive my latest "these things take time" sermon. Raul knew nothing about Brent, the shoot, or my dream of achieving financial independence via modeling. I saved tidbits about Amelia's progress and my small achievements decoding my father's calendars for Wednesdays, when we met for dinner at the Sea Shanty, and Sundays, when we went sailing.

On the third Friday Brent called to say that he had news for me. I visualized the cigarette between his nicotine stained fingers as he spoke.

"I heard from Rudy Martin — Supreme Modeling. Rudy liked your portfolio, thought you had a look, but he's chin-high with blondes at the moment."

I'd reached a giddy high with expectation in the first half of his message only to have my hopes flattened. "So I guess that's it," I said, trying to keep the desperation from my voice. "Well, thanks for trying. I shouldn't have expected anything to come of it."

"Supreme is just one agency, kid. I still haven't heard from Sid Gluck, at Beaux Art. Like Rudy said, you got a look. You just have to find the right agency. Maybe Sid will give you a shot."

I replaced the phone and considered my options. I could send the portfolio Brent had put together to other agencies — at additional expense, naturally. Or I could go to New York, stay with a friend, and haul myself from agency to agency, spending money I couldn't afford. Or I could place an ad in the newspaper and sell the MG. The sale of my jewelry, I'd recently discovered, wouldn't provide a month's expenses. Selling my car would buy time.

I glared at my mirror searching in vain for the elusive *look* Rudy and Brett agreed I possessed. The blond hair helped. The stylish cut had been long overdue. My skill and knowledge of makeup had increased tenfold. And God knows, I was tall enough. I simply wasn't pretty enough.

Chapter Twelve

A few days after fishing Nicole out of the Seine, as they set up work stations on the cold wind-swept street, Henri pressed Alan for more information about the girl he'd rescued.

"She refuses to tell you her family name," Henri observed, removing a flier that got caught against the leg of his easel. "Strange. Tell me, is she pretty?"

"Yes. She's pretty," Alan admitted, annoyed that Nicole had resisted every proposal he had made to contact her family.

Henri chuckled and slapped his companion. "Would her breasts drive a man mad with desire? Is her face the face of an angel or a wild gypsy woman? And how does she feel about your other lady friends? You can hardly keep that part of your life a secret."

"I'm not sleeping with the girl and non-paying guests don't tell their hosts who they may entertain."

"For now, my friend. No woman can live with a man and say nothing while others share his bed."

When Mimi brought their lunch, she had her own ideas. "The butcher promised me a fat fresh chicken this Saturday. Bring her for dinner so we can meet her."

"I'm not planning to keep her very much longer. I don't want her to become too comfortable."

Three weeks later Alan lost one of his patronesses. Celeste sadly explained that she would no longer be able to continue their arrangement. Her husband was becoming suspicious. Alan suspected it was more likely that she had lost interest. Some women preferred variety. That didn't trouble him. Other women paused to admire his lackluster work, and if he desired, he was certain a replacement for Celeste could be found. But for some inexplicable reason he lacked the will to do so. With only two women providing the rent, and another mouth to feed, he could use the money. Fortunately, Henri's work was selling well, so Alan was able to manage.

Mornings, as Nicole swept or cleaned, Alan left. Afternoons she was gone as ordered. When he arrived home at night she would serve him dinner and silently watch while he ate. He found her gaze unnerving, her presence disturbing, so he would go out for a glass of wine and companionship. Late at night, as he lay in bed he imagined that he could smell her scent, could hear her breathing. By the beginning of March her slender waist had thickened and her girlish breasts had grown full.

Alan was making tea when he decided to confide in Georgette. For the first time ever he was unable to perform. In view of the circumstances, there seemed to be little else to talk about.

"I've tried to teach her how to cook, but she ruins everything. She scorches my shirts and she keeps me awake at night with her incessant weeping."

Georgette scowled. "Weeping?"

"I swear on my mother's soul I haven't touched her. I took her in because she had nowhere to go."

"What did you intend to do with her?"

"I thought I could reunite her with her family. But she won't even tell me her last name. All I could find out was that some distant cousin forced himself on her. The simpleton thinks because she agreed to be alone with him, and allowed him to kiss her, what happened was her fault. Do you see what I'm up against?"

Georgette tossed her head and laughed. "I think, my handsome young friend, that you've fallen in love. The Thief of Hearts has finally lost his. How fitting."

"Ridiculous! Weren't you listening? She's a half-witted overindulged child, spoiled beyond reason. I never touched her."

She moved his hand to her breast. "Not even like this? A little touch? You've never thought about holding her? Making love to her? Not even once?"

Alan could feel himself responding, growing hard as he visualized Nicole gliding from room to room, or daydreaming as she brushed her hair.

Georgette lightly kissed the top of his head and her perfume-scented shoulder brushed his cheek. "A lovely young thing just out of reach."

"I didn't pull her out of the Seine to take advantage of her."

"How does she feel about you? Can she be the first woman in Paris to be immune to your charms?"

He buried his head in Georgette's lovely neck. "I should throw her out. The miserable ungrateful brat criticizes me. She calls me a peasant. She says that I chew with my mouth open."

Georgette reached for his groin and laughed when she located what she sought. "And so you do." He involuntarily stiffened. Georgette drew him back to her breast. "Don't sulk. I find your peasant ways exciting."

"I want to learn how to eat like a gentleman. Teach me!"

"Later. For now it seems your shy little friend wants to play."

As promised, following their lovemaking, Georgette tutored Alan on the proper etiquette while dining — from helping a lady into her chair, to dabbing at the corners of his mouth with a napkin. To their complete amazement Alan was an adept pupil. It seemed he had all the makings of a gentleman: from his delicate hands and soft voice, to his innate lack of ambition and distaste for labor.

*   *   *

Things continued as they had. Nicole padded about the apartment, always watching him, accusing him with her soulful eyes, a noticeable bulge on her sylphlike frame. Alan did everything he could not to notice her, not to think about her, not to examine his motives for continuing to shelter her.

In mid-March, as he lay waiting for sleep one night, he heard soft mewing. Was it a neighbors' cat or Nicole crying again? He slid out of bed to investigate. The sitting room where Nicole slept was still. In the dim shadows Alan was uncertain if she was awake or asleep. He crouched beside her and touched her temple. It was damp. She had been crying. Her hand grasped his.

"Go back to sleep," he whispered, removing her hand. "Everything will be better in the morning."

She pulled herself up beside him, placed her head under his chin and began kissing his chest. "Stop!" He gently pushed her away. "I didn't take you in so that I could make love to you."

She inched back beside him. "You make love to those other women. Why not me? Am I so dreadful to look at?" she asked, her tiger eyes fixed on his.

"I make love to women. You're still a child."

"I'm not a child. I'm a woman who loves you. I've loved you from the first day you carried me home. Why do you think I won't tell you my family's name? If I told you, you would find my father. It's just as you said; my family wouldn't abandon me. My mother would insist he take care of me."

"You're confusing gratitude with love. I can't make love to you. It would be wrong."

"I see the way your eyes follow me when you think I'm not watching. Kiss me. Kiss me the way you kiss those other women and tell me that I'm wrong." She took his head in her hands and pressed her moist lips against his.

Despite himself he no longer resisted as she removed her nightshirt and covered him with kisses. He felt her nipples grow hard against his chest and heard her breathing quicken. "Maybe you're not the innocent little girl you pretend to be. Maybe you lied to me. You weren't seduced. You're a temptress determined to drive men mad by toying with them." He forced her beneath him, crushing her with his weight, deliberately holding her too tight, scraping the delicate skin of her face and neck with his beard. To his surprise, she met his intensity with her own. Only when his tongue found hers did she stiffen. He lifted his head and pushed himself off her. This was wrong.

"Don't stop! Teach me." She rolled on top of him and demanded his mouth, this time with lips parted and tongue searching for his. "I want to learn everything I can to please you."

"Are you sure this is what you want? I won't be bound to one woman. Not you, not any woman."

"This is what I want. You want me too. Deny it. You can't."

As she awkwardly pressed her open thighs against him, her scent almost stripped his determination to proceed slowly. "Nicole, wait. Not yet. It will hurt if I make love to you now. It's too soon. You're not ready."

"Now!"

"Wait. Let me show you." He pulled back so that he could reach the delicate area below her downy pubic hair.

"Now!" she said, grasping his shoulders to pull him on top of her. "I've waited long enough. Make me yours now."

Alan was powerless to resist. Her body wasn't prepared to receive his. She half-gasped half-cried as he entered her. Even if it was her decision, it distressed him to cause her pain, but her ferocious desire soon corrected the problem.

*   *   *

"You draw with your left hand. In France it's considered gauche to write with the left hand," Nicole told him the next day as she posed for him.

Alan had set her on the kitchen table in front of a window so he could show the sunlight filtering through her hair. He had draped a sheet around her naked body to expose only her head, throat, and shoulders. "In America no one cares which hand you use. And I'm an American. Now sit still and let me sketch you."

"When are we going to get married?"

"We're not getting married. I like my life the way it is."

"But you love me," she insisted, pursing her upper lip in that way he found maddening. "You adore me, you told me so repeatedly."

"Let me give you some good advice. Never believe anything a man says in the heat of passion. Fix the sheet. I want to show your shoulders, not your breasts."

"We weren't making love when you offered to marry me," she reminded him, with a smile that said the display was not accidental. "You told me that you would give the baby your name."

"That was before we made love. I can't marry you now."

"But that makes no sense."

"I offered to marry you and leave you in your father's good hands for a generous reward. I'm not cut out to be a husband. I have no job and no intention of finding one. Ask yourself, how would I support you and a baby?"

"You're an artist."

"I'm an artist without talent."

She dropped the sheet, leapt off the table and ran to embrace him. "I think your work is wonderful."

He kissed the top of her head and led her back to the table. "That shows how little you know about art. Are you going to pose for me or not?"

She tossed her head, eying him suspiciously, and refused the sheet. "How do you support yourself?"

"I take a percentage from what I sell of Henri's work and I live off women. If you're not going to cooperate, I have other things to do. Don't think you're going to change my mind. I like my life just as it is. Is that what you want in a husband?"

Nicole followed him, dragging the useless sheet behind her. "You take a part of what you sell for Henri. You're an agent. You can sell others' works as well."

"Don't you listen when I talk to you?" he scolded, forcing her to face him, while trying to ignore her unclad body. "I'm not cut out to be a husband — anyone's husband."

She undid his shirt button and inserted her hand. "You could learn. We can exchange lessons. I will teach you how to be a proper husband and you will teach me the ways of love. I am a good student, no?"

"A very good student, but not now. You've sapped all my strength. I need twenty-four hours to recuperate." As he bent to kiss her cheek she brushed her lips against his.

"Twenty-four hours." She laughed softly in his ear. "Liar!"

"If I'm ever rid of you, you daughter of Eve, I swear I'll never allow myself to fall into this trap again."

*　　*　　*

In the weeks that followed Nicole revealed her family name was Strauss, though she still refused to tell Alan where her parents lived. He ended his arrangement with his two remaining sponsors. So feverish was his desire for Nicole that it was unlikely he would be able to perform had he not. Every gesture and glance, the most casual contact, and the fire in him rose. If she whispered his name when he held her, he lost all restraint. The break with Brigitte was warm but final. He asked Georgette to meet him from time to time as a friend, and the philosophical Parisianne agreed. Regarding marriage, Alan remained firm. When they were not making love, they argued.

"You have to contact your parents," he told her. "Have you no pity? They must be worried sick about what happened to you."

Nicole inexpertly folded a towel and added it to the uneven pile before her. "I left them a note."

"Saying what? That you planned to drown yourself?"

"That I had done something awful and was going away."

"Oh, that must be huge comfort."

"You left your family. You never write them. Not a single letter. And they don't write you. You have no right to lecture me."

Alan spent little time wondering about the family he had left. Oh, perhaps he did think about Daniel once in a while, the second eldest male in the Fitzgerald clan, and the least likely to punch him. And maybe he did remember Fiona fondly when he saw a rough-knuckled, tall girl with a ruddy face. But Nicole was the spoiled daughter of aging parents. In the tender moments following their lovemaking she would tell him about her home, her family, her life — a life of comfort, servants, ease. A life he could only dream about.

"If I go home now they'll never let me marry you. I'll be shipped off to Switzerland to live with relatives until this thing is born. Only after it's safely disposed of will I be allowed to return."

Alan refolded the items that offended him the most. "Would the baby be sent to an orphanage or adopted?"

"Adopted, I suppose." She took the folded linens and shoved them onto a closet shelf. "There are always Jewish families who want babies."

"You would give your baby away? Just like that?"

"What choice do I have?"

"There must be someone who would marry you. Your parents

could find a young man from a poor family."

Nicole caught his sleeve and wrapped her arms about his chest. "You don't have to marry me. I won't leave you."

At that moment the child inside made its presence felt with three sharp kicks to Nicole's right side. Lying next to her at night Alan had felt this strange creature moving and imagined its tiny arms and legs reaching out to him. "What do you think? Is it a boy or a girl?"

"How would I know?"

"Doesn't a mother know these things?"

She shook her head.

"But what do you think?"

"Men prefer boys, no? Would you marry me if it's a boy?"

Alan considered the question. Boys were noisy worthless creatures who beat each other for entertainment and rolled about in the mud like pigs. Even the plainest girl from the poorest family had a dignity about her, was aware of her uniqueness. "No."

"Then why don't you help me get rid of this thing? You must know what to do — something bad to drink, a kick, a knitting needle —"

"Are you a complete fool? Do you want to die? Don't even think of such a thing! You're too far along. If I ever hear you talk like that again I will beat you until you bleed. Your skin will be raw. Do you understand me? Raw!" Alan didn't hit women. Even the animal that had sired him didn't hit women. Alan and his brothers were the frequent object of his father's drunken rage, but his sister Fiona was spared. No man or boy was permitted to raise a hand to Fiona.

The threat was sufficient; Nicole didn't suggest aborting the pregnancy again. Money grew scarcer. They sold her earrings and gold bracelet. A week before she gave birth they had their longest and loudest argument — with the same results. She refused to contact her family and he refused to marry her. When her time came Alan took her to the Catholic clinic for the poor and stayed by her side until they took her away.

Hours later a white robed nun led him through the ward past bed after bed. "Nicole has given birth to a girl," the nun said. "I understand she won't be keeping her. There are papers she'll have to sign. She's admitted that you're not the father."

Nicole was sleeping when he reached her. Beside her lay a

wrinkled, tightly wrapped, pink-skinned infant. "Is there a family waiting to adopt her?" he asked.

The nun gave him a sad smile. "Not yet. We'll do what we can."

Alan moved a battered chair beside Nicole and sat down to watch the baby open and close her mouth, trying to bite her fist. Nicole had no interest in this poor fatherless bastard with the near-white gauzy hair and iridescent pearl skin. Nicole would drop it by the side of the road, with no more thought than a chicken taking a squat. For what? For the privilege of living the life of a pauper with him. The baby wasn't his. Why should he care what happened to it? The infant uttered a sound, not a cry, more like a squeal. Alan placed his forefinger on her cheek. She instinctively turned looking for a nipple. As the tiny ruby mouth sucked his finger, the exquisite miniature hands with their ten perfect fingers folded and unfolded. A fatherless bastard indeed! Not while Alan Fitzpatrick was alive.

Alan shook Nicole awake. "You tell the good sister we'll be keeping her. She'll have my name, she will. You are to sign no papers, you hear? I'll marry you in any church you please, by any holy man you choose. One of them rascals is as bad as another. She is to be named Margaret Noreen Fitzpatrick, the same as my blessed mother, God rest her soul." In times of great emotion Alan accent became a bizarre amalgamation of brogue and burr.

"Marguerite Fitzpatrick," Nicole repeated, using the French equivalent. "I knew you wouldn't make me give her away."

"This wee bonnie lass doesn't belong to you." Alan scooped up the baby. "You gave her away the day you tried to drown yourself, and again when you wanted to do away with her. This little lady belongs to me. Margaret Noreen Fitzpatrick is mine. And don't you forget it!"

* * *

On the walk back to his flat through the narrow twisting cobblestone streets, Alan considered the possibilities of his new situation. Having made his decision to marry Nicole, he saw no reason not to capitalize on it. Indeed, with three mouths to feed he would be a fool not to. But he would have to proceed carefully. Approached wrong, Nicole's family might decide to disassociate themselves entirely. They hadn't seen or spoken to Nicole in nearly seven months. They might be furious at her. She could be disinherited – cut off without a sou. Who would benefit from that?

Most certainly not him. A man might not have all the answers, but if he was smart, he knew where to get help. Alan knew just that person. She was kind, wise, and a lady herself. Doubtless, she could predict their reactions.

A discreet phone call to Georgette and the appointment was arranged for the following afternoon at Notre Dame. Alan found her in the last pew quietly saying her rosary, her lovely brow transfixed in beatific adoration. The massive stone building smelled of incense and candles. A small tour led by an Italian guide prowled its perimeters. Alan waited until Georgette ceased praying before approaching her. He quickly genuflected and took the seat next to her, then explained his dilemma.

"I'm not the kind of man rich parents want for a son-in-law. Tell me what I must do to make them more agreeable. You know such things."

"My dear friend, what has love driven you to?"

"Madness and despair."

"Since I see you are so determined, I'll try my best." She patted Alan's hand. "First of all, you must convince them that the child is yours. If they believed their daughter was pregnant by one man, moved in with another, and went seven months without contacting them . . . Well, you can imagine . . ."

"You are right, of course. The child is mine."

"You must have Nicole swear that you were always prepared to marry her, and that it was she who was unwilling. They'll sooner forgive their daughter than a stranger. Will Nicole agree?"

"Nicole will do what I tell her."

"And they must believe you are a gentleman from a good family. It helps that you're an American. No one can say for certain whether you are descended from savages or nobility. Invent an old aristocratic family. It's done all the time."

"Scotch or Irish?"

"Hmm." Georgette tucked her beads inside a black velvet bag. "Scotch. I've never met a person from Scotland. If I haven't, chances are Nicole's family haven't either."

"How am I going to convince them that I'm a gentleman? There has to be more to it than not speaking with your mouth full and taking small bites."

For the next two hours, as they sat in a café, Georgette

educated Alan on what his new family would expect.

"A gentleman's manners are impeccable. His voice is neither too loud nor too soft. He never loses his temper in front of a lady, or an inferior, no matter how great the provocation. He is profuse with expressions of gratitude to his peers and above for any courtesy extended him. To people beneath him, he is polite but not familiar."

Alan accepted each rule and committed it to memory.

"A gentleman tips generously, but never calls attention to it," Georgette went on, as they drifted down the boulevard. "Nor does he boast."

"Would you say that I boast?"

"Never! In this you've always been a gentleman. Nor have I ever seen you lose your temper. Above all, my love, a gentleman has an income. Naturally it's better to have an inherited income, but nowadays a business which earns huge sums of money is acceptable. For this I have no solution."

"I am hoping my future father-in-law will suggest a suitable vocation."

Georgette took a cloth purse from her pocket and pressed it into Alan's hand. He refused it. "For you," she said, "and your new wife, and baby. A wedding gift from a friend." On her third attempt he sheepishly thrust it into his pocket. "Use it to buy new outfits for the three of you. Don't be pig-headed and skimp on yourself. A gentleman is judged by his appearance no less than a lady — hair, nails, clothing. See that you are all perfectly groomed when you meet Nicole's parents."

Alan embraced her. "Thank you for everything. You are my sanity, Georgette. How would I ever manage without you?"

She pretended to frown, the fine lines around her mouth overshadowed by her natural beauty. "You would find a way. Men with your charm always do."

Chapter Thirteen

In South Florida, from December to February, the weather was unpredictable. It could be sunny and warm or damp and chilly. But by mid-March days were longer, and unless it rained, evenings were reliably delightful.

As it was a Wednesday, at ten o'clock Raul and I were once again in the Sea Shanty's dim parking lot lingering next to my soon-to-be-sold car. I leaned against it deliberately blocking the door handle. We were standing within inches of each other. I could smell his aftershave and feel the heat from his body. For a moment, I thought he was going to kiss me. His head dipped forward toward mine, then lifted.

"There's a full moon. Let's take a walk on the beach," I suggested, reluctant to end our time together. Raul had been exceptionally quiet during dinner.

"I don't think that's a good idea," he said, still close. "Remember I said that I'd tell you when that guy you're sort of seeing was bothering me. Well, it's bothering me. In fact, I think we should limit our conversations to the telephone."

It was decision time. I could speak now or . . . *"Or"* was not an acceptable alternative. I reached for his hands. "I was seeing someone but not anymore."

"When did you break it off?"

"You'll be angry if I tell you."

"Tell me anyhow."

"Before we met."

"Before we met!" He clenched my fingers, just tight enough to let me know his displeasure. 'You're right. I'm angry. You're either a tease or a sadist."

"I'm not a tease or a sadist, I'm a coward. There were too many things happening in my life – all very confusing. I didn't want to get involved with anyone. I'm sorry. I feel differently now."

"And now you think you can simply admit that you're a coward and it's going to make everything right." He took my hand, wrapped it behind me and drew me to him until his head reached mine. The side of his face was firm and warm; his lips were soft. It was a long, slow, tender kiss. As irrational as it might seem, after waiting so long for this moment, my initial thought was how well we fit together. Raul claimed to be five foot ten. My guess was closer to five nine. But we fit together perfectly: faces, lips, arms, torsos, hips — like two sides of a zipper. My second thought was, when the next kiss was more intense than the first, and my face, neck, and chest were searing like molten lava, Bruce Hoffstat had never made me feel like this after two kisses. Not even when ...

Raul opened my car door, abruptly ending my daydream. "After due consideration, I've decided to accept your apology. Saturday night will be our first official date."

"Why can't tonight be our first official date?" I asked, my lips still tingling. "It's not that late."

"I have a twelve hour day tomorrow starting at seven."

"Oh."

"If you shared your little news bulletin earlier, we'd be doing some serious holding and grabbing by now. I was ready, willing, and able. The way I see it, you've only yourself to blame if you have to wait until Saturday night for more."

He was punishing me for lying to him. The man was too confident, too damned smug. And why was I the only one breathing hard? I wrapped myself around him and kissed him — this time with lips moist and parted, nails clawing his back, tongue darting at his, and a soft suggestive moan for drama. Only when I was quite certain that he was as disturbed as I was, in the one undeniable manner of men, did I back away. "You might consider arriving on time."

*   *   *

Raul and I spent our first date at the movies watching *Love in the Afternoon*. As Audrey Hepburn plotted and schemed to win Gary Cooper's heart, we found any excuse to touch. With his arm casually resting on the back of my seat, turning to whisper allowed us to brush cheeks. Holding hands, grazing knees, leaning against each other — tame stuff for two people who exchanged looks that could touch off a forest fire.

After the movie Raul drove Esmeralda into my driveway, turned off her lights, and tucked me under his arm and kissed my temple.

"Would you like to come in? I could fix you a nightcap," I mumbled. It was difficult to speak clearly. Raul had moved to my lip and was nibbling it.

"Not a good idea."

"I wasn't asking you to stay the night." I raised my face to his. "Just a nightcap." I'd always thought those passionate movie clinches were wild exaggerations. I felt like a cut-glass bell that had been struck for the first time: quivering with waves of excitement and astounded by its ability to make music.

Raul lifted my hair and delivered a series of moist kisses to the back of my neck. "If I go through that door right now, neither of us is going to have any interest in a nightcap. You know what's going to happen."

I wasn't certain what would happen, only that I wouldn't object. A formerly benign section of my anatomy was sending the most erotic messages to my brain. I tried another tack. "I'm not very good at it. You might not want me."

Raul laughed — his musical laugh. "Charlie, haven't you been paying attention? I want you."

"So then what's stopping you?"

"The other night I was angry and hurt. But I've had a chance to think about what you did. Diabolically clever, you figured out a way that we could continue meeting without getting too close. If I hadn't pressed the issue, you might've kept me dangling for months. Doesn't that tell you something?"

"I admitted that I was a coward."

"You're pouting again. I can see that adorable upper lip in the dark. I don't think you're a coward. Your entire world has been turned upside down."

I snuggled next to him. He was right, of course. My father's suicide. Guilt. Anger. Depression. Fear. Learning that I was a destitute orphan with no talent, skill, or means of supporting myself. A sick dependent sister. An identity crisis based on a mountain of lies.

"You need time. We're going to wait."

"What are you? The last man in North America with principles?"

"Don't give me so much credit." He brought his nose to mine and kissed me. "I'd rather wait and not mess up our chances."

"Okay. Where do we go from here?"

"We can stop now like the two intelligent adults we are. I'll call you every day and we'll meet on Wednesday."

I shook my head. Having achieved a height far beyond my

previous experience, I wasn't willing to interrupt the experience this soon. We were fully dressed. He hadn't as yet reached under my blouse, touched my thigh, stroked my . . . "Don't go yet."

"Or we make out like two teenagers until one of us can't take any more."

I kissed his Adam's apple and slipped my fingers between the buttons of his shirt past the soft curly hairs on his chest to his nipple – his erect nipple. "That someone is going to be you."

"Sweet Jesus," he sighed, collapsing against the car's seat. "You're probably right."

*   *   *

The money from the sale of the MG went directly into my checking account. The impressive balance pleased me until I sat at Daddy's desk and wrote my first check to Silver Glades. Even with careful monitoring, the money wouldn't last long. Lacking motorized transportation, I rode my bike. Twice a week I borrowed Esmeralda so I could visit Amelia. Raul had offered to take me on Sundays, but I had mixed feelings about having them meet.

Euro Classique, a local art gallery, has offered to hire me to assist with sales next season — from November first through the end of March. But the salary was miniscule and by mid November Petal would return and I'd no longer have a place to live. And I had no way of knowing how much longer Amelia would require care.

Brent has promised to call me the minute he hears from Beaux Art Modeling and the thus far unresponsive Mr. Gluck. Whenever I considered my chances, my mood fluctuated between tentatively hopeful and panic.

On May 2nd I received a call from Peter Brent. Sidney Gluck wanted to meet me.

"Do you think Mr. Gluck simply wants to interview me, or is he truly interested in hiring me?" I asked, bobbing around the kitchen in my slippers, trying to sound calm and think clearly.

"I told Sid, 'This kid can't afford to schlep herself to New York for a go-see.' I said, 'You have her pictures. Make a decision!' He's going to give you a try. You're to meet with him Monday."

"The next time I see you I'm going to kiss you."

"Yeah, yeah, that's what they all say," Brent muttered. "By the way, I told Sid that you're nineteen. Don't go and blow everything."

"I'm only twenty-three. Why would you tell him that I'm

nineteen?"

Brent coughed — or perhaps laughed. With his raspy voice it was difficult to say. "In this business youth is everything. The camera makes every line look like a crater and every wrinkle like the Grand Canyon. A year on a fashion model is like dog years — seven to one."

I wasn't worried about how old I'd be in dog years. I was afraid that Amelia wouldn't be able to manage without me — and Raul would.

Chapter Fourteen

When I told Maria that I was planning to go to New York in less than a week, she became frantic. She was convinced that my starved skeleton would be found crawling back to Palm Beach. To quell one mutual fear, I readily agreed to learn a few rudiments of cooking. At the moment, we were preparing dinner, something I could reheat later. Raul was coming to dinner.

Both Maria and Carlos were aware that I'd been dating him. They had strong opinions about that as well.

"Your father wouldn't approve," Maria had informed me the previous day.

"Why do you think my father wouldn't approve? Because Raul is from Cuba?"

"Because he's from Cuba. Because he's Catholic and you're not. Because Raul Francesco isn't your kind of people. Because he's not the man your father had in mind for you or your sister. Mr. Jack was a gentleman. He didn't raise you to marry a — a —" Maria waved her hands in exasperation. "A common lawyer."

I haven't told her, or anyone other than Raul, that Jack Morgan wasn't the man people thought they knew. He wasn't even Jack Morgan.

Despite the lecture, she and Carlos had agreed to go out for the evening and leave Raul and me alone. Coral and watermelon-pink hibiscus flowers floated in the pool. I'd placed the flares and candles used at dinner parties strategically about the garden. The night air was scented with gardenias. Two albums of Spanish love songs recorded by Xavier Cugat's band were on the hifi. Petal's silver and fine china sparkled on the patio's round table. I might not know how to cook, but I'd picked up a few tricks from two exemplary hostesses — my stepmothers.

From our second official date, Raul and I started every meeting with the same goal. We would say good night with a simple kiss. Petting, making out, whatever one calls it when two people do everything they can to arouse each other without a satisfying conclusion, was too frustrating. Despite noble intentions, we always ended dates the same way: at the beach scandalizing the land turtles or steaming up Esmeralda's windows. Sometimes we did both before Raul called a halt. I was tired of being protected. Tonight I was determined to overcome his stubborn objections.

My hair had been fluffed and fussed over. The thin straps of my dress exposed my bare shoulders. Its turquoise color flattered my eyes. Everything was in place for a seduction — including my newly acquired diaphragm.

"You're up to something, Charlie," Raul said, after he finished the beef consommé, cold duck salad, and whipped cream and strawberries dessert — the only dish I knew how to prepare entirely unassisted, besides tea and coffee.

"What makes you think I'm up to something?"

"A home-cooked dinner, fine wine, dim lights. Carlos and Maria out for the evening. You don't have to be Sherlock Holmes. I thought we decided to hold off until July Fourth."

I must have been mad to suggest July Fourth. Maybe it was the idea of fireworks going off over the water as we made love on the beach that had appealed to my romantic nature. "You forgot Xavier Cugat and his romantic love songs."

"Xavier Cugat. Nice touch. Okay, something made you change your mind. What?"

I played with my coffee cup. "I have to leave in five days. A modeling agency in New York wants to hire me."

He turned away and glared into the darkness.

"I thought you'd be excited for me. You're the one who made me realize that I needed to be self-sufficient. Modeling pays well. It was one of your suggestions."

"Forget everything I said." Raul reached across the table to stroke my cheek. "Don't go, Charlie. You must know how I feel about you."

"I don't want to leave. I have to. The money from the MG won't last forever. Amelia's treatment costs a fortune."

"Take any kind of a job you can find locally. Between the two of us we can manage Amelia's care."

"Sure. And you drive Esmeralda because your Mercedes is in the shop for repairs."

"Forget Esmeralda. Cars don't mean anything to me. I keep Esmeralda to rattle the natives."

"I'll still need a place to live."

"Move in with me. I'll sleep on the couch."

Good Lord, he was hardheaded. This wasn't going to be easy. I unzipped my dress, stepped out of it, and tossed it on the chair. He pretended indifference.

"If all you're planning to do is sulk I might as well take a swim." I wriggled out of my half-slip and kicked my sandals in his direction. Now down to a strapless lace bra and panties, I removed the barrette from my hair and shook it free. Raul reached for my leg, but I was too quick for him.

"Do you ever fantasize about me?" I asked as I stepped into the chilly pool and preened. "What I'm wearing and doing? Taking a shower or getting dressed?" The cool water made the tiny hairs on my arms rise.

A sly grin slowly replaced his frown. "I've spent days thinking about your sublime long legs. Enough time to cross the Atlantic by rowboat, imagining you naked or sunning yourself in a skimpy bikini right before I make love to you."

"I don't own a skimpy bikini."

"In my fantasies you do." He unbuttoned his shirt, removed it, then unzipped his pants. Socks and shoes quickly followed. "What about you? What am I doing in your fantasies?"

"I can't say it out loud. Come here and I'll whisper it in your ear." I waded into deeper water.

One dive, three powerful strokes and Raul was next to me, shaking his head and sending droplets in all directions. "You're a Jezebel – manipulating men with your will."

"A Jezebel? Me? That's a laugh! I'm practically a virgin." I tugged at his shorts before swimming away. "It's quite possible that

I'm frigid."

"Stay put." He caught my hand. "Frigid? Frigid means that you're unresponsive, that you're incapable of passion. Not unless you're the world's greatest actress." Using two fingers he drizzled pool water on the nape of my neck as he kissed my temples, the side of my mouth, and behind my ear.

My head dropped back. My eyes closed. I could hear myself making funny squeaky noises as I clung to him like a jellyfish.

"Frigid?" he whispered. "Try again."

I could feel him growing aroused as he nearly circled my waist with his hands – but no more so than I was. Lord, he knew how to make a point. "I've never had an orgasm," I half moaned, my voice lacking the intensity it needed for a decent challenge.

"You're kidding." He leaned away to study my face. His hair had formed ink-black wet ringlets that circled his head.

"It's not something a woman brags about." I reached behind my back and unhooked my bra. That caught his attention. The bra floated away and was sinking before he stopped staring at my breasts long enough to grab the strap and toss it out of the water.

"I wish I knew sooner, Charlie. I didn't bring protection. Unless you . . ."

"It's all taken care of."

"All taken care of?" he whispered, locking my legs between his and sliding his hands down my spine until he reached the cushioned portion of my bottom.

As I nodded Raul's wet lashes brushed my cheek — an unexpectedly arousing sensation.

"You've never had an orgasm?"

"Nope."

"Well, in that case, you're going to have one before you leave. How much time do we have? Five days? At least one. Maybe a dozen." He needed no further encouragement or assistance to remove my panties.

My nipples felt like spiked darts against his chest. "Didn't anyone ever tell you that it's childish to boast?"

"I don't boast. Boasting is when you can't produce what you say you can. I'm confident. Big difference," he told my neck between kisses.

When he started to remove his shorts, I reached to help, just for the chance to run my hands down his solid thighs, over the equally firm curved calves to his slender ankles. We stood, flesh against flesh. For the first time, there was nothing between us but the silky water. Like Adam and Eve. And like Eve, I felt no need to hide my nakedness. Raul's eyes assured me that I was beautiful, sensual, desirable – and just maybe a little wicked. The night air was warm and still – so still we could hear a nearby sputtering flare over the music. Cool waves licked my shoulders, back, and breasts. I leaned back against Raul's supporting arms to watch his approving gaze float over me.

"When was the first time?" he coaxed in his bass cello voice. "Were you crazy about the guy or just curious?"

"Curious. It was after the spring formal in my junior year."

"And you both had too much to drink?"

"I was tipsy. Dickie was polluted."

"Hold me here — like this."

"Here?" With all our petting, we hadn't ventured below the waist. I tentatively felt around. Apparently, a man's height was not indicative of the size of his plunger. Both Bruce and Dickie were taller, but Raul was . . .

"Oh yes! That's very good! Now, did you give little Dickie another chance or was that it for him?"

"I don't remember agreeing to testify, counselor."

"Every attorney has to ask questions. I assume the other guy was boring."

"Why?"

"Because you stopped seeing him."

"Mmmmm." Raul was investigating the demanding little tickle between my legs. It became impossible to concentrate on anything else. I buried my face in his neck.

"No competition."

I involuntarily trembled when he reached my . . .

"Now rock up and back a little like you just did." With his free hand he gave my rear end an encouraging tug, release, and tug. "Follow the music. Listen to the rumba."

It seemed very forward. Were women supposed to be this aggressive? I was accustomed to being passive. That's what I had intended. To arouse Raul until he agreed to make love to me? And it did feel sensational, perhaps in part, because I had control over what felt nice – and what felt even better. I was making mewing sounds when he covered my open mouth with his. Perhaps I had latent talent and was better at this than I'd thought.

We drifted to the shallow end and onto the stairs. There was no awkwardness, no reservations. It astounded me that Raul could say anything — what he wanted, where he enjoyed being touched, when to wait and when to begin again, tender words of love. I didn't know what moved me more: the sweet intense sensual satisfaction, the joy of giving pleasure, or the intimacy. The elusive orgasm I had used to entice Raul seemed of zero importance when at last he shuddered inside me. Orgasms were probably a literary creation, a product of some writer's imagination. If they did exist, they were highly overrated.

Taking my hands in his, Raul kissed each before placing them against his heart. "It's still early. You were very close."

"Just as long as you're not tired of me," I said, pretending to be coy and not shamelessly honest. I was happy, content, and sated beyond all expectations.

Raul wasted no time making it vividly clear that he wasn't tired of me. Ten minutes later I was leading him to my bed. Thirty minutes later I was astride him, pressing his hands to my breasts, my head flung back. Gone were all thoughts of modesty. I was a wanton woman demanding pleasures of the flesh. Soon my ankles were above my head and around his neck. Another first for me – and very erotic. And then Raul was where I liked him most – on top of me, where I could feel the length of his frame writhing hard against mine. His brow, lips, tongue meeting mine. Torso to torso. Pelvis to pelvis. Embraced. Enfolded. Wet with perspiration. Open, vulnerable, blanketed, and protected all at the same time. I heard myself sigh and whimper.

"Close your eyes and count backwards from twenty."

"Why?"

"Just do it. Not to yourself. Out loud. Slowly. And with each number, feel yourself becoming more excited. You're almost there."

"Twenty, nineteen . . . " I closed my eyes and pictured our nude bodies below. I was somewhere else. Another planet. I was ready to soar upward like a Roman candle and detonate in one mighty astounding explosion. "Why are you stopping?"

"I can't give it to you, Charlie. You have to go after it. Just go after it and it's yours."

"Twelve, eleven, ten, nine, eight, eight, seven, seven. I . . . I . . . " *I need you*, was what I wanted to say. *I can't do this alone.* But I didn't have to verbalize the thought. Raul had joined me again, meeting my thrusts with his own. "Five, six, four, three, three, I . . . You . . . Two, two, one, I . . . Ohhhhhhh." It wasn't a SWOOSH! BOOM! like a Roman candle, the way I'd imagined. It took a long swooooooooooOOOOOOCHHHH before I was rewarded with a spiraling string of dazzling explosions each detonating the next.

Raul arched his back to gaze down at me, irresistibly handsome with his tousled hair and teasing cave-dark eyes, before dropping his head next to mine for a series of triumphant spasms.

My body responded with several milder but decidedly delightful explosions. I felt an overwhelming exultation: joy, accomplishment, peace, gratitude, and incomparable tenderness for the man holding me. Was this true love or afterglow? I couldn't permit the question. I was leaving in less than a week. But I didn't need additional convincing. Boasting was when you couldn't produce what you said you could. And orgasms weren't overrated. "Stay with me tonight," I begged. "I want to wake up and see you lying next to me."

He kissed my forehead. "Try and make me leave."

"If you're going to stay, can we do it again? I only did it once. Maybe I need more practice."   He chuckled low — distant thunder. "More practice," he echoed. "We can do it again only if you let me rest a while. And that means you have to stop doing what you're doing with your toes. It isn't very restful."

*   *   *

Over the next two days Raul left me only to go to work. When I was alone, I packed, made innumerable lists, explained to Amelia where I was going and when I would return, delivered the kiss I had promised Brent – and cried.

Friday afternoon, while Maria cooked, I prepared an ice pack for my swollen eyes and waited for Raul's return. Maria no longer attempted to dissuade me from seeing Raul. She was too distraught about other things.

"If you ask Mrs. Morgan nicely, she would let you stay at her house. Mrs. Morgan always liked you. She don't like stables and she don't like horses, but she likes you. She always tell me that you were the smart one. 'That Charlotte has a good head on her shoulders.' That's what Mrs. Morgan tell me. And she got plenty of room for you in New York. You be much better off with her. You don't have to stay with strangers."

The smart one. Good head on my shoulders. News to me. I switched the ice pack to my left hand so that I could stir the stew with my right. "I'm not staying with strangers. I'm staying with my friend Carol Mehring until I can find an apartment of my own."

"Are you paying rent to this girl?" Maria eyed me suspiciously. "Did you find out how big her apartment is?"

"I insisted on paying for my share of the food and a bit towards the rent. Carol wouldn't have invited me if there wasn't enough room."

Maria slashed at an onion with homicidal enthusiasm. "New York isn't a safe place for a girl like you to live alone. Coming home late. Modeling. Letting men take pictures of your body. What would Mr. Jack say? If Mr. Jack were alive, he would turn over in his grave."

"How many onions and how much celery?"

"One large onion, two stalks of celery. Don't forget, lots of paprika. As I was saying, if your father were alive . . ." The lecture and the cooking lesson continued unabated until Raul returned.

*   *   *

That evening by the pool as we shared a recliner Raul and I planned trips. He would come to New York over the Memorial Day weekend. I would return the July Fourth weekend. We could make love on the beach under exploding fireworks as we originally planned. Saturday we went for one last sail and reminded each other that Memorial Day was only weeks away. Later, we made love, even though our insatiable desire had left us raw.

It amazed me that Raul was able to express himself eloquently and effortlessly, in Spanish, in English, devoid of embarrassment. I, on the other hand, wanted so much to express my feelings, but the best I could do was whisper a pathetic "me too" in the dark. It had to be the difference in our cultures, mine clearly the inferior. Sunday morning Raul drove me to the airport.

"Vaya con dios, mi corazon. Go with God, my heart," he said, as I turned to leave. "Remember, you can always change your mind."

I made it through the plane's door, at which point the tears could no longer be contained.

Chapter Fifteen

On May 3rd, less than twenty-four hours after moving in with my old college roommate Carol Mehring, I realized that I'd made a mammoth mistake. Brian, the wiry, dark-bearded, grubby man who greeted me at the door, wasn't a guest. He lived there. In my experience, respectable single girls resided with their parents, shared an apartment with another single girl, or stayed at a residence designated "Women Only." Living with a man was unthinkable. But where was I to go? I had mailed a check to Carol before I arrived. Why hadn't I listened to Maria's advice and questioned the living arrangements before I agreed to this ménage a trois? Now, thanks to my friend's poor judgment and my stupidity, three people occupied the one bedroom apartment. Three people vied for the sole tiny bathroom. I slept on the lumpy, too-short couch.

I soon discovered that wasn't the worst part of the arrangement. Apparently, Brian thought I found men with scruffy beards and pasty skin devilishly attractive. The miserable letch leered at me whenever he thought Carol wasn't watching. He accidentally brushed against me while I fixed breakfast. He wandered into the living room clad only in his shorts and meaningfully scratched himself. His vulgar antics didn't go unnoticed. Carol's thin lips disappeared as her mouth turned down. Her yellow-green eyes clouded. Her chin and forehead grew increasingly blotchy. And the Oreos she consumed to treat the condition weren't helping.

*   *   *

Monday morning I was seated in Beaux Art's busy reception area waiting to meet Sid Gluck, my first boss. For the past hour Mr. Gluck had been either on the phone or meeting with supplicant after supplicant. I knew this from the conversations I heard through the thin walls. Some left his office with red eyes. Others left grim. None left happy. Two people remained – me and a man wearing a uniform that informed the world his name was Pete, and he was employed by *Cool It*, the world's finest air conditioning firm.

"Listen, give your boss this message!" Pete and I heard Gluck say. "T-t-tell him nobody threatens me. T-t-tougher than him tried.

Let him play games with me and I'll cut off his balls and shove them down his throat."

I actually trembled when I heard the receptionist say my name.

"Don't worry," she whispered as I approached the door. "His bark is worse than his bite, and he never uses bad language in front of the girls."

Mr. Gluck was a short man with broad shoulders, cropped dark gray hair, and plump florid cheeks. He handed me a notepad and a pencil. "Sit d-d-down and write w-w-what I tell you. I say this only once, the first d-d-d-day we meet, and then I don't say it again. You're getting a chance, a chance, not a g-g-guarantee. You get paid a salary for six weeks, after that if you're not getting enough calls to make it worth my keeping you, you're on your own. You're out. Do you understand?"

I nodded.

"Good. You show up for every call, prepared to work, on time, no excuses. You make a list for yourself every day that you keep in your purse, with names, addresses and phone numbers. At the top you put the scheduler's name and phone number. You call her if there's any change to your schedule. Any change! If you get lost walking, you call her. If you get hit by a car, with your last dying breath you beg someone to call your scheduler. Okay?"

I nodded again and scribbled on the pad.

"If you need time off for any reason," he said, glaring at me ominously, "you give me at least a month's notice, more is better. Now, about personal hygiene: use deodorant, look clean, smell clean, shave your legs and under your arms — every day, no excuses. I don't care what your grandmother told you. Shaving under your arms does not cause cancer. You're shocked that I say such things? G-g-girls come to me from all over the country — some who've never been off the farm. Just because they're pretty doesn't mean they have any common sense."

I kept my head down and focused on writing — anything to avoid eye contact with this terrifying crude man. I couldn't believe my ears. No one had ever spoken to me like that. If I weren't so desperate I would get up and walk out. Mr. Gluck was either unaware of my distress or indifferent. He continued spelling out the terms of my employment.

"I don't want to hear about any Beaux Art single girls getting pregnant. Do not get pregnant! Talk with one of the girls if you need advice. Look at her blush. I never knew a person could turn such a color."

I had been blushing since he handed me the pad. The latest tirade simply poured oil on the existing fire.

"As long as you're blushing anyhow, while you're with Beaux Art you will not take any assignment that I wouldn't want my daughter doing. No dirty pictures. Be careful. Some of these guys are pretty slick. You don't know what a pile of BS they can dish out. Some girls fall for it. I'm a family man. I don't want my name connected in any way with dirty pictures. Do I make myself clear?"

"Very clear," I croaked.

"Now, walk for me."

I stood, not knowing what was expected of me.

"Walk! Across the room! Left to right and back again."

My limp. He had noticed my limp when I'd entered. But in three-inch heels my walk was more a rolling gait than a distinguishable limp.

"Different. Jazzy. Tell the scheduler that I said to send you for runway work. They'll either love it or they'll hate it. I'm guessing they'll love it."

"Yes, sir."

"Welcome to Beaux Art. I hope you'll be very happy here."

*   *   *

Thursday, my fourth day as an unbooked model, I decided not to wait until Raul called me for our prearranged twice-weekly phone calls. Since my living arrangements permitted me no privacy, I grabbed a handful of change and found a nearby sidewalk pay phone. I was determined to sound calm, cheerful, and confident.

"You'll get something soon," Raul said, after I admitted that after seven go-sees, I still hadn't been selected for a shoot. "Give yourself a chance. It takes time to break in."

"Is everything all right with Amelia?"

"All quiet. I'm going to see her Sunday."

For the first time since we were little girls, I was jealous of my sister.

"I wouldn't be disappointed if you changed your mind and came home," Raul went on. "If you're determined to be a model, I'll buy a camera. You can pose for me."

"I can't give up without a fight. I may be spoiled, but I'm not a quitter."

"When did I say you were spoiled? Over-indulged and pampered maybe, but not spoiled. Spoiled is what happens to milk. Now, tell me how much you miss me — that other men can't compare – that you have erotic dreams where I make mad passionate love to you and you wake up dripping in perspiration."

"You are impossibly egotistical."

"Egotistical, am I? Last night I walked into the shower with my shoes on. That's right. I ruined a perfectly good pair of shoes because I was thinking about you – wondering what you were doing. Just hearing your voice makes me want to quit my job and jump on a plane."

"I miss you too," I said, trying to pour all the emotion I felt into four inadequate words.

"I suppose that's about as much racy conversation as I'm going to get from an uptight Brahmin WASP."

"It's only two and a half weeks until we see —" The operator interrupted us for the third time. "I dropped my change, operator. Another minute," I pleaded. My coins were gone.

"Find us a hotel with room service and a queen-sized bed," Raul said. "I'll call you Sunday morn—"

The line went dead. We had exhausted the operator's patience.

*   *   *

Ten days after I arrived, after enduring Brian's irritating attention, Carol's obvious unhappiness, and my increasing anxiety, I was actually pleased to hear Petal's voice on the phone.

"Maria tells me you found a job modeling. Very enterprising. I told your father that you were more resourceful than he gave you credit for."

"It's not quite a job yet," I admitted. Carol, in the kitchen dipping into her cache of Oreos, and Brian, watching cartoons on television, pretended not to be listening. "So far I've been turned down for every assignment. But the other girls warned me that it wasn't easy to get started. Clients and photographers prefer experienced models."

"Remember to always be gracious, smile, and you'll do just fine. You're not planning to model lingerie, are you?"

"Model lingerie? Certainly not."

"Good girl. But that isn't why I called. Maria told me that you would be staying with Carol until you find a place of your own. It occurred to me that she might not have enough room for you. So many Manhattan apartments are frightfully small."

"It's a lovely apartment and Carol is the kindest hostess." I smiled at Carol, whose eyes delivered a message that even Lassie would understand.

"While it was darling of Carol to invite you for a brief stay, longer isn't necessary. You know you're welcome to stay with me for as long as you wish. In fact, I expect you to."

I considered the offer. Not very long ago Petal had shown her displeasure at my detective efforts. Now she was inviting me to live with her. Was she merely being thoughtful, concerned that by overstaying my welcome it might embarrass her socially, or seeking to monitor my activities? For the moment it didn't matter. Earning a living had effectively curtailed my investigative work. "How very kind of you, Petal. Are you certain that I won't be an inconvenience?"

"An inconvenience? Jack's daughter? Hardly. And do tell Carol that I send my love to her mother. I suppose she told you that Nadine and I attended the same finishing school."

Carol's sad-clown-smile couldn't mask her relief when I relayed Petal's invitation and my acceptance. Brian responded with a characteristic burp.

*   *   *

The next afternoon I kissed Carol good-bye, smiled my best sorority girl, head-tilted-to-the-right smile, waved at Brian, and lugged my two suitcases to the elevator. My emotions were mixed. Fleeing the cramped awkward living arrangement and replacing it with free room and board at my stepmother's brownstone was heavenly. On the other hand, it was a step backward on my long road to independence. But only temporarily, I reminded myself, as I paid the taxi driver. A temporary sidestep. My goal continued to be an apartment Amelia and I could share, entirely paid for by my job.

"Mrs. Morgan is at a bridge tournament," Joseph explained as he took my bags. "She said you could stay in your old room, or the guest suite on the third floor, whichever you prefer. Would you like Theresa to help you unpack?"

"No thank you, I can unpack myself. And the guest suite would be wonderful."

I inspected the sunny yellow and white suite. In the bedroom, a cut-glass bottle of sherry and matching glasses had been thoughtfully placed on the triple-sized French provincial dresser. A yellow vase filled with fresh white tulips sat on the night table next to the bed. The gleaming bathroom contained innumerable fluffy yellow towels and a large white wicker basket overflowing with assorted toiletries. As for the adjoining sitting room, a pair of inviting chairs done in quilted chintz occupied the windowed side of the room. On the wall a recessed television set was flanked by a pair of floral prints. A side table held a white telephone that assured blissful privacy.

My laundry would be washed, ironed, and put away for me. Delectable meals would appear and dirty dishes would be whisked away. The furniture would be dusted, the carpet vacuumed, and the bathroom scrubbed. All done, as if by magic. People considered cigarettes, alcohol, and drugs addictive. Cigarettes! Alcohol! Drugs! Hah! Comfort was addictive. Ease was addictive. Luxury was addictive. I was its shamefaced, but all too willing victim.

*   *   *

"Sign in and take a seat." An overly made-up, fortyish receptionist with thick lavender eye shadow handed me a clipboard and pointed to a row of Danish modern chairs.

I used two lines and scrawled "Charlie." Since I was accepting my stepmother's hospitality, to respect her morbid fear of publicity I'd decided to use only my nickname.

The receptionist glared at me through her thickly clumped lashes and simpered, "Charlie! Easy to remember."

I no longer wore a hat and gloves to potential jobs as I'd done my first week. Determined to appear seasoned, I tossed my head and slouched in the bored manner I've observed on more successful job-seekers. Twenty-five minutes later I followed the hall to the third door on the left, as the receptionist had instructed.

A bald man wearing a torn gray sweatshirt took my portfolio. He flipped through the photos. "You call yourself Charlie, eh? Catchy."

"Thank you."

He held up the photo of me in riding clothes. "Do you actually know how to ride a horse? Profile!"

I turned my head as instructed and smiled. "I ride well." I'd learned that modesty was considered dumb, and since some shoots involved sports, I added, "I also ski, play golf, and swim."

"She also skis, plays golf, and swims. What else do you like to do, society girl? Anything a red-blooded guy like me might be interested in? Lift your chin."

I thrust my chin forward and inverted my shoulders. "Nothing you wouldn't want your sister to do."

"Snappy answer. You don't mind if I tease, do you? Walk to the door and turn around."

"I was five eight when I was twelve and five eleven at fourteen. I've had more than my share of opportunities to get used to teasing."

"I've seen enough."

I sighed and returned for my portfolio. "Thank you for your time," I recited automatically, trying not to think about my bank account, which was shrinking at a dizzying pace.

"Not so fast, society girl. Talk with Rhoda at the desk and let her know I've given you the okay. She'll tell you what to bring with you and where to go."

"Does that mean I have the job?"

"That's what it means. Next!"

*   *   *

Ironically, living with Petal, free from the responsibility of cleaning, cooking, food shopping, and laundry, allowed me the time to resume my investigation as well as access to information. In fairness to my gracious hostess, I decided not to question the staff. However, anything overheard or witnessed was fair game, and that included the telephone book she'd left lying about. I still hoped to decipher the remaining coded names in my father's appointment book. Since Daddy hadn't altered phone numbers, comparing my father's cryptic calendar and telephone book against Petal's intelligible one made sense. After hours of cross-checking I had substantially reduced my list of unidentified names. Because of the increasing frequency of their meetings, I was particularly curious about the woman Daddy dubbed the Crab. Based on my knowledge of my father's preferences, I believed her to be approximately my father's age or older, attractive but not necessarily beautiful, and if not wealthy, financially independent.

With Petal's rigorous social schedule, I was alone most evenings and weekends, which was good for my detective work, but after two weeks of luxurious solitude, I was lonely. Luckily, I met Belinda.

A portion of the steps of the colossal New York City Public Library had been blocked off for our use. Ordinarily, the massive stone library with its signature carved lions was a tranquil setting. Ordinarily, one could still hear pigeons cooing and fluttering over the sound of pedestrians, and car, taxi, and truck engines. Ordinarily. That day, men with jackhammers were blasting the street and generally interrupting traffic. The pounding jackhammers competed with frustrated drivers beeping their horns. Jerry Voorhee, the shoot's photographer, had to shout to be heard. Jerry was delighted with the weather, which had cooperated to the fullest. We had ideal conditions – overcast without rain.

Belinda's real name was Natasha Wolanski. Professionally, she was known as Belinda Young, and she was undeniably the most stunning woman I'd ever met. She was nearly my height, with perfect features, handfuls of glorious auburn hair, porcelain skin, and jade green eyes. Zeus would have chosen her over Athena, until she spoke.

"I noticed you're walking funny today. Did you hurt your foot?" Belinda asked in her nasal, high-pitched voice, as we waited to be called.

"It's nothing. I have a slight limp."

"Geez, I'm sorry. I have a big mouth. Sometimes I say the dumbest things."

"You didn't say anything wrong. No one notices the limp unless I'm rushing or really tired. Yesterday was a long day."

"Maybe it's those shoes. Let me try them on. I may have a pair that'll fit you."

My shoes? Girls at school exchanged shoes. Not me, of course. "They'll be too big on you." I leaned against a stone column, removed my shoes and handed them to her. "They're a size eleven."

Belinda stepped into my navy flats. "Look, they fit. I knew they would. And I'm a size ten. Where do you buy these?"

"They have to be ordered. No one carries an eleven."

"Hmmm. Italian. Probably custom-made."

I nodded and smiled my apology.

"Don't you know Italians all have itsy-bitsy skinny feet? That's why they hurt. They look great, but they're too soft. No support. I buy American." She passed me hers. "I buy the cheapest ones I can find so I can throw them away when they scuff. Size ten. Here, try them on."

I slipped on her beige pumps. It might sound silly, but I was like a child with a new toy. I was normal – more or less. "They fit. Perfectly! And they were comfortable."

Jerry, the shoot's director, gestured for us to take our places.

"Do they always treat you so impersonally?" I asked as we once again waited for the photographer to adjust his equipment.

Belinda stared at me blankly for a moment then brightened. "Yeah. First they tell you that your forehead's shiny and your boobs are too big. Then, when they got you in front of the camera, they're oohing and ahhing that you're perfect, you're beautiful, you're gorgeous."

"This is only my second time at this. I'm extremely self-conscious."

"Well you don't have to be self-conscious, or nervous even. You got a look — a special something that makes you stand out. Your mouth is different, baby-doll looking, and your cheekbones are sensational. Me, I'm just like a thousand other pretty girls." Belinda checked her mirror, frowned, and rearranged an errant curl. "Freddy says you live on Fifth Avenue in some swanky building and don't need the dough. You're lucky. I gotta work for a living."

Since this was delivered without a trace of animosity, I responded in kind. "I work because I have to, not because I want to. I'm temporarily staying with my step-mother because I can't afford a place of my own."

"No kidding!" Belinda checked the mirror again then tossed it aside. "Some of us girls are going out later to Schrafft's. You can get a hamburger there or a salad if you're like me and gotta watch everything you put in your mouth. You think you'd like to come?"

"I'd love to. Thank you for inviting me."

"Freddy's right," Belinda said, flashing those amazing green eyes. "You got class."

* * *

When I returned from dinner with Belinda, I took advantage of Petal's generosity and used the phone in my room to call Raul. The second thing that I intended to do, as soon as I could save enough money, was head to Steuben and pick out a sensational piece of crystal for Petal. The first thing was to get an apartment of my own.

"I made a new friend," I told Raul. "I met her at a shoot we did for Saks. She introduced me to some of the other girls."

"Another assignment. Good for you!"

"How's Amelia?"

"It's hard to say. I've only seen her three times and once was with you. She seems quiet. Then again, I'm a stranger, so I guess that's to be expected. Any progress in looking for an apartment?"

"Not really," I admitted, as I sat on my bed and wrapped and unwrapped the phone line around my finger. "Even studios are expensive in a decent building. I've been thinking about looking for a roommate."

"A roommate? How are we going to be alone if you have a roommate?"

"I can't impose on Petal indefinitely, and at this rate, I won't be able to save enough to get my own place for a year or more."

"Well then, just make certain your roommate uses perfume, and not aftershave."

"I made reservations for this weekend. I found a small hotel – "

"I have bad news."

I stood. "No! Don't say it. Don't say that you're not coming."

"I want to be there, *cara mia*, you know I do. But there's a legal matter I have to take care of for one of my cousins."

"No!" I'd never met any of Raul's family, but I knew from our conversations that he had innumerable relatives living in Miami. They were always calling him for favors. "Why can't one of your cousins or uncles take care of it?"

"I'm the only attorney in the family."

Probably the only one who spoke English, had an education, and a job. My imagination supplied a roomful of bearded men, their chests crisscrossed with ammunition belts, rifles in one hand and grenades in the other. I wondered if this cousin required bail. "What about Neville? He has an entire office full of attorneys."

"Neville normally doesn't go out of his way for the Cuban side of the family. I'm lucky he hired me."

I fell onto the bed. "I'm so disappointed. I've been counting the minutes. Now I won't see you until July Fourth."

"How do you think I feel? I've thought of nothing else since the day you left. Every inch of my body is longing for you. Should I be more graphic?"

Since Raul sounded as miserable as I felt, I changed the subject. I had no one else with whom to discuss the one subject that haunted my nights. "When I look at the picture of my mother, the house she's standing in front of looks so familiar. I keep thinking about Paris. If I was there, I know I could learn something — maybe why my father killed himself."

"Have you given any thought to what we discussed? If his suicide was somehow related to forgery, it's reasonable to assume that he was on the verge of being exposed. Keep digging and you may be opening Pandora's Box."

I sighed. "I know."

*   *   *

A shoot in Central Park involving horse-drawn carriages ended early due to a sudden thunderstorm. I used the opportunity to call Amelia's doctor during routine office hours.

"Your sister is making fine progress," Dr. Mendelson said. "A nice young man comes to see her. Aides tell me there's a noticeable improvement the days he visits."

Raul? My Raul? I suppressed a mean wave of jealousy. My sister was getting better in part because of Raul's kindness, and I was being irrational and petty. "Is she ready to be discharged? I'd like to bring her to New York to live with me."

"New York? Oh my, no. And leave Amelia alone while you're at work? At this point, she shouldn't be alone for more than a few hours a day."

"I expect to have my own apartment soon. What if I hired someone to stay with Amelia while I was out?"

"Patience, Charlotte. Amelia is getting stronger every day. Give it some time."

I didn't want to be patient. I missed my sister. I missed my father. I missed Raul. I didn't like living in big bustling Manhattan where everyone had someone to be with except me. I didn't like being an objectified plastic mannequin. My investigation had come to an abrupt halt. I had eliminated only three women from my Crab list. Petal happened to mention Olivia Marchand had taken a month-long safari last November. I checked my father's calendar and saw two meetings scheduled with the Crab that coincided with Olivia's trip. Hardly a heart-stopping breakthrough. I'd met some nice women to spend time with, and I took advantage of the many museums the city offered, but I was still lonely.

Did I mention I missed Raul? I longed for him. I missed the conversations we have without speaking. I missed the way his shoulder felt next to mine and the excitement of his presence. Every millimeter of me missed Raul.

I did, however, like the money I earned. It pleased me that I now worked more than I was idle, that jobs came easier than they had. Like miserly mad Midas, I pored over my growing savings account and gloated. Every dollar I deposited made me feel less like a sparrow trapped in a wind tunnel.

*   *   *

I descended the portable staircase at the West Palm Beach Airport, rushed through the terminal's double doors, and found Raul waiting for me. We kissed and grinned at each other, both trying to look like a normal civilized couple instead of sexually deprived psychopaths.

"I have a surprise for you," Raul said as we stepped out of the cooled air into the humid jungle I still considered home. "Two surprises. First one is in the parking lot."

"You sold Esmeralda without letting say good-bye?"

"She passed away peacefully in her sleep from natural causes. I had no choice. The Buick up ahead is mine."

The Buick was a shiny midnight blue convertible.

"Very nice. And the second surprise?"

"We're invited to my parents' home for a Fourth of July party. You're pouting. Tuck in that lip and tell me what's bothering you."

I fanned myself with my free hand to indicate my unintended response was caused by the heat. "I wasn't aware they knew about me."

"I had to tell my mother that I'm seeing someone or she would insist I call her friends' beautiful single daughters. It's a traditional Cuban parent's right to meddle in their children's lives. Is there a reason my parents shouldn't know I'm seeing you?"

"These single daughters are all beautiful?"

"Beautiful, brilliant, talented, and fantastic cooks — every last one. Naturally I tell my mother that I'm not interested — that I prefer to spend my time sitting at home. Waiting for you. Living from call to call. All alone."

I weighed the alternatives. The underlying threat was clear. If I accepted I would be moving our relationship to another level — something I was reluctant to do. If I refused Raul would be angry and hurt. Both choices were laden with danger. A vision appeared: a circle of sloe-eyed nubile women clad only in filmy veils, sensuously snaking their way around a dazed and dazzled Raul. I made my decision. "Please tell your parents that I thank them for their kind invitation and would be delighted to attend." I looked for the predictable smirk and wasn't disappointed.

"That's tomorrow afternoon. What do you want to do today?"

Twenty-three years of indoctrination prevented me from admitting I would like to find us a bed – that and guilt. "Can we go to visit Amelia?"

"Absolutely."

An hour later, happiness at being with the two people I cared for most prompted me to ask my sister, "Would you like to come home with us tonight? We could go out to dinner and you could sleep in your own room. How does that sound?"

Amelia shook her bent head.

"Then what would you like to do? You get to choose."

Amelia slyly looked at me from under her bangs. "We could go for a ride in Raul's new car and stop for ice-cream sodas."

Raul laughed. "A black and white with sprinkles and a cherry."

*   *   *

"What should I expect?" I asked Raul, as we approached a modest one-story house ringed by coconut palms.

"An interrogation worthy of the KGB. At least two of my very inquisitive relatives will ask if you speak Spanish and when we're getting engaged. Unfortunately, after we go in they won't let me near you to run interference. You'll be on your own."

Which was precisely why I hadn't wanted to come. "Be truthful. Am I going to tower over everyone?"

"I don't know. I never think about your height."

I fired my most dubious stare.

"My parents may have invited tall friends. My uncle Ramon is taller than you. That's probably it." When the door opened I knew immediately the aristocratic woman facing us was his mother — the arched brows, the aquiline nose, the possessive air.

"You must be Charlotte. And you," she said, turning to Raul, "are late again. He's always late, but surely you know my son's faults by now."

"Mrs. Francesco, so nice of you to invite me."

"Relax, everyone's going to love you," Raul breathed in my ear before surrendering me to his mother.

Gabrielle Francesco led me to the back of the house and outside, to a group of women speaking Spanish. They immediately switched to English when she introduced me.

I looked around. No one looked like the sort who might require bail. The men wore white plissé Egyptian cotton shirts over their slacks rather than tucked in, a fashion I found both neat and sensible for a tropical climate. Most were clean-shaven. I'd expected beards, or at the very least, long droopy mustaches. As for the women, no matter what their age, their posture was regal and more aware of their femininity than women I knew. The many children were starched, neat, and well behaved. Only infants and the youngest toddlers dared to interrupt an adult. I was ashamed of every bigoted notion I'd ever entertained.

"My son tells me that you're a model," Mrs. Francesco said as we chatted with her niece and daughter. "That's not the sort of job I would expect for a woman of your background."

"Actually, it was Raul's suggestion."

"Raul suggested that you become a model? Surprising! We never really know our children, do we?"

"Had I known earlier that I would have to support myself and my sister, I would've chosen a different education. Unfortunately, a bachelor's degree in art history isn't very practical."

"You must enjoy being a model."

"I like runway work. It's hectic, nerve wracking, and chaotic, but it's fun. It's also very limited. Designers only do a few shows a year."

"What about the glamour, the attention, the travel?"

I had to smile. "Some girls find it glamorous. The majority will tell you being a model is far less exciting than people imagine. Most of the time it's boring. There's a lot of standing around waiting for the light to change, or equipment to be set up. Most times I feel as glamorous as a Thanksgiving turkey."

"To be a model you have to live in New York," Gabrielle Francesco continued.

"Or London, or Rome, or Paris — any city that's a fashion center."

"Have you considered doing movies or the theater?" Raul's elder sister Toni asked. "I've read that a lot of actresses start as models. Lauren Bacall was a model."

"I have neither the desire nor the talent to be an actress. But even if I did, where would they find a leading man tall enough to play opposite me? They would either have to dig a trench for me, or have him stand on a box."

Gabrielle Francesco threw back her head and laughed, her face relaxed for the first time since we'd met. "You're beautiful and you're quick — a dangerous combination. I can understand my son's fascination."

Miguel Francesco, Raul's father, joined us. He was a broad man, with dark rough skin and thick eyebrows. Although no taller than Raul, he seemed to occupy an inordinate amount of space. Perhaps it was the cigar he flourished as he spoke. "My dear Gabrielle, are the women of this family planning to monopolize our lovely guest? Others are waiting to meet her."

"I was just about to see what's happening in the kitchen," Mrs. Francesco said. "Perhaps you'll introduce her."

Miguel Francesco led me to a trio of men engaged in an animated conversation. One had to be Uncle Ramon. We stood eye to eye. "Please welcome our guest, Charlotte Morgan," Miguel Francesco said. "Charlotte is an accomplished horsewoman. Raul tells me she's participated in many state and national riding events."

The men he addressed half nodded, half bowed. Smiles were formal. I felt like the too-tall outsider I was.

"You may not be aware," a pock-marked man said, "before that communist dictator seized control, Cuba's Olympic equestrian team was known around the world."

After I acknowledged both the justifiable renown of Cuba's horses and sportsmen, and the tragedy of Fidel Castro seizing control, I was rewarded with friendly smiles. And more introductions.

"What do you think about children?" Raul's Aunt Susanna asked shortly after we joined a group of women. Susanna's dress won the prize for the tightest one I'd ever seen. Copious cleavage rose and heaved as she spoke.

"I'm in favor of them," I teased. "Oh, you mean do I want children? I would like a carload when the time is right."

"Are you planning to work after you're married?" she persisted.

"A respectable man supports his wife and children," Miguel Francesco declared, leaving no room for argument. He gently guided me aside. "The pictures you pose for — they don't make you wear . . ."

Petal would be shocked to learn that Miguel Francesco had asked the very same question she had. "I don't accept assignments that would require me to pose in lingerie, and I'm rarely asked to model swim suits. They prefer me in tailored clothes, evening gowns, or sportswear."

"Anyone can see you are a lady."

"Thank you."

"I couldn't help but notice that you don't smoke. Look around. Some of the women smoke cigarettes. Not my wife or daughters, but some do. Your sister, does she smoke?"

"Occasionally, when she's out with friends. But *never* in front of my father. He didn't approve of women smoking either."

"Do you think it's odd that I grew tobacco in Cuba and I don't approve of cigarettes, just cigars — and only for men?"

"My father wouldn't find that odd. He enjoyed a good cigar now and then, but he never offered me one."

"I think I would have liked your father."

"I'm certain that he would have liked you."

"Turn around! Behind you," Miguel Francesco said. "The fireworks have started. A lovely way to celebrate freedom."

I looked for Raul. He was surrounded by a bevy of winsome creatures all vying for his attention. They couldn't all be related to him. His eyes met mine. Months ago we had made entirely different plans for tonight — plans that involved just the two of us.

"Later," he mouthed.

*　　*　　*

My last evening in Palm Beach Raul and I were alone in the library listening to music. After spending almost every minute of the weekend together, the frantic need for sex had been replaced with a delicious warm glow. He looked so right in my father's massive wing chair smiling down at me. I decided to ask Petal for it.

Raul rubbed his finger against my cheek. "I managed to get the first week in August off. It's slow in the summer and I volunteered to take it without salary. That gives us eight full days together, depending on how much time you can free up."

"That's when I'm planning to go to France."

"Don't make mean jokes."

"It's not a joke. I have to go to Paris."

He took my chin in his hand and studied my eyes. "For your job? Are they doing a layout in Paris?"

"It has nothing to do with my job. In fact, I'll have to ask for a sabbatical, or whatever it is they call it when you want to take time off."

"If it isn't vacation time, which you've earned, your boss will call it a lack of professional commitment. You could get yourself fired. You do know what fired means don't you?"

"Please don't be angry with me."

"I hate it when you're in New York and I'm here. When you're in Paris, even a phone call will be impossible."

I avoided his eyes. "I have to do this. There's still so much I don't know."

"Why Paris and why now?"

"It's maddening knowing so little about my mother – what she was like, what she enjoyed doing when she was a girl. I plan to cover every street in Paris until I find the house in the picture. Someone has to remember my mother – neighbors, shopkeepers. People in Europe don't move around like they do in the States."

"What if the whole thing turns out to be a wild goose chase?"

"Do you remember my telling you about Georgette, the woman we met in Cannes? She was married to a Russian conductor. His first name was Nicholas. We had dinner together the night before they had to return to Paris."

"She addressed your father as Alan."

"Right! After a private little conference with him, they explained it was a joke they had between them? I couldn't remember their last name until it came to me a few weeks ago – Torchinsky. And Georgette was no casual acquaintance of my father's. I saw what passed between them. They'd been lovers. Everything I've learned about my father has come from women. The key to my father will always be women."

"But she was old. She's probably dead by now."

"I met her ten years ago, when I was thirteen. Everyone looks ancient to a thirteen-year-old. But now that I've had a chance to think, Georgette must be in her late sixties. Now do you see why I have to go? Time may be running out."

"If you can find her. And that is a big if. Why can't it wait until I can go with you? Paris would be a great place for a —"

I touched my finger to his lips. I couldn't let him say it. First the party and now this. Too soon.

He pulled me into the massive wing chair and onto his lap. "I'm trying to be patient, Charlie, but I hate when you're away. We are going to be together at some point, aren't we? I'm not just kidding myself, am I?"

I buried my face in his neck. How could I reply to a question for which I had no answer?

Chapter Sixteen

In the drawing room of one of the grand homes on the Avenue de Montaigne, Alan looked past Nicole's stern father and her slender disapproving mother, to the luxurious expanse beyond. The windows were elaborately festooned with wine-colored moiré drapes that matched the upholstered couch. Ivory silk curtains beneath kept out the afternoon sun. A pair of Chinese cloisonné vases, the height of a five-year-old child, flanked the marble fireplace. Nearby, and more imposing, was a parquet mahogany gramophone, its lid open and its arm poised, ready to play one of the records undoubtedly concealed in the cabinet below. Several large paintings done by celebrated artists hung from the dark paneled walls.

As described to Alan in advance, Maurice Strauss, born Morris

Strauss fifty-six years earlier in Stuttgart, was a gaunt man with a narrow face and pointed beard. He traded in rare books. Heavy, thick glasses pressed hard against his nose.

"It's good to see my daughter again and know that she is safe. You can't imagine how frantic we were."

"A daughter, with a daughter of her own, but no husband," his wife snapped. A pair of spectacles, attached to a gold pin by a lavender ribbon, hung from Hortense Strauss' gray silk dress. Unlike her husband, a naturalized French citizen and the first of his line to possess wealth, Madame Strauss came from a family of successful French importers. Nicole said her mother often boasted that she could trace her family's business back to the Silk Route. She was a handsome woman with silver-blond hair that curved fashionably under her chin.

"It is my fault, Papa," Nicole said. She was dressed in her new pale blue cotton dress with a pleated bodice and elbow length sleeves. Instead of the young mother she was, she looked like a lovely schoolgirl holding a younger sister. "Alan wanted to present himself to you and ask your permission to marry me. I was ashamed that I had acted so recklessly. I refused to tell him who my family was."

"Until it was too late," Madame Strauss added. "Don't think we will give you a sou, monsieur. You have robbed us of our only daughter, bewitched her with fairytale stories of romance."

"Now, now, Hortense, let us not be too hasty. Monsieur Fitzpatrick appears to be an honorable man. He has not asked us for anything."

"Nor do I intend to, sir," Alan answered before Madame Strauss could interject.

"I apologize for my wife's outburst. You can see how distressed she is — how distressed we both are. But that is behind us now. Come, let us sit down and have tea." Strauss located a funnel-shaped speaker hidden beneath a tapestry and spoke into it. "Mignon, we're ready for tea."

"No doubt you were disappointed with a girl," Madame Strauss commented. "Men prefer a son to carry on their name."

Alan took the baby from Nicole who had grown bored with her fussing. As the infant had scarcely left his arms since birth, Alan handled her with easy confidence. He smoothed the white hand-embroidered dress which Nicole had purchased for the occasion, and readjusted her socks. "On the contrary, Madame. I can truthfully say with all my heart, I prefer a daughter. Boys grow up and leave home. Girls, even after they marry, belong to their family."

"The child of a Jewish mother is Jewish in our religion," Madame Strauss informed him. "You would not object to seeing your daughter raised in our faith?"

Alan did his best to suppress a smile. "I assume Jews worship the same God as lapsed Catholics."

"What about the wedding?" Madame Strauss asked. "Were you planning a civil ceremony or a church wedding?"

"I've given Nicole my word that we would be married by a rabbi. We were hoping you would make the arrangements."

Madame Strauss gave Alan her first guarded smile of the day.

After a lavish tea was served Monsieur Strauss became more direct. "The life of an artist, even the most gifted artist, is uncertain. Please forgive me, Monsieur Fitzgerald, but Nicole's mother and I are concerned. You have not mentioned another source of income."

Alan knew that so much depended on his response. "Despite what your daughter may say to the contrary, I will never achieve success as an artist. However, I'm a fine agent. I currently represent only one artist, Henri Puissard, a talented young man with excellent prospects. Perhaps you've heard of him."

"Is it possible to support a family representing only one artist?" Strauss inquired, apparently neither convinced nor appalled.

"I hope to find others to represent as well." Alan waited.

Strauss looked first at his daughter and then at the infant. "Would you be willing to work for a gallery? I could make inquiries for you. The Strauss name is well known."

A job! Alan had hoped for something that would leave him a measure of independence. But Strauss had suggested a job — a job with fixed hours as regulated as a prison. A job with a demanding superior who would expect apologies and groveling. A job with arrogant pompous patrons. The very notion of it was enough to sicken him. If he refused the Strausses would turn their backs on him. The house was even grander than he'd imagined. Nicole was one of only two children. The old man looked frail, sickly. Nicole had told Alan of the paralyzing migraine headaches and poor vision that plagued him. He wouldn't live forever.

"You would work on salary plus commission," Strauss added. "And you wouldn't have to give up Puissard either. If he's as good as you say, any gallery would be willing to display his work from time to time. "

Nicole sat across from Alan pale and silent. Only her eyes spoke. Say "yes" they pleaded. Alan nervously patted Marguerite's back. The scent of flowers blended with her baby powder and fragrant skin. They awaited his decision. "You are most kind, sir. I would be very grateful if you would make inquiries for me."

The baby chose that instant to loudly break wind. Strauss chuckled and was soon joined by Alan. The women covered their mouths to hide their laughter.

"It seems my granddaughter already knows how to entertain guests," Strauss joked.

"Did I not tell you, Alain, that my papa is a most amusing man?"

"That's exactly what you said, my dear." The first battle had been waged and deflected with endurable consequences, Alan told himself. What else would be required of him?

"I see my beloved Hortense is eager to hold her grandchild," Strauss said. "Would it be possible, my son, to share her?"

Alan smiled broadly at all present, and with a flourish worthy of a dauphin, lowered his daughter into Hortense Strauss' open arms.

* * *

Alan halted when Georgette paused to contemplate a particular painting. He had married Nicole seven months earlier, before he began working at Debarge's gallery. From time to time he would meet with Georgette, typically at a museum. Today they had chosen the Louvre.

"I adore Boucher," Georgette commented, dimpling as she spoke. "Madame de Pompadour looks as delicate and fresh as she did when she was alive."

"The lady has her charms, but I don't like Boucher. His work looks like the top of a birthday cake, all sugary pastels and no substance."

"You're jealous."

Alan allowed a group of uniformed schoolgirls to pass in front of him. "Oh, I'm jealous of his skill. I simply don't admire his work."

"It's not like you to be irritable, Alain. What makes you so cross? Are they mistreating you at work?"

"Do you know what Debarge has me doing? Not sales, which I might excel at. No. He has me crawling through dusty papers checking provenances. He doesn't trust me with his precious clients."

"Remind me what a provenance is."

"A provenance is a history of a painting's present and past owners, exhibits where it has been displayed, and any awards it may have received. Debarge's family has been representing artists since the eighteenth century. For all we know, Debarge's great-great-grandfather sold Louis the Fourteenth this very portrait."

"And you hate this paper work. Are you any good at it?"

"Tolerably. If all the papers are provided it's fairly routine. But when there are gaps in ownership, or supporting documentation is missing, it can take weeks of boring research to resolve."

"My darling, you are most impressive." Georgette stroked the base of her throat. "All this is done to protect the clients?"

"All this is done to protect Debarge's reputation. Selling a fake can be ruinous. So I compare signatures and dates, and make endless trips to churches and museum libraries where I pore over dusty tattered catalogues. And for this I take home scarcely enough money to pay the rent. Honest work is detestable. I really should have gone into politics. I can lie as well as any prime minister. You never see a poor politician. Do you suppose it's too late?"

Georgette laughed, a lilting laugh. Two nearby gentlemen turned and smiled their approval. "And your wife and baby? They are well?"

"As soon as I leave for work Nicole drops Marguerite at her parents' home. My daughter is cared for by servants while her mother goes off to spend the day with her mindless friends. At night Nicole returns home to sigh about their new dresses and the trips they have planned."

"Nicole is young. That is the way of young women of her class. The poor and the rich spend little time with their children. It's the merchant class that spoils them. Your daughter is being well cared for."

Alan considered Georgette's assessment. Perhaps he was being unfair to Nicole. She loved Marguerite. But marriage to a rich woman wasn't what he had imagined. Nicole's family was polite but cool — and certainly not generous. His job, which required an expensive wardrobe, paid a meager salary. A tiny flat in the least fashionable district was all he could provide for his family. The weekly dinner at his in-laws' home was their sole luxury. "You're a good friend, Georgette."

"Only a good friend? I must be getting old."

"I was just wondering if we could slip away to some lovely hotel room for a few hours. I miss your tender attentions."

"Not unless my husband gives up this silly nonsense of having me followed."

Alan had known in advance that Georgette would demur. He gave her his most Gallic shrug and feigned disappointment. Her smile told him that he had accomplished his purpose. More would have been impossible. He wanted only Nicole. There were times when he felt like a man living someone else's life – like a spy in a movie.

*   *   *

"She's teething," Nicole told him when he arrived home. "All babies cry."

Alan lifted the ten-month-old infant from her crib and placed her on his shoulder. "How long has she been crying?"

"Hours."

"What have you done for her?"

"I've tried everything: feeding her, changing her, putting her to sleep. Nothing helps."

"You could hold her and walk with her as I do. It seems to comfort her." As if to underscore his point Marguerite located her thumb and sucked loudly.

"Mignon says that we spoil her, that we hold her too much and that's why she cries."

"A maid decides how to raise my daughter, and you, her mother, listen to her. See, Marguerite is drifting off. Look, she's rubbing her ear."

While Alan patted and paced Marguerite slept, but if he attempted to put her in her crib she woke up screaming. He ate the dinner Nicole had prepared holding his daughter. Hours later, she was awake once more, refusing anything but an occasional sip of water from her bottle. Alan tried every distraction he knew: hiding his face behind his hands, shaking his keys, singing, dancing. Through glazed eyes Marguerite alternately smiled and whimpered.

"Something's wrong with her," he told Nicole. "She's never been this unhappy."

"It must be her teeth. What else could be wrong?" Nicole asked. "You'd better give her to me so you can get some sleep. You have to go to work tomorrow. I can stay home and rest."

Alan weighed the offer. It was nearly eleven o'clock and he did have to get up early. But Nicole would fall into a deep sleep as soon as Marguerite quieted. Napoleon and all his troops could rise from the dead and take Paris while singing the national anthem and Nicole wouldn't awake. If something was truly wrong . . . "You go to bed. I'll be in soon."

Nicole yawned and left. He could hear her brushing her teeth as he paced the small room and hummed to Marguerite. In thirty minutes both his women were asleep. Alan placed the baby in her crib. Her little body seemed unusually warm. He took a blanket and pillow for himself and lay down on the floor next to her, drifting in and out of sleep until two a.m. when Marguerite began sobbing. Her nose was stuffed and she was having trouble breathing. Her plump cheek felt fiery against his. Pacing the floor no longer quieted her. Alan put her down long enough to heat her milk bottle, which she refused. The sound of her labored breathing distressed him even more than her crying. Marguerite had never been sick. She had always been a healthy happy baby.

As she alternately coughed, choked, and whimpered, her face and palms reddened. Her skin was fiery compared to his. High fevers were dangerous — even he knew that. Frantic with fear Alan searched his brain for a way to her cool her. Water. He dampened a small towel and wiped her burning brow, face, and hands. Startled by the cold water Marguerite stopped screaming. Alan continued mopping the length of her little body until her skin felt cooler to his touch. He alternated holding her and pacing with bathing her. Just before dawn Marguerite fell asleep in his arms.

"Call a doctor and then your mother," Alan told Nicole when she awoke. "Better yet, have your mother call one. Doctors don't come quickly to a poor neighborhood like this. Tell her that her granddaughter is dangerously ill."

*   *   *

A grim man with deep-set eyes, wearing a fine dark suit and carrying his identifying black leather bag, arrived within the hour.

He took the infant from Alan and went into the bedroom. "Wait here. I'll be with you shortly."

The sound of his daughter crying as the doctor examined her tore through Alan. He ran his hands through his hair as he waited for the diagnosis.

Hortense Strauss arrived minutes after the doctor. "Alain, are you sick as well? You look dreadful. Perhaps you caught something from the baby. Have the doctor examine you when he finishes."

"I'm not ill — just tired."

"Alain didn't sleep at all, Mama. He was up all night taking care of Marguerite. He insisted."

The doctor emerged from the bedroom. "She has pneumonia. She's still feverish but not dangerously so. You saved her from convulsions or perhaps worse, Monsieur, with the cold compresses. I recommend that she be moved to a hospital where she can be watched around the clock for the next few days."

Madame Strauss fingered her steel-framed glasses, which hung from a ribbon to her waist. "That won't be necessary, Doctor. Hospitals are filled with germs. My granddaughter and her parents are moving into our home on the Avenue de Montaigne. If you would be so kind as to recommend a private nurse, I would be most grateful."

The doctor nodded formally. "A competent private nurse in your home might be just the thing. Please allow me to send one."

"Pack as many things as the car can accommodate, Nicole," Madame Strauss ordered. "You won't be coming back here to live."

"What will Papa say? Have you discussed this with him? He will not be pleased."

Hortense stared into Alan's exhausted bleary eyes. "I will inform Papa that I'm bringing our children home where they belong."

Chapter Seventeen

Paris in August. It was strange being there without my sister and father. We had come to France after Daddy and Norma's marriage ended. My father said it was to expand our minds and polish our underused French. The real reason, I suspect, was to lessen the impact of the divorce. As the taxi drove to my modest rented room, I tried to imagine my parents strolling these very streets: my young handsome father in his early thirties holding hands with my radiant mother, who was gazing up at him. It's easy to imagine couples falling in love in Paris. The city seemed designed for lovers. The sidewalk cafes, the Eiffel Tower, the flowing Seine, the carved and gilded bridges, are perfect settings for flirtations, unhurried conversations, and clandestine kisses.

I was an American in Paris. *An American in Paris.* Was it possible for an American tourist not to hear Gershwin's brilliant ode to Paris repeating in her brain? It scarcely left me. Gershwin had captured the street sounds perfectly. They were different – softer, more subtle than Manhattan's. They didn't echo off towering steel and glass buildings. Car horns were tenor, not bullying baritone or bass. And the police sirens' BEEEEEP beep BEEEEEP beep BEEEEEP beep, though insistent, was less shrill.

I had to repeatedly remind myself that I'd come on a mission and not as a tourist.

As soon as I unpacked I started looking for my father's old friend in the telephone directory the hotel's day clerk had provided. Fate intervened, and I reached her that evening. After some animated conversation Georgette invited me to her apartment the following day.

The Torchinskys lived on the Left Bank, an easy walk from my hotel. In their small cluttered apartment, threadbare antique furniture competed for space with stacked rattan trunks. Several well-executed paintings and three portraits of the still-lovely Georgette, done at various times of her life, hung on the walls. Framed photographs were scattered throughout the sitting room.

For a woman I guessed to be seventy, Georgette was agile, her spine remarkably straight. The lines on her forehead and around her eyes gave her once classic features the suggestion of wisdom. Nicholas' right side had been devastated by a stroke. His speech was slurred and his handsome Tartar face was a cruel caricature from the one I remembered.

"How splendid of you to find us," Georgette said. "How is your dear father? I haven't heard from that rascal in years."

As simply as possible I repeated the story of my father's death.

Georgette seemed to age as I spoke.

"It must be a mistake," she insisted. "Your father was not the sort of man who would kill himself. Believe me. I knew your father well."

"There was proof. His body was found. And he mailed letters to us before he died."

"Tell me, cheri, what is it that you are hoping to learn from me?"

"I want to know why he did it. I want to know the truth."

"The truth. Whose truth? Your truth? My truth? Sometimes the truth is ugly. Your father is gone. Let his secrets die with him."

I turned to a photograph showing Georgette receiving a medal from the imposing Charles De Gaulle. "You weren't awarded the *Croix de Guerre* for turning your back on ugly truths."

"Forgive me, *cheri*. It's such a shock. When I knew your father he was full of life. Throw him into the most troubled waters and he would float to the top. You know, of course, that your father pulled your mother from the Seine."

"My mother? You knew my mother?"

"I never actually met your mother, but your father talked of her always."

"Not to us. Amelia and I know nothing about her."

"Your father adored your mother. There was no one he loved more, except perhaps you and your sister."

I wiped away a single tear that had slipped down my cheek. "My mother's last name. Do you remember it?"

"Of course. Her name was Nicole Strauss. She was the daughter of . . . Give me a moment to think. Ah yes, my memory has not left me entirely. Her father was Maurice Strauss, a man who dealt in rare books."

"Strauss is a German name. I thought they were French."

"They were French. They were loyal Frenchmen. Not like some traitors who turned against their country when the Nazi Huns invaded. The Strausses were French Jews."

Jews? My mother was a Jew? The blood drained from my face. I began to cough uncontrollably.

"Nicholas, quick, get her some brandy!" Georgette said, waving her hands.

Nicholas's response was unintelligible.

"Oh Nicholas, what was I thinking? Stay with her. I will get the brandy."

"No, no," I said. "I'm quite all right. There's no need to trouble yourself. On the other hand, perhaps a brandy would be nice." I used the time that Georgette was out of the room to compose myself. She soon returned with three glasses. Nicholas raised his and with the left side of his face, grimaced at us.

"To your health." Georgette turned to Nicholas. "And all my love to you, *mon cher.*"

"Please go on," I said after taking a sizable swallow of the potent liquor. "You were telling me about my mother."

"Are you certain you wish to go on? We can talk more tomorrow."

"Very certain. Please start with how Daddy came to pull my mother out of the Seine." I removed a wad of carefully folded tissues from my purse. "Please don't stop if I start to puddle. As you can see, I've come fully prepared."

I learned about the pregnant girl my father had rescued, and that Amelia was my half-sister and not my father's biological child. Though I yearned to hear every detail Georgette could recall, I realized it would be necessary to leave some information for my next visit. Recalling an emotional past had exhausted my hostess. To change the mood I rose to inspect the portraits of Georgette done years before — mementos obviously kept for their sentimental value. Only one displayed artistic merit.

"Your father did the oil on the left," Georgette said.

The oil on the left? The least skillful of the three. I looked closer. There it was — "A. Fitzpatrick" in the corner of the painting. I mentally compared it to the two landscapes hanging in Petal's bedroom. Another lie. Daddy couldn't possibly have painted them. He most definitely wasn't a forger. "Did you happen to know if my father took any canvases with him when we left in '41? I was particularly thinking about a Renoir."

"I was able to help him with transportation and papers to leave Paris. I don't know what he took with him. We never discussed it."

"Did he have access to fine art?"

It was Georgette's turn to redden. "Your father worked for a distinguished gallery in Paris, one that most certainly would handle Renoirs, but I would swear on my life that Alain Fitzpatrick was not a thief. Never! Impossible!"

"I agree. I was simply wondering if he'd been asked to take artwork to the United States as a means of protecting it or of selling it for someone."

"Ah yes, I see. However, Claude Debarge wasn't the sort to permit anyone take his treasures abroad. Like so many others, he hid his treasures in France. After Paris was liberated he immediately reopened the gallery. Your grandparents had a large fine home where you all lived. Perhaps the paintings were theirs."

I not only had a mother, I had grandparents. "Is it possible they're still alive?"

But all Georgette could give me was their address when we left Paris without my mother. Thrilled but shaken, I invented an excuse to leave and quietly absorb all I'd learned.

Explaining she needed to buy bread for dinner, Georgette walked me to the street. "It's wonderful to see you again. Just the sight of you, your gestures, your graceful long fingers, the way you carry yourself — you remind me so of your dear father. You will return tomorrow, won't you?"

"Tomorrow. I promise."

* * *

The next morning I faced the building where my parents had lived. There was no point in asking permission to see it. After the war the building had been divided into four apartments, with four separate bells, but the exterior hadn't changed. The black metal railings were freshly painted and the window boxes were filled with scarlet geraniums. Squinting in the strong morning sun, I could imagine my mother standing by a window with open shutters and fluttering lace curtains. She was holding a baby — a baby I decided was me. My father came and stood behind her, his hand resting lovingly on her shoulder. He was thirty and had a pencil-thin mustache. I thought, if only they would look down and see me, I would wave and they would wave back. I waited. But they were too absorbed in each other, blind to my presence. I permitted the bittersweet image to fade.

Turning my concentration to the street, I considered the nearby ground-level shops. I tried to guess which ones might have been in business twenty-five years ago and then gave up. I would have to systematically go up and down the street, photo in hand.

The dress shop's saleswoman could tell me nothing. The store had been sold twice in the last twenty-five years. Nor could the shoe shop's owner, the tailor, or the restaurant's employees provide any information. I'd almost exhausted all hope when I reached the *patisserie*, the bakery. The shop was new. The woman behind the counter was too young to remember my family. The pastry in the window and the heavenly smell of fresh croissants lured me inside.

"I'm trying to learn about people who lived on this street many years ago. Perhaps the owner would remember," I told the neat young woman.

The woman's thin lips curled into a scowl before she disappeared into the back of the shop. Moments later she reappeared, an ancient man beside her, with bushy erratic eyebrows and powerful arms. Flour dusted his body, clothes, and hair.

"Who are you looking for, Mademoiselle?" he asked, wiping his massive hands on his apron.

"The Strauss family. They lived here —"

"The family Strauss — the Jews — I remember them. They've been gone for many years now."

Although I had been half-Jewish for less than twenty-four hours, that part of me flinched.

"The old book dealer scarcely left the house those last years. Terrible times."

"What else can you tell me about them? Did they move? Is there anyone in the family who's left?"

"Why are you looking for them? They were loyal French citizens. They had a son, like mine, who died serving France. They were Jews, but they were French Jews. Many Jews lived on this street then."

"Nicole Strauss was my mother. My father was Alan Fitzpatrick."

The old man came around the counter and stared at me. "My eyes are not so good anymore. I should've known. You are the image of your mother."

"I'm trying to learn something about them. We left France when I was two. My mother stayed behind to look for her brother."

"Ah, yes. Tragic. You're lucky that your father was an American and could get you out when he did."

"Do you know if any member of my family survived?"

He shrugged. "The last one to live here was Madame Strauss — your grandmother. She moved away after the old man died. I don't know where she went. Those were desperate times. You can believe me when I tell you that some unscrupulous bakers added sawdust to the flour to make it go further," he added, as he turned to leave. "Sawdust!"

"I realize you're busy, but could you spare a little time to tell me what you remember of my mother and grandparents?"

He frowned and then nodded. "Come back in an hour. I'll tell you the little I know."

When I returned an hour later, Monsieur Bernard took me to a tiny table in the back of the bakery. Over coffee, crusty bread and cheese, he told me stories about France before the war, and the little he could recall about my family. My grandfather was dead. He died not long after my mother. The Vichy government had stolen everything of value. My grandmother was left with nothing. She moved away soon after.

I took one last look at the *patisserie* where my grandmother had shopped, the narrow sidewalk where my mother and her brother would have played, and the house where my grandfather had smoked his pipe, before walking away.

*   *   *

After trying unsuccessfully to find any trace of my grandmother, I spent my remaining four days in Paris visiting as many spectacular museums as my feet could cover and time would allow. I purchased a large bottle of Chanel #5 for Amelia, a cashmere sweater for Raul, and an elegant Lalique vase for Petal. I planned to give it to her when I moved out. The excellent rate of dollars to francs, coupled with absence of import tax, made my purchases irresistible.

I met with Georgette three more times. Just as I'd told Raul, women would always be the key to my father. Though she knew my mother only from my father's conversations, Georgette was able to fill in some details about their life together.

With regard to the explanation my father had given for changing our names at our meeting ten years earlier, Georgette said, "Your father said that he had hidden his daughters where Hitler couldn't find them. When I reminded him that Hitler was dead, he told me, 'That's what we'd like to believe. If only it were true.'"

"What do suppose he meant by that?" I asked.

"That bigots and bigotry is still alive."

"You think that's the reason my father changed our identities?

"Your father was a complicated man. I believe your mother was the only woman he gave himself to completely. His eyes filled with lead when he told me that she was dead. He was furious at her for not leaving Paris with him. Furious at her for dying. I suspect that he wanted to symbolically hurt her, by cutting himself off from whatever members of her family survived."

An interesting theory. I wasn't certain if I believed it. But I was eager to return home. I loved Paris. Paris, where each of the five senses was celebrated. The music of the street performers, the smell of brioche baking, the reflections in the Seine of the building and bridges above it, the statues and monuments, not one carelessly executed or placed. Paris didn't take herself lightly. She was the timeless and ageless courtesan. Nevertheless, I longed to be home. Every couple holding hands or kissing in a doorway reminded me how much I missed Raul. Paris was best shared.

Chapter Eighteen

December, 1938

Alan watched in mute wonder as Nicole stepped out of her dress and left it on their bedroom floor as she headed for her bath. Shoes, chemise, and underwear followed in succession. Now twenty, her slender naked body denied that she was the mother of two.

"You leave your things on the floor. How can you be so sloppy?"

She turned to mock him — sashaying to the left, then the right. "Claudine will be in to straighten up after we leave. Stop being silly."

"What sort of example are you setting for the girls?"

When they had shared Alan's flat Nicole had kept the small apartment clean and reasonably neat. However, now returned to her native habitat she resumed her position as the indulged daughter. But her hold on him was not to be denied. Alan followed her helplessly to their bathroom, already aroused. He caught her arm and pulled her to him. When her feather-soft hair brushed his jaw, he knew the internal battle he continuously fought was lost.

"We'll be late if we don't hurry," she said without moving away. "There's no time for your little games."

"There's always time." He dropped his hands to her soft bare buttocks. "Do it for me, Nicole."

"What is it that you want me to do?" she asked, affecting innocence while toying with his ear.

"You know what I want. Do the gasp you do when you're startled. Do it, Nicole. Do it for me."

"Like this? Aaahh." She inhaled sharply. "Aaahh. Is that what you want?"

He undid his trousers with his free hand and let them drop without releasing her. "Now pretend you're seventeen and sleeping in my sitting room and I've come in to check on you."

"The Varnes will be annoyed if we're late."

"They'll recover. Do it. Beg me to make love to you just as you did that night."

Nicole shrugged and assumed the pout that she knew excited him. She was no longer a girl, but a siren pretending to be a girl. "I see the way your eyes follow me when you think I'm not watching," she said in a breathy whisper. "I'm not a child. I'm a woman. Kiss me. Kiss me the way you kiss those other women."

Alan buried his face in her hair. "There are no other women. There is only you."

"But that isn't what you said. You said —"

"Only you, Nicole. You have stolen my soul."

*   *   *

Indeed the Varnes did recover, but not before Madame Varne inquired if her guests had had difficulty obtaining a cab.

Nicole's baby eyes were so innocent no one could doubt their sincerity. "I'm sorry that we're late, but Michelle insisted on having her daddy's attention before we left. Hearing the fuss, her sister Marguerite was not about to be ignored. Alain spoils them dreadfully you know."

Madame Varne clucked sympathetically and led them into a drawing room filled with guests. "How old are the girls?" Her brown eyes heavily outlined and mascaraed, and her dark hair stylishly bobbed, the elegant Madame Varne was cousin to the French branch of the Rothschilds. Not nearly as wealthy as the famous Jewish scions, Helene Varne was still a noted hostess. Like four generations of French Jews before him, Maurice Varne manufactured furniture. Originally from Poland, Varne was the name his grandfather had chosen. Their apartment, though small, was filled with the classic furniture produced by the Varne firm, past and present.

"Maggie, our Sarah Bernhardt, is just past two," Alan said. "Michelle, whose career has yet to be determined, is ten months."

Madame Varne favored Alan with her most maternal smile.

The Fitzpatricks completed the party of twelve. They were part of a circle of married couples in their twenties and thirties brought together by status and commonality. Discussions normally covered politics, books, the theater, and domestic gossip. Tonight, despite the best efforts of the host and hostess to divert talk to a more agreeable topic, conversation throughout dinner was the frightening event that had taken place in Germany a month earlier, November 9, 1938 — Kristallnacht. Dinner over, all returned to the drawing room. Three gentiles were present: Alan, Edward Pentergast, an Englishman, and Anna Grossvelt, a Swiss woman, all married to French Jews.

"Germans have always been anti-Semitic," Madame Grossvelt said, settling her ample frame into a comfortable chair. "Nothing like that could happen here. The French are civilized people. They wouldn't tolerate it."

"I beg to differ, my dear Anna," her husband replied, gesturing with his glass. "Have you read how our so-called enlightened press, the *Figaro* and *Le Temps*, reported this disgraceful crime? There was no sense of outrage, no suggestion we condemn this action. Even worse, we hear no talk of how we can stop this insane demagogue before he invades France."

"He wouldn't dare. The Maginot Line and the French army are impenetrable," Madame Varne insisted.

"Chamberlain thinks Hitler can be bought off, but this chap Churchill claims Hitler is a madman determined to rule the world," Monsieur Pentergast asserted in his harsh French.

"Rule the world, indeed." Madame Varne held up a cut-glass decanter. "Who would like another liqueur? Alain? Louis? What you about you, Nicole? Surely a little liqueur . . ." All present demurred.

"Ribbentrop is in Paris to sign a pact of French-German friendship with Bonnet," another guest said. "Those of us who emigrated to France in the past are fortunate. France will no longer accept foreign Jews."

"It was inevitable," Monsieur Varne said. "France cannot support an endless stream of immigrants."

"Where will they go?" Alan asked, entering the discussion for the first time that evening.

"England is admitting some," Monsieur Pentergast said from his perch near his wife. "The United States is taking others. I've heard people talking about emigrating to South America, Australia, the Caribbean, even Africa."

"Every country has quotas. People applying for entrance far exceed those permitted to enter," Monsieur Soral, a university professor, added. "Many will be left with nowhere to go."

Monsieur Wiener, who had been standing quietly near the doorway, spoke, "Our government just passed a law revoking the citizenship of certain naturalized citizens under the 1927 laws. It won't affect anyone in this room, but others . . ."

"I know nothing of politics," Alan said, feeling once again the outsider. "But is no one present concerned about safety? Is there not one of you considering emigrating? Edward, you've retained your English citizenship. What about you and Clarice? You have children. Wouldn't you be safer in England, at least until this madman is stopped?"

Every eye coolly rebuked Alan. He had dared to speak the truth, and they reacted as though he had committed an unpardonable faux pas.

"We are loyal French citizens, Alain," Claude Varne quietly explained. "My father and my grandfather, and no doubt my great-grandfather, honorably defended France's borders. France would never allow what has been going on in Germany to happen here."

Monsieur Pentergast cleared his throat. "There have been incidents. Our youngest was singled out by schoolmates — kicked, spat on."

"Claude is right," Nicole said. "We Jews are loyal French citizens. Why should we desert our homeland because of a few isolated incidents? I will never leave France."

"I hope you didn't mean what you said," Alan said later that evening when he and Nicole were once again in their bedroom. "I'm a U.S. citizen, which makes you and the girls citizens as well. I think we should leave France as soon as possible."

"Never! If you're frightened, you go."

"How can you say such a cruel thing, Nicole? Would I ever leave you and the children?" His question received a scowl and a pout. "Think of our babies, Nicole. They may not be safe here. Paris is not the same city it was five years ago. Paris is nervous and worried. Every day I hear another anti-Semitic remark from people I thought better of. They frighten me. When people are panicked they do crazy things. If we leave now, I promise we'll return when all of this unrest is over."

"How can I leave my family? They can't manage without me."

"Your father runs his book business without help. Your mother oversees the entire household accounts, the staff, and still finds the time to meddle in our affairs. Your brother is away at school. The maid cleans. The nanny sees to the girls. The cook cooks. What is it that you do that no one else can?"

"I am the daughter. My children are the grandchildren." Nicole pulled back the blanket and sat on the bed. "Philippe called me today and asked me to tell Mama that he has enlisted."

Alan turned away in disgust. Their educated friends denied the obvious. German Jewish refugees spoke lovingly of the homeland they had been forced to leave. His wife was determined to be intractable — a woman who would rather throw herself in the Seine than disgrace her family. And eighteen-year-old Philippe had enlisted. Was there ever a more unlikely candidate for soldiering than his girlishly-thin, soft-mannered brother-in-law? Were all Jews insane — or only the ones that he knew? Within the month Alan had an answer. Without a word to their neighbors and colleagues, the Pentergasts had left for London.

*   *   *

September 1, 1939, Germany invaded Poland. On September 3rd, France and Great Britain declared war on the aggressor. Like Philippe Strauss, thousands of French Jews enlisted in numbers far exceeding their negligible proportion of the population. In return, the government promised the families of enlistees protection from expulsion or interment. It was a promise not to be kept.

Debates in the Strauss-Fitzpatrick home on whether to leave or to remain continued, with Alan standing alone. Maurice Strauss refused to leave Paris, his home, or his precious books. Hortense

Strauss would not leave her husband's side, and the country her son now valiantly defended. Nicole would not leave her parents. Perhaps in defense of her superfluous position in the family, she had become Maurice's assistant. The crippling migraines Maurice Strauss had suffered occasionally in the past were growing increasingly frequent. Nicole appeared determined to learn the intricacies of an exacting business before her father became totally incapacitated.

By May 10th, 1940 Germany was goose-stepping through Luxembourg, Belgium, and the Netherlands. "It's only a matter of time," Alan pleaded with Nicole. "Leave with me now, before it's too late."

"The Maginot Line is impregnable. France will not fall."

Alan's employer lacked Nicole's confidence. Debarge feared if the Nazis took Paris his treasures would join others being scooped up by Hitler's advancing army. As no one in France was buying art, only selling it, Debarge released all his employees with the exception of Alan. It was Alan's job to crate anything of value, help hide it, and revise the accompanying paperwork.

"The *chosen people*," Debarge declared one day as together they crated a large oil. "We can blame this on them,"

"Blame what on them?" Alan asked, hiding his outrage. His angry employer had forgotten he was married to a Jew, that he lived with her family.

"The invasion. We French have rid ourselves of every dictator and that Teutonic would-be Napoleon knows that. Hitler knows that he can't hold France long. He wants the Jews. If we turned them over to him, he would leave France alone."

"If he only wants the Jews, why are we hiding the artwork?"

Debarge sneered. "Hitler's crazy but he's not stupid. Once he takes control, he will grab everything he can."

Maurice and Hortense listened in shock when Alan repeated the conversation to them. They knew Debarge, had purchased artwork from him. Jews living in Paris had considered him sympathetic. Maurice had arranged Alan's employment with Debarge. Had the man become part of the insanity taking hold of the city?

Only Nicole insisted that Alan was exaggerating.

"You should have walked out when Debarge said France should

turn over her Jews," she accused.

"And where would Alain go?" her mother asked, surprising Alan by taking his side. "Do you think there are so many enlightened employers in times like these? Jobs are impossible to find. Your husband did the right thing by saying nothing."

On May 15th Nazi Germany broke through the Maginot Line. June 11th the Italians declared war and invaded the south of France. The Germans entered Paris on June 14th, and established the Vichy government. A number of brave soldiers kept fighting after the occupation. Some were killed by furious French civilians afraid their resistance would bring retaliation from the Vichy. Acts of cowardice and bigotry took place next to those of defiant courage and patriotism.

As Parisians struggled to make sense out of the bedlam, tens of thousands of desperate refugees poured into France — Jews, gypsies, intellectuals, homosexuals, artists, people who found themselves without a country. Essentials of life became even more difficult to obtain. The refugees were held responsible for any and all troubles. Alan heard stories of people he knew being taken to internment camps, their belongings confiscated. He witnessed Jews being harassed, spat upon, and beaten in the streets. Marguerite and Michelle were no longer allowed to leave the house without their father. Arguments between Alan and Nicole were long and heated.

One sunny day in June, as Nicole worked upstairs with her father, Hortense cornered Alan and led him into the butler's pantry. Over the last several months his relationship with his mother-in-law had improved. She no longer threw disguised barbs that suggested he lacked ambition or avoided hard work. Her anger was now reserved for the detested Vichy.

"Have you ever noticed that Marguerite looks very little like her mother and not at all like you?"

Alan scrutinized Hortense's face. So she knew. He was being tested again. "It's not important. Nicole is my wife. Maggie and Michelle are my daughters, now and forever. Do you doubt that I love them? What else matters?"

"Nothing, I suppose."

"Does Father Strauss know?"

"I haven't told him. There seemed no point." Hortense

examined a silver water pitcher and frowned at the tarnish that had accumulated.

The unused fine china and stemware were hidden from sight and dust by cloths, but tarnish couldn't be prevented. Without a full staff to scrub, clean, cook, dust, polish, wash, and iron, the house no longer looked the way it had when Alan first saw it. He waited for the testing to continue.

"While walking around the city your father-in-law was knocked to the ground and viciously kicked and beaten," she said, her face now tight and pained. "The old fool tried to keep it from me, but he couldn't hide the bruises. They heard his German accent and assumed he was one of the refugees. A kind gentleman, who was there fortunately knew him and interceded, or Maurice surely would have been killed. Paris is no longer safe. France is no longer safe. You, Nicole, and the children must leave."

Alan snorted his irritation. "How very amusing. That sounds exactly like what I've been saying for the last three years."

"So, you see, you've had an ally for some time. I've kept my silence to preserve the family. The family is everything."

"Until Father Strauss was attacked."

"Yes. Until my husband was ruthlessly beaten and nearly killed. Do you know why I insisted you move into this house when Marguerite was ill?"

"You thought you could care for her if she was living here," Alan replied, taken aback at the question.

"Wrong! I insisted you come to live with us because I knew you were a better parent than my daughter. I knew I could always rely on you to protect my grandchildren. You're a strange man, Alain, but in this you have always been consistent."

"It won't be easy. Vichy officials will do everything they can to prevent our leaving. They will deluge us with red tape."

"Money, Alain. Money is the knife that cuts through red tape. I will help you get papers and bribe those who would stand in our way."

"What about you and Father Strauss? Come with us."

"Maurice is a sentimental patriot who will never leave France. Nor is he well. The headaches are worse than ever. And I? I cannot leave my husband and my son."

"How will we convince Nicole? Nothing I say gets through to

her. If I didn't love her so much I would've taken the children and left."

"Nicole is headstrong and naïve but anyone can see my daughter adores you. Together, we will convince your wife, my foolish daughter, that she must think and act like a mother. A mother protects her young."

Alan looked at the small elegant woman with newfound admiration.

*   *   *

When Alan returned home from work one afternoon in July, Maurice Strauss was in his bedroom hiding from the light. Since the beating, his migraines never ended. The children were napping and their nanny was nearby darning their socks. Nanny was one of the two remaining servants. The cook had been dismissed months before. Claudine, the maid, a woman all alone in the world and too old to find another position, had gratefully opted to stay on without salary. With so many adults housebound, Nanny should have been dispensed with ages ago. But Michelle had been born with a twisted right leg, and Nanny was the sole member of the household who could administer the hour-long massages the doctor had prescribed, without the infant's pitiful screams piercing the air and gnawing at everyone's nerves.

Alan found his wife and mother-in-law in the study. Hortense was working on a petit point canvas destined to cover a throw pillow. Nicole was examining a leather-bound book, white cotton gloves on her hands. In less than two years she had become indispensable to her father's business. An enameled clock on the mantle ticked loudly. Outside the draped windows, on the street below, passing military vehicles could be heard rumbling over the cobblestones.

Maurice, when he was strong enough to be called upon, had supported his son-in-law and wife's stance. With persistent badgering, the three had convinced Nicole of the need to take the children and flee. Three weeks earlier Hortense had begun implementing her plan.

"You're home early," Hortense said, lifting her head from her needlework.

"We've packed and hidden the last piece." Alan walked to Nicole and kissed her cheek. "I have created my last fraudulent invoice. My services are no longer required. Where are my girls?"

"Taking a nap," Nicole said. "They'll join us later."

"Is the book particularly special?"

She gently placed the book on tissue paper. "An original edition by Victor Hugo, with notations by the author — excellent condition. A year ago, the right collector would have traveled half of France for the privilege of buying it. Today, if I had a book handwritten by Cleopatra herself, I couldn't sell it for enough money to pay a month's rent. Now you've been laid off. When will this war be over?"

"It's just as well that Alain has been laid off. He will be less likely to be missed," Hortense said. "The last greedy friend-of-a-friend I had to bribe came through. Everything has been arranged. You are leaving eight days from today."

Nicole gasped. "So soon? Is that enough time to prepare? Does Father know? What do we tell the girls?"

"You will tell the girls nothing!" Hortense tapped her wooden embroidery frame nervously with her needle. "The less they know the better. At the last minute you say that you are taking them for a little vacation. And I shall tell your father later this evening when we are alone. Make no mistake, Nicole, he is in complete agreement. Now would you be a dear and prepare a pot of tea for all of us? A cup of tea would be so nice."

Hortense waited until Nicole had wrapped the book, put it away, and left the room before addressing Alan again. "I've raised some money, enough to get you to the United States if you're careful. This family doesn't have diamond tiaras or such, but I'll give you some jewelry to take with you. You can convert them to cash when you arrive at your destination, or God forbid, if for some reason you are detained, you can use it for bribes."

"You would entrust me with all this?"

"I am entrusting you with the lives of my daughter and grandchildren. Is there anything I treasure more?"

Alan stared at his hands. "Forgive me, Mother Strauss."

"Father Strauss and I have been thinking. What if Debarge is right and the Nazis confiscate artwork? Wouldn't they be most likely to single out Jews first? The Vichy government won't protect us. We've decided it would be wise to take some of the better oils with you. They can be rolled to occupy little room and are light to carry."

They could hear Nicole approaching with the tea.

"We shall talk more later," Hortense said, rising to meet Nicole. "Ah tea. Just what the afternoon needed. See, Alain, your wife is learning to be a perfect American wife. She has warmed the croissants and found us some butter. Now where are my darling girls?"

Alan was already halfway out the door. "I'll have them here in a minute."

* * *

Over the remaining days there was little opportunity for private conversation between Alan and Hortense. Little details, like obtaining lightweight sturdy luggage, gathering hard to obtain food that would travel well, and sewing gems into the linings of their clothes, consumed the precious time remaining. And it all had to be accomplished in secret. It was impossible to know which acquaintance or servant might purposefully, or inadvertently, give them away. With only three days to spare, a drawn, tight-lipped Hortense drew Alan aside to tell him that the farmer who was supposed to get them safely out of Paris had been arrested.

"What will we do?" Hortense said. "Everything has been arranged."

"Someone I know may be able to help," Alan said. "Please don't question me and try to keep Nicole calm. I may not return tonight."

Hortense solemnly nodded.

* * *

Alan reached Georgette's home after Claude Pelletier had returned for the evening. Through the windows, he could see him pompously parading about the house. Rather than compromise Georgette, Alan decided to hide in a side doorway until morning after Pelletier left. Typical self-serving politician, Alan thought bitterly. The man had supported the Vichy government and had been awarded a post. It was that post's authority that Alan sought. Would Georgette do this for him? It was a lot to ask of a friend. Favors involved risk. In these tumultuous times surely scores of people had gone to her for favors. But he was desperate. Pelletier left at eight o'clock. Alan knocked on the door.

"I'm here to see Madame Pelletier," he informed the maid.

She scowled and silently took his card. He waited outside until she returned and led him to Georgette.

Alan explained his problem. "Even those of us with American

passports are being stopped and detained. I have two precious little girls. We need safe passage out of Paris, Georgette. Everything else has been arranged. I know it's dangerous for you, but I have no one else to ask."

"My dear Alain, in all our years as friends I have never seen you more attractive. A protective role is very becoming to you. Of course I'll help. Tell your wife that I hope she will be very happy in Philadelphia."

He took Georgette's hand in his, brought it to his lips, and tenderly kissed it. "What about you, Georgette? How will you get through this madness?"

"How will I get through this madness? I've discovered my true love's identity, darling Alain. It's France. I will use my mind, my body, and my soul to fight for her until she's free once more or until I die."

"What about your husband? He serves the Vichy."

"After I'm done using whatever money and influence he has, that traitor can go to hell, where he belongs."

*　*　*

Nicole occupied the children in another part of the house while Alan and her parents decided which paintings he would take. A massive landscape was eliminated because of its size. A pair of small, early nineteenth century landscapes of excellent quality were taken down and set aside. Two family portraits and several other lesser works were not considered because of their limited value. The brittle nature of one of the oils excluded it. It couldn't be removed from its frame and rolled without causing irreparable damage. Three exceptional still-lifes, two florals, and one portrait were selected. Only a few works remained, including an outstanding Renoir in the front parlor and a magnificent van Dyck in the dining room. The Strausses had not mentioned them.

"What about the Renoir and van Dyck, or would you rather not part with them?" Alan asked. Perhaps his in-laws were reluctant to entrust their finest pieces to a mere son-in-law.

Hortense clapped her hands and laughed — the first hearty adult laugh heard in the Strauss household for months.

"My dear, what is so funny?" Maurice asked from the other room. "Alain, what is she laughing at?"

"Alain thinks my uncle's masterpieces should be protected from the Hun invaders," she said between bursts of laughter.

"They can't have been done by your uncle," Alan insisted. "They're too good — the subject, the execution. Look at the van Dyck." He pointed at the full-length portrait of a nobleman with a broad hat, boots, and spurs. "Seventeenth century. Part Elizabethan, part Baroque, entirely van Dyck. Could your uncle have copied with this precision?"

Maurice had joined them. "They're not copies, my son," he said laughing. "They're originals."

"But if they are not copies . . . "

Maurice addressed his wife. "Tell him, my dear. Tell Alain about your prissy uncle Gaston."

Alan walked to within of a foot of the Renoir. It was the top half of a seated, lovely brown-haired young woman, holding a glass. He stared into the subject's eyes and then stepped back. The lush muted blue sky background gave no indication of the setting. It could have been a study for one of Renoir's larger, more encompassing works. Breathtaking. "The brush strokes. The exquisite facial coloring, the way he layered his oils and blended them. Can it be true?" he asked Hortense. "Did your uncle really paint both of these?"

"It's true," Hortense assured him. "They are the family jokes. I thought Nicole had told you about them ages ago."

"The artist, is he still alive? Did he do any others?"

Hortense fingered the ribbon which held her glasses. "Always the renegade, my uncle Gaston amused himself by imitating whichever artist took his fancy that day. He was a scandalously naughty boy who died at the age of forty-four when the carriage he was riding in overturned. After his death the paintings were divided among whichever family members wanted them. I chose these. My sister, who lives in Switzerland, has more. You're not thinking of taking them with you, are you?"

"Would you object?" Seeing her hesitation Alan added, "They are family heirlooms, of a sort."

Hortense looked at Maurice. "What do you think, Maurice? Shall we allow Alain to rescue Uncle Gaston's family heirlooms?"

Maurice smiled broadly. "I think the United States is a perfect place for your uncle's absurdities. Just be certain to tell your friends, Alain, Gaston was Hortense's uncle. He was no relative of mine."

From the floor beneath they heard Nicole's scream.

Alan raced downstairs and found Nicole slumped on the floor hysterically crying. In her hands was a letter. The children were poking her.

"What's wrong with Mommy?" Maggie asked Alan. By this time Claudine and Nanny had arrived and were soon joined by Hortense.

"Mommy's sad," Alan told the four-year-old. "You and Mushy be good girls and go with Nanny. I'll find out why Mommy is sad and make it better."

"Don't be sad, Mommy," Maggie said.

"Sad Mommy." Michelle's upper lip protruded. Nanny attempted to lead them away, but neither was willing to leave.

"You're frightening the girls," Alan told Nicole. "Tell them you're going to be fine."

"Go with Nanny," Nicole said mechanically. "Mommy will be fine."

The girls allowed themselves to be led away — Maggie reluctantly, Michelle limping behind.

Hortense took the letter from Nicole and began reading, her face blanching as she did.

"What is it?" Alan asked. "What's in the letter? Who sent it?"

"It can't be. Not my son! Not Philippe! Wounded. Badly wounded."

"When?" Alan asked. "Look at the date! When was the letter written?"

Hortense shuffled the pages until she located what she sought, then mumbled days and dates to herself. "Five weeks ago. Oh merciful God. Not my son. Not Philippe."

All discussion halted until the children had been put to sleep for the night. Alan resumed removing the oil paintings from their frames while Maurice solemnly lectured him about the background of the artists, and when and how each work had been acquired. Nicole sat nearby reading and rereading the letter. It had been written by Jacques Levinson, a soldier who had served with Philippe. Though Levinson had tried not to alarm the family unnecessarily, it was clear Philippe's injury was grave. Levinson also suggested that Philippe might be sent to an internment camp to recuperate. All reports of internment camps were harrowing. People had been known to disappear.

Maurice spoke. "This information in no way alters our plans for you and the children. Who knows if we could make the necessary arrangements again? Nicole, you, Alain, and the girls will leave tomorrow as planned. Mama and I will go and look for Philippe. When we've located him, and as soon as he's well enough to travel, we'll all go to Switzerland where we'll stay with your aunt and uncle until this ungodly war has ended."

"No! I'm not leaving," Nicole said. "Alain will take the girls. You and Mama will stay here in case Philippe tries to contact you. I will find Philippe and bring him home."

"Nicole, your father is right," Alan said. "We must leave tomorrow. All of us. How will I manage the girls without you?" But Alan recognized the same infuriating stubbornness that he had seen before.

"Listen to your father and your husband," Hortense said, her voice cracking with emotion. "Look after your children. They may be all this family has left."

But no amount of cajoling, pleading or badgering would change Nicole's mind. Ten minutes past two it was finally agreed. Alan would take the girls, the paintings, and the small amount of cash Hortense had collected, and leave for the United States. The jewelry would now be used to finance Nicole's mission to move Philippe to safety, preferably to Switzerland and their family. As soon as that was accomplished, Nicole would join Alan and the children.

Chapter Nineteen

The day I landed at La Guardia Airport the temperature was near one hundred. New York's five boroughs were experiencing a scalding summer's end heat wave. After a cooling shower I called Raul to tell him that I had arrived home safely. Since telephone conversations lack intimacy, I wanted to wait until the upcoming Labor Day weekend, when we would be together, to tell him more.

I received an unexpected call around seven o'clock that evening from the former caretaker of Treetops, Woody Wilson. He was calling from Ramapoka, a small town in upstate New York. He and his sister Essie had purchased a lodge consisting of twelve guest cabins and a two-story house that they shared.

"It gives me something to do besides fish," Woody said. "And it brings in a few dollars as well. You're welcome anytime. Course it's pretty rustic here, but the cabins have hot water and plenty of it. Seen to that myself."

"It sounds very nice."

"What?"

"It sounds very nice," I shouted into the phone.

"Thinking of heating a couple of the cabins. Wouldn't be much of an investment. Might bring in some hunters in the winter. Make it a year-round resort."

"You can't know how pleased I am to hear from you. Give me your phone number and address so I can contact you."

He did, then said, "I found this hatbox filled with letters and such at the house in McLean. At first I thought I should throw them out, because they weren't really sent to your father. They're written in some foreign language. I didn't know what you wanted me to do with them."

I recalled finding the box with its odd contents. Perhaps I'd dismissed it too quickly. "Please mail the box to this address. Better yet, send it Casa Buena in Palm Beach." Raul might be able to add another perspective.

"Will do. Just want you to know, I get plenty of use from your father's things. Essie says I look real spiffy on Sundays when I go to church."

"Daddy would be pleased."

"Almost forgot to mention it, before we closed down the house a lady came by asking about your father. Name of Brighton. Had to tell her your father was gone."

"Do you remember the lady's first name?"

"Christine. Nice looking. Kind of perky. Said she was a stewardess. Said your father forgot a book he was reading on one of her flights. Asked how he died."

"And you told her?"

"Had no reason to lie. She took it kind of hard — considering."

"How hard?"

"Surprised. Real surprised. Sad."

Miss Christine Brighton had considerately made the trip from the airport all the way to the house in McLean, simply to drop off a lost book and then appeared sad when told of Daddy's death. Another of Daddy's playmates. "Did Miss Brighton mention what airline she worked for or where she lived?"

"Nope. Didn't ask."

I still hadn't identified the Crab. First initial C, last initial B. Daddy might have created an acronym using initials. His relationship with the Crab had gone on for years and meetings had become increasingly frequent. If Christine Brighton was the Crab it would explain why she took Daddy's death so hard. Damn! Without the name of the airline or a point of origin it would be impossible to trace the perky Miss or Mrs. Brighton.

I raced to find the address books but none contained an entry for Christine or Brighton. It wasn't Daddy's style to leave incriminating evidence. And then I remembered how much I'd learned calling a single mysterious name – Fiona Hagan. In total, there were approximately twenty listings I couldn't identify. All I needed was a few credible fibs that would provoke useful discussion.

"Hello, this is Charlotte Morgan," I explained to R. Simons, the first candidate – a Virginia phone number. "As you probably know, Jack Morgan, my father, died in early January. We're still going through his things and I found an unmailed letter with your name on it, but no address."

After Robert Simons revealed he was our blacksmith, I suggested the envelope probably contained a Christmas card and the conversation ended.

The next nine calls were equally fruitless. Two phone numbers were out of service. Three well-meaning, but unenlightening people, a man and two women remembered meeting me. Four well-spoken women that I instinctively knew had been romantically involved with my father, couldn't wait to end our conversation, sighed with relief, and thanked me profusely when I offered to throw away what had to be a Christmas card. At nine o'clock, I decided to make one last attempt for the evening and reached S. Weiss. Sylvia was a widow and had met my father five years ago, at Sak's, where she had sold ties "for something to do" after her husband's death. She and my father had remained friends until his death.

"Did you notice any changes in him that last year or so?" I

asked.

"Now that you mention it, I did. He seemed far away and – somewhat melancholy. I'd appreciate it if you would forward that card."

After we hung up, I made a note to myself to find a lovely holiday card, add my father's signature and a wish for a happy new year in my father's handwriting, and mail it to the nice lady.

*　*　*

Although I'd planned to continue my telephone exploration the following evening, a week passed before I had the opportunity to try the remaining unidentified listings. After the predictable *out of service* calls, unanswered ringing, two tries where I learned I had reached the right number and wrong individuals, I located J. Randall.

"When I read the *Times* obituary," Jeremy Randall said in a distinctive and educated English accent, "you can't imagine how distressed I was. I don't know why your father would be contacting me, but I can give you my address and you could send it on, if you would be so kind."

"Would it be rude to ask how you happen to know my father?"

"Not at all. We met at an art gallery – a show for an upcoming young artist. We chatted for a while, discovered we shared a number of interests, and decided to meet from time to time. Just two chaps having a bit of man-to-man. I travel a good deal. I regret those meetings weren't more often."

"About how long ago did you meet?"

"Eight to ten years ago. I can't be certain."

I was disappointed. I'd been hoping to find earlier links to my father's past. "Did my father ever mention Amelia and me?"

"My dear, he liked nothing better than to tell me about his two lovely and talented daughters."

"Would it be possible to meet, Mr. Randall? Unless you're too busy. I work and only have evenings and weekends free. No doubt you have plans."

"I'm a lonely old bachelor, and you must call me Jeremy. I'd be delighted to meet you. What do you enjoy doing on weekends?"

"Mostly I do dull practical things. When I have some free time, I like to visit museums."

"Splendid! You're your father's daughter. Shall we meet at the

Frick? I'm a past member of the board. We won't have to pay the admission fee," he confided, like a guilty little boy.

"I adore the Frick."

I hung up smiling. I would be going to the fabulous Frick, an early Twentieth century mansion, now a museum, and meeting a good friend of my father's, one who shared our love of art. The endless hours and dreary evenings spent poring over papers and making futile calls had paid off.

*   *   *

When I entered the museum, just off Fifth Avenue, I found a dignified man in his early sixties, wearing a white linen suit and neatly trimmed beard, apparently waiting for me. It wasn't until I drew closer that I realized the sorely twisted torso, partially hidden by the Panama straw hat on his lap, wasn't a trick caused by shadows.

"Charlotte, Charlie, how lovely to meet you," he said, his gray-green eyes twinkling. "Your father's description doesn't do you justice. Please forgive me for not standing."

It was only then that I noticed his bowed legs and misshapen hands.

"Thank you. I've been looking forward to this all week."

"As you can see, I have our day passes. Now, if you would be so kind and summon my manservant, we can proceed. He should be lurking in the next room. But before you go, I must warn you. Disraeli is rather frightening to look at and severely retarded."

I was glad that Randall had warned me. The poor bearlike creature with his mouth hanging open, staring up at a Corot painting of a pond, was unnerving. "Paint! Paint!" he was saying in a loud voice.

"Mr. Randall needs you."

Disraeli stared at me uncomprehending. His blackened teeth crisscrossed one another in random confusion. Then, apparently, his brain processed my message for he left me to get a nearby wheelchair. I followed him back to Jeremy Randall, whom he lifted into the chair as easily as if the man had been an umbrella.

Jeremy rearranged his clothes. "Shall we proceed?"

"Disraeli seemed impressed by a Corot," I said, still unnerved by the manservant's appearance. "He was staring at the oil saying, "Paint, paint."

"Yes, yes. Disraeli likes to play with oils. He saw me painting many years ago and decided it was great fun to make a huge mess. If he's a good boy and minds me as he should, I occasionally permit it."

Viewing the Frick with a man who turned out to be an art authority was wonderful.

"And now we must stop for an afternoon aperitif or tea," Jeremy announced when we'd nearly completed viewing the last room. "You will join me, won't you? I know a small bistro that can accommodate us."

I quickly decided the errands I had planned to do could wait. It was impossible to say when I'd have another opportunity to talk with this knowledgeable and fascinating man.

While we sat in the front of the tiny restaurant where we could watch passers-by, Disraeli was in the dim rearmost booth. Jeremy had explained to me that many restaurateurs disliked seating Disraeli where customers could see him. Some refused to seat him at all.

Since I could imagine that distorted mouth tearing at his food, I could understand their concerns. "How did Disraeli come to be in your keeping, Jeremy?" I asked when our tea and sandwiches had been served.

"A number of friends and I had gone on a picnic on my family's estate. I found the wretched creature hiding in the brush. He was filthy, near-naked, and starving. He couldn't have been more than ten or eleven. His parents must have led him into the forest and left him there to die. Since he spoke no more than a few words, it was impossible for me to learn where he came from. I had no choice but to take him home. The staff fed, bathed, and deloused him. After that, I couldn't exactly return him to whence he came. Since no one claimed him, I kept him. I was twenty-three then, and though it was barely debilitating, I had already been diagnosed with this sorry disease. I knew I would eventually need the sort of assistance he could provide."

"How fortunate for him to find you."

"I was engaged to an exquisite creature at the time, the daughter of an earl. You remind me of her. When her family learned that I had rheumatoid arthritis, naturally the engagement was broken. They would never permit her to marry a helpless cripple."

"I'm so sorry."

He leaned toward me conspiratorially and said in a low voice, "To be perfectly honest, I miss my painting more than I miss the young lady. I've become accustomed to being a bachelor. Now tell me about yourself. Is there a particular young man who makes your heart beat faster? An eager suitor determined to win your hand?"

"There is someone I care for, who cares for me, but there are complications."

"Complications?"

"We come from different worlds. I don't think I can live in his, and he wouldn't be accepted in mine." Had I been asked to explain why I chose to share my most private thoughts with a total stranger, I wouldn't have been able to do so. But after Jeremy's soliloquy, sharing confidences seemed natural. "Tell me how you became an art expert."

"It's a long tale. Are you sure you want to hear the sordid saga? You can look at your watch, shake your head, and politely beg off. I won't be offended."

"You're a wonderful storyteller. Nothing could make me leave."

"In the States birth order is irrelevant. On the other side of the pond, the first son inherits the family estate. I was the first son, but I was also an impractical artist. Critics predicted a brilliant future for me. My work was exhibited at some of the finest galleries in England. My brother William was the financier. Together, we could have ruled the world, but then I lost my brother."

I waited for Jeremy to continue.

"I don't know if you're aware of what has been happening in England these past years. Taxes, my dear. Taxes and the ever-increasing costs of maintaining large homes. Many estates have been sold, gone forever. But William and I would never let that happen. He loved our home as much as I did. I was still able to paint when William was alive. After his death, I had to find a way to retain the family legacy. When I realized that my career as an artist was coming to an abrupt end, I made shameless use of all my friends and acquaintances who were busy disposing of their valuables at a dizzying pace."

"To pay taxes."

"Precisely. You see, they needed guidance on which family heirlooms to dispose of, and how to accomplish it discreetly."

"You were perfectly situated to advise them."

He lightly tapped his cane in approval. "Let's not overlook new money, my dear. While family fortunes were being lost, others were being amassed. Two world wars produced a flock of Alfies, with grimy hands filled with banknotes who wished to gain quick acceptance."

"What better way to accomplish that than to acquire fine art? And who better to help them than a knowledgeable gentleman, such as yourself?"

He smiled his approval. "But in my defense, I am diligent about the services I provide. I spent many years immersing myself in study."

I took a breath and plunged where perhaps I shouldn't have. "Do you ever come across forgeries?"

He appeared surprised, if not shocked. "I do," he admitted.

"How do you protect your clients from forgeries?"

"Oh, besides looking for style, brush strokes, and execution, modern science has given us chemists who are able to provide invaluable assistance. I frequently make use of their skills."

Twenty or more questions bombarded my brain, but discretion prevented me from asking them. "Your brother must have been quite young when he died. Was it a result of the war?"

Jeremy's face darkened. "William was a perfectly splendid fellow — ruddy with health, admired by old and young alike. But he said he heard voices. I blame myself. I should've insisted he see a doctor. Should've taken him myself. He would still be alive today if I had. William hung himself. My beloved brother hung himself. You have no idea of the grief and guilt I live with every day of my life."

The boulder in my throat nearly prevented me from speaking. "Oh, but I do. My father died by suicide," I said hoarsely, before I could stop myself.

"You poor child," Jeremy said, reaching across the table to pat my arm, and looking nearly distraught as I felt. "Please forgive this fool for reopening a fresh wound. I can't tell you how shocked I am."

Although I was unable to respond, it was comforting having him there, another human being who had lived through what I had, shared the same doubts, and grieved as I did.

"You have no idea as to what drove him to this tragic decision?"

"None."

"All I can advise is, carry on with your life as he would've wanted you to do. That would be the most fitting memorial to the father that adored you, don't you agree?"

"I do," I agreed. "And thank you. You are the kindest man."

As I climbed the stairs to Petal's townhouse, I thought how nice it was to meet and spend time with a compassionate and knowledgeable older gentleman, like Jeremy Randall. I didn't have a single acquaintance over the age of forty with whom I felt comfortable discussing anything personal – and certainly not the circumstances surrounding Daddy's death. Before, lacking aunts, uncles, and grandparents had seemed unimportant. My school friends had grumbled when they were forced to attend deadly dull family functions, where their hopelessly out-of-date elders doted on them and foolishly praised them for the simple biological process of growing. They thought me lucky. It was only now that I realized how silly my friends' complaints were. How wonderful it must be to have a large caring family.

*   *   *

Petal believed I was staying with friends in the Hamptons over the Labor Day weekend. Unless I did something outrageous to bring attention to myself, she wouldn't be outraged or upset that I'd checked into a hotel with a man. I'd lied because it was easier than trying to explain Raul and his place in my life, something I had difficulty defining for myself.

The family who owned the weathered brownstone offered clean, cheap, convenient rooms. I'd found the poor man's bed-and-breakfast, minus breakfast, advertised in the *Village Voice*. Since New York City was a vast unknown for Raul, I wanted to show him as many marvelous tourist attractions as we could fit into our days together. At two o'clock, Raul and I left our unpacked bags and headed for The Empire State Building.

Later, rather than dine indoors on a perfect afternoon Raul and I found a restaurant on Mulberry Street in Little Italy, with an awning and sidewalk seating. As we ate our spaghetti and meatballs, we talked about Jeremy Randall, work, and finally what I'd learned in Paris, information I had been consciously, and unconsciously withholding. I began the story in what I considered to be a logical order, but Raul's questions sent it in every direction.

"Did you call Fiona and ask her if she remembered seeing any paintings among your father's things when you came to the States?"

"Yes. As soon as I got home," I fibbed. The call was made five days later — when it finally occurred to me.

"And did she?"

"Not at first. Not until I realized she would be imagining framed paintings. When I described a canvas removed from its frame and rolled, she remembered seeing tubes of various sizes covered with wrapping paper."

"Did she say how many?" Raul reached for my hand under the tablecloth, or maybe my thigh.

"She guessed there were between six and ten of them. Maybe more. The Renoir and the two he gave to Petal make three. So there were others."

"They would've had to be valuable. Nobody goes to all that trouble to bring in mediocre paintings. That would explain how your father supported the three of you without working, and how he financed his foray into Palm Beach society. Where do you suppose he got them? Do you think they belonged to your grandparents?"

"My grandparents lived well, but based on Georgette's description, it was unlikely they owned masterpieces." I wasn't certain if I wanted to divulge that my mother was a Jew. I weighed my words. "We left France after Germany invaded. The Vichy government was in control. Everything was chaotic. Jews were badly treated. Many had priceless family possessions confiscated. He might have smuggled the paintings out of France as a favor for someone."

"What about after the war? Wouldn't that someone try to reclaim them? Your father had changed your names and disappeared. How would the owners know where to find him?"

"I knew that you would jump to that conclusion, but don't even think it. Daddy would never betray a trust. Steal from desperate helpless people who relied on him? Never!"

"I have to admit it would be entirely out of character." Raul brushed his forefinger down my cheek. "Besides, he held onto at least one of the most valuable paintings for years after he returned to the States. Thieves don't do that."

"What if he tried to locate the owners after the war, and when he discovered they were dead, he decided to sell them and keep the proceeds?"

"A possible and logical assumption. But if there was no one to claim the proceeds . . ."

"Where's the crime? How would killing himself protect Amelia and me?"

"Forget modeling. Become a private investigator."

I blushed at the praise — or perhaps it was the heat generated by Raul's leg tucked over mine. It was a miracle that the water glasses on the table weren't boiling.

"Can I bring you coffee and our dessert menu?" our waiter asked.

"Just the check," Raul said.

At eight-thirty, the streets were filled with people savoring what New Yorkers considered the last weekend of summer. Juxtaposed against the balmy weather, storefront windows incongruously displayed winter clothes: corduroys, tweeds, wools, and furs. As we threaded our way through the crowds I was pleased to note, unlike a stroll in Palm Beach, we attracted minimal attention.

"I saw an oil that I know for certain Daddy painted – a portrait of Georgette. Mediocre, at best. He couldn't have done the two landscapes he gave Petal. Which means he was incapable of producing a decent forgery. No wonder he never pursued his painting after he returned from Paris."   "If we walk a little faster we can make the light."

We walked a little faster and just made the light on West Broadway. "Did I tell you that Georgette was awarded the *Croix de Guerre*?"

Raul slipped his arm around my waist and pulled me close. "I want to hear everything, later."

"Are we walking fast, or is it just my imagination?"

"We're walking fast. Do I have to explain that your man needs attention?"

We still had blocks and blocks to cover before reaching our room. For weeks I'd had visions of being held, kissed, nibbled, bit, nuzzled, stroked, and fondled. I've dreamed of passionate sex with Raul until our bodies glistened with sweat. I might not be able to say it, but I intended to do everything on that list and more.

"Follow me!" I took his hand and led him through the clusters of less motivated pedestrians until we reached the rooming-house and flew up the front stairs. A middle-aged couple standing in the tiny vestibule turned to stare as we raced past them trying not to giggle like adolescents. We practically fell into the room in each other's arms. Without thinking, I reached for Raul's pants, undid the zipper, and delved inside — an extraordinary, impetuous, and brazen act for me.

Raul stopped what he was doing, which was kissing my neck while simultaneously tugging my blouse loose from my skirt. "Do you know what I love about you?"

"No."

"Everything."

Why couldn't I say things like that?

*   *   *

We had opened the eight-foot high top windows to let in the breeze. An electric fan poised on a dark Victorian dresser helped stir the air. Blankets and spread lay in a heap on the plaid armchair; the sheets askew from our impatient lovemaking. In the semi-darkness we could hear two men in the hall arguing. It seemed they both had romantic designs on a man named Demetrius. This was the Village, after all.

As Raul lay on his side to hold me, his knees against the back of mine, his head resting against my shoulder, I admitted, "My mother was Jewish. That's what made me think the paintings might have belonged to Jews."

The argument outside was so loud that I wasn't certain if Raul had heard me. Before I could repeat myself he responded. "Why did you wait until now to tell me? Did you think I would feel differently about you?"

"I'm having trouble accepting it."

"Accepting what? You were baptized, weren't you?"

"I don't know. Probably. I don't have any proof. I was raised Episcopalian. But one half of me is a Jew."

A door slammed. Another door, from the far end of the hall, opened. "Ladies, ladies," a new male voice chided. "Please. I can scarcely hear the radio with you screeching at each other. Believe me, Demetrius is simply not worth it. I happen to know that he voted for Richard Nixon in the last election. Richard Nixon! Can you believe it?"

The two took their argument, now being conducted at a reduced volume, downstairs.

"What's the big deal?" Raul said. "In Cuba, we have people of every religion and color. It doesn't change who you are."

"I feel like an outsider. I think I've always felt like an outsider. Now that I know I'm half Jewish, it all seems to makes sense."

"Everybody feels like an outsider sometimes."

I thought about what he'd said. Would I ever feel as though I belonged again? "What do you think Petal's reaction would be if she found out that Jack Morgan's daughters were half Jewish?"

"You know her better than I do. What do you think?"

My stepmother didn't have a single Jewish friend, employee, or business acquaintance. She belonged to half a dozen clubs that didn't allow a Jew on the premises, much less had one as a member. "I think Petal would prefer having a leg removed without anesthesia. I have to get a place of my own. The time has come for me to bid a fond farewell to my life of ease and luxury."

*   *   *

Sunday afternoon we viewed the island of Manhattan from a Circle Line boat. So our yacht wasn't privately owned, and it sold hot dogs, beer, and souvenirs, and we had to share it with a shipload of other sightseers. In our rail-side chairs it offered a fresh salt air breeze and breathtaking views of the city. We couldn't hear the city's unmistakable dissonance: the blaring horns, the screeching subways, or the buzz of a million or more hearts beating. While we enjoyed the spectacular display of steel, concrete, and glass of the financial district on our left, we heard only the dull hum of the engine below and an occasional cheerful gull. It was all so lovely, so untroubled. The Statue of Liberty in the distance inspired strangers to smile and nod at one another – another New York City miracle.

"It seems to me that Amelia is doing very well," Raul said, taking my hand. "Don't you think it's time she left the clinic?"

"Dr. Mendelson insists she isn't ready to leave."

"She's willing to leave the grounds and talk with me. She walks with authority. I haven't seen the sudden panic in her eyes for months. I can't think of a single reason why she shouldn't be released."

I had independently come to the same conclusion. She would need some help, of course, but I would provide that. "On my next trip, I'm bringing her here to live with me."

Raul turned and reached for my other hand. "That wasn't what I was suggesting," he said, staring straight into my eyes. "I was thinking, without the additional expense you could come back to Florida. If not immediately, then soon. I'm leaving tomorrow night. You know that I hate having you so far away."

I looked away. "Me too."

"Then come back with me."

"And do what? I'm a model — a model who's starting to make a very nice income. Models live in Manhattan. You promised to be patient."

"I'd feel a whole lot better if you looked sadder."

I forced the sides of my mouth as far down as they would go. "Do I look miserable enough now?"

"Maybe."

"The next time you come, I'll have my own apartment. A quiet place without slamming doors and noisy hallway arguments."

"The next three bridges," our guide said over the loudspeaker are the Brooklyn, the Manhattan, and the Williamsburg, all connecting Manhattan to Brooklyn. In 1898, the five boroughs joined to make New York *the largest city in the world*. At the time, Brooklyn," he paused while a small contingent cheered, "Brooklyn was fourth largest city in the United States."

For the rest of the cruise we relaxed and allowed our tour guide and the city to entertain us.

"What do you want to see now?" I asked as we pulled up to the pier.

"A museum. An art museum."

"Any particular reason?"

"I know some names — Delacroix, Rubens, Picasso, Degas. But they're just names to me. I want to see a painting through your eyes."

"Well, it's too late today to go to the Met, my favorite museum in all New York. But I can take you to 57th Street. There are a number of interesting galleries between Lexington and 3rd Avenue, and one I'd particularly like you to see."

The first gallery we reached specialized in avant-garde art. Since my enthusiasm for the genre was limited I could stimulate little interest from Raul. Looking at a large metal mobile created out of auto parts, he said under his breath, "Truly moving."

"Very funny," I whispered back, leading him toward the front door. "You'll like the next gallery better. It's more traditional. I know that because Jeremy Randall sells works there."

"You mean I'll actually know what I'm looking at?"

Gallery Three Fifty-Two was less than a block away.

Raul pointed to a canvas, a well executed but predictable rendering of a crumbling Roman ruin. "Now this is more like it. You're the expert, tell me what I should be looking for."

I selected concepts that I thought Raul would find interesting: the symbolism of the broken columns, the slavish reproduction of the classic style, as well as the artist's nice use of shadow and light.

"You see all that in one painting," he said as we moved to the next grouping. "I'm impressed."

Just before we left the main salon I saw an extraordinary study of sunflowers. The impact was immediate. I felt disoriented, as though I was trapped in an optical illusion. Nor was it the first time I experienced this bizarre reaction looking at a painting. Ignoring the shifting floor and undulating walls, I inched back until I reached the far wall.

We were quickly joined by a portly man in a pinstriped suit, who apparently had noticed me hugging the rear wall. "It's exquisite, isn't it? An outstanding example of van Gogh's artistry." He handed me his card. "I can see you are quite taken with it."

"Exquisite," I agreed.

"And very well priced, considering the artist. We've had tremendous interest in the piece."

"Do you happen to know the owner?" I asked.

"If you give me a moment to check my records, I might have some information for you."

The salesman soon returned with a woman. "I'm Madame Ivanavich, owner of Gallery Three Fifty-Two. I understand you've inquired about the van Gogh. How may I assist you?"

The woman facing us packed a general's authority into a five foot three inch frame. The sidepieces of her large dark-rimmed glasses led directly to a thick black hair-bun. Slashed across her forehead were bangs cut with military precision. Even her smile had an exactness about it — just so wide and lasting for just so long.

"I was wondering who owned the van Gogh," I said.

"The owner wishes to remain anonymous. However, the work is represented by Mr. Jeremy Randall."

"Really. I know Jeremy Randall. He was a friend of my father's."

Madame Ivanavich graced first me and then Raul with a warm smile. "And your name?"

I introduced myself and Raul.

"Then you're aware of Mr. Randall's international reputation," she continued. "He's often called in to authenticate important works."

"I know."

"We're most fortunate to be able to display Mr. Randall's pieces here in the States. Were you interested in making an offer on the van Gogh for yourself or a client?"

"It's a lovely piece, but I'm not representing a client," I said. "And unfortunately, a work of this magnitude doesn't fit into my present plans. Perhaps in the future."

"What was all that about?" Raul asked, when we left.

"I'll tell you later."

Chapter Twenty

Since our room provided only a single chair, and no table or air conditioner, Raul and I sat on the floor in our underwear and ate the Chinese food we'd brought back. A blue bath towel was our tablecloth. Matching washcloths were our napkins. From an adjacent building, we heard a soprano practicing scales. For the last few minutes I'd been trying to explain my objection to the painting we had seen earlier, without appearing demented. I glossed over my physical reaction and concentrated on facts.

"The subject is one van Gogh did many times, and the interpretation is consistent. But there are certain irregularities that disturb me."

Raul handed me the shrimp in lobster sauce. "Define irregularities. And please keep in mind, I was a political science major with a minor in psychology."

"Subtle or not so subtle differences in style, brush strokes, and shading. The emphasis on a color or hue the artist never used.

Proportions."

"Do artists stick with the same style their entire career?" he asked. "Don't they change from time to time?"

"Absolutely! Artists often experiment. They go through periods, trying this and that. Some are so diverse, like Picasso, their work can range from classical to inventing absolutely new and visionary ways of depicting people, places, objects. But they don't change styles mid-painting."

"And the van Gogh we saw today was . . . "

"Was not entirely consistent, in my humble opinion."

"You suspect the painting is a forgery."

"No. Yes. No. It was only a thought – which a model with a bachelor's degree in art history should keep to herself."

"Why don't you ask your new flame about these inconsistencies? The esteemed and respected Mr. Randall."

"I can't believe that you're jealous of a kind old man," I taunted.

"Only that he gets to spend time with you when I can't."

I crawled to Raul's side of our tablecloth-towel and licked the duck sauce from the side of his mouth before kissing him.

*   *   *

All the inquiries to the friends I had made at work for a decent but inexpensive apartment in a safe neighborhood finally paid off. Less than two weeks after Raul returned to Palm Beach, Deirdre Saxon, known throughout the industry for her waif-like beauty and bizarre eating habits, told me about a fabulous apartment that had been suddenly vacated by two aspiring actors she knew. I freed up an hour and raced over to see the plum find, checkbook in hand.

The fourth floor apartment had one large bedroom and a dining alcove that could be converted into the second bedroom I would need for Amelia. The view from the windows was the backs of other buildings and a small courtyard. While the courtyard was more concrete than leafy green trees, the apartment was quiet, unlike those that faced the hectic street. The kitchen was the size of a closet and the bathroom fixtures were archaic. Every wall was painted a different hideous color, but the elevator worked and glorious daylight flooded the rooms. "Will the landlord paint before I move in?" I asked the slouching superintendent picking his teeth.

"No. If you're not ready to give me a check, I got two other people who want to see it," he informed me.

"I'll take it." My hand shook as I wrote out my first check for two months' rent. Self-respect does not come cheap.

It required two cab rides to move my belongings from my old residence to my new one. As planned, before I left, I presented Petal with the Lalique vase and thanked her profusely for her kindness. Newly acquired items, purchased with a credit card, included a queen-sized bed, a single chest of drawers, all necessary linens, a card table with two folding chairs, and dinnerware for four. Luxuries, like a couch, would have to be added after I addressed the more pressing issue of ridding myself of the nightmarish color scheme.

As soon I was put away my few belongings, feeling immensely pleased with myself, I rang Jeremy's number hoping to plan another trip to one of New York's museums or galleries. My wacky imagination had been adding distortions to the van Gogh since Raul and I had done our gallery tour. If I could find the courage, I wanted to ask him about it. The dear man surprised me by inviting me to his home for dinner.

*   *   *

In early October, Manhattan's autumnal leaves were mottled green, burnt copper, and brick red. I spent nearly thirty minutes taking the leisurely walk to my host's New York residence on 72nd Street and Central Park West. This was my first visit to The Dakota and I was looking forward to viewing it from the inside. It had been built in the gilded age, the late eighteen hundreds, and was a grand building known for its distinguished residents and luxurious accommodations.

I gave my name to the concierge and was directed to the elevator. Going up I remembered a story that Petal had told me about a resident at the Dakota. It seemed that a woman had unexpectedly come home early and found her husband in high heels and about to slip on one of her chiffon dresses over an extra extra large black lace teddy. Maintaining complete control she coolly asked him to replace her things and meet her in their study when he'd finished. Then she asked for and was granted the title to the apartment, a house in the Hamptons, and a large share of stocks. I later heard the tale again with the names of Sybil Landry and gubernatorial hopeful Jay Watts Landry attached to it. I exited the elevator wondering how I'd react if I happened upon either the unflappable Sybil Landry or her husband.

When I rang the doorbell Disraeli opened the door. I froze for a moment. He could be quite frightening. "I'm here to see Mr. Randall."

"Coat," I thought he said.

I removed my coat, handed it to him, and tried a smile. "Thank you."

At that, Disraeli pointed to my arm. Bobbing and grinning, as though we shared a huge joke, he grunted, "Paint! Paint! You paint."

I lifted my arm to inspect it and found a white patch I'd missed when cleaning up earlier. My hideous walls had required coat after coat to cover. I'd worked continuously until it had been time to dress. "Yes, paint. I was painting my apartment — making it pretty."

He reached to touch my hair. "Pretty."

I stood motionless and forced myself not to flinch while he lifted a curl and examined it. "Pretty."

"Disraeli, bring Miss Morgan here," Jeremy called from the other room. "Don't be concerned, my dear, he won't hurt you."

Rebuking myself for acting so childishly and possibly hurting the poor soul's feelings, I walked through large double doors. Like the entranceway, the room had a fourteen-foot-high ceiling and elaborate inlaid wood floors, topped with antique Persian carpets. It appeared to be used as both a library and sitting room. Three walls were covered with floor-to-ceiling walnut bookshelves. On the fourth wall, several old portraits hung on the sides and above the door. My host waited for me on a large French tapestry chair.

"Do sit down. How good of you to come. Isn't it lovely for late October? When I left London the weather had turned cold and rainy. Now tell me everything that has happened since we last met."

Within minutes I found myself spellbound by this captivating man until Disraeli entered the room. He had changed his shirt, and if I wasn't mistaken, he had combed his hair as well.

"Dinner's ready," Jeremy announced. "Disraeli, help me into the dining room."

Disraeli supported Jeremy as he covered the short distance to the small but elegant room. Light from a leafy Murano glass chandelier with matching wall sconces glistened off the upholstered pale peach silk moiré walls and furniture.

After we sat down and Disraeli left us it seemed the right time to ask my silly question. "Jeremy, I saw a van Gogh at Gallery Three

Fifty-Two. I was told that you're representing the owner."

"And I heard that you had asked about it." Jeremy lifted the soup spoon to his mouth with his sad clawed fingers. "It sold a fortnight ago."

"It occurred to me . . . That is — This is so silly of me, but did you have any concerns about the painting's authenticity?"

"You're not only beautiful and intelligent, you have a gifted eye. The oil was badly damaged in transit years ago and required extensive repair. Regrettably, the restorer was not equal to the task. Naturally, I felt it was my duty to inform prospective buyers. But I'm pleased to say the purchaser, a splendid chap who's taking it to Australia, wasn't the least bit dissuaded."

"Restorations! Of course. I should have realized that immediately. A clumsy restorer can ruin a painting. Not that the van Gogh was ruined. It's a lovely –"

"The remarkable thing is that you noticed it, my dear. Do you realize how many people, knowledgeable people, have examined that painting without comment? Remarkable!"

I flushed at his approval.

"You know," he went on. "I've often thought about taking on a protégé here in the States at some point. We could work together while you trained. Surely a career as a model doesn't go on indefinitely. Would you fancy such an offer?"

"You would consider training me to work with you? What can I say? I'm overwhelmed. I'm thrilled."

"I would be delighted to have a talented young woman like yourself working with me, although I suspect that before that comes to pass, one young man or another will win your heart and erase all thoughts of a brilliant career." Jeremy dropped his head and lowered his voice. "Now tell me about your Cuban chap. Should I assume you're still seeing him, or has a battalion of admirers replaced him?"

Once again, I found it easy to confide to Jeremy that I was no closer to resolving my relationship with Raul, though my feelings for him continued to deepen.

*　*　*

I'd just thrown out the last unclaimed Halloween candy and was about to eat my take-home sandwich when the phone rang.

"Amelia left yesterday afternoon and hasn't returned," Dr.

Mendelson informed me. "The clinic has called every number we had for Mrs. Morgan, but she hasn't responded. And we've been unable to reach you as well. Needless to say, we're very concerned about Amelia. Have you heard from her?"

"We had a two-day shoot out of town and I just came home. There would be no way for her to contact me." Now that I had my own apartment, I no longer had the luxury of a butler who took messages. Because of that my sister might be in danger. Slowly inhale! Exhale! Inhale! Slowly! Don't panic, I ordered myself. I wasn't allowed to panic. Not while my sister needed me. "Have you searched the grounds, called the police?"

"The first thing we do is search the grounds. We try to avoid calling the police before we contact family members," Dr. Mendelson said. "In the rare instance this happens, it's usually a misunderstanding. Someone has forgotten to sign a patient out or in."

"Did she just wander away or was she with someone?"

"She was with someone. It's not the policy of this institution to permit —"

"Who?"

"She was with that nice young man who's been coming to visit her."

It was as though an icy blade had been driven into my chest. So this was what jealousy felt like. It was horrific. I was bathed in sweat. Could it be? Raul and Amelia? No. No! I had to calm down. To regain control. Maybe Raul had taken Amelia for a ride and they had a flat tire. A flat tire could be fixed. A minor traffic accident. Or worse. God, they could be lying in a hospital. A ditch.

"Charlotte! Charlotte! Are you there? Have we been cut off?"

"No. I'm here. Have you tried calling the local hospital?"

"Not as yet."

"Then I suggest you do so. If I don't hear from you in an hour, I'll be on the next flight available." I replaced the phone. The confidence I had so painfully acquired over the past few months had vanished. The endless flattery heaped upon me as a model was meaningless. I was Alice again: ugly, skinny, plain, and growing taller and taller with each breath. God, just let the car be in a ditch. Let them be shaken but uninjured — safe but unable to get to a phone.

I started packing. Packing was the wrong word. I threw my

clothes in a suitcase as I wandered from room to room forgetting the reason for many trips. Twenty minutes after my conversation with Dr. Mendelson, the phone rang.

"This is Harold Holmes. Amelia and I . . . That is to say, we've been trying to reach you since yesterday."

My brain scrambled to catch up with my racing pulse. "We! What's happened to Amelia?"

"Amelia's fine. She's with me," he said, in a pathetic attempt to sound dignified. "I hope you weren't unnecessarily frightened."

"I most certainly was frightened. What was I to think?" While I was delivering the tongue lashing that Hasty deserved, I was simultaneously thanking God that my sister was safe and that Raul wasn't somehow involved. "I can't believe you took Amelia off the grounds without my permission."

"It was Amelia's idea."

"I have nothing more to say to you, Hasty. Let me talk to Amelia."

"She's afraid to speak to you on the phone. Is it possible for you to come to my family's home in Palm Beach?"

"It's not only possible, it's imminent and inescapable." For once Hasty had the good sense not to cackle.

*   *   *

"We want to get married," Amelia told me at the Holmes' house, clutching Hasty's hand as though she were drowning and he was a life-preserver.

"Oh Amelia, I know you think this is the right thing to do. But it's too soon after your illness to be making an important decision like marriage. Dr. Mendelson insists you're not ready to be discharged. You may think you're fully recovered, but Dr. Mendelson says you could have a relapse if you're thrust back into things too quickly."

"Oh, but I am better, Charlie. That's why I wanted you to come. To see how much better I am. I've been doing so well for months."

"Don't believe everything that quack Mendelson tells you," Hasty advised me. "One of the orderlies told me they had to let some of the staff go. There aren't enough patients at the clinic so they're looking for ways to keep them. Maybe the fruitcake business is seasonal. Heh-heh, heh-heh."

Damn that irritating laugh, and damn Dr. Mendelson! If I'd

moved Amelia to New York when I originally wanted, this never would have happened. "With all due respect, Hasty, please let me remind you that you walked out on the fruitcake sitting next to you when she needed you most. I don't think you're the right man for a delicate girl like Amelia."

"No one calls me Hasty anymore. I'd prefer it if you called me either Harold or Hal. And as for my past actions, what I did was despicable. I listened to bad advice from friends. Amelia understands. Why can't you?"

Before Amelia could interrupt I tried another tack. "We're broke, Harold. Daddy left us nothing. There'll be no trousseau, no elaborate wedding, no honeymoon, and no lavish gifts. Amelia and I are penniless orphans. Why do you think I had to get a job?"

"I know that. And I also know that you've been taking care of Amelia's expenses. I'm hoping you'll allow me to repay you."

"Did you know that my father's death wasn't an accident? He killed himself. It could come out at any time. Are you prepared for that kind of notoriety?"

Harold limited his irritating laugh to a snicker. "Everyone in Palm Beach knows that. He wouldn't be the first guy to kill himself because he went bust."

I decided to try another ploy while I weighed whether I should unleash the ultimate weapon and risk my sister's mental health. "What do think your family will say when they learn your plans?"

"My parents adore Amelia. She'll stay right here in this house until the wedding — in a separate room."

Naturally. He couldn't have brought Amelia here without their approval. I had no choice. "Here's something that isn't old news and is guaranteed to be of interest. Our mother was a Jew. Amelia and I are Jewish." I turned to Amelia. "I'm sorry, darling. I know I should have told you before this, but I was afraid you'd have a setback."

Amelia's face darkened. Rather than looking distraught she appeared angry. Very angry. At me. Now I personally have never considered Hasty/Harold/Hal Holmes handsome. But he never looked more attractive than the moment he laughed that annoying laugh.

"Heh-heh-heh, your mother was Jewish. Well so was Nathan Finkelstein, the furrier – my mother's father. Who did you think started Romanoff Furs? Peter the Great?"

"Harold and I loved each other before and we love each other now," Amelia told me when Hal went to tell his parents the wonderful news and we were alone. "You almost ruined it for me, Charlie. Please don't do that again." Her words were delivered softly, but I could hear new determination in her voice.

"I meant well. You know I did. I don't want anything bad to happen to you ever again."

"I know Harold isn't an Adonis, or terribly witty, and that some people think he's . . . well, silly. But he's kind and gentle and he loves me – and he's very rich. My plans were always to marry Harold. I know he'll take care of me."

"Is that what you want? To be taken care of? I can take care of you. I have a good job and my own apartment."

"I'm not independent like you are, Charlie. I don't want to be on my own. I want to be Harold Holmes' wife. His parents are very kind to me. They've asked me to think of them as my parents."

"Were you shocked to learn Mother was Jewish? I didn't intend to spring it on you like that. I planned to tell you when the time was right."

"I never worry about things like that. I loved you, Daddy, and Harold. Now that we don't have Daddy anymore, I can love you and Harold and his parents."

Any frustration I had felt toward my sister for her illness or sudden disappearance evaporated. "I was wrong to stand between you and Hal. Will you ever forgive me?"

My sister smiled, a smile known for its ability to leave the strongest man defenseless. "Only if you'll agree to be my maid of honor."

* * *

The sudden and unexpected trip to Palm Beach provided me with an unscheduled weekend with Raul. My brother-in-law-to-be volunteered to drive me to Raul's home — a place I'd never seen. We followed the directions to a portion of the island inhabited by the sparse year-round population.

"In case Amelia hasn't told you, the man I'm seeing is from Cuba," I explained as we approached the small white cottage, set next to and back from a larger white two-story house. "Dark hair, dark eyes, Latin complexion. He works for Byrd, Regis, and O'Dell. He's a lawyer. Raul Francesco is his name. Since we're going to be related, I thought you should know."

"You're seeing a lawyer? Oh no, not that — anything but a lawyer. Heh-heh-heh." Hal winked at me. "You know I'm just kidding, don't you?"

Like it or not, Hal Holmes was growing on me. I'd have to find some way to block out that annoying laugh. "I sorry that I misjudged you, Hal. I know you and Amelia will be very happy together."

"Thank you, Charlie. That means a lot to me."

I kissed his cheek before saying goodbye.

"You look exhausted," Raul said when he opened the door. He reached for my overnight bag. "How about a glass of wine? Red or white?"

"Anything, doubled." I quickly glanced around the room — tacky mismatched furniture, industrial strength fabric, a worn carpet. Doctors' waiting rooms were more tasteful. But it was cozy.

"The house came furnished. You don't think I picked this stuff, do you?" Raul said, as though he was reading my mind.

"You're in better shape that I am. My apartment has only the bare essentials."

The fatigue and strain lifted as I sipped the wine and related the events of the past day. Needless to say, I omitted my initial confusion and subsequent fright over the identity of the "nice young man."

*   *   *

The next morning Raul and I removed the last of my belongings from my stepmother's home. I would have to sort and decide which items to discard and which I would ship to New York. For a change of scenery, we drove to Lake Worth and spent the day at the beach and walking around the town. Before we left, I suggested we shop for the ingredients I would need to make dinner for the two of us. Meatloaf was a recently acquired skill and I was looking forward to showing off.

As dinner cooked, I received an excited telephone call from Amelia. Chatting with my sister, the way we used to do several light-years ago, made me feel like a carefree girl again.

"The wedding will take place in May at the Holmes' country club in Newport," I told Raul after I'd hung up. Amelia and Hal wanted to get married sooner, but Hal's mother wouldn't hear of it.

"Nice girls don't marry helter-skelter unless there's a pressing reason to do so," I said, quoting Amelia, who had earlier quoted Faith Holmes. "You'll never guess who's giving Amelia twenty-four place settings of any sterling silver pattern, plus whatever china she chooses, as a wedding gift."

"Your stepmother."

"Okay. Which one?"

"Too easy. Petal Morgan," he said, cocking his head and looking smug.

"How did you know?"

"Elementary, my dear Watson. Your sister is marrying a Holmes. A pricey gift will insure any hard feelings resulting from past treatment will be forgotten, and Petal will be invited to the wedding."

"Nice work, Sherlock. But if you're so smart, take a look at the contents of that box in the corner and tell me what you make of it."

Raul thoughtfully examined the puzzling papers. "Blank stationary, assorted letterheads. Some of this is so yellowed with age the companies probably aren't in business any longer. There're several pages that are written on, but they're nearly impossible to read. Here's one, either in Italian or French, I'm not sure. The script is very odd. You speak French. Can you make out what it says?"

I wiped my hands on a towel and walked over to inspect the letter. "It's French and it's a letter between friends. It's dated August 2nd, 1895 and it was done with a quill."

"How can you tell?"

"Just for fun, when I was in high school, I tried calligraphy using a quill. There's scarcely any deviation in the width of lettering with a ballpoint pen. With a fountain pen, the harder you press the wider the imprint. The same holds true for a quill, except there are even more variations. The results can be very artistic."

"Are we talking about a feather?"

"I suppose we could be, but what's more commonly meant is a metal pen point inserted into a holder. It's also referred to as a quill."

We exchanged the pages and separately inspected them. There seemed to be nothing to link them. The letters were written by several apparently unrelated people. "My question is, where would Daddy find papers like these?"

"He might have bought an old desk or found the box in one of your stepmother's antiques."

"Then why hang onto them?"

"I bought the old bureau in my bedroom from the Salvation Army. The top drawer contained an envelope filled with an old woman's memorabilia: snapshots taken when she was young, postcards from Atlantic City, a pressed corsage, and a packet of love letters tied with a faded ribbon. There was nothing in her things to indicate a husband or children. She must have died a lonely old maid. I couldn't bring myself to throw it away."

"You sentimental old thing."

"One large envelope — all that was left of a entire life. How could I throw it away?" Raul patted his lap. "Come here. I want to discuss something important with you. We have decisions to make."

"Can't it wait? We can talk after dinner. The meatloaf must be done by now."

I used every ploy I could think of during dinner, short of doing a striptease, to distract and delay. I knew what was coming. We had decisions to make. Another request not to return to New York. But no amount of chest stroking, coy smiles, or my other blatant hints were going to deter this conversation.

"Now," he said, as he dried the last glass I'd just washed.

"Bedroom? I bet you're dying to show me your bureau, the one with your little old lady's love letters."

"Living room now," he said, tugging my hand. "Bedroom later."

"Where should I sit?" His lap would provide more opportunity for diversion.

"Anywhere I can see your face where we can't touch. It's too easy to be distracted."

I chose the floor next to his chair.

"Topic Number One, you asked me to help you discover the reason your father killed himself. I think I have the answer. We were very close when you told me about the paintings your father brought from Paris. I think the paintings he sold when he first returned to the States belonged to your mother's family. It would make sense for them to entrust their valuables to your father under the circumstances."

"So why did he change our names?"

"All three women your father married, including your mother, were socially and financially above him. My guess is he wanted to reinvent himself in order to fit into Palm Beach society. Alan Fitzpatrick was an uneducated man from a blue-collar neighborhood in Philadelphia. Jack Morgan could be anyone he wanted to be."

"If he changed our names, how would my grandparents contact us after the war?"

"When your father took you and Amelia to Paris, did he ever leave you to run an errand or to visit someone by himself?"

"Amelia and I shopped and went to movies a few afternoons, and I know what you're thinking. Daddy took us to Paris to look for my grandparents. But my grandfather was dead and probably my grandmother as well. I know that because I was unable to locate her."

"Maybe he was looking for more than your grandparents. I don't think the Renoir belonged to them or he probably would've sold it sooner. I think you were right when you guessed it belonged to Jews who wanted to smuggle valuables out of the country. That would explain why your father hung onto it. After Norma divorced him, he was desperate for money, so he sold the only thing of value he had left."

"But if the owners were dead, where's the crime?" I asked, repeating what so often had been asked of me.

"Ah, but maybe the owners hadn't died. Maybe they'd moved, or they left heirs who later came looking for the paintings. They may have hired a professional to find Alan Fitzpatrick. It would've taken a private investigator years to uncover the switch in identities. By that time, the paintings were long gone and so was the money. If the newspapers uncovered the story, your stepmother would have instantly divorced your father. You know how she detests publicity. A man who changed his name, who's accused of stealing priceless works of art from helpless victims — helpless Jewish victims? He could've been sent to jail."

Daddy's note had said that he was trying to protect Amelia and me. Raul's explanation made sense. It not only agreed with what I'd uncovered, it fit my father's character. We had the last piece of the puzzle.

Raul reached over and brought my head to his knee. "Are you okay?"

"Yeah."

"You should be relieved. Your father had his faults, but he wasn't unprincipled."

"But that doesn't mean I'm not heartbroken. What a waste! A crazy, stupid, idiotic waste."

"Come here," he said, pulling me onto his lap. "You look very tired."

With my cool cheek resting on Raul's warm shoulder I agreed, "Tired, sad and disappointed."

Chapter Twenty-One

Knowing in advance the attention we would attract as a couple, but determined not to be deterred, after breakfast the next day we toured Palm Beach. Raul took my hand and smiled genially at every person we passed. When we reached Worth Avenue I joined the game.

"I have plans that I want to discuss with you," he said. "You know that I've always wanted to go out on my own. Well, I decided it's time. I have some money saved, and I've found a location in Miami. I know enough people there to practically guarantee me a clientele the day I hang up my shingle."

"Have you given notice?" I asked, matching the expectant excitement in my voice to his.

"Not yet. You're part of my plans. Within the year I want to make Hal Holmes my brother-in-law."

It took a moment to register. He had proposed. I had anticipated another request to return to Florida, not this. It wasn't until Raul turned to look at me that I realized I'd stopped walking. My feet had temporarily forgotten their purpose. "I can't. Not now," I whispered, as I resumed walking.

"I don't know about you, but I'm not willing to go on like this, seeing you for a long weekend every other month, and then having to separate."

"It's not as though we don't talk in between," I said. "I thought you loved our telephone conversations."

"They leave me frustrated and angry – angry with you and angry with myself."

"I can try to come down more often. I don't like being separated either."

"It's not enough. I'm a traditional man from a traditional home. We get married and we have a family. What did you think I had in mind?"

I squeezed his hand. "It's just that I don't want to stop working yet and I can't work in Miami."

"You hate modeling."

"I don't hate modeling. I find it boring. But I like being independent. I like having my own apartment. I'm just starting to get control of my life. What I hate is being broke and helpless. I'm never going to be broke and helpless again. When I'm no longer in demand as a model, I'll find something else to do." My strong words sounded far more confident than I felt. I felt sick. And pushed. And panicky.

"Then change careers now," he coaxed. "I'm not saying you have to stay at home and do nothing. You can work if you want, until we have children. You do want children, don't you?"

"Of course I want children, but I'm not ready to make that sort of decision right now. Everything is happening too fast."

"I'm sorry, Charlie. I can't go on like this. I can't watch the world passing two-by-two and come home to an empty house every night."

"And I don't like Miami. It's too hot in the summer."

Raul halted. "Miami's too hot in the summer, but Palm Beach is fine. Try being honest with me."

"Fine, I'll be honest with you. I can understand that you want to live in Miami to be near your family. But I don't feel comfortable there. I don't fit in."

"It's all right to date me, to be seen walking with me like this, but not to marry me," he said, his voice severe and his face tight with resentment. "I can tell you how much I love you, how much you mean to me, but when it comes right down to it, I don't make the grade. I can never be a part of your world. That's why you can't say that you love me, isn't it?"

"It's not like that. I'm not like that," I said, looking down at the pavement and then back up at his sad reproachful eyes.

"But you are like that, Charlie. How many people have you told that your mother was Jewish? You're ashamed of it. You're ashamed of me. You may not realize it but you've never gone out of your way to introduce me to a single friend?"

The accusation stung like angry wasps. Was it true? I'd told Hal about Raul, but what about other people? Was Raul right? I hadn't introduced him to my friends in Palm Beach or New York. Was I keeping him to myself, or hiding him? All I knew for certain was that I wasn't ready to get married and I was hot. Hot, damp, and drained. The combined heat from the sun and pavement was oppressive. It was hard to breathe.

"Would you like me to drive you to the Holmes' this evening?" Raul asked when we reached the ocean.

Was this how it would end? Would I always remember watching the waves lapping the sand while two thugs took turns pounding on my chest? I was losing more than a sweetheart. I was saying good-bye forever to my best friend. "I'd appreciate it if you would drive me to the Holmes. I'm sure they can make room for me." I was very good at polite. It was honesty that I needed to work on.

Raul nodded.

I turned away. I couldn't bear to see his face and wouldn't allow him to see my burning tears.

Chapter Twenty-Two

October, 1940

With a signed letter on Claude Pelletier's official stationary and Georgette's chauffeur driving, exiting Paris proceeded without incident. From there, they traveled by rail. Alan did what he could to divert the girls, walking them from car to car, permitting them to chatter with the other anxious passengers. The monotony was interrupted by nightmarish stops when German soldiers boarded the train and reviewed passengers' documents. Those travelers whose papers were considered suspicious were removed from the train at gunpoint. Tensions escalated. Both girls grew fussy and irritable. Michelle wet herself while sleeping — something she hadn't done for months. The children repeatedly asked why their mother wasn't with them until Alan stopped responding. He silently cursed Nicole's obstinacy.

Two days out of Paris, at a routine station stop, the conductor once again demanded their traveling documents. The young German soldier who accompanied him appeared agitated, his eyes continuously scanning the passengers. He fondled his pistol with his thin elegant fingers as the conductor examined their papers. "You are Jews?" he asked in German.

Since Paris had been occupied Alan had learned enough German to understand the crucial word. *Juden.* "A Fitzpatrick, that's a Jew?" he answered in English, praying his interrogator understood the gist of what he was saying. "That's a good one. I'm as Catholic as the Pope. But more important, I'm an American citizen. *Americanishe!* We are all *Americanishe* citizens! President Roosevelt does not take kindly to American citizens being harassed."

"Your Jew-loving Roosevelt can go to hell," the soldier spat at Alan. He bent to stare, first into Maggie's face and then into Michelle's.

Maggie tried a tentative smile and received a frown in return. Michelle stuck out her tongue.

"Michelle, that's very rude," Alan told his daughter in French, tugging her hand. "You must apologize. Repeat after me in English, '*I'm sorry.*'"

"I sorry."

The conductor returned their papers, and he and the soldier moved on to the next passengers, a gray-haired couple who held hands as they were questioned. Strangely, as the miles separated him from Paris and Nicole, in spite of the many discomforts, the never-ending needs of the girls, and his fears for their safety, despite a thousand unforeseen hazards he imagined Nicole facing, Alan felt a rebirth of energy. He no longer felt like an actor playing a role.

*   *   *

The first thing Alan noticed about Bea Loomis was her short, stocky legs — noticed them before he observed her smiling at him from a park bench across the path. He and the girls had been staying with his sister and her family for more than a month, a temporary arrangement. Bea was a woman in her mid-fifties with short, coarse dark hair and a warm gap-toothed smile.

"Would it be all right if I gave the girls a lollipop?" Bea opened her purse and waited until Alan nodded. "I seen you out here every day the last few weeks – you and the girls. I live across the street." She pointed at a recently painted brown two-story house with a porch, little different from others on the block.

Michelle and Maggie interrupted their game of tag to turn to look at him. "One each," he said.

"*Merci, Madame,*" Maggie said, eyes twinkling, every dimple fully flexed.

Michelle took the next one. "*Merci, Madame,*" she whispered.

"In English, please," Alan said.

The girls repeated their thanks as directed.

"They speak French. Heavens, what lovely children. You're very welcome." She waited until the girls had skipped away. "If someone from Hollywood took one gander at your older girl she'd be a movie star like Shirley Temple."

Alan chatted with the pleasant woman while the girls took turns showing off for her. Maggie sang a song and Michelle did a succession of somersaults which tangled her hair and rumpled her clothes. Both performances received hearty applause. Indeed, everything they did seemed to delight her.

When Alan and the girls had moved into Fiona's already overcrowded house, he had forgotten the noise and confusion that accompanies a large group of people living in close quarters, sharing a single bathroom. He soon discovered that unlike his sister, Bea Loomis lived alone. She had inherited the house, as well as several other properties in the area, from her recently deceased husband, the hard working teetotaler Frederick Loomis. Mr. Loomis had no other heirs.

"So you see, Alan, having you and the girls in the upstairs bedrooms would be no trouble at all. I would enjoy the company and . . . Well, I'm sure you can see that I love children. Fred and I never had any of our own."

"About the rent," Alan said. "I would have to ask you to be patient. I'm an art dealer. I should be closing a sale on one of my works within a week or so."

"You're an art dealer, are you? I knew right away you was a gentleman. I've got an eye for these things. I also see a great sadness when I look at you." Bea lowered her voice. "It's those little girls' mother, isn't it? She's ill, isn't she? That's why you're always alone with the girls?"

"She should be in Switzerland by now with her brother. He was wounded while fighting for France. She was supposed to have come with us, but . . ."

"I knew it. I knew the minute I laid eyes on you. You're worried about your wife. And it's all that blasted Hitler's fault. He's the devil, Alan. Satan with a mustache."

Alan moved their belongings to Bea Loomis's home the following day. She cooked for them, cleaned for them, and over his objections, did their laundry as well. The girls saw her as another nanny, patient and affectionate. In return, Alan insisted upon assisting her with her packages and twice weekly hauled two large garbage pails to the sidewalk. When he did finally sell the first of the paintings, he paid her the paltry sum that Bea resolutely maintained was all he owed.

Fall turned into winter. The ground became hard and cold. Mounds of dirty snow refused to melt. Fear for Nicole's safety combined with anger. Three months had passed since their arrival without word from her. Messages from Hortense were increasingly desperate. Alan no longer trusted himself to read her letters while the girls were awake. They watched his face and became anxious and clingy.

In Paris, the price of food and fuel had soared, Hortense wrote. Many items were unavailable at any price. The Vichy government, eager to placate their oppressors, surrendered their immigrant Jews. New laws and reinterpretation of old laws, including the definition of immigrants, changed daily. The two words his in-laws had come to dread were "immigrant" and "Jews." People who had lived in France for twenty and thirty years and had married French citizens, were being reclassified as immigrants. Men, women, and children were taken away and not heard from again.

Every letter required the same purifying ritual. Alan would put it in his drawer with the others, close the door to his room, ask Bea to watch the girls for a few hours, and take himself to the nearest saloon for a night of drinking himself numb. The next morning he would appear at the breakfast table pleasant and alert. After three torturous months he received a letter forwarded to him by Hortense, written by his wife.

It had taken Nicole six weeks to reach the town where Philippe had been taken. When she arrived there French troops had vacated. Fortunately, the area was still part of the so-called "free" section, so there were no German encampments. Desperate to learn where Philippe had been taken, Nicole had showed his picture and questioned whoever she met. Farmers told her the soldiers had left weeks before. A priest looked at the formal photo taken of Philippe and told her he didn't remember seeing anyone who resembled the young man. The letter ended with Nicole explaining she intended to continue questioning people in the area. She sent her love to him and the children.

Alan threw the letter on the dresser, slammed the door, and strode past gentle Bea Loomis without a word of explanation.

The next letter from Nicole arrived three weeks later and was a month old. She had written from Lyon, only miles from the Swiss border. God alone knew what had led her there. Obviously, she'd written other letters that had never arrived. In this letter she acknowledged the futility of chasing rumors. She swore if she didn't have concrete evidence about Philippe's location, she would head for Switzerland and her family. She sent kisses and love and asked them all to pray for her. Hortense's accompanying letter began so hopelessly, Alan put off reading until the next morning.

As time passed he saw less of his sister and her family. The inevitable questions about Nicole were too painful to answer. Even the girls no longer mentioned their mother. As young as they were, they knew any reference her would catapult Alan into a daylong depression.

Three of the paintings had been sold at auctions and brought enough money to carry them for the next several months. Two landscapes and a still-life remained — and the two family jokes. Alan refused to consider taking a job. His girls were too young for school and still needed him. When their mother arrived, he would look for employment.

There was one place where he went to relieve the monotony, a long bar at one of the finer hotels. There he could enjoy the company of men, not only locals with their familiar complaints, or soldiers on leave, but men who traveled, dabbled in politics, and hobnobbed with the elite and powerful. One blustery evening in February Alan found himself listening to a series of entertaining anecdotes told by a recently retired butler named James Forsythe. Forsythe was the real McCoy — clipped British accent, buffed nails, droll sense of humor, as engaging a gentleman's gentleman as any Hollywood producer could manufacture. He was on his way to Canada to visit his married daughter. As the evening wore on, and the whiskey they consumed had time to take its effect, the two men became increasingly informal.

"As a young lad I lived through far drearier than this," Forsythe confided. "Nonetheless, it's difficult getting oneself adjusted to the cold weather again. My people wintered in Palm Beach."

"That's in Florida, isn't it?"

"Technically, my boy, Palm Beach is in Florida. In truth it's an independent principality owned, operated, and run by the very rich for the very rich."

"And these people live in Palm Beach?"

"Winters they reside in Palm Beach. The rest of the year they have homes in New York, Philadelphia, Chicago, Boston, Newport. Did I say homes? Palaces are more like it. Sultans don't live as well."

"This Palm Beach, is it anywhere near Miami?"

Forsythe leaned conspiratorially closer. "Miami? Hah! Riffraff compared to Palm Beach. I happen to know for a fact that coloreds are free to live in Miami."

"There are no colored people in Palm Beach?"

"Protestants preferred. Catholics tolerated. Jews and coloreds can't go into a hotel or buy a cigar. Against the law. And if you don't live on the island of Palm Beach, you're required to present official documents allowing you to cross the bridge. Coloreds must have documents simply to haul away trash. I knew you'd be shocked when I told you. I could tell you were a decent sort when I met you. There's the look of a gentleman about you too." Forsythe sipped his drink. "Have you ever been on a yacht the length of a rugby field? That's a sight you don't see every day."

Forsythe prattled on with Alan drinking in every word. He could almost see the sandy beaches, the palm trees, bathrooms with gold faucets – homes with glittering ballrooms that could hold two hundred people or more at one time. A lush oasis. A Shangri La. He could almost feel the balmy warm breeze, taste the champagne.

"These people know how to spend money, not that they ever sent any my way. Raspberries in the middle of winter, caviar, mansions, Packards, Rolls Royces, limousines — five for every one they need. Thirty-six years in service, nineteen of them here in the States, and I still can't get accustomed to it."

"The money?" Alan asked.

"Not just the money. I can understand that money means nothing to them — they have so much of it. What I find hard to accept is that the world can't touch them. Nothing touches them. Not the Depression. Not Prohibition. Prohibition came and went and these people never missed a dance step. Not even this bloody war affects them. Hardships? Rationing? Coffee, sugar, butter? They've got it. Anything you want."

"I've had trouble buying shoes for my girls. They outgrow them so quickly."

"Not these people. Ration cards mean nothing to them."

"After Pearl Harbor didn't any of the men enlist? I'd be at the recruiters in a minute, if it weren't for my girls."

"Some of the men did. I think they fancy the uniform. Not that they're in the bunkers with the enlisted men. They go on to be colonels and generals and such, like that MacArthur chap. Married above himself and left his beautiful young wife to kick up her heels at one soiree after another, with one man or another, while he was off liberating the Phillipines."

"There must be a lot of lonely ladies with the war going on."

"Ah, the ladies," Forsythe leaned close. "I haven't even begun to describe the ladies. The perfume. The clothes. The diamonds. All the goodies and no morals. Hundreds of them desperate for some manly attention, if you get my drift."

Alan nodded. He was quite familiar with the drift.

*   *   *

Alan read Hortense's letter again. Nicole was dead. Had been dead for more than a month. Hortense had received word that her daughter's body had been found by the French underground near the Swiss border. She had been shot. They had found her address in the papers she was carrying and thoughtfully contacted the family. There was still no word of Philippe.

"We are beyond grief," Hortense had written. "Maurice refuses to eat. If you were to see him now you wouldn't recognize him. We take refuge in the knowledge that you and the children are safe and well. We yearn for the day when you can return. Our girls are all we have now. Protect them. In them Nicole lives on. May g_d bless you and look over you all."

Alan sobbed into his pillow, holding it against his face to muffle the sound, just as he had done when he was eight and had taken another whipping from his father. How could she do this? How could Nicole do this to him? Abandon him. Abandon their daughters. He had warned her, argued with her, begged her. If she had agreed to leave . . . Her brother! She had chosen her brother over her daughters and himself. And what had she accomplished? Nothing! Less than nothing!

Hours later, with the throbbing pain in his temples threatening to explode, Alan made himself a promise. He would never lose himself to a woman again. Never!

*   *   *

Alan unrolled one of the Strauss family jokes, the bogus van Dyck portrait of a nobleman in riding clothes, for Maxwell Muller, the dealer who had sold his other paintings for him. The work had fooled Alan, but could it deceive an expert? His plan required a large sum of money, certainly more than he could acquire from the sale of the two remaining legitimate oils. If he succeeded, humble Alan Fitzpatrick and his darling daughters would no longer exist.

The two men pinned the canvas to a board so that Muller could examine it. Alan assumed a look of polite indifference while the dealer scrutinized the painting at several distances and from numerous angles. "Hmm. Interesting." Muller walked to his desk and removed both a magnifying glass and a jeweler's loupe. First he employed the glass and then the loupe. "Aha! Yes. Very interesting."

He was suspicious. Alan knew it was a damn good forgery, but perhaps this man wasn't as easy to deceive as he'd been. Alan waited. If Muller declared the painting a fake, he would claim ignorance. How was he to know it was a forgery? Surely, possession of a forgery wasn't a crime, was it?

Muller finally turned to him. "I assume the painting belonged to your late wife's family, the same as the others?"

"Yes."

"Were there no survivors other than yourself?"

"No other survivors."

"You do have proof of ownership, a transfer from your wife's family to yourself?"

A pause. Less than a heart-beat. "Of course."

"It's one thing to dispose of a good quality painting without proof, but a major artist like van Dyck requires a complete provenance. Without a provenance . . ."

Was Muller suspicious or simply being prudent? "The provenance, of course. Naturally I keep all provenances in a vault. I didn't think you'd need it today just for a preliminary viewing."

"Here's my advice. Leave the painting with me. I'll have it mounted and framed at my expense. We can deduct the cost later, after it's sold. It'll command a better price if it's framed properly. There are some people I'd like to show it to. Naturally I'll give you a receipt with an estimated value, any amount you wish. And you needn't be concerned about additional insurance. I'll call my agent immediately."

Alan unpinned the van Dyck and rerolled it. "I have to travel to New York. Some personal business I have to attend to. I should be back in . . . let's say two weeks."

Muller watched nervously as Alan rerolled the painting. "I hope you're not planning to show it to another dealer. I'm sure you'd have to agree that I've always dealt with you fairly. Not every dealer is as trustworthy as I am. I thought we had established a nice working relationship. In truth, I consider you more a friend than a client."

Alan made no attempt to interrupt. He had wanted to see if the oil would convince an expert. Apparently it had. He had not considered the necessity of a provenance. None had been requested before. But as Muller had pointed out, the sale of a van Dyck wasn't an everyday event.

"With an item as valuable as this," the dealer continued, "I would consider a more modest percentage. Please don't be fooled by the size of the shop, my friend. I have access to museum directors and private collectors that would astound you. If we can't get the sum that you have every right to expect, we can always resort to an auction."

Obviously, Muller had no reservations. An unqualified success. "I have complete confidence in you, Maxwell. Rest assured that I'll return with the painting and the provenance in two weeks, perhaps three." Muller walked him to the door and gravely shook his hand.

Two weeks to create a provenance. Two weeks should be sufficient time for a resourceful man like himself.

*   *   *

The car rattled rhythmically as the train cut through the night. Alan glanced appreciatively around the stateroom. The compartment was like those in movies — but better. He could touch the velvet benches and run his finger along the polished wood trim. The girls slept in the berths the porter had prepared for them. Michelle's sylph-like face, with her irresistible pout was so much like Nicole's it was almost painful for him to look at her. Maggie's thumb was tucked in her mouth. Nearly five, she was too old for such things. Both girls had clung to their baby ways since leaving Paris. Their luggage was filled with newly purchased clothes. They would start their new lives in style.

Hortense would get half of what she had asked of him. Her grandchildren would be safe and well. They would grow up to be ladies — pampered, accomplished, and accepted by society. No psychotic Jew-hating monster would ever touch them. The half she wouldn't have was their presence. Nicole was dead. No fanatic family member ready to give his life for God-knows-what would ever lay claim to his children. No Strauss would find them. They would have new names and lives. He was taking them to Shangri-la, to become part of the world of the insulated rich. The sale of one of the family jokes had financed this initial leg of his grand plan. Surely Uncle Gaston, the Strauss family scallywag whose artistry and imagination had facilitated this transformation, would wholeheartedly approve.

Constructing perfect provenances — after the first it seemed only sensible to produce one for the quasi-Renoir as well — from the painting's creation to subsequent exhibitions and acquisitions, had taken Alan a month's work. Rummaging through antique furniture he had found blank pages with letterheads, quills, sealing wax, and ink bottles whose contents had discolored with age. A shop that advertised "Serviceable Used Office Furniture", had supplied him with an ancient typewriter and two cartons of yellowed invoices. With a bit of practice he was able to imitate a few kinds of old-fashioned handwritten script. Duplicating engraved seals proved a challenge — but fortunately, thanks to a metalworking class taken in high school, a surmountable one. Personal letters used to substantiate transfer of ownership were his favorites, particularly those between family members or lovers. Though time consuming to compose, the letters provided the greatest opportunity for creativity.

He had improvised devilishly clever tricks to add authenticity, such as holding a page over a flame to age it and allowing ashes from his cigar to burn pinholes. Libraries and museums seemed to be run by the bored, guileless, and gullible. Administrators were happy to accommodate a charming amateur art historian like himself, who wished to use their facilities for research. Uniformed security guarded the priceless artwork. Scant attention was given to the seemingly worthless supporting documentation. It was childishly easy for him to leave with catalogs and pamphlets in his briefcase, and just as simple to return after he had amended them.

It was rather like a game, a game made just for him – a practical application of his assorted, and heretofore unvalued talents. Deliciously irresistible! A lackluster painter with a tolerable knowledge of art, a gift for invention, and a dash of irreverence, could make an outstanding forger. It was a pity his newly discovered skills would be wasted.

Chapter Twenty-Three

Confused and depressed back in New York, with Amelia well, safe, and happy, and the mystery of my father's suicide solved, I only had my work for distraction. Determined to exhaust myself into numbness, I accepted every last minute, weekend, inconvenient, and undesirable assignment. I covered more pavement than any New York City mailman.

A Budweiser beer ad for television shot at a dude ranch in the Catskills was only a one-day shoot, but because of the traveling involved, we left the city at six a.m. and returned after midnight.

I needed a hard-hat for another commercial, the brainchild of Mayor John Lindsay Wagner, the *"I Love New York"* campaign. The building we used was under construction – no walls, only steel beams and a temporary platform for a floor. Luckily, I don't suffer from a fear of heights or open spaces because the view was awe-inspiring.

I agreed to do a magazine layout for *Vogue* with Lance Kreisler, the most unpredictable and volatile photographer in Manhattan, a man I'd managed to avoid in the past. Considering Kreisler's reputation, the day went relatively smoothly. He had only one tirade that fortunately wasn't directed at me.

Falling asleep was difficult. Staying asleep was impossible. At two, or three, or four in the morning I wandered about my apartment and tortured myself with thoughts of Raul smiling, laughing, his arm around one of the buxom beauties I had seen at his parents' home. Ten pounds slipped away. My clothes no longer fit. I once again weighed what I had in the weeks following my father's death. I felt as though I was confined to a sunless maze. If I saw an elderly couple help each other cross the street, my eyes filled with tears. The unexpected sentiment in a movie made me weep uncontrollably. When I spent an evening with friends, I was a spectator and not a participant. I often thought of contacting Jeremy Randall, but I wasn't ready to answer the unavoidable questions about Raul. I was afraid Jeremy's heartfelt concern would cause me to burst into tears. I didn't want the compassionate man – who seemed eager to take me on as an apprentice after my career as a model ended – forced to watch me bawling like a baby. It seemed decidedly unprofessional.

It was ironic. After years of wanting suitors and lacking them, now that I no longer cared, I was pursued. Friends arranged blind dates. Belinda was seeing a Broadway producer and he had a friend, a recently divorced friend – very nice, very handsome, very successful. The evening ended early. He was handsome. Nice was debatable. As for successful, I lost patience with his bragging and invented a migraine headache.

I refused most invitations, but when I was once again feeling particularly low, I accepted one from Stan Greystone to a gala cocktail party. It was to be held at the Guggenheim Museum. I'd met Stan at lunch during a work break. He knew the model I was with, called her and got my phone number. He was four or five inches shorter than I was in my stocking feet – a detail that didn't seem to disturb him. In fact, since I'd begun modeling, I'd noticed my height was no longer a dating liability. Apparently, models were permitted deviations from the norm other women weren't. Stan proudly paraded me around, introducing me to people he knew. I felt more like an accessory than a date. I didn't return Stan's next call.

Facing Thanksgiving was particularly hard. I had no desire to fly to spend the holiday with Amelia and the Holmes. Sunny Florida didn't match my dark mood. And it would be too painful to be in Palm Beach and not see Raul. So while others were dining on cranberries and turkey, I occupied the single orchestra seat I'd purchased for *West Side Story*, having forgotten it was a modern-day *Romeo and Juliet*. By the tragic ending, I had a pounding headache.

When I was alone I put myself on trial. As prosecutor, I hurled Raul's worst accusations at myself. I hadn't introduced him to friends. I'd refused to marry him because I was a snob, a bigot, and materialistic. As the defendant, I systematically refuted every accusation. I wasn't looking for a rich man to take care of me. I wanted to take care of myself. If I hadn't introduced Raul to my friends, it was because we had so little time together. I wasn't a bigot or a snob. I hadn't chosen how and where I'd been raised. It wasn't my fault that Raul and I were no longer together. It was entirely his doing. He was the one who had demanded all or nothing. I needed time. My father had taken his life less than a year ago. My entire existence had been turned inside out. Everything I'd known to be true had turned out to be a lie. It was unreasonable of Raul to demand an immediate decision. So why did I feel so empty? Why did I long to be warm and safe in his arms?

When Christmas approached, I called Amelia and gave her a plausible excuse about not being able to join her for the holiday because of a critical shoot. Once again, the lie was easier to deliver than the truth. I could hear the disappointment in her voice, but she would be with Hal and his family. I would be alone. Damn Raul! Damn Daddy! Damn men who made you care about them! I bought myself a gift — the best and largest television set I could find. I would spend my late nights watching Jack Paar — a man who could neither see nor touch me.

In my fervor to contest Raul's accusation that I was ashamed of my heritage, I decided to interview the only Jewish person I knew well. I reasoned that if Sid Gluck had no qualms about telling me to shave under my arms and not get pregnant, the very least he could do in return was answer a few questions.

I waited until everyone had left for the day and then knocked on his door. Seated behind his desk, Mr. Gluck glowered at me from under his bushy eyebrows. He motioned for me to sit. My courage evaporated. "I'm not sure how to say this, Mr. Gluck. Maybe this isn't a good time."

"W-w-w-what is it, Charlie? Someone made you a better offer? You're leaving me? I gave you a chance when no one else would, and now you're leaving me."

"No, nothing like that, Mr. Gluck. You've been very kind to me. I have no plans to work for another firm."

"You're getting m-m-married," he bellowed. "Another one who wants to get married. Tell your boyfriend that it's no disgrace to have a wife who earns more money than he does. Believe me. I know. A couple of good years with me, and you'll be able to buy a house. How many young people today can afford to do that? Children you can have later. Oy, don't tell me. Not you too. You're pregnant. F-f-franklin Delano Roosevelt, I never saw a person get so red."

"I'm not pregnant, and I'm not getting married," I said, wondering what the late president had to do with my proclivity to blush. "I would like to talk with you about something else entirely. Would it be all right if I closed the door?"

He leaned back in his chair and covered his eyes with his stubby hands. "Sure, c-c-c-close the door. So what's on your mind?"

I returned to my chair, took a deep breath and gave myself a mental kick. "It occurred to me that you're Jewish. I don't know any Jewish people — person, other than yourself. That is to say, I've met a few, but none that I can ask . . . "

"And?"

He looked both impatient and suspicious. I called on the Holy Spirit to guide me. As usual, He remained elusive. I plunged on. "Both my parents are deceased. I've recently discovered that I'm half Jewish —"

"Your mother was a Jew."

"How did you know that?"

"How do I know? I'm c-c-clairvoyant. With a name like 'Morgan' I should think your father was a Jew? Well, Charlie, according to our laws, if your mother was a Jew, you're a Jew."

"I am?"

"According to our laws. Also according to Hitler, a p-p-pox on his head, may he rot in Hell for all eternity — to Hitler, you'd also be a Jew."

So it was true. I was officially Jewish. Two wildly divergent authorities agreed. No wonder the Holy Spirit refused my calls.

Gluck rolled up his sleeve and pointed to numbers tattooed on his forearm. "Do you know what this is?"

I couldn't describe the wave of nausea, the acrid taste in my mouth, the horror at seeing numbers burned into human flesh. My mouth hung open. Speech eluded me. I'd heard about such things, seen them in newsreels and on television, but I'd never given them much thought. Suddenly, pale, skeletal people with sunken tragic eyes staggered across the stage of my mind – frail, barely-alive men, women, and children.

"Oy, look at you! First red, now white as a ghost. You're not going to be sick, are you?" Gluck didn't wait for my reply. He frantically fanned me with his newspaper. "I didn't mean to upset you."

"You were in a concentration camp?" I croaked hoarsely, as soon as I could speak.

"I was at Dachau for seventeen months."

"Your family?"

"My parents, my sisters and brother, my uncles, my aunts, g-g-gone. Taken away. K-k-killed. All of them. Everyone but a cousin who lives in Israel."

"I'm so sorry."

He rolled down his sleeve. "My Rosalie is right. Sometimes I don't think before I talk. But you needn't be upset. It's not so terrible to be a Jew. This is America — land of the free, home of the brave. Where a poor immigrant like yours truly, with fourteen dollars in his pocket when he walked off the boat, can work hard and become a big shot." He smiled at me from under his unruly eyebrows. "You're not afraid of me anymore? You used to be afraid of me."

"I was never afraid of you — well, I was a little afraid of you, but mostly you just embarrassed me."

"You think you're the only one who was embarrassed? You think it's so easy for me to say those things? B-b-believe me, it's a lot easier to talk like that before I get to know a girl. You'd be shocked how many of the things I told you that day, girls coming to New York for the first time need to be told. What about you? Are you feeling better now?"

"Much. Thank you."

"It's funny, Charlie, you don't look Jewish. You must look like your father."

I smirked. There was no other word for it. I smirked. "Actually, I strongly resemble my mother."

"You look like your mother. That's a good one on me. I forget. Like ice cream, Jews come in all flavors. So, *shayna yiddisha maydelle*, that's pretty Jewish girl translated, you came to me for a reason. So tell me what you want."

"I want to know what it means to be a Jew."

"To me you came for such an important question? B-b-better you should talk to a rabbi. I could tell you the wrong things. In my house we don't even keep kosher."

"I'll understand if you'd prefer not to." But I stood firm without looking away. After all I'd endured to get to this point, I had no intention of leaving now.

"Oh, what the — There's more to being a Jew than keeping kosher. You have p-p-plans for tonight? Someplace you have to go?"

"No. No plans."

He reached for the jacket hanging on the coat rack to the right of his desk. "You'll have dinner with my Rosalie and the children."

*   *   *

I took a cab home that night. As I sat in the rear seat, the smoke from the driver's cigarette drifting back to me, I reviewed what had transpired earlier that evening. Sid Gluck and his wife had a twelve-year-old daughter named Judy and a ten-year-old son named Barry. The Gluck family embarrassed me with their blunt questions, astonished me with their uninhibited bickering, and overwhelmed me with hospitality. Barry said that I talked funny. Judy declared my accent elegant. Mrs. Gluck, who wanted to be called Rosalie, thought I was too skinny and kept refilling my plate.

Mr. Gluck defended my weight and declared me lucky because I didn't have to starve myself like other models he employed. There was a great deal of discussion about whether anyone present knew a Jewish girl as tall as me. No one did.

If the Glucks were typical, although I had no basis to believe my solitary sampling was indicative of the larger group, Jews *were* different from the people I'd known. For one thing, Jews seemed to enjoy poking fun at themselves. They spoke louder and with more intensity. They kissed a great deal. Descriptions of holidays involved food — either one fasted or feasted. Indeed, food seemed of preeminent importance. Kosher laws – rigid rules about food selection, preparation and consumption – were too complicated to contemplate. The Glucks explained that *some* people still kept kosher kitchens, but they considered the practice outdated.

I learned that Jews don't recognize the divinity of Jesus Christ. No Gluck had any understanding whatsoever of the Trinity. In fact, the God the Glucks described seemed rather uncomplicated by comparison to the one I knew. Do this! Don't do that! The basic ten commandments, as far as I could see. And the concept of Heaven and Hell I had been taught was fundamental, seemed extremely fuzzy. None of the Glucks was certain if earthly behavior either guaranteed reward or punishment after death. Really! What reason would a person have to be good if not to ensure better treatment after death?

I couldn't wait to resume my investigation. It was hard to remember a time when I had eaten so much or laughed more.

"*Shalom aleichem*," I told the tired driver when I paid my fare — a phrase I'd been taught earlier that evening. He returned a blank expression.

I translated. "Peace be with you."

"Yeah, lady, same to you."

* * *

My friends were either busy with last minute shopping or attending Christmas parties. Gifts on my list had been purchased, wrapped, and mailed weeks earlier, and my weekend calendar was empty. Rather than resume useless self-pity I decided to call Jeremy. Luckily he was in town.

"I would invite you to my apartment but I'm still decorating," I said, eyeing the tiny tree I'd set on an upended wastepaper basket.

"It's not very comfortable as yet. But there's a nice little Italian restaurant just down the street. I'd be delighted if you'd be my guest."

"That's very thoughtful of you, my dear, but entirely unnecessary. Restaurants are so crowded this time of year. It would be much simpler if you came here."

I wrote the date on my calendar and underlined it twice. The next day, feeling festive, I purchased two extravagant bottles of champagne. As I walked home I remembered Disraeli. No doubt Jeremy, as his employer, would remember him with a Christmas gift, but I doubted that anyone else would.

*   *   *

"Merry Christmas. This is for you." Before allowing Disraeli to help me remove my coat I handed him a small package. He looked at it and then returned it.

"A Christmas gift for you," I repeated, placing it in his hands. He stared at me. This would take some doing. I removed the paper, opened the box, and removed a pair of lined leather gloves. "These are for you. Put them on. See if they fit."

"Disraeli, bring Miss Morgan here," Jeremy called from the other room.

"I'll be there in a moment," I replied. It took a bit of body language and considerable persuasion, but I finally convinced Disraeli the gift was for him and that I wouldn't move until he tried them on.

With the index finger of his gloved hand he touched my forehead and then his own. Inordinately pleased with myself, I hummed as I walked down the long hall. Deck the halls with boughs of holly, fa, la, la, la, la, la.

I presented my host with the brightly wrapped bottles of champagne and kissed him on both cheeks. "Merry Christmas, Jeremy."

"My dear, aren't you the most delightful young lady? First you grace me with your presence, and then you insist on bringing gifts."

The evening was extraordinarily pleasant. Disraeli served the dinner the cook had prepared and the conversation never lagged. There seemed to be no point on the globe Jeremy hadn't visited — Europe, Asia, South Africa. His was an extraordinary life for a man plagued with such a debilitating disease. He had been entertained by shahs and princes, presidents and prime ministers. Jeremy had actually asked an African potentate if he had difficulty remembering the names of his many wives and concubines. The potentate confessed that he'd never addressed them by name, only by terms of endearment.

"What about your many sons?" Jeremy had pressed.

"They are the sons of a king. I gave them my name," the potentate had said, chuckling and immensely pleased with his solution. "That way I only have to remember one – mine."

As we laughed and chatted a thought came to me. "My father sold a valuable painting about ten years ago. A Renoir. It's only natural that he would've wanted you to handle the sale, or at the very least, requested your opinion."

"He did ask me to advise him what it might bring," Jeremy said, apparently surprised I knew about the painting. "It wasn't one of the artist's finest efforts. Nevertheless, the appearance of an unknown Renoir caused quite a stir."

"A German industrialist bought it."

"I don't remember the details. I was spending most of my time in London, the Middle East and Asia around that time."

"Did my father say how and when he had obtained it?"

"Ah, now I understand your curiosity," Jeremy said smiling. "He told me that it was part of a settlement between him and his former wife. I didn't inquire how it came to be in her possession. Should I have?"

"No. Certainly not." The story my father had given him more or less matched Raul's theory. The former wife was my deceased mother.

At ten-thirty I rose to leave.

"Please allow me to engage a car service for you," Jeremy said. "You may not find a cab."

"I'll walk. I live only ten minutes from here." It was a bit of a lie. Twenty minutes was more accurate. "With so many people out shopping and going to Christmas parties, the streets are quite safe."

"Well then, I must insist that Disraeli accompany you. The very notion of your leaving my home this late at night alone is unthinkable. Your father would never forgive me if something happened to you. I would never forgive myself."

As no amount of protest could dissuade my earnest protector, I agreed. The order was given and soon Disraeli trailed silently at my side, a bulky article under his jacket. Feeling somewhat frightened I reminded myself of the beatific smile I had received earlier. And Jeremy trusted the man. When we arrived at my home I thanked him and turned to go inside. A hand stopped me. Disraeli flung his head back. Darkened deformed teeth gaping at me, he reached under his jacket. I waited, poised to bolt. A large book emerged. He handed it to me. "Paint. You paint."

I took the book and moved to a spot on the sidewalk with more light. It was an illustrated book of Impressionist paintings. Disraeli had seen the paint on my arm and assumed that I was an artist. Or perhaps he remembered our first meeting at the Frick. The gesture was incredibly touching. The book had to belong to Jeremy. Disraeli had nothing to give me, so he had taken a book from his employer.

"Thank you, but I can't keep this."

Disraeli looked hurt and confused. I could hardly accuse him of stealing. It would be kinder to simply surreptitiously return the book on my next visit. "Thank you so much. It's a wonderful gift."

He dropped his head, smiled shyly, and ambled off.

Back in my apartment I examined the book. Many of the pages were soiled. It had obviously been heavily used by Jeremy. An odd choice. Had Disraeli observed Jeremy either giving or receiving books as gifts? Considering his limited use of language, I'd probably never know.

Chapter Twenty-Four

I had told friends who were certain to feel sorry for me that I was spending Christmas Day with family, so I couldn't very well admit to anyone that I had no plans whatsoever. I decided to hand-deliver gifts to Petal's staff — people who had taken care of my father, my sister, and me. I purchased large boxes of pastries at Ferrara's, a wonderful bakery in Little Italy, and gift-wrapped the boxes myself, taking great care to make them as festive as I could. My stepmother was in Palm Beach, but the staff was pleased to see me. The hour I spent there was the high point of a long lonely day.

Fortunately, I had my choice of New Year's Eve invitations. I chose the escort and party that seemed most likely to be superficial, frivolous, and frenetic. Neither disappointed.

Toward the end of January, Ted Jensen, my eighth grade buddy, called. He had been working in Manhattan since graduating from Duke. When he'd heard that I was living in the city, he contacted my stepmother for my phone number. Ted was the only person who had ever been able to talk me into anything — well, almost anything, certainly more trouble than I would get into on my own. We cut classes — something I had never done before, and didn't do after he moved away. We caught frogs in Central Park and held jumping contests with them. We had teachers searching frantically for erratic electrical devices, by humming softly while seated in the back of the classroom. Naturally the humming ceased when our victim approached. The last time I saw Ted he had been my height and hadn't begun shaving. I wonder what he looked like now. After twenty-five minutes of animated phone conversation we decided to meet for drinks the following afternoon.

Oh my, how he had changed! I looked across the tiny table in wonder. My old friend had the sort of clean-cut good looks women sighed for: strong jaw, broad forehead, clear light eyes, engaging smile. And tall — taller than I was. "I'm very glad you decided to look me up," I said, grinning for all I was worth.

"Give me a minute to restart my heart and I'll tell you how tickled I am that I managed to locate you. You were always cute but when did you get to be so gorgeous? And why wasn't I around? You should warn a guy who hasn't seen you in — how many years is it?"

"Ten, almost eleven."

"Ten years! Let's go someplace where we can eat while we talk. I'm starving."

We spent the rest of the evening catching up on time spent apart: schools, friends we'd lost touch with, friends we still knew. I told him my father was dead, that he died in a car crash. Ted had lost his mother to ovarian cancer while he was still in his teens. He had two brothers, a sister, and seven nieces and nephews. His father had remarried and lived in California. Ted was a stockbroker.

"Stodgiest firm on Wall Street," he said. "Banker's hours. I wear suits — all navy blue or gray. Conservative trading. Totally dull and predictable. Bet you five dollars that's not what you would have predicted for me."

"My turn," I said. "Independent career woman. Model. Five foot eleven and holding. Bet that's not what you would have predicted for me."

"I don't know what I expected. I'm delighted with what I found. Tell me you're not seeing someone special."

"I'm not seeing anyone special."

"Great! Me neither."

After he handed the cab driver a few bills to cover my fare, and before he closed the door behind me, Ted bent over to kiss me good-bye. A nice kiss. On the lips. More than friendly without being sloppy. I knew he would call again.

Later that night I woke up and discovered I'd fallen asleep with the television on. As I got up to turn it off, I glanced out my window. With the lights out, my sheer curtains hid me from view while allowing me to see through them. Four stories below I thought I saw a shape moving in the shadow. It was just after two-thirty. Too nervous to go to bed, I remained staring into the dimly lit courtyard hoping I was wrong. Forty-five minutes passed. A figure emerged. Disraeli was watching my window.

*   *   *

It was amazing how quickly the weeks flew after Ted and I started dating. Our conversations had none of the awkwardness associated with first dates. We talked about the things we had done in the intervening years: school, camp, travel, friends. I was astonished at how many people we both knew. Ted seemed to fit into any group, any situation. I felt comfortable meeting his many colleagues and business acquaintances. It was fun watching his face as he introduced me and mentioned that I was a model. But after two months of dating I wasn't ready for the Final Step. Thankfully, Ted was a perfect gentleman. Nearly a perfect gentleman. A perfect gentleman with hot breath, busy hands, and a recurrent, detectable physical condition. To be perfectly honest, it would be difficult to put him off much longer. Nor was I certain how much longer I wanted to wait. My hitherto dormant libido had reawakened and was nagging me.

*   *   *

Raul's call came shortly after I arrived home from work. We hadn't spoken since . . . I didn't want to think about our last meeting.

"Where are you calling from?" I asked, my voice scarcely more than a croak.

"Home. Palm Beach," Raul crooned in that voice that made my cheeks burn.

"So you're still with . . ."

"Byrd, Regis, and O'Dell."

"Oh," I said. It was the best I could manage until my pulse steadied.

"December, I brought in two important clients. One is the owner of the second largest cattle ranch in Argentina, who's been investing enormous sums of money in the United States. He specifically requested that I handle the details. Apparently, the issue of race decreases as my value to the firm increases. My Christmas bonus was embarrassingly generous and I got a raise."

"Wonderful."

"There've been broad hints about making me a partner."

"I thought you planned to move to Miami."

"I'm not sure what I'll say if I get the offer, but I've decided to stay put for a while. I thought you would be down for Christmas — spend some time with Amelia — look up old friends. Should I assume you're involved with someone?"

"I am. What about you? You dividing your time between any of those winsome creatures I met at your parents' home?"

He laughed — a rumbling bass cello. "Completely against my will I've been forced to escort every female between the age of fifteen and fifty who lives on the east coast of Florida — sometimes two or three a night. Of course they have to meet my parents' stringent criteria: beautiful, educated, and from a fine Cuban family. Exceptions are made for Spanish nobility. What about the man you're seeing?"

"His name is Ted. I've known him since grade school. He's a stockbroker."

"Is it as good with him as it was with us?"

"Don't you think that's a very personal question?"

"I wasn't talking about making love. I meant all of it — being together, talking, arguing. When are you coming down? Maybe we can get in some sailing."

"I don't know. It's March. Maybe Easter. I'm spending Passover with my boss and his family." Considering past accusations, I couldn't resist throwing that in.

"Let me know when you'll be here. It will give me a chance to show you my new office."

"Sure. I'll call you."

"Damn! Double damn!" I said after I hung up. He was the one who had demanded all or nothing. It had taken me months to recover from our break-up, to find reasons to smile again. Why did he have to call now? To find out if I was seeing someone? To try again? Damn! Just when things were going so well with Ted — a man who belonged to the world I knew. Perhaps it was time to take our relationship to the next plateau.

*   *   *

"I'd be very happy to advise you on some investments," Ted said, pulling me down next to him on the couch. "Long term or short?"

It wasn't as though I hadn't warned him that I was inviting him over for a home-cooked dinner in order to pick his brain. I had. Any additional notions were entirely his own. My plans were still conflicted. The bottom half of me was shouting "Yes! Yes!" Thanks to an expert teacher, and dare I say it, a reasonable amount of innate ability, I was no longer the blushing innocent hoping to be led to my first orgasm. Today's Charlie had trouble ignoring the heat generated by her persuasive companion.

"What are you looking to do? Financially."

"I'm a model. A model's day in the sun is about as long as a gardenia's. I'm twenty-four. I probably have another really good year at this, maybe two or three. I'm trying to be prudent and plan for life after modeling."

"What then? Marriage? Retirement? Live off your trust fund?"

"All I have is what I earn. When I marry — if I marry — I intend to continue working." I took hold of the hand that was reaching around my shoulder and hung dangerously close to my breast. Another inch and all intelligent conversation would cease. "I'm trying to think of something else I can do to support myself. Any ideas?"

"Why not open an agency of your own?" Ted asked the nape of my neck. It had taken him all of two dates to discover how sensitive I was there. And he'd become proficient at exploiting it.

I dragged his face to mine. "I can't open an agency of my own." I returned a kiss — a kiss that warmed my face and made thinking difficult. "I don't know anything about running an agency, and even if I did, I would never compete with my boss. Mr. Gluck has been like an uncle to me. And what are you doing?" I asked when he removed my three-inch high heel.

"Relax. I'm going to massage your poor tired feet. I don't know how women can walk in these things."

I gratefully surrendered. Ted knew just exactly how to knead my toes, instep, ankle, and calf to loosen the knots. My eyes were closed when he finished with my soothed right leg and moved to my left. "You don't think it's odd that I want to work after I'm married?"

"Should I?"

His hand had passed my knee and was on my thigh and inching upward. When it reached my garter I stopped it with mine. "You are supposed to be advising me on investments."

He smiled and sat up. "Write down everything you spend in a year: food, rent, insurance, everything. Divide it by twelve. Leave three to four months expenses where it's readily accessible, like a savings account. Put the rest in six month certificates of deposit. Almost any bank that is FDIC insured is fine. Jesus! When, Charlie? How much longer am I supposed to wait? You know how I feel about you."

"How *do* you feel about me?"

"We're together every minute we're not working. I introduce you to all my friends. You've met my sister and one of my brothers. Come with me to California and I'll introduce you to every Jensen in the phone book. What do you want me to say? That I love you? That I'm crazy about you? You must know that by now." Using his forefinger he tipped my face to his. "Maybe I should be asking you that question. How do you feel about me?"

"I spend every minute that I'm not working with you. I introduce you to all my friends. I ask your advice about money. I laugh at your jokes, even the ones I've heard before. And haven't you noticed? I really like kissing you." To prove it, I did just that — one of my better efforts. "I just need a little more time."

"How much time?"

"Isn't your birthday in June? What day?"

"That's three months from now. Too long. Two weeks from today. April first."

"Too soon."

"Then April 15th. It'll make paying my taxes something to look forward to."

"Easter," I countered. "That's only six weeks away. It can be your Easter present from me."

He pulled me to him, reached under my sweater, and with one hand expertly undid my bra. "If I have to wait until Easter I'm going to need a lot of encouragement."

So I encouraged him. In the process, I almost convinced myself.

* * *

I received a call from Jeremy about a week later. Disraeli was missing.

"I arrived back in New York three days ago and the ingrate disappeared that same night," Jeremy said.

"Have you called the police?" I asked, looking out my bedroom window, half-expecting to see him there.

"I haven't called the authorities. Disraeli has done this before. He always turns up in a few days."

"What if he's lost and can't find his way home? Wouldn't it be wise to alert the police? It's so difficult for him to make himself understood. They might not realize that he's harmless. They might hurt him."

"He's not lost. That monster enjoys torturing me like this. Considering his hideous appearance, it's incredible how the cretin manages."

"Do you have any idea where he goes or what he does?"

"No. Of course he's always starving when he finally does return. Who would take him in or feed him? This is the way he repays my generosity."

"Besides calling if I see him, what else can I do to help? My stepmother could recommend some excellent agencies if you need temporary assistance."

"Just call me if you see him. I'll send someone to pick him up and bring him home."

After I hung up I wondered why I hadn't told Jeremy I had seen Disraeli two nights earlier, once again standing beneath my window. Something in Jeremy's tone: his anger, his lack of concern — it was a side of him I hadn't seen before. His stories had been so entertaining. I envied his expertise, admired his spirit in the face of his horrid disability. I was flattered by his attention and comforted by his paternal interest and concern.

Now I was confused. If Disraeli returned, should I call the police or do as Jeremy had requested? Would I be in danger if I brought the retarded man into my home simply to question him? I knew virtually nothing about people like Disraeli. I needed an expert. A psychiatrist. The only psychiatrist I knew was Dr. Mendelson. I decided the doctor owed me a favor. I called his office the following morning.

"Amelia hasn't had a relapse, I hope," Dr. Mendelson said. "Do remember that I cautioned against removing her too soon."

"Amelia is doing very well, and thank you for inquiring. This call is about another matter entirely. I have a professional question I hoped you could answer."

"How may I help you?"

"I gave a retarded man I know a small gift for Christmas. Well, I'm afraid that little act of kindness might have been misinterpreted. I've seen him standing beneath my window late at night."

"Yes? And what's your question?"

"Four days ago he left his guardian without notice — or to be more accurate, he's run away from him. I was concerned that I might be in danger."

"I couldn't possibly know that without a complete work-up, or at the very least a look at his psychiatric history."

"No, I don't suppose you could. Actually, I was wondering . . ." I searched for the right words. "Since he seems to like me . . . In a general sense, are retarded people capable of extreme emotions?"

"I think what I'm hearing is, do retarded people have sexual drives? Are they likely to force themselves on an unwilling partner?"

"I guess that is what I mean."

"They are certainly capable of sexual arousal, and yes, even a fixation on a particular individual. But unless they've exhibited violent tendencies, it's highly doubtful they would hurt someone. Perhaps you should tell me about the behavior that you've witnessed."

I related Jeremy's tale of finding Disraeli and what I had observed between them.

"You realize of course, the selection of his ward's name is very telling?"

"Is it? I'm afraid you give me more credit than I deserve."

"Think about it, Charlotte. Naming a retarded man after a brilliant Jewish statesman is insulting, demeaning, dehumanizing, and probably anti-Semitic."

"I see."

"Have you ever heard or seen Mr. Randall exhibit any warmth to Disraeli? A touch, a smile, even a sincere 'thank you'?"

I thought for a moment. Had I? "No. Never. And he did use some nasty language to describe the poor man, but I thought that was because he was very upset."

"Exactly what terms did he use?"

"He referred to him as a cretin and a monster."

"If I had to make an educated guess, based on what you've told me, I'd say most likely Disraeli has been mistreated in some way, perhaps even beaten. Repeatedly leaving his guardian and hiding, indicates gross mistreatment, not just verbal abuse."

"I can't imagine Jeremy Randall abusing a helpless creature. How could anyone do that?"

"A dog licks the hand of its master after it's been reprimanded. This unfortunate man had to have a reason to repeatedly run away from the only home he knows."

"So my being kind to him had nothing to do with it?"

"He's run away before. He only returned because he was starving and no one would take him in. His guardian has admitted that to you. Disraeli might come to you for help."

"Me?"

"You may be the only person who's been kind to him, showed him compassion."

"If he came to my courtyard and I took him in, what do you recommend if he should try to — to touch me?"

"Distraction and dissuasion. If he tries to touch you in an improper manner, gently remove his hands and firmly tell him that friends don't do that. Reassure him that you want to be his friend. Remain calm. Exhibiting fear might confuse him."

"If Disraeli is being abused, what alternatives are there?"

"I'm afraid you're in a very difficult position, Charlotte. If Randall is his legal guardian, unless you can prove physical abuse, such as beatings, withholding food, water, or medical treatment, convincing a court will be very difficult. Obtaining custody will be almost impossible. And if he is taken from Randall, you have to think about what's to be done with him. The care given at state institutions leaves a lot to be desired."

"But what if he's being abused?"

"All I'm saying is that the problem is more complex than you realize."

That evening I made a large pot of strong coffee, turned on the television, moved my easy chair to where I could see out the window, and sat down to wait. Had I misjudged Jeremy Randall? Was he a fiend or the kind, caring man I believed him to be? Was it possible to be caring to one person and mistreat another? While I questioned my conflicting feelings toward Jeremy Randall, and my feeble understanding of the contradictory nature of man, I continued searching the shadows, looking for a lifelike silhouette. About one o'clock I spotted Disraeli in the darkness huddled against a wall. I shoved my feet into boots, grabbed my winter coat and house keys, and raced down four sets of stairs. The back door screeched as I opened it. The figure lumbered toward the alley.

"Wait! Don't leave."

The night was brutally cold. Disraeli turned to face me. I was greeted by the smell of rancid sweat, dirt, and fear. "Don't be frightened."

"No Randall. No Randall," he begged, his eyes widening.

"I'm not going to call Mr. Randall. You're going to come upstairs with me. I'm going to feed you. You must be very hungry. After you eat, you can rest. Do you understand?"

I led him like a puppy to the back entrance. When we reached the door and light, I could see his torn jacket provided little warmth. His head and hands were bare. What I could see of his face and hands were covered with grime.

"Just a few more stairs," I said. "Here, down this corridor. This is where I live. You'll be safe here."

I made him sit at my table and brought out whatever food I could find. Where had he gone, slept? From the way he devoured the food, he must not have eaten since he'd left Randall's home — four and a half days ago. Between bites I could see the gratitude and childlike trust in his eyes. Still, bathing him worried me. He had to bathe. Now that we were inside, my eyes were watering from the stench.

When he finished eating, I led him to my bathroom and filled the tub. For good measure I poured in a generous amount of bath salts. I had no idea if he would understand what actions were desired and which were not.

"You have to take a bath," I explained. He watched me without moving. "Wait until I've left the room before removing your clothes. Get in the tub and wash yourself. Use these towels afterwards. Don't put your dirty clothes back on. I'll give you a bathrobe. You can wear that until I have a chance to wash the clothes you're wearing." Without waiting to see if I was understood, I closed the door behind me and mentally crossed my fingers.

When I heard splashing I congratulated myself on this first small step. I found my roomiest robe, a coral print, and shoved it through the door. Please God, I prayed, grant him understanding. I didn't want to have to deal with a naked man, and in particular, not this man. Fifteen minutes later he emerged smelling of my bath salts and wearing my robe — a sight too comical to describe. I showed him to the makeshift bed I had assembled while he bathed. He lowered himself to the floor and wrapped the blankets around him. Within minutes, his tree-trunk neck ringed in coral ruffles, the sweet scent of lilacs hovering above him, Disraeli was snoring peacefully.

His filthy clothes were neatly folded in the bathroom. I left them for the morning and went into my room, locked the door, and wedged a chair under the knob. I had reached this far safely, but without the additional cautionary measures, I knew I wouldn't sleep.

In the morning, while Disraeli slept, I took his pitiful wardrobe to the basement laundry room. Inside his jacket pocket, still wrapped in red tissue paper, were the gloves I'd given him. Despite the bitter cold, he either hadn't realized their purpose, something I doubted, or treasured them too much to use. As his clothes were being washed and dried, I called one doctor after another until I found one willing to see him that day. Purchasing some new clothes and taking Disraeli to a doctor were as far as my plans extended.

* * *

I waited in the doctor's waiting room for the results of Disraeli's examination. It seemed an inordinate amount of time had passed since I'd left him in the examination room with the doctor's nurse, a cheerful woman about my age. I must have looked overly concerned because she came out an hour later to reassure me that all was well. The X-rays would be available shortly. Fifteen minutes later I was shown to Dr. Daniel Pagano's consultation room. He was younger than I expected, in his early thirties, a tall man with the blackest of black hair and empathetic dark eyes. He invited me to sit, and I chose one of the two steel chairs facing his desk.

"I estimate Mr. Disraeli to be in his late forties." Dr. Pagano said. "As far as I can see, in a general sense, he's healthy. I'll need the complete blood work before I can say for certain."

"Your nurse said you had X-rays taken."

"You asked me to look for signs of abuse. X-rays can provide a history the eye can't see. In this instance it did. Mr. Disraeli's right tibia was broken and not reset, probably when he was five or six years old. That's this bone," Pagano pointed to his calf. "Currently, he has some minor scrapes and bruises – what you might expect on someone who has been living on the street for a few days."

"So your opinion is that he hasn't been abused?"

"It's not that simple. Many bruises heal and leave no trace, but other forms of neglect and mistreatment don't. He was born with ankyloglossia, which means his tongue isn't attached properly. It's a simple thing to correct and should have been done when he was an infant, but it could have been done later."

"Would that affect his speech?"

"To some extent, but more important, it prevents the tongue from cleaning the mouth. Consequently, his teeth are horribly decayed. Several should be extracted as soon as possible. They must cause him great pain, yet there are no indication of any dental work. None. As far as his poor enunciation is concerned, that has more to do with his bone structure. He has a prograthic jaw — a jaw that is badly out of alignment. That too should have been corrected, and still can be. In addition to improving his ability to communicate, he would be more normal in appearance. Being retarded is enough of a handicap. He frightens people and that affects the way they respond to him."

"I was afraid of him at first."

"But the most significant signs of mistreatment are those to his skeleton. To put this simply, in layman's terms, his X-rays indicate that he performed heavy labor at an early age. The bones in his spinal column, shoulders, and arms show extreme stress. Anthropologically speaking, he has the skeleton of a slave, like those forced to work in stone quarries."

"Can you tell how old he was when that took place?"

He nodded. "In general terms, as early as eight and continuing through adulthood."

I couldn't be certain how long I sat there unable to speak. As Dr. Mendelson had pointed out, a punished dog doesn't run away unless it's been badly mistreated. The enormity of the abuse was chilling. I no longer considered Jeremy Randall my friend. "Would you be willing to testify to what you've told me?"

Dr. Pagano smiled at me sympathetically. "Morally and ethically I would have no choice. But I doubt if you'll be granted custody. Neglect isn't abuse."

"He doesn't want to return to his guardian."

"I'm sorry I can't be of more help. Given his limited intelligence and speech, without witnesses, it would be virtually impossible to prove criminal activity. If you're serious about pursuing this, you'll need a first-class lawyer and a small miracle."

Chapter Twenty-Five

My shopping completed and my fury calmed, I used the time on the subway home to think. It would have been easier taking Disraeli with me to purchase clothes for him, but I was afraid he might be recognized. By this time, Randall should have alerted the police. Instead, I'd left my guest with strict instructions not to answer the phone or let anyone in — particularly not Jeremy Randall. I was learning the degree of comprehension I could expect from Disraeli. He understood simple concepts and was eager to please.

The subway car was more than half-occupied. Facing me was a heavy woman with coarse wrinkled stockings, and a Negro man in a denim blue uniform. Like all well-mannered New Yorkers they adhered to the Rules of Behavior in Confined Quarters — they ignored me.

I had discovered on my countless trips crossing the city that the monotonous motion of the subway helped clear my mind. I had a lot of decisions before me. Should I return Disraeli to Randall and hope for the best? Or should I provide him with a safe place to stay and try to persuade Randall to relinquish guardianship? A year ago, I'd been unable to support myself and Amelia, and now I was considering taking on a monumental responsibility that would never end. What sort of care could I provide for this man? I had to be insane.

The car went black as it rumbled through another narrow tunnel and momentarily lost electrical power. I thought back to the first time I'd met Jeremy Randall. So much of what he had told me about his life echoed mine. Financial upheaval. Depression. A beloved family member who killed himself. What I wouldn't give to know how much of that was lies, because I no longer believed his stories. The car screeched to a halt and the man in uniform stepped out. A gentleman wearing a beret and carrying a violin case entered and took the nearest seat. I returned to my musings.

I needed a place to hide Disraeli before Randall discovered he had come to me for help. But where? Silver Glades? An institution filled with troubled people. Hardly a cheery environment. It was too bad we no longer had the house in McLean. There was lots of open space there, undemanding work, and Woody . . . Woody Wilson who ran a hunting lodge in a quiet little town in upstate New York. Woody Wilson and a sister who had raised and lost a child with Down's Syndrome. If only they would agree to take in a lodger who needed a bit of looking after. It would give me time to decide how to proceed.

*   *   *

"I'm taking you to my friend's house," I explained to Disraeli as I drove. "You're going to stay there for a while. My friend's real name is Clarence, but we call him Woody. He's a very nice man who will treat you kindly. His sister's name is Essie. They own a small bungalow colony."

"Bungalow. Bungalow. Bungalow." Disraeli cradled the art book he had given me and I'd insisted he take with him.

"A bungalow is a small house. You've stayed in hotels, haven't you?"

"Hotel," he said, nodding.

"A bungalow colony is like a hotel, but instead of having a lot of rooms in one building, there are many little houses. It's very quiet there and safe."

"I want to be with you."

I'd improved deciphering Disraeli's speech. "We've been over that before. Mr. Randall knows where I live. It's only a matter of time before he figures out that you're staying with me. If he finds you, he will make you go home with him. I won't be able to stop him. But if he can't find you . . ."

"I don't go with Randall."

"Right. Woody and Essie will give you lots to eat and will see that you're warm and safe. I'll come to visit you as often as I can. You must promise me that you won't run away and frighten me. Now promise me. I have to hear you say that you promise you won't run away."

"I promise. I don't run away."

"Good."

"I don't go with Randall. Never! Say you promise I don't go with Randall."

"I promise." It was a promise I hoped I could keep.

*   *   *

For the next two weeks, I avoided all contact with Jeremy Randall as I questioned my decision to harbor Disraeli. But my daily calls to Woody and Essie only reaffirmed my decision.

"He wants to help," Woody said. "Follows Essie everywhere. Likes making beds, sweeping, helping me bring in firewood."

"Does he ask where I am and why I don't come to see him?"

"Asks about you. I tell him you have to work. I can't always make out what he's trying to say, but Essie understands him right fine. He told us his name is William. We call him Willy."

William! Jeremy Randall had told me that was his brother's name. His brother! Had Randall repeatedly and cruelly mistreated his own brother? Would their kinship make gaining custody even more difficult?

"Essie gave him Amos' toys — stuffed animals, building blocks, a set of watercolors. Fiddled with them some. Liked stacking the blocks and watching them crash. Had to laugh. He got real mad at the watercolor set though. Threw it across the floor."

"I can't tell you how much I appreciate your help, Woody. If there's anything you or Essie need, any additional expense, you must tell me."

"Took him to the surgeon like you asked. He sent me to a special kind of dentist. Seems like they're planning to work on him together. You'll be getting the bills any day now. Gonna cost you some."

"That's fine."

"Essie wants to talk with you now."

Essie wanted to thank me for the ham I'd sent, and to tell me how much she enjoyed having Willy there. As we spoke, I realized that I not only missed Willy's company, I was just the tiniest bit jealous. But he was safe and happy, and if I wished to keep him that way I would need a lawyer.

*   *   *

I wasn't using Willy as an excuse to speak to Raul again. I simply knew that he would be sympathetic and helpful. Jeremy Randall and Willy were foreigners, in the United States on visas, I planned to explain. That was the reason I'd decided to call him, as opposed to another attorney. As a naturalized citizen Raul was familiar with immigration laws. My intention was to get some general information about how to proceed. I had promised to stay in touch. I made extensive notes and rehearsed what I would say. Still not ready, I ate lunch, picked up the dry cleaning, and vacuumed the living room carpet before I managed to dial his office. A secretary took the call and promised to relay my message.

Raul returned my call in ten minutes. Despite all my advance preparation, when I heard his voice, my pulse tripled. I steadied myself and concentrated on my notes. He listened quietly as I explained the situation.

"The man you described is wealthy," Raul said. "He could afford to hire a valet. It seems incredible that he keeps Willy solely as an unpaid servant, unless he truly feels some responsibility to the man."

"But he mistreated him."

"I understand. People form all sorts of bizarre symbiotic relationships. Some divorce cases I've seen would make you sick."

"Isn't there anything that can be done? What sort of lawyer

should I be looking for?"

"It's a complicated case. Willy isn't an American citizen, which means dealing with the INS, Immigration Naturalization Services. Proving neglect and obtaining guardianship involves family law. If physical abuse can be proven, Randall can be charged criminally."

"I'm determined to try. Willy's happy where he is. He doesn't want to return to Mr. Randall. What do you recommend?"

"Me. Acting as your friend and attorney, I should sit down with you and Randall and see if we can come to a reasonable agreement. I'll be there as soon as I can make arrangements with my office — probably before Sunday."

"I wasn't asking you to take the case. I just needed some general legal advice. Leaving your office on short notice could jeopardize everything you worked so hard for."

"Let me worry about that. I'll get back to you with my plans in a day or so. In the meantime, don't discuss the case with anyone. I have an idea that might force Randall's hand."

I imagined Randall's grasping misshapen hands reaching out for Willy, and in that instant I knew. The twisted spine. The bowed legs. The tortured walk. The crab claw hands. Perky stewardess Christine Brighton wasn't the Crab. Jeremy Randall was. And I strenuously doubted the fiend was my father's close friend and confidant.

"Charlie, are you still seeing that stockbroker?"

"Am I still seeing the stockbroker?" Raul's voice jolted me back to the present. "Yes, I'm still seeing him. His name is Ted Jensen."

"I had to ask. It doesn't affect my decision to help."

"I know."

"What does Jensen think about you battling Randall for custody?"

"He's all for it," I lied. I hadn't discussed the possibility of taking on Willy's care with anybody other than Woody and Essie. I was still hoping to find a simple compassionate solution. There had to be a place for people like Willy.

"What did you want me to do with that box of stationery that was your father's?"

I had forgotten the box and its inscrutable contents. Logic said scrap it. I had examined the letters before and found no common link, no shred of useful information. But after breaking the Crab code I was feeling decidedly clever. "Bring it with you. Just the stationery. Not the box. I'd like one last look before I toss it out."

Chapter Twenty-Six

New York, 1951

During the preliminary divorce proceedings, to her attorney's barely-concealed surprise, Jack made no demands on Norma. He regretted his marriage was ending, preferring a stable environment for his vulnerable teenage daughters. And he genuinely liked and admired Norma. She had been a generous, entertaining, and loving wife. He probably would have been faithful even if she hadn't made it explicit from the onset that she wouldn't tolerate less.

Even before the split was finalized, Jack decided remaining in Maryland would be unwise. Norma knew *everyone* worth knowing. Gossip and prying questions would be inevitable, and would harm the girls. He considered moving to Palm Beach, where the winters were wonderful, but the summers were intolerable – thick with heat and humidity and devoid of population. Manhattan seemed the best choice. It offered fine private schools, a full range of cultural events, and scores of luxury hotels, all of which led to opportunities for meeting the right people. Since the move would take place in June—Norma had thoughtfully suggested the separation correspond to the school year—Jack planned a long weekend in New York in April to search for new quarters. Beverly Larson, a charming older woman he knew from duplicate bridge, volunteered the use of her Manhattan apartment. Her son had recently accepted a business assignment in Italy. He and his family would be spending the next eighteen months in Rome. The widow Larson would be joining them; she had always wanted to take an extended visit to Italy.

Her apartment was small, she said, but the location was excellent. Her only request was that Jack care for her many plants. After subtle questioning, Jack learned that her Upper East Side "small" *a*partment contained two bedroom, one and a half baths, full living and dining rooms, and a large kitchen. He promised her plants would receive his unfailing attention and the "search and procure" weekend proved unnecessary.

Upon their arrival in Manhattan, seeing the veritable jungle consigned to his care, Jack called a residential plant service he found in the Yellow Pages. The service's fee was a pittance compared to rent.

If he'd had to provide solely for himself, the divorce settlement he hadn't requested, but had gratefully accepted, would've done nicely until the next Mrs. Morgan could be identified, wooed, and won. (Jack was already considering two or three potential candidates in Palm Beach, and one in New York.) However, a man living in Manhattan with two daughters enrolled in a pricey academy couldn't survive long on the current contents in his checking account. Food. Entertainment. Transportation. Clothing. School uniforms and supplies. If necessary, his wardrobe could last years. The girls' wardrobe, on the other hand, would soon be out of style or too small. Charlie was growing at an alarming pace. Jack needed cash.

It was time to sell Uncle Gaston's Renoir – the only item of potential value he possessed. Formerly stowed in Norma's attic, the locked Louis Vuitton trunk that hid it and the materials he had used for forging documents now served double purpose as a bench in his bedroom.

One night while the girls were safely asleep, Jack assessed the provenance he had created nine years earlier. Bills of sale, either handwritten or typed on the decrepit typewriter, were flawless. The handwriting and signatures were distinct. The letters he had composed with a quill had the stilted language and touching personal references worthy of a Mark Twain or Edgar Allen Poe. He was delighted with his efforts.

While the girls were at school Jack carefully stretched and mounted the canvas. Would the painting deceive an expert? It had fooled him – a man who had spent his entire adult life admiring the genius of others. Knowing the oil would be more desirable, credible, and valuable if it was suitably framed, he devoted a month to canvassing Brooklyn and Queens for the right sized carved gilt frame until he located the perfect one.

To handle the proposed sale, Jack selected a prestigious

Manhattan gallery. He visited it and talked with George Landau, the proprietor, several times, as though to assure himself the facility was worthy of handling his treasures. Landau made it known that he was eager to view, and possibly sell, the paintings the distinguished Mr. Morgan had acquired in France before the war. He graciously offered to "stop by for a quick look." Equally gracious, Jack refused, citing the servants' love of gossip as a reason. In truth, although the apartment was comfortable, it was hardly a setting for the collection he had described. Instead, Jack allowed himself to be persuaded to deliver for consideration the one oil he was prepared to part with at the moment, a Renoir.

Jack had prepared himself to hear a range of responses, from doubt and dismay to total acceptance. But watching Landau dip and bob around his office as he studied the painting he had placed on an easel under a stark white light, and hearing his "Oh, my! My, my!" reactions, made Jack uneasy. It would be simple to explain he had been duped. There would be some polite apologies from both sides and the matter would be forgotten. On the other hand, it would be infinitely more complicated to produce a means of financing the next year or more until his future consort could be bedded and wedded. Wealthy widows and divorcees, of a certain age and open-handed temperament, were not a commodity to be found in the classified section of the *Times*.

"I'd be happy to take it on commission, if that's what you'd like," Landau finally said, to Jack's great relief. "But not until I have a colleague of mine examine it. With your permission, of course."

"I'd be delighted to hear your colleague's opinion. Perhaps he can suggest an opening price."

"Excellent! Why don't I take your number and have him contact you?"

Jack left his phone number and Uncle Gaston's Renoir with Landau. Within the week he received a call from Jeremy Randall, who suggested Jack meet him at his home. Despite thinking the choice of location odd, Jack agreed.

*   *   *

Jack was happy he had not pressed for a more conventional meeting place the moment he entered Randall's luxurious Dakota residence on Central Park West and saw the bent-over man, a cane in each hand, awkwardly lurching to greet him.

After they had settled in Randall's splendid library, his host offered tea – the British version – with a gleaming silver service, fine china, dainty sandwiches, scones, and sherry.

"Now tell me about yourself," Randall urged. "Are you married? Any children? I don't get out as much as I'd like. I travel, naturally. My work requires it. Regrettably, I don't have the freedom I once had to socialize as much as I'd like."

Jack began with the barest rudiments of his personal history. He was a widower with two young daughters, and was now divorced.

"Tell me about the girls. I hope you're not in a hurry. Everyone seems so rushed nowadays."

He willingly told the lonely man about his beautiful and gifted daughters. Jeremy—they had advanced to Christian names—seemed so eager to hear the slightest detail. He laughed heartily at Jack's recanting of childish antics and warmly admired the girls' accomplishments.

"I must sound awful," Jack finally said, "going on and on like this. I usually have the good sense to keep my paternal pride to myself."

"Nonsense! You can't know how good it is to hear a man speak so affectionately about his children. You must have loved their mother utterly and completely."

Jack was both startled and moved by the insight. "I did."

"When I was a lad of twenty-three and not the cripple you see before you, I was engaged to an exquisite creature. It was one of those marvelous matches – two equally old and prominent families. But it was true love for both of us. That silly darling girl adored me. Then I was diagnosed with rheumatoid arthritis. The engagement ended. My ring was returned. I was heartbroken. The earl wouldn't permit his daughter to marry a man destined to be dependent on others."

"I'm so sorry."

Randall waved a hand. "Years ago. Now she's simply a lovely memory. Time heals and corporeal beauty fades. I expect she married well, had a brood of five or six, and grew stout. Only art is timeless."

"Perhaps that's why we're drawn to it."

"You're an artist then, are you? I suspected as much."

"A bad artist – and I'm not being modest." It was getting late. Two hours had passed quickly. While the girls each had a key to the apartment, Jack liked to be there when they came home from school – to hear the day's events while they were still bubbly and ready to talk. "About the oil," Jack hinted. "I assume you've had a chance to examine it."

"I suppose we must discuss the oil," Randall said, his voice and enthusiasm drooping. "And we were having such a lovely visit."

Jack saw his hopes for the future diminish as he read consternation on his host's face.

"Amateurish forgery," Randall advised. "Salable, but only to the right customer, and at the right price, somewhere it won't get much exposure."

"I don't understand," Jack bluffed.

"The oil's a forgery. Now don't be hard on yourself. Perhaps as much as twenty percent of what I come across isn't genuine. Dealers, auction houses, private individuals, like yourself, pass along works a washwoman could spot as fake."

"Really? You're certain the Renoir . . . I bought it from what I believed was a reputable dealer. But I'm not an expert, like yourself. Nor, apparently, was he."

"Now the provenance, on the other hand, is brilliant – simply brilliant. First rate! Perhaps the best I've seen. I wish some of the authentic works I represent had provenances half as good."

Jack didn't want to talk about the provenances. "You mentioned there might be a market for the oil, despite your concerns of its authenticity."

"I have a few customers in the Middle East, oil-rich shahs and sheiks, who don't know the difference between a Titian and a triton. Objects of art are merely props. They have absolutely no appreciation or understanding of western art – or middle-eastern art, for that matter. The Sphinx and the pyramids were all but obscured by sand. If Napoleon hadn't happened along, they would still be buried."

"And let's not forget Howard Carter and Lord Carnavon, two countrymen of yours, who discovered Tutankhamen's tomb."

"Landau deserves a commission for his participation," Randall said, returning to the original topic. "Do you have any other works you're looking to sell?"

"None," Jack admitted.

"Unfortunately, I won't be traveling abroad for some time."

Jack did his best to hide his disappointment with a grim smile.

"If you need some . . . That is to say, Jack, I'd be very willing to give you an advance."

Jack considered the unexpected and tempting offer from this kind and intuitive man he had known so briefly. His checking account was in rapid descent. But he couldn't accept the offer so soon and not appear desperate. Better to leave the door open and return if it became absolutely necessary. He declined the loan and rose to leave.

"I thank you for a most enjoyable and enlightening afternoon."

With a wave of his clawed hand, Randall indicated Jack should sit again. "We are both gentlemen, are we not? Two gentlemen with common interests. I feel I can speak directly. Is it possible to contact the dealer from whom you obtained the oil? Any chance he knew the actual artist?"

"I doubt it."

"Regrettable. I would love to have asked him who prepared the provenance. A great painting with lackluster credentials is harder to sell, and most often commands far less than it deserves. Needless to say, I frequently come across these situations. I have a genuine Pissarro at this very moment with nary a scrap of paper to substantiate its authenticity. It belongs to an old, old friend and fellow Mason. His father bought it years ago because his mother liked it. They're both gone and he wants to sell it – gambling debts, I think. Would you care to see it?"

Jack's mind raced ahead. Paintings that lacked provenances. His only true artistic talent. Would it be wrong to take advantage of his gift? He had profited from it before with the sale of Uncle Gaston's van Dyck, and he was hoping to profit from it again. Could Jeremy Randall be trusted?

"If it wouldn't be too much trouble."

"It's hanging in the dining room over the mantle. Take a right when you exit this room." Randall pointed to the door. "I'll wait here for you, if you don't mind."

Jack entered a plush apricot dining room with a Murano glass chandelier, so different from the masculine library he had left. Above the Greek-columned mantle made of milk-white marble was the Pissarro, its shadowy landscape transformed by rays of sunlight piercing dense tree branches. Small, simple, and perfect. He returned to the library and praised the painting.

"What are you thinking, Jack? I can see sparks darting behind your eyes."

As Randall had observed, they had much in common. Two men with a love of art who appreciated comfort and beauty – both willing to bend a few rules. "I believed the Renoir was genuine. It lacked a provenance. I fabricated one. Apparently I did a good job."

Randall tap, tap, tapped his cane on the floor in apparent delight. "A good job? A brilliant job! Every field has its experts and in this, you are the consummate expert."

Twenty minutes later, a handshake sealed the agreement. Jack would be paid a nice sum for a provenance for the Pissarro – enough to support the girls and himself for a month or two. When Uncle Gaston's Renoir finally sold, Jack would receive seventy-five percent of the purchase price. Ten percent would go to Landau, who had done little more than introduce them, and an equitable fifteen percent would go to Randall, for his part in locating a buyer and finalizing the sale. A conservative estimate of Jack's share could support his family for a year or more. When Randall identified another fine work missing decent credentials, Jack would enhance the existing provenance or create a new one. A few such commissions and he could take his girls to France – something he had always dreaming of doing. Randall had called his work "Brilliant" "First rate." Being praised for talent was exhilarating.

Before Jack left, Randall expressed his desire to meet Charlotte and Amelia. He adored children and to his everlasting regret, he would never have any of his own.

"Please don't be offended," Jack said, hoping to convey his sincere distress. "Under any other circumstances I'd love to introduce you. But they've just been through a divorce. They had to move, change schools, leave their friends. They would ask questions about how we met and I'd have to lie. I try to spare my daughters the concerns of the practical world. Can you . . . "

"Say no more about it, dear fellow. I understand completely. We shall follow a fine old tradition and keep trade and family separate. Perhaps that's the better idea after all." Randall rang the bell on the table beside him.

The manservant who had let Jack in and had served tea appeared. God had cruelly treated this pitiful soul, Jack thought, as the hulking man showed him to the door. He was both hideous to look at and mentally feeble. How fortunate he had been to find employment with this understanding and kind man.

Chapter Twenty-Seven

Ted knew about Raul — that he had been a good friend to me after my father's death, that we had dated for a while, and that he was coming to New York to represent Willy and me. When Ted offered to drive me to the airport, I immediately accepted. Ted's presence would underscore the finality of our breakup.

As I located Raul's face among the passengers exiting the plane, I squeezed Ted's hand and leaned into his shoulder. Raul handled it well — a momentary pause upon spotting me, followed by a wave and a broad warm smile. He kissed me on the cheek before he shook Ted's hand.

Ted glanced at the raincoat Raul had over his arm. "Don't be fooled by the mild weather we're having tonight. It's still winter."

"In a few days it'll be April. I figured this would be warm enough over a jacket," Raul explained.

As we walked to Ted's car I directed the conversation to Willy. We decided that Raul and I would meet with Randall in an effort to settle the matter privately. Failing that, Raul would pursue it legally. Ted deferred on matters involving law, but offered practical suggestions that Raul listened to attentively. Eager to please both, I labeled every contribution brilliant. I was attentive, appreciative, and bubbly. I smiled so hard my jaws were starting to ache. And just to make certain there was no misunderstanding everyone's role in this threesome, I clung to Ted like a suntan.

After we dropped Raul at his fraternity brother's home I congratulated myself on how well things had gone. Perhaps it was the evening's excitement, or the anticipation of the impending battle, but I was wide awake. "It's still early," I said to Ted as we approached my building. "Would you like to come up for a while?"

He maneuvered the car into the first convenient space — a driveway. "It's late. We both have work tomorrow. Besides, I'll never find a parking spot."

"You have work tomorrow. I have off."

He leaned across to kiss me good night. Instead of the simple kiss he expected, I drove my tongue between his lips. He returned my advance with a few moves of his own. With both parties' enthusiastic participation, things quickly became heated.

"You're in a romantic mood," Ted whispered. "Anything I said?"

"You don't have to say anything special for me to feel romantic." I put my right hand on the back of his neck and moved my left hand to his upper thigh. "Are you sure you won't change your mind?"

He stopped kissing me to study my face. "If I put the car in a garage, how long shall I say I'll be?"

"I'll leave that up to you."

"Then I'll tell the attendant I'll pick it up tomorrow morning."

Once inside my apartment Ted needed no encouragement to resume where we had left off in the car. It occurred to me that making love was a bit like dancing. First times could be awkward. You may be hearing the tender rhythms of a waltz, and he may be hearing jazz. The results could be disastrous. There was always the inevitable question as to who would lead. I'd done all the leading I was capable of in the car. Fortunately Ted needed no further encouragement to take the initiative. I did all I could to keep in step. As we exchanged kisses in my entranceway, he undid my blouse and bra. Both hands circled my nipples before one left to help me remove my skirt. Two long sweet kisses, the first on my lips and the second at the base of my throat, and Ted tugged his shirt loose and undid the buttons. His bare upper torso was lean, muscular, and double the size of mine. I leaned forward to kiss his shoulder and then his jaw.

"Move over here," he said, "in front of the mirror."

As requested, I stepped to the left. I was viewing my very first pornographic movie. It was arousing watching the half-naked couple: the bare-chested man with intense eyes and the pale woman whose breasts he cupped with his hands. Dangling in long tendrils, curling in wisps around her face, her hair sought to escape its severe French twist. She watched him kiss the nape of her neck while he removed hairpins and let them fall until her eyes closed.

Like drops of dry rain, pin after pin slid down my neck, spine, shoulders and breasts, then fell silently to the carpet below — a sensory experience unlike any I'd known.

"Why don't you see what you can do with my trousers?" Ted suggested. "And take your time." I opened my eyes, turned to face him and obediently opened his belt and undid the zipper, slowly, as requested. Before I could continue, he stepped back to remove the slacks and then his shorts. His was an efficient and well proportioned body. I self-consciously covered my breasts with my arm. Ted removed it.

"I'm going to finish undressing your luscious self and you're going to watch."

I shook my head. The mirror was too disturbing.

"Don't be a baby. Watch!"

I watched — my pale skin juxtaposed against his, my blond hair next to his brunette. I watched my skirt and then my slip slowly slide down my hips. I could feel his erection hard against my thigh. I watched his head drop out of sight as he kissed each vertebra until he reached the base of my spine. I fought the urge to look away at the sight of him on one knee, undo my garter belt and sliding my stockings and panties off my legs. The reflection revealed a woman at first self-conscious, then a curious voyeur, and finally lost to everything but her lover's presence, scent and touch.

"Now," I breathed, when excitement exceeded fascination. "We should . . . I should . . . The bathroom."

"We have lots of time. I'm not going anywhere."

Lots of time! I wasn't certain how much longer I could contain myself before I turned into a crazed rapist. I attempted to pull away. "I really should go now, before . . . before . . . diaphragm. I don't want to have to stop later." I had found the magic word — diaphragm. He released me.

After I finished fumbling with the damn thing and washing my hands, I discovered the bedspread folded and removed, and Ted atop the sheet and grinning at me.

I was ready. Good Lord, I was ready. I had been ready since that first kiss in his car. But Ted wasn't. Not that he had trouble regaining an erection – that took no time. He wanted to prolong foreplay – apparently indefinitely. Every time I attempted a direct landing, he decided another part of my anatomy needed attention. "Could we do this now?" I pleaded, as he licked the back of my knee. He moved up beside me. "For as long as you'd like."

And that wasn't empty bravado.

*   *   *

"Why last night, Charlie?" Ted asked the next morning after returning from the bathroom. "What made you change your mind?"

"What was wrong with last night?" I lifted the blanket and backed my warm sated body against his cooler one. "I thought things went quite well, didn't you? Especially for a first time."

He reached around to hug me and laughed — a liquid, meaningful laugh. "No complaints here. Still, I was wondering if I might've had some help."

"What kind of help?" I stiffened.

"All along you said that you wanted to wait, that you weren't ready. Then suddenly you changed your mind." He kissed the back of my neck. "It occurred to me it might've had something to do with your charming lawyer friend."

"Why would you think that?" I asked, pulling away.

Ted flung his feet over the side of the bed and sat up. "Come on, Charlie. You were smoking before we left the airport. I don't remember ever having that affect on you."

"How about what happened between us in this apartment?" I asked, turning over to face him. "What did you think that was? An Oscar-winning performance in the category of pornographic art? I can't believe you're saying this to me."

"What went wrong between you and Raul? One woman didn't satisfy him? The old machismo factor? He wasn't ready to settle down?"

"If you have to know, Raul proposed and I refused. I didn't think we were right for each other. It ended well before I met you."

"Don't ever take up poker, Charlie," he said, standing. "A blind man can see there's still something between you — both of you. I'd like to think it was something I did, or said, that triggered last night's explosion, but I don't believe in kidding myself."

Now I was angry. I sat up. "If you thought that, why did you agree to come up? No one forced you."

He shrugged. "I thought I'd even up the playing field, to show you what you'd be missing. Latin men have quite a reputation as lovers. Besides, you invited me. Tell me, how did I measure up?"

"That isn't fair."

"Life isn't always fair, Charlie. If life was fair we wouldn't be having this discussion. You would feel about me the way I feel about you." He bent to stroke my hair. "But it's obvious that you're not certain how you feel, and I have no interest in being hurt."

I caught his hand. "I would never hurt you, Ted. Never."

"Not intentionally. Unintentionally, you might. That's why I'm going to give you some time to work this through. We're not going to see each other for a while. When you're absolutely sure it's over, *if it's over*, call me."

As Ted dressed to leave I turned my face to the wall. He wanted to even up the playing field. I was angry. Used and manipulated. Tossed in the garbage like a tennis ball after a match. How did he measure up? The gall of the man. He didn't want to be hurt. Well, who wanted to be hurt? I knew what that felt like. Still, it was impossible to deny that seeing Raul again, knowing that he was near, made everything more vivid. Changing the way one felt about a person wasn't as simple as turning off a tap. Our affair was over. We had agreed. So why had Raul called to ask if I was seeing someone? It was his fault that I was feeling this miserable. This whole damn thing was Raul's fault. But I had returned his call. Had asked for his help. Double damn! I was still furious, except I wasn't certain at whom.

"Come closer. I have to go to work," Ted said.

I flipped over. Seeing him standing there smiling down at me: impossibly handsome, knowing that we wouldn't be seeing each other again was almost physically painful. My anger evaporated. He bent to kiss me — a long, hard, bittersweet kiss.

"When it's over," he said.

Long after the front door closed, I got out of bed, took a shower, and ate breakfast, doing my utmost to erase Ted's accusations from my thoughts. Raul and I were scheduled to meet with Jeremy Randall at one o'clock. My pulse increased in direct proportion to the remaining time. Nerves. Just nerves, I reassured myself. I was very troubled about Willy. His entire future was at stake. As for me, I was taking on an enormous responsibility for which I had little preparation. My erratic respiration had nothing to do with Raul. Just nerves. Our affair was over. History. Ted was the man in my life now. I was still glowing from our lovemaking. How many men would understand my confusion and be willing to wait? Only Ted. He had so many qualities that made him the right man for me. I would let a few days pass and then call and tell him so.

Chapter Twenty-Eight

We sat at my new wrought iron kitchen table with its two matching chairs, my latest acquisition, to plot our campaign. Randall had canceled that afternoon's meeting, rescheduling it for the next day. He had called Raul that morning to say the appointment couldn't be kept. I inspected the ancient yellowed stationery that I had asked Raul to bring with him. In addition to the assorted blank pages and several unused invoices from unknown companies, there were six personal letters and five itemized bills, all handwritten, all unrelated. There had to be some reason my father had kept them.

Raul dated the top of his legal pad and added my name and Willy's. "Randall's not going to give in without a fight. He's up to something."

"The first time I met him, so much of what he told me about his life echoed mine. Financial upheaval. Depression. His brilliant and dear brother William who killed himself. Then it turned out that Disraeli's real name is William. What I wouldn't give to know how much of what he told me was lies. I no longer trust anything he said."

"Maybe Willy is his brother. Skillful liars often weave bits of truth into their stories."

"Willy says that he's not, but he may not understand the concept. We don't know the extent of his intelligence."

"He'll have to be examined and tested by a psychologist."

I took a sip of my coffee and glared at the mute documents. "Does he get tested before or after I have his teeth and jaw fixed?"

"Before. You'll have to wait until you're granted custody before proceeding with surgery. The only dental work that can be done is emergency treatment. We have to be very careful so that no charges can be filed against you, in case this thing doesn't go our way."

"What are my chances?"

"I couldn't even guess before talking to Randall in person."

"I'm quite certain that Jeremy Randall is the mysterious Crab in my father's appointment book. But I doubt if it was a case of two old friends getting together, as he claims. He might fool a gullible creature like me, but an accomplished teller of tall tales, like Alan Fitzpatrick, alias Jack Morgan? Not very likely."

"You used to like Jeremy Randall. Do you think there's a possibility that you're only angry at him because of the way he's treated Willy? Your father might not have seen that. He may have simply enjoyed the company of a kindred spirit."

*   *   *

Having agreed to meet with Randall at his apartment, I was agitated and at the same time excited. Raul handed my ruglike full-length coat, and the lightweight raincoat that he claimed was all he needed, to the unfamiliar valet, a florid beefy man.

Randall's greeting to me was as welcoming as though this were simply a social call, but when I introduced him to Raul, I noticed the subtle change. Beneath the smiling exterior and practiced courtesy, I saw a tinge of contempt.

"Please sit down." Randall indicated chairs. "I hope we can dismiss this matter quickly and go on to more pleasant subjects."

I reminded myself that we were hoping to learn more than we divulged, and as Raul could be more objective, I would let him speak for both of us.

"We're also hoping for a quick resolution." Raul took the chair next to mine. "As you may have surmised by now, William wishes to stay with Miss Morgan."

"So he now wishes to be known as William and has expressed a desire to stay with Charlotte? Rubbish! That's absurd. William isn't capable of making those decisions. He has the mind of a child."

Randall had used the name William, that Raul had slipped into the conversation. I was amazed by the success of the ploy. Randall obviously had forgotten that he had told me about his tragic suicidal brother.

Raul ignored Randall's outburst. "Are you representing yourself to be William's guardian or his employer?" he asked. "If you're claiming to be his employer, I'd like to see some canceled checks or signed receipts of payment —"

"I'm his guardian. Any trivial services he performs are done voluntarily and don't begin to cover the cost of maintaining him."

"If she's granted custody, Miss Morgan is prepared to provide for all William's needs — present and future."

"I've consulted an attorney," Randall cautioned. "He informed me that Charlotte can be charged with kidnapping. Naturally, as an old friend of her father, I am most reluctant to do so. Provided she returns William within the next twenty-four hours, we can forget this entire matter."

"Miss Morgan is not holding William against his will," Raul reminded him. "He came to her for help and doesn't wish to return to you. He has made himself quite clear in this regard, to Miss Morgan and to others."

"Young man, you know nothing of William, and neither does the well-intentioned, misguided Miss Morgan. William is a willful balky child given to hysterical fits. He requires constant attention. Miss Morgan might think of herself as his champion now, but she'll soon tire of the obligation."

"I'm prepared to take on William's permanent support," I said, my first contribution to the conversation.

Randall turned to me. "My dear, can you prove that you're financially capable of providing for William for the rest of his natural life? How? In your current position as a model? Hardly an enduring career."

I'd told Jeremy Randall many things, but I'd never discussed my financial situation. Did he know that Daddy had died penniless?

"William isn't a young man," Raul said. "He won't be able to assist you in the way you require forever. Considering his appearance and limited ability to communicate, surely the valet you've hired is far better suited to serving you."

"I don't have to explain my actions to you. I expect you to return William as I've requested or face the consequences."

"William claims that he's your brother," Raul bluffed.

"Impossible!" Randall said, obviously startled. "William would never say such a thing."

"But he did," Raul pressed. "A man of your obvious means using his brother as a servant and then mistreating him and ignoring his needs – we take serious issue with that in the United States."

"William is my ward. While he has been in my care he's never been mistreated. You can't prove such an absurd accusation."

Randall's voice was strong but his hand visibly trembled. Raul had shaken him.

"We have doctors willing to testify that William was both physically neglected and abused," Raul continued.

"Physically abused? How dare you accuse me of abusing William." Randall reached for a nearby bell. "I've tried being patient with you, Charlotte, out of friendship to you and your father, but your actions have exceeded my tolerance. Since you refuse to return William as requested, this meeting is over."

During the exchange some pesty little questions had been nagging at me. I decided that I might not get this chance again. "I never asked you about the provenance for the Renoir."

Randall glared at me before replacing the bell in his lap. "What is it that you wish to know?"

"You said that it wasn't one of the artist's finest efforts, and that the appearance of an unknown Renoir caused quite a stir. No doubt you asked to see the provenance." I scanned Jeremy Randall's face for the smallest sign — a twitch, anger, fear. He actually smiled — a cold, hard smile.

"Naturally I examined it. It was beyond reproach." His eyes narrowed and the cold, hard smile disappeared. "I don't see what this has to do with William. Since you're not willing to return him I have no choice but to advise my attorney to take action." Randall rang the bell and the valet appeared. "Edgar, please show Miss Morgan and her companion to the door."

Chapter Twenty-Nine

1960, Palm Beach

Jack followed Petal through The Breakers' two hundred foot long, pillar-lined Italian Renaissance lobby, heading for the palatial Palm Courtyard for cocktails and hors d'oeuvres. The fabulous oceanfront hotel, built at the turn of the century and modeled after the Villa Medici in Rome, was acknowledged to be one of the most magnificent hotels in the world. Symmetrically placed around the expansive multi-tiered stone Courtyard were a dozen or so eight-foot-high ice statues of Greek gods, goddesses, and nude athletes. Poised on their columned pedestals and shimmering in the moonlight, they towered over the tuxedo-clad men and glittering gowned women. Circling the central cascading fountain six toga-clad female harpists, and an equal number of male violinists in white jackets and black ties, provided Debussy's ethereal *Clair de Lune*. The air was heavy with the scent of potted gardenia bushes.

The season had just begun – like the others before, a series of endless theater parties, balls, galas, and silent auctions orchestrated by the Grand Dames of Palm Beach society, like Marjorie Merriweather Post, the cereal heiress; or Sue Whitman, whose great-grandfather developed Listerine, or Mary Sanford, wife of "Laddie" Sanford, who had made his fortune selling rugs, and earned his reputation bedding young beauties.

"Tom, Alice, Mary, Marshall, so good to see you again." Petal smiled and paused as she passed through the throng in her classically-cut silver satin gown with matching mini-cape, designed for her by Pierre Balmain. Combined with her diamond starburst tiara and earrings, inch-wide sapphire and pear-shaped diamond choker and matching bracelet, Petal was a regal figure. "Dahlia, you look perfectly divine."

The elderly woman Petal had addressed, with the surgically altered, too taut face, and ill-fitted cobalt blue chiffon gown, better suited to a younger and more buxom woman, was being half-led/half supported by Leonid Clapton, her regular walker.

Walkers were single, well-mannered men employed to escort widowed and divorced women to Palm Beach events. They had to be competent dancers who owned and looked good in a reasonably up-to-date tuxedo. When they weren't leading their hostess/employers around the dance floor, they were expected to make light conversation. For their services, walkers received all expenses the event incurred, plus disparate and imaginative bonuses. They might be provided with a suite or small apartment on estate grounds. They might be awarded a lightly used automobile. They might have their medical and dental bills paid. A high percentage of walkers were homosexuals. They collected orchids,

Broadway memorabilia, stickpins, cufflinks, antiques, small dogs and art. Some, like Leonid, were as dull as the women they escorted, but many were interesting individuals with fascinating stories to tell.

"Jack, please be a dear and get us drinks," Petal requested. "You know what I like."

"Wait, let me find chairs for the ladies and I'll join you," Leonid said, as he guided Dahlia to an unoccupied table.

Petal's eyes fired an unmistakable message at Jack. Be quick! She didn't want to be saddled with the dreary woman one minute longer than necessary. When Jack returned with her double Chivas Regal, single ice cube, Petal was already standing. She took the proffered drink, agreed to an undetermined lunch date, and waved away a toga-clad waiter carrying a tray of tempting appetizers before Jack could reach for one. Petal rarely ate between meals, and then minimally. Trim, stylish, and impeccably groomed, she could fit into dresses she had worn thirty years earlier.

Jack had considered himself the luckiest of men when Petal had agreed to marry him. She was capable, efficient, loyal to friends and family, courteous to servants, careful never to embarrass him in front of others, conveniently ignorant of the women he saw, and of course, unfailingly generous to him and his girls. His meager earnings as a forger merely allowed him the pleasure of providing his daughters the odd indulgence that Petal considered unnecessary, like the beaver coat Amelia had received at graduation, and the MG Charlie had received at hers. It was Petal who provided everything else, without criticizing his girls' behavior or choices.

On the other hand, Petal was bigoted, narrow minded, humorless, irate when challenged, ruthless when crossed, and regrettably asexual. Jack hadn't anticipated Petal's desire to maintain a chaste relationship a problem. She had made it understood from the beginning that she didn't care about his fidelity, as long as he was discreet and chose women outside their social circle. Finding willing and desirable lovers was easy. What Jack hadn't considered was his pride. He had always relied on his virile good looks, magnetism, and sexual prowess. With Petal indifferent, he lacked power over her. He was an accessory – little more than a walker – a way to show the world she could successfully compete with any woman.

"What table are you at?" Petal inquired of Teddy and Lane Reinhardt, when it eventually became time to leave the Palm Court and proceed to one of the hotel's three ballrooms for dinner. "We are sitting at Corinth."

"We're at Athens with the Duke and Duchess."

Petal did her best to suppress a gasp by lightly touching her lip.

"You may have heard," Lane continued, "they were our guests at Serendipity." She was referring to their noted Long Island Gold Coast estate.

Jack inwardly cringed. He might be in the minority, but he wasn't alone in his distaste for "the King who gave up his throne to marry the woman he loved." While most Americans were enchanted with the Cinderella story, most Palm Beach proprietors were not. They wisely hid their finest merchandise when they saw the restless royal couple approaching. Royalty didn't carry cash, nor did they write checks for the items they "purchased." Shop owners could send invoices, but they wouldn't receive responses. Jewelers visibly trembled when the pair took their daily afternoon stroll down Worth Avenue. Everything in their path was fair game. Even treasures borrowed from their hosts during their stays were presumed to be gifts.

"You simply must introduce us," Petal said, displaying her widest smile. "I shall never forgive you if you don't."

To dine with the royal couple was to preview heaven. If the Duke and Duchess agreed to stay at your estate or mansion, your position as a society icon was guaranteed for life.

"Of course, my dear," Lane said. "Stop by when we're dancing. The Duke and Duchess are ever so gracious, but they don't care to have people hovering over them while they dine."

Suddenly, as if the mention of their names could produce them in the flesh, the diminutive Duke and Duchess swept past them, then were lost in the crowd. Jack didn't need to see the pair to visualize them. The Duchess' coiffure would be sleek. She would be clad in a beautifully tailored gown cut close to the body, with minimal embellishment, which would flatter her petite figure and showcase the spectacular, world-renowned jewels the Duke had commissioned for her: a tiger, or leopard, or flamingo brooch, or her almost twenty carat emerald engagement ring, each stone as perfect as nature could produce and man could fashion. As for the slender elegant Duke himself, he had redefined men's fashion. Black tie and jacket formal wear was his innovation.

Jack dreaded the inevitable request to join others on the dance floor so that Petal could be introduced to the restless pair. His reason for hating the former King Edward VIII went beyond his empathy for the local tradesmen. Jack keenly remembered the European leader Edward had admired and praised before Germany launched its first attack of World War II, against neighboring Poland. Adolph Hitler! The insane monster who had declared his *final solution* for every Jew alive, the vile despot responsible for the loss of six millions of lives. Adolph Hitler – the evil scourge Jack personally blamed for the loss of his beloved Nicole. The Duke and his consort were still not welcome in England.

The dance floor was already occupied with a dozen couples doing society's version of swing, an upbeat dignified fox trot, to Les Brown's renowned orchestra. Under the hand-painted vaulted ceiling, the tables were covered in white-on-white striped damask, candles, and marble urns filled with all-white flowers. Wrapped in etched silver paper and tied with white satin ribbon were favors for the ladies – probably French perfume from their size and shape.

When they reached their designated table, still half-empty, Petal walked around it so that she would be seated next to the daring Wall Street tycoon Doug Burson. Petal was not above picking the brains of those men she thought could be useful. But before plunging into more serious matters, she reminded Burson of an escapade from their past. Elsa Branff, seated to Jack's left, was busy talking to the walker on her left. Jack tried his crab soufflé garnished with Beluga caviar. It was outstanding , but too filling and rich to finish. At least four additional courses would be served before a sampling of desserts, chocolates, marzipan pastries, and after-dinner liqueurs.

Scanning the palatial room it once again occurred to Jack that Versailles, during the reign of Louis XIV, had never contained more decorative wealth at one time than could be found at a typical Palm Beach charitable event. By itself, the choker Petal wore was equivalent in value to a fully staffed ocean-going yacht. Five hundred guests, two hundred and fifty of them women . . . The early morning hours before the Harry Winston and Tiffany masterpieces could be replaced in vaults would be a perfect opportunity for a daring cat burglar, Jack mused. If only he was a competent, conscience-free thief instead of Jeremy Randall's hostage forger.

As a novice producer of provenances, Jack had found his first efforts an entertaining challenge. Every handwritten document had to be unique and consistent. As time passed, he discovered that while signatures were relatively easy to vary, he could produce no more than six distinct styles of handwriting – and that required intense concentration. What was more, his inventory of yellowed invoices had quickly disappeared, and decent replacements were near impossible to find. He had tried to explain to Randall that new paper was a sure giveaway, and he couldn't use invoices from defunct hardware or dry goods stores. Since his paintings had fooled professionals, Randall was unconcerned about the credibility of their provenances. They were simply window dressing.

When Jack had been desperate for cash and believed the paintings were legitimate works of art, the sporadic requests had been appreciated. But after Randall was certain his accomplice dared not betray him, he became increasingly greedy. Formerly undiscovered masterpieces began turning up as regularly as Jack's monthly copy of *Esquire*. Someone was producing damned good fakes. Experts accepted them without question. Galleries vied for the privilege of handling them. Jack's fear of exposure increased with every passed forgery. Randall could take off in the middle of the night leaving him to face charges. From the onset, as a favor to the severely incapacitated man, Jack had delivered the paintings and their accompanying documentation to galleries and private clients. It was Jack the buyers would remember and could identify. And every dispute produced increasingly overt threats.

"I have passports to a dozen countries in a dozen names. You have your precious daughters. Let's not forget that you're doing this for them," Randall enjoyed reminding him.

"You do remember, don't you, Jack?" Petal said, interrupting his thoughts. "One of the young people had too much to drink and decided to go into the pool fully dressed. Or perhaps he was pushed, I can't say for certain, but before long, half the guests were diving in and splashing the rest of us. Hap Hapsburg lost his Rolex that night. We didn't get home until daylight. It was the leukemia function. Or was it the Red Cross Ball?"

"Leukemia," Jack supplied. "Two years ago, I think."

"Come, Jack! The Duke is going to waltz with Lane, and Teddy is right behind him with the Duchess. I've been dying to have a small dinner party for them, perhaps two dozen close friends."

Petal hadn't waited for Jack's response. She had taken his hand and begun the seemingly impromptu trip to the dance floor the second she had spotted her prey. There was no escape. The dance floor. The dreaded introduction. The polite smiles all around. The invitation that he prayed the Duke and Duchess would decline. If not, he would spend an entire evening being gracious to a man he despised.

Jack knew what he had to do. He had been thinking about it for more than a year. He would have to leave the two most precious people in his life knowing the anguish it would cause them. He would have to do it in a way that would squelch questions or tracking. Every day he found another excuse to put it off.

Chapter Thirty

"Still think my father was meeting with Jeremy Randall because he enjoyed the company of a kindred spirit?" I whispered to Raul when we were inside the Dakota's elevator. We descended one floor and were joined by three passengers speaking Italian. Our conversation would have to wait.

"You definitely hit a nerve when you asked about the Renoir," Raul said as we walked back to my apartment. "That stopped him dead in his tracks. I'm thinking that your father and Randall were involved in something criminal and Randall was blackmailing him."

My brain was being bombarded by a dozen disturbing and conflicting theories. "I don't know. I have to take another look at that stationery. How fast can you walk?"

"Faster than you."

We half scurried/half ran as we tried to avoid colliding with the surge of people walking, shopping, pushing baby carriages, and unloading trucks. By the time we reached my building we were both flushed and breathless. The dials above the elevators told us that one was stopped on the fourteenth floor and the other was in the basement — no doubt still under repair.

"The stairs," I panted. Four flights later we were gasping for air. I knew what had been missing from my life since we broke up: the rush, the thrill of tackling the unknown. The key shook in my hand when I opened the door. I flopped onto my kitchen chair and spread the assorted stationery across the table. Looking past the obvious I saw the common thread. Why hadn't I noticed it before? The box of pen points, the scissors, the paste, five bottles of ink. I must have been blind, but my eyes were used to seeing script produced by ballpoint pens. Suddenly, the answer was obvious. "These were all done by the same person. My father."

"How do you know that? What is it that you see?"

"Look!" I said, pointing at the top page. "They're all done in a different script, with different colored ink, some in French, some in English, but one thing is the same. The script doesn't fade. Quills have to be continuously redipped. The script goes from dark to light as the ink runs out. Look at this page and this one. No fading. Whoever wrote these redipped his pen frequently, perhaps as often as every word, well before the ink ran out. One sheet could be attributed to a personal style, but not all of them. My father created these," I said, with more than a trace of pride. "They're practice pieces."

"So that's why you asked Randall about the provenance."

"When Daddy brought the paintings to this country it's logical to assume that he lacked supporting documents. My guess is that he decided to manufacture his own. If Randall realized the provenances were fake, he could use that to blackmail Daddy."

"But why would he think the provenances were fakes? Your father's handiwork fooled even you. Unless . . . Unless one or more of the paintings were forgeries."

"My father wouldn't pass off a forgery as genuine," I stubbornly insisted.

"Not even if he was desperate? Not even if he had two expensive daughters to support? Maybe he didn't realize they were forgeries but Randall did. Or maybe he didn't he see it as stealing. What makes any painting worth a million dollars? Can't a man like Randall find someone to produce good copies? A good copy would be a piece of cake to sell if it had convincing documentation."

Raul's theories were hard to dispute. I could remember seeing many disturbing paintings hanging in galleries and museums and never dreamed of questioning their authenticity.

"Think about it. He was blackmailing your father to make provenances for his forgeries. Do you think Randall is capable of that?"

I shook my head. "Absolutely! The man's a parasitic maggot. Look at the way he mistreated Willy."

"Maybe your father wasn't entirely innocent, but at some point he wanted out. He probably feared they would be caught. They could go to jail. But Randall wouldn't let him out. He demanded more and more. Remember the ever-increasing appointments with the mysterious Crab."

"My father chose death over disgrace. That's what he meant in his letter when he said he was doing this to protect us." The empathy I saw in Raul's eyes was making me feel entirely too vulnerable. "Damn Randall! A pox on his head!"

Raul laughed. "A pox on his head? Where did you hear that?"

"It's one of my boss' milder epitaphs — a literal translation of something he mutters under his breath."

"I don't think I've ever heard you curse before."

"That does it. I don't care what it takes. Willy is not going back to that vile unscrupulous man. Could I really go to jail for trying to protect a helpless abused man? Could Randall charge me with kidnapping?"

"Relax! I'm going to contact him and let him know that if he even thinks about going to the police, we'll go directly to the DA and charge him with fraud and blackmail. He doesn't know if we have proof of his involvement. As bluffs go, it's a reasonably good one."

*   *   *

For the next two weeks, I met with Raul every third or fourth night for a brief update at a Hamburger Heaven — a neutral location. I no longer trusted myself to meet him at my apartment. I recognized the signs: the shared jokes, the teasing – the erotic dreams. It would be too easy to forget what had driven us apart, too easy to end up rolling about in my queen-sized bed. He might be ready to try it again, but I wasn't. Nothing had changed. It was a risk I couldn't chance. Every time I heard my voice grow mint-julep and Georgia-peach-pie sultry, I made certain the next time I spoke it was in my best clipped, time-is-money New York accent.

As for progress, advances were small, setbacks were frequent. Randall had hired a team of attorneys who were inundating Raul with a trainload of paper. Apparently, he was not easily bluffed. Things were not going smoothly for our side.

"Any thoughts as to where Randall might have gotten the forgeries?" Raul asked, as I was about to bite into my chili cheeseburger. "It would be terrific if we could prove criminal activity and put him in jail."

"Randall must know hundreds of people in the art world. The forger might be in the same position as my father, forced to participate or be exposed and just as unlikely to come forward."

"I intend to rent a car so I can drive up and meet Willy this Sunday. It's important that he's comfortable with me if we have to go before a judge. I was hoping you would like to come. He likes and trusts you."

"I really should," I replied, far too quickly. "I haven't seen him in several weeks. He must think that I abandoned him. Besides, you may not find the place without me."

"Terrific. Should we ask Ted? Maybe he'd like to come."

I pretended to cough so I could hide the lower half of my ketchup-red face behind my napkin. I hadn't spoken to Ted since the morning he left. But I had thought about him. And when Raul left New York I fully intended to call him.

"Ted will be away, in Boston, the entire weekend, visiting an aunt," I lied, the best one I could produce under pressure.

Chapter Thirty-One

Sunday, as planned, Raul drove and I did my best to retrace the route to Woody and Essie's lodge. A light dusting of snow had turned the landscape into a Christmas card. I was looking for a rusted Yoohoo sign where we should turn, but when we reached it all that was identifiable was a brown and white can of soda. The twisty mountain road was narrower than I remembered. A pothole sent me sliding to the center of the car, shoulder to shoulder, thigh to thigh with Raul. I caught his smug smile and crept back to my original position — hugging the doorknob.

"Take a left."

"Where?" Raul asked. "That break in the trees? That can't be a road. It doesn't look paved."

"It isn't paved, and we're almost there. If that large rock on the side of the road wasn't covered with snow you would see the white paint."

A half mile later we pulled into Woody and Essie's driveway. Willy was waiting for us. As we followed him to the main building, I realized the bottoms of Raul's thin shoes were soaked, and despite all efforts to hide it, he was shivering. I had worn boots, gloves, my voluminous shaggy overcoat, and a hat. Some things never change – like hardheaded stubborn men.

When Willy removed his coat and hat I saw that his hair was neatly trimmed and his nails were clean and clipped. He was wearing a pair of pants and a shirt I'd purchased for him, thick-soled work shoes I didn't recognize, and a navy cashmere sweater that had been Daddy's. I was as proud as a mother peahen. Woody and Willy took Raul to see the rest of the lodge. Having seen it, I stayed with Essie, a tiny woman with faded blue eyes and tightly curled, coarse gray hair, in the main entry before a huge crackling fire.

"Wait till you see Willy's cabin," Essie said. "He has a surprise for you."

"Do you know what it is?"

"I'm not allowed to tell. It would spoil Willy's surprise."

The men returned in a few minutes. "Willy wants to show me his cabin," I told Raul. "You'd better stay here with Woody and warm up."

"I'm fine," Raul said. "You don't think I'm going to let a little cold weather scare me."

The four of us followed Willy to the nearest cabin. On one side of the room was a rough-hewn chair, a braided rug, and a bed covered with a tan chenille spread. On the other side stood an easel with a brilliant study of water lilies on it — one Monet would have been pleased to claim as his own. It was not an exact duplicate, not one that I was familiar with, but it could fool a lot of people. Art students the world over slavishly copying the maestro couldn't produce this. This was the work of a truly gifted artist. I was too stunned to move, let alone speak.

"Mine. I give it to you," Willy announced. "Merry Christmas!"

"He thinks when someone gets a present, that it's for Christmas," Essie explained. "Isn't that precious?"

"Go on and take it," Woody said. "He made it for you. The next one's for Essie and me."

"Monet," Raul said softly, taking my arm to steady me. "Are you all right, Charlie?"

"I'm terrific," I laughed, my voice as giddy as I felt. "Randall didn't have to look far to find his forger. No wonder he's so desperate to get him back." I turned to Essie, who obviously had no idea what was being discussed. "How did you discover Willy could paint?"

"He didn't like the watercolor set my boy Amos used to play with. He tried fiddling with it — adding things, trying to thin it and change the colors. When he smeared it on paper with his fingers, we finally figured out what he was trying to do. Had to drive almost sixty miles before we found an art store. This fellow knew just what he wanted. Pointed to colors on a chart, and tubes of paint, brushes, oil, spirits."

"It's pretty good, don't you think?" Woody asked.

"He's more than good, Woody," I said. "He's God's own miracle."

I tried questioning Willy. Where did he learn to paint? Had someone taught him? No one had taught him. Did he paint from memory or from a picture? Both, but mostly from pictures. Had Randall brought works of art home for him to study? No. Had Randall often taken him to museums, like the Frick where I'd found him staring at a Corot? They had spent a great deal of time in museums and galleries, and if I understood correctly, museums all around the world. As to the mechanics, a vision he might have before he began a work, or what he thought about as he painted, Willy was unable to explain.

"Go on and show her, Willy," Essie urged, when he balked at my request for a demonstration. "He's shy — frightened to let anyone but me see him paint."

That didn't surprise me. Randall must have threatened him with beatings, imprisonment, or death if he revealed his talent.

"Go on," Essie encouraged. "Take out your canvas and paints.

Miss Charlotte is your friend. No one's going to hurt you. You want her to be proud of you, don't you?"

Willy dug out his supplies, including his book of Impressionists, and set up his work area with a fresh canvas. I thought we had lost his attention as he rifled through the pages, but finally he stopped at a still-life by Cézanne titled "Fruit Bowl, Glass, and Apples." He used his fingers and nails as much as he did a brush. Despite his bizarre facial contortions, it was apparent the artist was lost in his work. After forty minutes we could see the bowl and apples taking shape. Willy had selected a different perspective from the original, and Cézanne's glass was missing. I would have liked to stay longer and watch, but I knew that many hours of effort would go into this new creation, and we had to get back to the city before the snow made driving too hazardous.

"Should we tell folks about Willy's painting?" Essie asked.

"Not yet. This adds a whole new dimension to the case," Raul said.

"Do you think it'll help or hurt?" she asked.

Raul put his hand on Essie's shoulder. "Help. We'll find a way to make it help."

"You folks should stay the night," Woody suggested as we walked back to the main lodge. "We have lots of room. It's coming down hard, and it doesn't look like it's stopping."

The snow, which had scarcely powdered the ground when we'd arrived, was now above our ankles. Drifts went as high as our knees.

"What about it, Charlie?" Raul said. "It's four o'clock. Why don't we stay and get an early start tomorrow morning? By then the roads will be plowed. Getting back will be a cinch."

You'd like that, I thought. A remote romantic setting, miles from civilization, blazing logs in the fireplace, a couple of hot toddies to melt inhibitions, and I would slide right back to the battle between my upper and lower halves.

"The weatherman only predicted a few inches," I said. "It should be stopping any minute. Raul and I both have to work tomorrow. Once we get on a main road, we'll be fine." I kissed my three friends good-bye and promised to return soon. Willy held Essie's hand as he waved at us.

The tires spun and the car skidded as we pulled away. After what seemed hours we reached the end of the long driveway.

"Let's hope the next road has been plowed," Raul said.

It hadn't.

"We can't be too far from the highway. Conditions will get better as we get closer," I promised.

"Let's hope so. I would hate being stuck out here. It's getting harder to see the road."

It looked like we were in a blizzard of goose down. Even worse, pockets of snow had accumulated in the corners of the windshield and were closing in on the fan-shaped center. My watch said five twenty, but the sky said later.

By six thirty we had covered no more than a mile or two and had seen no vehicles either coming or going. Raul lowered his window and pushed back the block of snow. Temperature within the car dropped radically. I waited until he was finished before doing the same to mine. With the window open, I could see no more than a few yards. I turned to the rear window — it was entirely covered. We inched forward. I prayed as snow crunched beneath our wheels. The snow on our windshield had become clumps of ice that now nearly obliterated our vision. The thrashing wipers groaned as they scraped the gritty surface. Raul stopped the car, jumped out and pulled several clumps of ice off the windshield. He returned seconds later covered in snow and shivering.

"Maybe we should look for a safe place to wait this out," I said, miserable with guilt.

"I didn't want to worry you but I've been looking for a safe place to stop for the last thirty minutes. I don't know how much longer I can keep this thing moving."

As if to accentuate the odds of impending disaster the engine coughed. I checked my watch. We had been driving two hours. "Look! Isn't that a clearing up ahead? If we can make it there, at least we won't have to stop on the road."

"Let's hope we have enough gas. We're going to need it."

I leaned closer so I could read the gauge. "The tank is a quarter full. That's more than enough to get us to a gas station once we're able to move again."

"I'm not worried about a gas station. We have to stay warm until someone comes to rescue us or we'll freeze." We made it to the clearing. After a few minutes of letting the engine run with the heater set to high, we reluctantly turned it off. Skiers hate this type of snow — driving, wet, icy, treacherous. Judging by the conditions, it might be days before we were rescued. I readjusted my collar. Raul had to be freezing. "Why did you have to wear that dumb raincoat?"

"It's all I have. There's not much call for overcoats in Florida. The parka I had when I was in law school was shot. Besides, you don't hear me complaining, do you?"

"You don't have to complain. You're shivering and your lips are blue. We're never going to get through this alive unless we keep each other warm. Slide over and open that pathetic excuse for a coat."

Raul slid to my side of the car. I unbuttoned my coat. He slipped his arms around my back. I could feel his icy hands through my bulky sweater.

"Now this was a great idea," he murmured. "I feel much warmer already."

"Don't look so smug. This is a simple act of mercy. I'd feel dreadful if you flew up to help me and froze to death in the process."

"As long as you're being merciful, would you mind very much blowing on my ears?"

I had a hat and gloves. Raul had neither. Frostbite was a real possibility. I removed my scarf and tied it over his head and under his chin, fully expecting a protest. I guess the threat of losing both ears to frostbite superceded the fear of looking absurd. He used the activity to resettle himself. Somehow his face came to rest against mine. It soon went from cold to warm. This was friendlier than I'd intended. There was a difference between hugging and holding. I was being embraced. The temperature in the car sank with each tick of the clock. At some point I fell asleep. I dreamed that Raul was kissing me, gentle comforting kisses. Perhaps it wasn't a dream. I awoke when I felt him move away. I checked my watch. It was after nine.

"What are you doing?"

He was buttoning his coat. "We both fell asleep. It's very cold in here. I have to turn on the engine before it freezes, but I can't start the car until I make certain the exhaust pipe isn't blocked with snow. The fumes could back up and we'll die of carbon monoxide poisoning."

"I'll go with you."

"Stay put. It only takes one person." Before I could argue he was out the door. He returned wetter and colder than before. Thankfully, the engine started. I brushed the snow from Raul's hair and eyelashes and once again opened my coat. We resumed our former position. The heater warmed my frozen toes. I fell back to sleep. The next time I awoke Raul was playing with my hair. When he saw me open my eyes, he kissed my neck, his lashes brushing my cheek. If someone happened to be watching, I appeared to be cooperating.

"You never answered my question," he said. "Was it as good with Ted as it was with us?"

I pushed his head away. "I don't believe it. Is there no limit to your arrogance?"

He replaced his head, lower this time, on my chest. His right hand slipped under my sweater, to my back just above my waist. "Not just making love. I mean all of it — being together, talking, arguing. I really miss the arguing. Admit it. We didn't need fireworks. We made our own."

I tried to envision Ted's face but the image refused to come. "Arguing. Sometimes I miss the arguing," I said. Making love was what I was thinking. That first time in the pool, in my bed, in the hotel room. Then it hit me. *Was*, Raul had said.

"*Was* it as good with Ted as it was with us?" I repeated. "You used the past tense to describe my relationship with Ted? Stuck in a snowstorm, dressed for the Easter Parade, waiting to freeze to death and you're as pigheaded as ever."

"Did you or did you not tell me you were seeing some guy long after you broke up with him? Do you think you could fool me twice? That ridiculous act at the airport – fawning all over the poor fellow. I can read you like a book, and not a novel, a comic book. Mr. Jensen is history. You haven't gone out with him since the day I arrived." He kissed the base of my neck.

"You followed me. I can't believe it. You followed me."

"Follow you? I would never follow you. I bribed your nosy janitor."

There seemed no point in quarrelling. I listened to the snow falling. You could hear snow falling by the absolute absence of sound. No birds chirping. No crickets. Just silence. We were locked inside another universe — dark, frozen, still. The car got a lot warmer after he started kissing me, hot little kisses on my forehead, neck, and lips.

"Just because I'm letting you kiss me," I said, desperately trying to sound stern, "doesn't mean I'd ever consider trying it again. Five minutes after we're back in the city, I'm going to forget everything that takes place tonight. It's back to business. I can't go through that again, and I won't."

"You need me. You're a vivacious sexy woman with an uncanny instinct for art, but you're a rotten judge of character. Face it! You need me."

A vivacious sexy woman with an uncanny instinct for art? "That van Gogh we saw that day was a forgery. 'Badly damaged in transit.' Another lie! It hadn't required extensive repair. It was a fake. I'd swear to it."

"I always believed you."

But what about the second part of that statement? Maybe I wasn't the best judge of character. But rotten?

As if he could read my mind, Raul said, "Jeremy Randall? An adolescent would have seen through his preposterous stories. Hal Holmes? You completely misread him. Wrote him off without giving the poor fellow a chance to tell his side of the story. And what about your own sister? What about Amelia? How well do you know her? Admit it! You're a rotten judge of character and you need me."

"It won't work. We're from two different solar systems."

"We'll make it work. We're a great team. Together we can do anything. I'll get a job anywhere we can be together. New York isn't such a bad place to live."

"For people who own overcoats. And what about Willy? Caring for him is a lifelong responsibility. I can't ask you to take that on."

"We'll adopt him. I promise to raise him like my very own."

"He's an artistic genius, you know."

"He's a savant."

"A what?"

"A savant. A retarded person with an inexplicable gift. There's a man in Miami who's a savant. He can barely read, but give him a date — any date over the last thousand years, and he can tell you what day of the week it fell on. I don't think I've ever heard of a savant who paints before, but I've heard about one who can play an entire piano concerto after hearing it once."

"Savant or genius, Randall will never let him go. Willy's the goose that laid the golden egg. What do we have? A few sheets of paper, a wild theory, my word against a respected art expert, and Willy's Monet. No one will believe us. We'll be laughed at. Daddy's name will be blackened. Amelia and Hal will be hounded by reporters. And in the end we'll lose."

"Look at that pout. Do you know that your upper lip drives me wild?" He kissed the aforementioned lip. "Stop worrying. I already thought of a way we can use Willy's gift to our advantage, and yes, maybe even put Randall in jail where he belongs."

I returned the kiss — and the next. "We've been in this car for days. How much gas do we have left?"

"A quarter of a tank."

"That's what you said hours ago. We must be empty by now."

"Don't worry about the gas. It's more important for you to tell me how much you love me, and how much you've missed me."

"I intend to continue working. Your family will have to get used to the idea. That is, unless we die out here frozen together like twin Popsicle sticks."

"I'll talk to my father. My sisters will back me up. They think you're fantastic."

"What about your mother?"

"She thinks you're fantastic too."

"Oh sure." I turned the door handle and pushed. The door wouldn't budge. I panicked. I knew the time was getting near when I would have to use the bathroom.'

"What do you think you're doing?"

"It's my turn to clear the exhaust pipe, but the door's stuck. The snow's blocking it. And it's cold." I felt a tear slide down my nose. "If we don't start the engine soon it won't start again." Damn! I hated to be seen crying. "This is all my fault. You wanted to stay. I was the one who insisted on leaving because I was afraid . . . And now . . ."

"Say the most romantic thing you can think of and I'll make it all better. I promise."

"How?"

"Never mind how. Just say the most romantic thing you can think of."

"I'm glad that I asked you to help me. And I'm happy that you came."

"You call that romantic? That's pathetic. You'll have to do much better than that."

"I'm a rotten judge of character and I need you."

He took my face in his hands. "Nice. Sweet. But still not good enough. Try harder. Let yourself go. Say something crazy. Something passionate."

"There's no way you can fix this. We're stranded in a snowstorm. No one knows we're here. No one's coming to rescue us."

"So then what does it matter what you say? Tell me how much you love me and don't spare the salsa. I want to hear it once before I die."

"If you ever leave me again, I will . . ." and then I whispered it — the worst and most vulgar threat ever, the one I'd heard Sid Gluck scream over the phone — the one involving a man's privates.

"Charlotte Michelle Fitzpatrick Morgan, that's the most romantic thing you've ever said to me. If it weren't for all these clothes I would make love to you right here and now."

"So how are you planning to get us out of here, buster?" I asked. "Or was that simply a mean manipulative lie?"

"The state troopers should find us pretty soon. Before we left I told Woody if I didn't call the lodge in three hours to notify the state police."

Then I heard it. The most terrifying sound ever – the growl of a nearby grizzly bear. My childhood summer camp was located in the Adirondacks. Anyone who ever camped there has heard stories about grizzly bears. In their quest for food marauding bears have been known to rip apart cars. On their hind legs they can stand ten feet high. They can tear a man's head off with a single swipe of a paw. And one was not more than a car length away. "Don't say anything," I whispered. "Don't even breathe. That's a grizzly bear. Oh my God, he's getting closer." Instead of looking frightened, the man holding me laughed. "Why are you laughing? Are you insane?"

"A grizzly bear? You hear a grizzly bear? You think you don't need me? That's the snowplow, you ninny."

Chapter Thirty-Two

Things I learned about Willy following the snowstorm: Raul was right, Willy was a savant. There was no other explanation for his extraordinary gift. And he didn't always feel like painting. He could be encouraged but not pushed. Not everything he produced was outstanding. He didn't do portraits. He could lose interest in a promising project and never complete it. It was wise to provide him with oversized canvases, because he rarely centered his works. After completion they usually required educated trimming. But some were truly spectacular!

A few days after we returned to the city I received an envelope containing my last two checks for Willy's care and a brief note from Woody. I called him.

"Essie's got her heart set on keeping Willy, and I don't feel right about taking your money. He more than pays his way by helping with chores."

"I'm happy to hear that everything is working out so well."

"Only fair to tell you Essie and I want custody. Aim to hire a lawyer if we have to."

I was speechless. Angry. Hurt. Betrayed by people I'd trusted.

"Before you get your feathers all ruffled, you think about it. People in Ramapoka don't make fun of Willy like they do in a big city. They're used to him here. He's made friends. He's happy. He's got us to look out for him. You go to work. Travel."

"But the cost of providing for Willy's surgery, dental treatment, hiring an attorney —"

"Willy's not going to forget you or what you done for him. You and your gentleman friend are always welcome here. Be our guests and stay as long as you'd like. Miss Charlie, you're still young. You'll get married, have children. I'm right fond of Willy, but Essie . . . Well, Essie's got her boy back. It would break her heart to give him up."

The lengthy speech Woody had delivered was rehearsed but honest. He and Essie were good people, eager to provide Willy with more than safety and paid concern. I was being unreasonable and selfish. "Tell Essie not to worry. Raul and I will do everything we can to help you."

*   *   *

Raul's plan involved publicity. He believed whoever could get the press on their side would win. Now that I knew my father's part in Randall's scheme, my dread of publicity rivaled Petal's. I tried to persuade Raul to think of another way.

"You said it yourself," he reminded me. "We can't prove a thing: not that Randall abused Willy or that he passed his work off as genuine. And we won't get cooperation from any gallery who carried or displayed Willy's work. They have too much to lose. The good news is the media loves a great human interest story, and we're sitting on the hottest one to come along in years."

"What about my father's reputation?"

"We'll try to keep his part in the crime secret, but I can't promise anything. If it does become public, the fact that he chose to kill himself rather than continuing, will make him sympathetic and put the blame squarely on Randall. If we don't do this, Willy will ultimately be returned to Randall. I'm afraid that I can't think of another solution."

It was a panic-provoking decision, but after considering both extremes, I decided that Willy's imminent safety and happiness were more important.

I laid out Raul's plan for Woody and Essie, who were so anxious to keep Willy, they would go along with anything. The three of us spent hours explaining the importance of the press conference to Willy.

Raul also persuaded the prestigious law office of Corbit, Lang, and Klein to get involved. When I questioned the firm's motives, the only response I received from Raul was "they have their reasons" and a enigmatic smile. I knew Corbit, Lang, and Klein represented the rich, powerful, and famous, but I was too frantic trying to juggle work, Willy, Woody, Essie, Raul, and rampaging nerves to waste energy on learning more.

Raul scheduled the conference at Marshall Corbit's sprawling Cold Spring Harbor estate. The tent, erected on the expansive lawn behind the house, held seventy to eighty expectant reporters and photographers. On the stage were two empty chairs and three of Willy's finer efforts, including a work-in-progress.

Woody and Essie said they preferred to remain in the house until the last reporter left. My job was to keep Willy calm and insure his cooperation. I held his hand and reassured him as we waited by the tent's flap, listening as Raul prepared the restive audience. Willy was an autistic savant, Raul explained, a mentally handicapped man with an inexplicable talent for imitating Impressionist masters. We believed his paintings had been sold as forgeries. Willy had come to me asking for protection, begging not to be returned to Jeremy Randall. I had placed him in a safe and caring environment. We didn't know for certain if Jeremy Randall was Willy's legal guardian. Substantiating documents had been promised, but not provided. Doctors were ready to testify that Willy had suffered neglect and abuse, though not necessarily at the hands of Jeremy Randall. Raul added that a deluge of direct questions would frighten and confuse Willy. Reporters were requested to submit questions in writing and remain quiet while I put those questions to Willy. Photographers were asked to wait until the end of the interview for photographs.

I led Willy to the stage. There was no way to predict his response. I prayed. I prayed that he wouldn't bolt. I prayed reporters would heed Raul's appeal for silence and patience. I prayed the photographers would cooperate. I prayed people watching would look past Willy's fearsome appearance and see the gentle soul beneath. I prayed that Willy would decide today was a fine day to paint.

Willy answered my questions as best he could, though often not loud enough to be heard beyond the first few rows. He didn't understand the need for the microphone or the echoes it caused, and pulled away when I moved it closer. I asked him to paint for us. After some prodding, he approached his half-finished vase of flowers, corrected an errant petal with his fingertip and pronounced it, "Good!" A ripple of polite laughter seemed to please him. I urged him to continue painting, but he was distracted. I observed several reporters checking their watches.

"Ask him about Jeremy Randall," a voice from the back called.

"I don't go with Randall," Willy informed the unknown questioner. "I stay with Woody and Essie."

A volley of questions attacked us from all directions. Willy froze. I could read the confusion and fear on his face.

"Please," I pleaded. "You're frightening him." The audience quieted. I knew I would have just one more opportunity to convince a tent filled with cynics before chaos reigned. I led Willy to the Monet he had given me. "Did you really do this painting?" I said, feigning disbelief. "Tell the truth. Someone helped you."

"My painting!" Willy announced, loud enough for the last person in the back row to hear. He forgot the spectators and began thrusting his finger at me. "Merry Christmas. You give me nice gloves – warm gloves. I make my painting for you. Merry Christmas!"

The entire room broke into laughter followed by spontaneous applause. It was thrilling to watch Willy's face as he slowly came to understand he was the cause of the enthusiastic outburst. "My painting!" Willy told the former doubters as he repeatedly pointed to his chest.

True artist that he was, Willy reveled in the attention by attempting to answer every question I relayed to him. He smiled. He laughed with his audience when he realized he had made a joke. As a finale, he returned to the work-in-progress and solemnly added a lovely peony. Jaded reporters rose to cheer.

We had won.

Photographers who had been impatiently waiting began snapping their cameras and calling out requests for poses. Though we had discussed the possibility, I feared Willy might be alarmed, but once again he astounded me. He was fascinated by the flashing lights.

"Pictures. They take my picture," he informed me.

I sensed he was disappointed when the hubbub ended and Essie and Woody came to fetch him.

Raul and I returned to my apartment, crossed our fingers, and braced ourselves for a barrage of lawsuits from Randall's attorneys. The six o'clock news carried the story.

Reporters attempting to interview Randall discovered he had fled. All efforts to reach him by phone at his London and Paris' homes were unsuccessful. His answering services had no knowledge of his whereabouts, and his attorneys' office had no comment.

We congratulated ourselves on a temporary victory. Raul and I called Woody to share the hopeful news then splurged on an expensive dinner to celebrate.

Joy and tranquility lasted twelve brief hours. The next morning the New York City Police *requested* I submit to an interview so that I could "shed light on a potential criminal investigation." Knowing the international implications of the case, Raul notified the FBI that I would be volunteering my help and suggested their agents be present at the police interview. Thankfully, Woody and Essie were spared, because Raul explained they had never met Jeremy Randall and were merely acting as Willy's caretakers. As for the artist himself, Raul had armed himself with doctors' signed affidavits attesting to Willy's physical condition and mental limitations. Willy received little more than a brief sympathetic questioning.

With Raul as counsel, I spent five hours detailing my knowledge of, and relationship to, Jeremy Randall and William Suffolk, the name on Willy's passport. We learned later that night from the televised news, that as I was repeating my suspicions of fraud and Willy's unwitting participation, the police had been searching Randall's residence and examining his bank accounts. Paint, supplies, and several partially completed canvases had been found. Ashes and scraps of paper, the remains of a fire in Randall's bathtub, showed he had tried to burn incriminating records. Interpol had been notified.

Apparently, Randall's brazen front had been a delaying tactic. The next morning the *New York Times* told the world that Randall's bank accounts, foreign and domestic, had been emptied the day prior to our press conference. And though Raul swore to me that he was innocent, somehow details reached the media.

Raul and I were dogged by reporters hungry for information to feed their insatiable readers. We had all been assigned grandiose labels. Jeremy Randall was the "Mastermind" or the "Fiendish Mastermind." Willy was the "Gentle Giant Genius." Raul was the "Rising Young Attorney." And I was the "Socialite Model and Art Expert."

At Willy's custody hearing, our doctors testified on our behalf. There were no doctors opposing. After a lengthy in chambers conference with the judge, Woody and Essie were granted temporary custody. Essie and I were named co-executors of Willy's trust fund — unsolicited donations had reached us. Provided Randall did not reappear to contest the decision, permanent custody was virtually guaranteed following a year's wait.

In the midst of the excitement, I received a call from the owner of Gallery Three Fifty-Two. "It's Madame Ivanavich and she's furious," I whispered to Raul, who could hear my side of the conversation from the couch. "She's threatening to sue both of us."

"It's going to be fine. Just tell her we'll meet her tomorrow morning at ten at the Gallery," Raul said.

*   *   *

By 10:10 the next morning we were closeted in Madame's small private office, and the object of her tirade.

"My phone hasn't stopped ringing since your circus sideshow." Madame's dark eyes glared at us through her black framed glasses. "I've been interrogated by the police. I've been accused of collusion. My customers believe every painting they've purchased from me is a forgery. They're demanding their money returned. My insurance company has informed me claims will far exceed my coverage. Do you realize what your little charade has done? You have ruined me. Retract everything or I'll sue you for every penny you have or will earn."

"We can't retract the truth," Raul said. "But I'd be happy to tell you how to restore confidence and turn what appears to be a calamity into a golden opportunity, unless you'd rather we leave."

Leaning against her desk, Madame Ivanavich patted her bun. "I'm listening."

I took the chair farthest from Madame while Raul remained standing.

"You'll explain to your customers, that you'll provide the services of Charlotte Morgan, the woman who single-handedly uncovered the forgeries and exposed the mastermind behind them," he counseled, momentarily stopping to smile at me.

Madame sneered. "If you're trying to be funny, I fail to see the humor."

"Not at all," Raul continued with the same even modulation. "Miss Morgan will examine any and all paintings you've sold and then provide a signed letter of authenticity stating the painting was either done by the stated artist or by William Suffolk, a once-in-a-century genius. After verification, the buyer can either opt to keep it or return it for the original purchase price."

"I might be able to hang on a year before having to declare bankruptcy."

"Madame," I said, "if the paintings are genuine and buyers want their money returned that would be ideal. You know better than anyone, the value of important pieces has skyrocketed. Many have doubled or tripled in value in the last few years. You can easily resell anything decent at a sizable profit."

"What do you suggest I do with the forgeries?"

"Inform your buyers that returned pieces will be priced higher than William's newer ones."

"Higher? Do you think people are fools?"

"Willy isn't a forger," Raul reminded her. "You've read what the newspapers are calling him. He's a genius and an international celebrity. Price his pieces high enough and every millionaire will trade in his Rolls Royce for the privilege of owning one. Look at the publicity he's already generated for the gallery."

"Top artists are commanding higher prices," Madame conceded. "Your Gentle Giant may be a celebrity, but I don't know. There's a risk."

Raul shrugged. "Or we can look for another gallery to handle William's work, and you can sue Jeremy Randall. He's the one responsible for your problems. We're only the messengers."

It took less than a heartbeat for Madame's response. "Gallery Three Fifty-Two has exclusive representation. I wouldn't consider handling William Suffolk without exclusive representation."

"Agreed."

"I determine the selling price and can limit sales. A sudden glut will force down prices."

"You handle all the details." Raul looked at me and received my approval. "Gallery Three Fifty-Two gets a two year contract subject to yearly renewals."

"A ten year contract with an option for another five years."

"A five year contract to start, with two year options. And you'll pay Miss Morgan a case-by-case consultant's fee for her time and expertise."

We watched Madame's eyes narrow. "How much?"

"I'm afraid I can't give you those figures at this moment. But it'll be fair to both parties. I'll have to get back to you after I've made inquiries."

*   *   *

The operation to correct Willy's tongue and realign his jaw was performed. As predicted, his appearance and speech improved measurably. We never did determine how he came to be a part of Randall's household. Based on discussions with judges and other attorneys, Raul assured me, if a routine custody battle had been held, we most assuredly would have lost.

As for the missing Fiendish Mastermind, rumors placed him in Australia, Egypt, Brazil, and Rhodesia. There was a side of me that would have liked to see Randall rot in jail because of his part in my father's death. Another side hoped the horrid man would stay buried. No one knew of my father's participation in the crime and I wanted to keep it that way.

As for Ted Jensen, it wasn't necessary to tell him my decision. He had seen Raul with me on television, read the newspaper accounts, and had drawn his own conclusions. My good friend called to wish us every happiness.

Raul joined the law firm of Corbit, Lang, and Klein. Unbeknownst to me, shortly after he arrived in Manhattan, he had used part of his free time to seek employment. I finally understood the firm's willingness to get involved in Willy's case. While I shunned publicity, law firms loved it. Raul would be providing his services to the rich, famous, and powerful, not defending the poor and the downtrodden. But he claimed, as I was an easy touch, he could always count on me to provide all the pro bono work he needed to satisfy his conscience. Which wasn't easy to deny — and Raul didn't even know that the proceeds of my first check from Gallery Three Fifty-two had gone to Carlos and Maria. Their granddaughter had been diagnosed with leukemia. The money would help with medical expenses.

Thanks to my father, Willy, and Jeremy Randall, I had a new career. My business card read, "Charlotte Morgan, Art Consultant, Specializing in Oil Paintings." So far, my services have not been sought by museums or auction houses hoping to correct past errors. Museum directors would rather be caught naked on Christmas morning, in Times Square,than admit they have been flimflammed. As for auction houses, I'd learned they were concerned with making money, not uncovering frauds. There were, however, a number of private individuals who wished to employ me.

Did I merit the title *Art Consultant*? A glance at a provenance and I knew instantly whether Daddy's fine hand was involved. For works minus Daddy's substantiating documents, I had to rely on instinct and research. I was learning to trust that queasy sensation I get when I see a fake. The difficulty is in finding supporting evidence to prove it to others.

Shortly after the snowstorm Raul moved in with me. We lived together without benefit of clergy. Naturally, our families were shocked, as were some friends. Frankly, I wasn't in a hurry to legalize the arrangement. Raul had some antiquated ideas of what a woman's role in marriage should be. We were still working out the details. Some time in the future, before we have children, Raul and I will wed. Maybe we'll have a priest, a rabbi, *and* a minister perform the ceremony.

One of my first non-essential purchases for our apartment was a floor-to-ceiling mirror for our bedroom. I claimed it made the room look bigger — which it did. Of course it served another function as well — a little trick I'd picked up from an old school chum. Raul did take down my hair, though the sensory experience never quite attained the heights it had that first time.

But there are so *many* things Raul did exceptionally well – including several a lady couldn't possibly discuss.

As for my father, there are times that I'm sad for no reason, but the rage is gone. There are times that I remember the many things I loved about Daddy and the fun we shared. There are times when I think he's still alive, because I can feel him looking over my shoulder pleased and proud.

Chapter Thirty-Three

Tijuana, Mexico

The rickety three-legged footstool held a pile of creased magazines and a day-old newspaper left by the whores. A slow moving ceiling fan provided little relief from the omnipresent heat and dank foul air. A sweating guard, a toothpick hanging from his lip, watched with detached interest as John "Jack" Caine, who used to be known as Jack Morgan, reclaimed the things he had surrendered when imprisoned.

Jack examined his money belt. It contained his doctored passport and an even one thousand dollars. He remembered losing twelve hundred or so playing poker, a Dallas back-street game that might have been fixed. He'd spent another thousand on a wild night in San Antonio that he'd like to forget. From there it was only a short hop to Mexico, where he'd had the bad luck of being in the wrong saloon at the wrong time.

"There's only a thousand dollars here," he said in acceptable Spanish, a language he had picked up during his stay. "What happened to the rest?"

The guard moved the toothpick to the other side of his mouth and shrugged. "Expenses, *senor*. You wanted better food, clean clothes, sheets, women. These things cost money. Not that any of it found its way to a poor man like me, a man with eight hungry mouths to feed."

"Expenses. Yes, of course." Jack pulled out a twenty, folded it and handed it to the guard. As he bent to retie his shoe, he bumped the shaky footstool. It toppled. Jack automatically righted it and replaced the scattered material. A picture in one of the magazines caught his attention. He picked it up and stared at the woman standing next to a silver Cadillac. The wind had caught her amethyst chiffon dress and her sun-drenched hair was swept from her face. An apparition. A ghost sent to haunt him. This was Nicole's doing. It was Charlie, but it was also Nicole.

He had dreamed about Nicole last night. In his dreams she would appear, only to vanish around a corner or dissolve into a fog. Last night she had turned to him and spoke. "Forgive me for leaving you."

"My love, find your way back to me," he had called to her.

Then she had faded into nothing.

"Can I have this?" Jack asked, holding the magazine. "I'll pay you for it."

The guard examined the twenty before putting it in his shirt pocket. "For a gentleman such as you, *senor*, what's mine is yours."

Jack carefully tore away the page, stared at it until it was locked into his memory, then folded it and tucked it into his money belt. Outside, he joined the guards and visitors waiting for the bus that would take them into town. As he leaned against a tree he daydreamed about his beloved girls. Who could have predicted his brainy introverted daughter would turn into a shimmering butterfly? Charlie. Always worried about her height, quick to hide behind her pretty older sister. He had pushed her to achieve. Charlie could ski with the best of them. The ribbons she had won for riding could fill a wall. She had excelled scholastically and in every sport she tried. And now she was a model acknowledged for her beauty, and undoubtedly pursued by princes and presidents. What father wouldn't envy him?

Nor could he forget gentle Amelia. Never had there been a better daughter. She would make Hal Holmes a loving wife. By this time, she must have married her dull but devoted millionaire fiancée. Knowing Petal as he did, Amelia's lavish wedding had to be the talk of Palm Beach society.

He had done this. The motherless boy who had to beg for food from working-class neighbors, had accomplished the impossible. He hadn't known how to give them the life they were meant to have, but he had managed to do it anyway. Everything he and Nicole had wanted for their girls: fine manners, opportunity, education, status, good marriages. He wasn't about to jeopardize it all to satisfy the insatiable greed of the devil's own son.

God had fathered only one son. The devil had many: the Marquis de Sade, Hitler, Genghis Khan, Stalin, and Randall Suffolk, also known as Jeremy Randall. He continued to use Randall as his last name because William couldn't, or wouldn't, be retrained to use another. He called the monster "Randy" – easily mistaken for Randall. It had taken Jack nearly a decade to learn what he knew about Randall and William Suffolk, a decade of creating letters of introduction, bills of sale, honorary degrees, and uncovering lies. It was only in the last few months that he had discovered their kinship.

Just as Cain hated Abel, Randall hated his brother. Providing him with the barest essentials a human being needed to survive. Treating him like a slave. Jealousy! Vile murderous jealousy! Cain had envied God's love for his brother and Randall envied the gift God had bestowed on William. Randall's motive for forcing the helpless prodigy to copy the works of others had to be more than simple greed. He couldn't bear to see the deformed genius receive the acknowledgment and acclaim he himself craved. He denied the world the opportunity to see where William's great gift might have taken him, had he been permitted to follow his artist's soul.

If God still heard prayers, He would punish the fiend by sending Randall Suffolk directly to Hell for all eternity. Jack's first priority, his girls, had prevented him from righting the wrong himself. He half-hoped someone would notice the little errors in the provenances. The limited styles of handwriting. The sole antique typewriter. His redipping the quill every few words. It had been five years before he had noticed the silly habit. By that time, he detested Randall and had decided to continue the practice as a means of defiance. It had been risky, but no one had caught it, and most likely, no one would.

When Jack saw the battered bus approaching he allowed himself to imagine a long hot bath, new clothes, and a shave — the kind that begins with a steaming towel and ends with a dusting of talc. He had a thousand dollars, not the twenty-seven thousand he had started with. A thousand dollars. A thousand dollars was a fortune to a starving man. He had a thousand dollars and a plan. Three months in a Mexican jail had stripped him of his illusions about the life of a vagabond. A man like himself was accustomed to better things. He would leave Mexico and head for the Paris of South America – Buenos Aires. Argentina was a modern country well stocked with two things that Jack admired: fine horses and fantastic wealth. Polo ponies, racehorses, thoroughbreds and silver mines. Ranches so vast they required airplanes to oversee them. Where there was landed gentry, there were certain to be lonely widows in need of comfort. Who better to console them? It was the life he was meant to lead. A thousand dollars would get him to Buenos Aires.

Someday! Someday he would see his girls again. Someday he would hold a wee bonnie lad or lass on his knee, and he would tell that precious tyke of the enchanted isle that was Paris before the war. Someday he would spin a tale of a dashing young artist and a beautiful fairy princess made of moonbeams and spun silk, lighter than gossamer, elusive as a shooting star.

Epilogue of *Exceeding Expectations*

~ and chapter in the sequel ~

Paradise Misplaced

Israel, 1962

Using the improvised field shower filled with sun-warmed water Naomi rinsed the sand from her body and hair. Unlike the others, she preferred a shower and clean clothes before joining the group at the evening meal. Youthful and trim at forty-four, she was able to do the arduous digging, sifting, and climbing required at an archeological dig without painful reminders the following morning. Work had gone well that day. They had unearthed two shattered but complete storage pots that she knew would be dated two centuries BC. The extra hands had helped.

In late June they had taken on five American volunteers eager to work on a dig over the summer: four college students, two boys, two girls, and a high school history teacher, named Michael. They had come to Israel to learn and become part of it. As though by handling the earth, replacing their pale pasty coloring with a rugged tan, and uncovering the artifacts of their ancestors, they could establish a link with their past. Soon she and the history teacher would become lovers. He was married. Naomi didn't know if he had children, nor did she care. She preferred married men. A married man could be counted on to leave at the end of the summer with a minimum of fuss. There would be no talk of staying and finding a permanent job. A good-bye, a kiss, and a soon-to-be-broken promise to write. No entanglements, no regrets.

From habit Naomi checked the small hand mirror. She no longer owned makeup, only salve to protect her lips. Her now-darkened hair was cut short and typically hidden under a hat. Lines from frowning in the sun creased her forehead and the corners of her eyes, but there were no signs of broken bones left to mend unset, no lurid scars or macabre tattoos like many survivors bore. She often thought that her body had fared better than her psyche. When she approached the spartan dining tent she noticed that

Michael had saved a place for her. She filled her plate with food and sat down beside him. Nearby, the two college girls were absorbing wisdom being shared with them by Shaul and Uri, the team's senior members – men more than double their age. Inevitably, they too would become lovers. The two boys would have to find young *sabras*, Israeli-born girls, who would consider their American cousins naïve but exotic strangers. Linda, a red-haired sophomore with a face full of freckles, grinned at Naomi. Her friend Jill, a broad-shouldered girl with dark eyes and braces, was too engrossed to notice her presence.

After Naomi had left Paris, when she was still Nicole, all her valuables, including her identification, had been stolen by a woman fleeing the advancing German army. Still searching for her brother, she had had to beg for food and shelter. As the occupying army grew in strength and numbers, food became increasingly scarce. When he caught her stealing moldy corncobs from his pigsty a collaborator turned her in to the Nazis. Her punishment was working as an unpaid prostitute, first servicing ordinary German troops, and later a major who claimed her for himself. Fortunately, she was not suspected of being a Jew, only a thief, or she would have been sent to a concentration camp. A year later she escaped.

For nine months she lived by hiding in fields, gleaning scraps of rotting crops and scavenging garbage cans. She developed a persistent racking cough. When the cold of winter drove her to seek the warmth of a barn, she was again apprehended, this time by a widowed farmer with five children. Seeing her emaciated skeleton he knew she was an escapee: either a criminal or a Jew. It didn't matter which. He needed a woman to cook, clean and warm his bed. She needed a place to hide. Preferring a woman with flesh on her bones, he insisted she eat enough to replace the lost weight. He also beat her when she displeased him. Nicole stayed until the war's end, then once again escaped. This time she made it to an Allied relocation camp.

Queries were made on her behalf. She learned that her brother and parents were all dead. Her husband and children's last known residence was in Philadelphia, where they live with an unrelated widow, but they had moved and left no forwarding address. Nicole was questioned again. Did she know where her husband might have taken the children? Without additional information it would take time to locate them. Months passed. Other camp internees located relatives and friends who had survived. One by one Europe's homeless obtained visas and fled: to the United States, England, Brazil, Argentina, Mexico, Canada, Australia, the Caribbean Islands, any perceived safe haven that would have them.

Yet another camp official came to speak to Nicole. Alan and her children had vanished. Could she think of a reason her husband might have for deserting her? Had they gotten along well? Had they argued? Often? About money? The children? Other women?

She didn't know where he might have taken her daughters, or why. They had argued. Often. Not about money. About the children. The camp worker frowned and promised to continue searching.

Nicole remembered back to the life she had had with Alain. For three and a half months, from the day she had managed to get rid of the last of his rich whores, to the day Marguerite was born — three and a half months – she shared Alain with no one. He had been hers alone for fourteen weeks. After that, the only time she had his complete attention was when they made love. She had lost him to her own daughter. If Alain were present there was no one else in the room for Maggie. When they moved into her parents' home, maids, cooks, nannies, all raced to attend to Alan's every whim. Even her cynical aloof mother had succumbed. No female was immune. And now this. He had taken their daughters and run off. She had suffered and fought to survive for this.

"Look around you," volunteers had lectured her. "You're not the only one who's lost everything. Others are starting new lives. Put aside the past. Live for the future. You're young and you have your health. Others are not so fortunate. You can find another husband. You'll have other children."

Nicole collapsed. A nervous breakdown, the camp doctors called it. But there was nothing nervous about it. It was a calm better than any she had known. No sounds, no nameless faces, no grotesque visions of her brother's exposed bones. No memory of the degradations she had endured, the endless line of men waiting to violate her. No images of her children crying, or of Alain leaving her. Nothing. Peace. Darkness. A black blanket enveloping her, hiding her from the piercing light.

Months later, as the blanket gradually lifted, the camp no longer contained familiar faces. The few people she'd known were gone. Those still there, the ones who lacked a country that would take them in or family seeking them, talked of going to Palestine. They would start their lives again in the promised land. A new beginning. A clean slate. Nothing to remind them of the past. Nicole decided to join them.

Shortly after she arrived in Palestine she was approached by members of the Haganah, the daring underground group fighting for liberation. Nicole was told that she was an ideal candidate: intelligent, fluent in English, beautiful, and mannered. Just the sort of woman British officers stationed in Palestine found irresistible. She could learn information from the British officers that would advance Jews' yearning for a safe homeland. Her people needed her. The Haganah needed her. They trained her. She was taught to kill with anything at hand: a rifle, a pistol, a bayonet, a knife, a pen, a water glass, the mirror from a compact. If working for the Haganah meant using her body for seduction, or if she was to die, it was of no importance to her.

In 1948 Israel became a state and Nicole's special services were no longer needed. She applied to a kibbutz. Some joined as a means of regaining a family taken from them by concentration camps. Others, because they believed in the ideals of a commune. Naomi joined because she wanted someone to make daily decisions for her. Swayed by her status as a hero of the Haganah, the kibbutz accepted her. Though she worked as hard as any, without complaint, she was a poor fit for communal life. She lacked the ardor, zeal, commitment. In 1953, after reading about an ongoing archeological excavation, she impulsively sent a letter offering her help and describing her interest in history, and her pre-war work with rare books. They invited her to join the project.

She was well suited for the slow-paced, hermetic, exacting work on a dig. She followed procedures, learned quickly, and possessed a keen eye for detail. Her notes were meticulous. Nine years later she was considered a valuable member of the team.

"Jill thinks you're a dead ringer for a girl we saw on television," Linda said, as they washed the dinner dishes.

In the last few minutes before nightfall, mountains in the distance softened and appeared closer.

"A dead ringer?" Naomi repeated. "What does that mean?"

"It's an expression. It means that you look just like someone else," Linda explained.

"It's true. She does that funny thing you do with your mouth, Naomi." Jill demonstrated the pout.

Naomi unconsciously touched her upper lip. "Why was she on television?"

"She was talking about this dumb guy who paints," Jill continued.

"He's not dumb," Linda argued. "He's retarded. They say he's some kind of a genius. I have a picture in my tent of the model who discovered him. It's an old magazine. She looks like Naomi, around the eyes."

"And the mouth, and the cheekbones, and her entire face," Jill said. "She looks exactly like you, Naomi. Go find the picture, Linda. She simply has to see it."

"That's all right," Naomi said. "There's no need to bother. I'll take your word for it."

Linda stood, quickly followed by Shaul. "You could have family that you don't even know about. Wouldn't that be exciting? To find a member of your family living in America, after all this time?"

"No one. I have no one."

"I'll get that magazine," Linda said. "You be the judge."

Shaul draped his arm over Linda's shoulder. "I'll go with you. It's not wise to walk alone after sundown."

"She's Naomi's double," Jill said, sliding closer to Uri. "I couldn't believe it."

"We'll go too," Michael said, taking her hand in his. "I want to see the American model who looks like Naomi."

Could it really be Michelle? Naomi wondered as they made their way in the semi-darkness, their path lit by flashlights reflecting off the stone. She would be twenty-three now. No, twenty-four. It would have to be her younger daughter. Marguerite had favored her father, the pedophile rapist. In the highly unlikely chance it was Michelle, what would Naomi do after all these years? Could she find her daughters? Would they allow her into their lives? Could she regain their love? Or would she seek a means of punishing the man who had stolen them from her?

~ Finis ~

Lisa April Smith

A Sample Chapter of
Dangerous Lies
By Lisa April Smith

Chapter 1

April 1979

The trial had everything an ambitious prosecuting attorney could want: a solid case against a known crime-lord and a seductively beautiful witness with a steamy past — ingredients guaranteed to pack a courtroom. From the minute the first photographer had caught a glimpse of Tina Davis the courtroom had been swarming with reporters. It was a plum assignment awarded for Jake Stern's fourteen years with the District Attorney's office and his impressive ratio of convictions. He should be savoring the certain win everyone had been predicting, jubilant with the publicity. Instead, as he watched her testify, he was irritated and agitated — irritated, agitated, and aroused — again.

He had specifically told her to dress conservatively — nothing low-cut or too short — appearances influenced juries. Today she was wearing a white knit turtleneck dress that flaunted every provocative curve — another outfit destined to make the six o'clock news. They couldn't get enough of her: the sexy walk, the clothes, the face. Her face. Each feature in itself was memorable: high cheekbones, delicately carved nose, precisely drawn mouth, and enormous, violet, heavy-lashed eyes. A mass of dark brown, writhing curls framed her face. Reporters battled one another describing her. One reporter insisted that she 'combined the sensual and the serene'. But despite their overblown sketches they all used the same label to identify her: *Tina Davis, Former Mob-Mistress.*

From the time she was fifteen until she was twenty-nine, Tina Davis, born Bettina Berenson thirty-nine years earlier, was the mistress of several underworld titans. At thirty-one, she had married Laurence Paxton Davis, flower-child turned drug-dealer. Jake had deliberately outlined her history in his opening statement. He had no intention of giving the defense an opportunity to shock the jury with the lurid details after she testified. Jake knew, if he told the jury right up front that Tina Davis had chosen to consort with the scum of the universe, they might not like her, but they would believe her. The maneuver seemed to be working. The eight men and four women of the jury nodded sympathetically as she testified. And she was a good witness; she spoke slowly and distinctly and her story was consistent.

The defendant's attorney was unable to hide his growing frustration. "You've testified that your late husband was a drug dealer. Wasn't he also an addict?"

Jake stood. "Objection, Your Honor. It's already been established that Larry Davis used drugs. Mr. Willard is repeating himself in an attempt to badger the witness."

The judge shot the cynical stare Her Honor was noted for at Tom Willard. "Objection sustained. Please get on with it, Mr. Willard."

Jake allowed himself a pleased inner smile, confident his stony face would mask his thoughts. It was almost fun watching him sputter like a defective firecracker as he attempted to derail her. Back in law school, Willard was an arrogant, pretentious ass — an ass who enjoyed waving his money in everyone's face. But he was no fool. The slightest indication of weakness and he would go for the jugular.

"You claim, Mrs. Davis, your husband died owing my client twenty-five thousand dollars, and that my client tried to collect the debt from *you*. Supposedly, he sent the two men who testified earlier, to threaten you. We've heard a lot of fuzzy, distorted tapes that supposedly support your assertion. May I remind you, those two convicted criminals have admitted, under oath, they're receiving consideration in the form of *reduced sentences* for their testimony?"

"Is there a question here, Mr. Willard?" the judge prodded.

"Just getting to that, Your Honor. As I was saying, twenty-five thousand dollars is a lot of money to most people. It certainly is to me," Willard informed the jury. "But as Mr. Stern pointed out, you have some powerful *intimate associates.*" A number of people, including three members of the jury, tittered. "Intimate associates with considerable financial resources. If what you claim is true, why didn't one of your *very close friends* come to your aid?"

Jake didn't wait for Willard to complete the sentence before standing. "Irrelevant, Your Honor."

"Sustained," the judge declared.

Jake would have loved to hear the answer to that one. Why hadn't she gone to one of her former playmates for help? Jake was aware of two who outranked the defendant. Either one could drop twenty-five thousand dollars on a bet and never flinch. Surely one of them could have given or loaned her the money, or at the very least, pressured the defendant to cut her a deal.

Instead she had waltzed into the nearest precinct and offered to get the cops enough evidence for a conviction — volunteered to wear a wire. Volunteers always made Jake nervous. Nervous and suspicious. What made her so anxious to repeatedly risk her life? Over a period of three months, with a recording device neatly tucked in her handbag, Davis had strolled into parts of the city that seasoned officers were reluctant to patrol. Then she had to pretend not to understand or hear, so the threats would have to be repeated. That sort of hot-dog heroics could have gotten her killed.

Jake shook his head. The cops she worked with idolized her. How could cops admire a woman who had chosen to live with gangsters, the very men they saw as their enemies? But cops have their own set of rules. If they had to list the traits they admired most, 'courage' would be at the top. Of course, her looks didn't hurt. When the detectives had first played a few of the tapes for him, they stood around laughing and punching each other — like kids reliving a Halloween prank.

Jake knew they viewed most prosecutors as educated, spineless, chicken-shits who got in their way — and that didn't exclude him.

Normally women with her sort of background had horrendous childhoods. But Davis' mother wasn't a prostitute and her father wasn't a pimp. She was born into a typical middle-class family — two parents, a brother, a sister — a family like the one Jake had lost. And she had grown up in Queens, less than three miles from his old neighborhood.

"My husband died trying to stop a fight," Davis said in answer to Willard's latest question. She crossed her legs and replaced a curl behind her ear. "My husband was a pacifist."

The gesture made the bulge in Jake's shorts quiver. She *was* a beautiful woman, an exceptionally beautiful woman. But he had a girlfriend, who was everything he wanted in a woman: educated, young, from a good family, attractive — not just attractive, pretty, very pretty. Tina Davis was not a person he would choose as a friend, much less a date. Maybe he could be more sympathetic if she was stupid or just ignorant, like most of the city's sidewalk hostesses. But she was neither stupid nor ignorant. During preparation for the trial, Jake had had a number of conversations with her. She asked intelligent questions and anticipated his strategies while taunting him with those searing eyes or smiling that knowing smile. And she always carried a book with her — good books, not junk — Tolstoy, Joyce, Proust. A Jewish mob-bimbo who read Proust. Nothing about Tina Davis made sense.

The judge consulted her watch. It was four o'clock on a Friday afternoon, an unseasonably hot Friday afternoon. They were minutes away from halting for the weekend. During their last break, the two detectives who had worked with Davis had unnerving news for Jake. There was a contract out on her.

She was gutsy, but she wasn't going to laugh that throaty little laugh when Jake informed her that someone planned to silence her permanently.